THE LIGHT BRINGER

Praise for
THE LIGHT BRINGER

"Superb!—*The Light Bringer* displays an outstanding supernatural adventure that will pull you into a world beyond life itself and make you wonder if it's really a work of fiction. A chilling movement across the threshold that separates this world and the next—*The Light Bringer* bridges the gap between the light and darkness, goodness and evil that exist in this world and our life beyond."

—**Dr. Tom Hill**, coauthor of *Chicken Soup for the Entrepreneur's Soul*

"In a powerful way, *The Light Bringer* helps the reader consider how well they are following the path of Light—and what temptations from the Dark Side they need to carefully turn away from. I recommend this book to anyone who is willing to honestly reflect on their life, and the life after."

—**Ron Brown, Ph.D.**, organizational effectiveness consultant
and author of *The Courageous Life*

"*The Light Bringer* is the story of Alan Crane, an ex-military man who discovers he has a gift of helping loved ones deal with the pain of losing a family member or friend through the perfect words, demeanor, and empathy. The reader is submerged into Crane's world as he faces countless cases of pained survivors, each one with their own story to tell about the beloved fallen. It is hard to put down *The Light Bringer* as you begin to sympathize with each one of the many character-driven stories and contemplate the various tragic and heartwarming encounters. *The Light Bringer* is chilling, moving, crushing, enlightening, compassionate and thought-provoking, truly tapping into the range of human emotion, making the reader reflect upon their own experiences with death and what might lie ahead."

—**Mitch Thrower**, CEO and founder of Bump Network, Inc.,
and author of *The Attention-Deficit Workplace*

"*The Light Bringer* creates for the reader a sense of possibility in a world of closed doors. The authors have described a reality outside of this reality and yet inside it at the same time, like an envelope inside of an envelope. The characters and the struggle feel bigger than life, but oddly familiar. I found this a compelling read."

—**Tom Searcy**, coauthor of *Whale Hunting: How to Land Big Sales and Transform Your Company*

"*The Light Bringer* by DiGiuseppi/Force was a real page-turner for me. I read over 100 pages without stopping and finished the book in two more sittings. The story is one of hope and reaping what you sow. It is well-written, and I was always anticipating what would happen next. Justice wins, although we may not witness the payoff. I would highly suggest this book."

—**Rocky Rowe**, broker/owner Select 1 Properties—Lake St. Louis, MO

"I lived this book as I read it from cover to cover. Having lost my daughter as the result of her brutal murder, I found that *The Light Bringer* uniquely captured the pain, despair, and ultimate hope and sincerity that can be found only through faith, family, and some very special friends.

"*The Light Bringer* is a must-read for anyone who has lost someone and has still not answered the question 'Why?'"

—**Carol Angelbeck**, Ocala, FL

THE LIGHT BRINGER

CHRIS DiGIUSEPPI
AND
MIKE FORCE

Health Communications, Inc.
Deerfield Beach, Florida

www.hcibooks.com

Library of Congress Cataloging-in-Publication Data

DiGiuseppi, Chris.
    The light bringer / by Chris DiGiuseppi & Mike Force.
        p. cm.
    ISBN-13: 978-0-7573-1573-2 (trade paper)
    ISBN-10: 0-7573-1573-9 (trade paper)
    ISBN-13: 978-0-7573-9175-0 (e-book)
    ISBN-10: 0-7573-9175-3 (e-book)
    1. Force, Mike.   2. Title.
    PS3604.I397L54 2011
    813'.6—dc22

                                                            2011010745

Publisher: Health Communications, Inc.
        3201 S.W. 15th Street
        Deerfield Beach, FL 33442–8190

Cover design by Larissa Hise Henoch
Interior design and formatting by Lawna Patterson Oldfield

*We would like to extend our sincere gratitude to
A. J., Joel, Mindy, and Nicholas.*

*In life they brought joy to many around them,
and in death they taught us to have hope,
inspiration, and the willingness to
think beyond our own mortality.*

Introduction

*"It is well that war is so terrible, else we
would grow too fond of it."*

—Robert E. Lee

SOME HAVE SAID THAT DEATH IS an invisible pattern, holding no definitive course or boundary, showing no bias, no profile or indicator, regardless of science, medicine, or statistics. The soldier, the police officer, the firefighter, the priest, the paramedic, and the doctor, who are often first to see death, are constantly reminded that there is no explanation of why it occurs. Many confuse the question of *why* death occurs with the question of *how* death occurs, and although the question of how is most often answered, why is never really satisfied. But perhaps there is an answer. Perhaps there is a reason. The truth is often too much for many of us to see or understand. Still, there may be those who find the answer and don't even know it.

Alan's mind balked at the thought of bringing home the charred remains of Antonio Rossi, his fellow Marine.

Why did this happen? he wondered, staring out the window of the plane. *How will I explain to the family of this brave warrior that his death came at the hands of those he trusted most?*

Adrift in sleep, Alan saw again a brilliant flash of light just before the thunderous explosion threw him from the armored personnel carrier. Dazed, he rushed back to the blazing pile of molten metal and pulled away the crumpled remains of the heavy door. To his horror he saw a charred, blackened body on the ground before him.

"No, no. Rossi…no, this can't be!" Alan knelt down and began to cry, overtaken with tremendous grief at the loss of another young hero.

Ash and smoke billowing around him, Alan barely noticed the hand on his left shoulder. He looked up and saw another Marine standing over him. From the insignia on his collar, Alan recognized him as his company commander.

He continued to cry. "He's gone—why was it him and not me?" Alan shook his head from side to side in disbelief, tears rolling down his cheeks to be consumed by the sand below. The captain lowered himself to one knee, keeping his hand on Alan's shoulder. "Corporal Crane, that's not your friend."

Alan tore his gaze from the charred remains as realization dawned on him.

"The body you see before you…is yours."

Alan awoke from the haunting dream with the captain's words still echoing in his mind. Once again, he looked out the window of the plane admiring the sunbeams that illuminated the clouds below and wondered where life's path would take him next. He seemed destined to deal with sorrow without ever understanding why that task had been appointed to him. He alone was meant to survive and comfort. He alone was tasked with making the reality of death less painful. But he often wondered: was he really alone?

CHAPTER ONE

"A man loves the meat in his youth that
he cannot endure in his age."

—William Shakespeare

MARINE CORPORAL ALAN CRANE stared at the dull tile floor of the chapel's vestibule. He pulled a small coin purse from his pocket and removed the rosary. Fingering its black, marblelike stones, he admired the silver cross that dangled from the end.

"What's that?" asked a voice. Alan looked up to see Lance Corporal Mark Jameson sitting on a short wooden bench on the other side of the room.

"A gift," Alan replied. "Something that was given to me a long time ago by a very close friend when we were kids."

"I had a friend named Bobby who used to call me from time to time—known him since we were four years old. Haven't heard from him since he went to jail about a year ago. I hope your friend made out better than mine."

"No," Alan replied. "He's dead."

Jameson dropped his gaze. Alan could tell by the look on his face that he wanted to say something sympathetic but had thought better of it.

1

The rosary caught the light and the silver cross flashed. *Like a snow-flake,* Alan thought, remembering that cold winter day so long ago.

Snow fell on the already icy ground as Alan followed his father across the top of the hill that everyone in their town used for sledding. Excitement surged through him as he glanced down at the fresh red paint on the runners of his new sled. The sled wasn't actually new—his father had found it at a garage sale and probably only paid a dollar or two for it. But it felt new to Alan and that was all that mattered.

Alan had inherited most of his father's physical features, including his dark brown hair and gleaming blue eyes. His calm and patient manner had come from his mother, who stayed at home and took care of Alan, his brother, and two sisters. They all lived in a somewhat cramped row home with three bedrooms; Grandma Crane occupied one of the rooms and the four kids occupied another.

His father had grown up extremely poor. Grandma Crane had been forced to sign custody of him over to the State of New Jersey to get him enrolled in a military school. After graduation he worked as a laborer for a scrap iron and steel company, or, as his father commonly referred to it, a junkyard. Thomas Crane always stressed the importance of family sticking together; Alan guessed that this was because he had been raised by an institution and knew the importance of family bonds.

Alan was thinking about his family when he noticed that his father was a good distance in front of him. As he hurried to catch up, he felt a hand on his shoulder and turned to see his friend Tommy McKelvy smiling from ear to ear.

"Take me for a ride on your sled, Alan. Please," he added. "Let's see how fast we can go."

Tommy was a year younger than Alan and came from a wealthy family. He was extremely intelligent and did well in school. At times Alan envied him; *Tommy had the world in his pocket.* Even though Tommy had everything going for him he was always friendly toward Alan and even seemed to look up to him.

"I have to catch up to my dad," said Alan. "Maybe later."

"Come on," Tommy whined. "Just one ride."

Alan let out a sigh. He could no longer see his father. Reluctantly he said, "Okay, one quick ride. I'll catch up with my dad at the bottom of the hill."

Tommy's smile grew even wider. "Cool, let's go!"

Alan set the sled down and Tommy lay flat on his stomach and let his feet dangle off the back. Alan lay down on top of him and the two kicked off from the flat crest of the hill. As the two boys whisked down the icy surface they picked up speed. Tommy, steering with the wooden slat at the front portion of the sled, looked up occasionally to adjust their course.

Alan enjoyed the cool sensation of the winter air rushing by, blowing at the tattered scarf draped around his neck. They were sledding on part of the hill where no one else had been. The snow beneath them was fresh and new. *Like my sled*, Alan thought happily.

As they rushed over the frozen ground, Tommy turned the slat to the left, aligning the sled with a pathway across the narrow bridge that traversed the hollow ravine at the bottom of the hill. Alan felt the back end of the sled beginning to slide out from under them. A slight sensation of fear overtook him as they slid sideways. He was just about to yell when Tommy corrected the slat, putting them back on track.

The newly fallen snow burst into clouds ahead of them, making it hard to see. The sled evened out and Tommy hung his head downward for a moment to clear his eyes. They were far off course, heading for a small stone building that served to house the park guards and their horses.

"Go farther left again!" Alan yelled to Tommy.

The bridge was now very close. They needed to turn sharply if they were going to make it. Alan reached down and grabbed the end of the steering slat, attempting to turn it, but his hands slipped and the sled jerked off course. They hit a slick patch of ice and the sled picked up speed. Alan opened his mouth to yell but the bitter, cold wind blasted the back of his throat, preventing any noise from escaping. The speed of the sled blurred their surroundings. It was dizzying. Suddenly the stone wall of the building loomed before them, terrifyingly close. A horrible sound, like cracking tree branches, was the last thing Alan heard.

CHAPTER TWO

"I look upon death to be as necessary
to the constitution as sleep. We shall rise
refreshed in the morning."

—Benjamin Franklin

S PECKLES OF LIGHT GLINTED IN THE DARKNESS. Alan heard a familiar voice.

"Alan," said Thomas Crane. "Alan, it's Dad. Can you hear me, son?"

Alan no longer felt the cold wind on his face or the icy ground beneath his body. He moved his head slowly to the side. The glints of light grew bigger and bigger. Slowly a dull, illuminating glow filled his entire view and he was able to make out the fuzzy outlines of figures standing a few feet away. As he struggled to focus, he noticed that the surface beneath him was not the wet feel of snow but the soft comfort of a bed.

"Alan, thank God. You don't need to speak, son. Just rest."

As he blinked he saw his mother and father standing on either side of the bed. He felt his mother's hand on his forehead and could hear her sobbing, but he saw as he glanced at her that her tears were those of relief, rather than sadness or pain.

Alan took a deep breath as he struggled to form a word. "Tommy?"

Two more figures drew closer to the bed and Alan recognized them as Tommy's parents, Mr. and Mrs. McKelvy. They both wore expressions of grief, as did his mother and father.

Nobody spoke for a moment or so. Finally, Alan's father spoke but seemed to struggle to find the words, "Alan, Tommy is…he didn't…"

Before his father could finish, Alan took a deep breath and said, "Dead. I know. I saw him."

Alan's father stared at him in disbelief but said nothing. Tommy's parents were also silent.

This time his mother broke the silence. "Alan, you've been unconscious for a long time."

Alan looked around. An IV bag hung close to his bed. He could feel the tape pulling at his skin where the needle was inserted into the top of his hand. The room was small and somewhat gloomy. In one corner there was a steel cart; Alan could see a stack of medical forms on top. His gaze rested on a small wooden cross on the opposite side of the room. The words "St. Anthony's Hospital West" were painted above it.

"I talked to Tommy." Alan's words came as though he was in some type of trance. "I walked with him."

His father looked at the others around the room, then back down at Alan with sympathy. "Son, you've been through a lot. You hit your head very hard. You need to rest."

"I saw Tommy after we hit the wall. We walked through a long tunnel. It was cold." He paused for a moment, straining to recall. "I remember how smooth the floors and walls were, almost like glass…dark glass." He trailed off. "Tommy said he had something very important to do, but that I couldn't come along. He said that I had to…" Alan said nothing for a moment. A tear welled up in his eye. "He said I had to go back."

As he spoke, Mrs. McKelvy approached the side of the bed.

Alan's mother looked down at him as she choked back a tear. "You must have been dreaming, dear. We all want to remember Tommy. He was a special boy." She rubbed his arm gently.

As Alan looked around the room he spotted his tattered winter coat hanging on a hook near the door.

"My coat, I need my coat," said Alan as he pointed toward it.

Alan's father looked down at him, "We can't go yet, son. You still need to rest."

"Please, Dad," Alan insisted. "I need to see my coat."

His father nodded and retrieved the torn jacket. He placed it on the bed.

Alan's hand found its way into one of the pockets. "I saw Tommy after we hit the wall. He gave me this."

He raised his right hand slowly to reveal a small brown pouch. Mrs. McKelvy gasped. Mr. McKelvy came closer to get a look at the object. "That's Tommy's rosary. He carried it with him everywhere."

"Tommy must have given that to you before you started sledding," Alan's mother said, though she sounded unconvinced.

"No," said Alan. "You've got to believe me. I saw him after we hit the wall."

Mrs. McKelvy took the pouch and opened the center pocket, revealing the black, marble-beaded rosary. She placed the rosary back inside and took Alan by the hand. "What else happened?" she asked softly.

"He said that he loved you and Mr. McKelvy very much and that he was going to help people. He was going to be okay. He said that he would see you again, and then he gave me this."

As Alan's mother and father stood speechless, Tommy's parents hung on every word Alan spoke. A tear ran down Mrs. McKelvy's cheek and splashed on the bed sheet. "I believe you," she said.

Alan made a motion to hand the rosary back to her, but she quickly pushed his hand away. "No, please, Alan, you must keep it. He gave it to you. There must be a reason."

CHAPTER THREE

*"Why is it that we rejoice at a birth
and grieve at a funeral? It is because we
are not the person involved."*

—Mark Twain

"ALAN. ALAN. CORPORAL." A voice from across the room jolted his mind back to the present.

Alan shook his head as if to fight off the remnants of the haunting images. Lance Corporal Jameson was now standing, eyeing Alan with concern.

"Sorry, Corporal," Jameson stammered as he tried to explain his actions. "You wouldn't answer and I was worried that you were, well…"

Alan held up his hand. "I apologize, Jameson. I was daydreaming, I guess. We need to concentrate on the reason we're here."

The two men were representing the Marine Corps in rendering military honors at the funeral for PFC Anthony Rossi, recently killed in combat. Rossi's personnel carrier had been struck by friendly fire, killing Rossi, who had been driving the vehicle. Alan had been riding in the back and had somehow survived the incident unscathed. Alan and Jameson had been directed to report to the chapel to assist the family and the minister with anything they needed. At the moment, the minister was speaking with the family, offering comfort and guidance.

The chapel doors swung open and a portly man dressed in priestly robes burst into the room, sweating profusely.

"I'm Reverend Arnold, and I think we have a problem," said the man, panting as if he were out of breath.

"How can we help?" asked Alan.

"Mrs. Rossi is extremely upset. She believes that I'm lying to her about her son's death. She fails to accept the truth. I've tried to convince her in the most"—he paused to think of an appropriate word—"delicate manner. She claims that the Marine Corps has lied to her, her family, their friends. She believes that everyone is in on it. She wants to open the casket."

The casket was closed due to PFC Rossi's condition after the accident. "I still don't think that would satisfy her," the reverend continued. "She was hysterical, practically screaming at me. I don't know where to go from here. I've seen her son; his condition is so bad that she wouldn't recognize him."

Alan could see that Jameson was cringing at the idea of dealing with a hysterical mother. "Let's talk to her and see if we can help," Alan suggested. The reverend looked relieved.

Alan pushed the chapel door open and Jameson followed. At the back of the church, sitting in the last pew on the right, was a short, large woman with curly black hair. She was sobbing. As they approached, Jameson slipped into the pew directly across the aisle from the woman.

"Ma'am, my name is Alan Crane. I'm a friend of your son's and I want to help you."

Rossi's mother looked up at him and said, "You can't help me. They're trying to say my son was killed. But I know they're lying to me. They won't let me see him because that's not really my boy in there. He's still alive. He's just lost. I know it!" Her accent was thick, her voice strangled by grief and anger.

Alan listened patiently. "Mrs. Rossi, that is your son. I know this to be true."

"How in the hell would you know?" Mrs. Rossi sneered. "You know nothing. You're lying to me, just like that stupid little reverend and those men who came to my house. They tried to tell me the same thing. I know these lies."

"You have to trust me, Mrs. Rossi. I knew Antonio."

She cut him off once again. "No!" She raised a tattered tissue to her eye, blotting away a tear. "Let me tell you about trust. When I was a little girl, I lived with my mama and papa in Sicily. My papa owned a vegetable market in town. One evening, a man came to the house dressed in a suit and said that he was from the government. He said that Papa needed to come with him because someone had destroyed our shop. Papa left with the man and I never saw him again. Mama and I went to the market and found it burned. I asked Mama where the man in the suit had taken Papa. She didn't know. She said we couldn't trust anyone. We had to leave our home. We spent many days and nights on the boat that brought us to this country.

"Now my son is gone and again I remember what Mama taught me about trusting the government. I trust no one. Only God." She dried another tear. "This is not my son." She pointed her finger at the casket as if she were insulted by its presence.

Alan took her hand and looked directly into her eyes. "Mrs. Rossi, I'm not lying. I know this is your son."

The woman studied him for a moment. "You prove it. You prove it to me."

Jameson heard Alan whisper something to her. The heavyset woman sat upright as if to direct her full attention toward Alan. Jameson watched from across the aisle as Alan tried to comfort her. Mrs. Rossi's demeanor slowly began to change. Jameson continued to watch in amazement as Alan went up to the casket and opened the cover. Placing his formal white hat with its shiny black brim on his head, completing the dress blue uniform he wore in respect, Alan saluted the casket of his fallen comrade.

As the fingers of his right hand stretched to reach the brim of his hat, the precision of Alan's slow-motion funeral salute caught Jameson's attention. Alan bent close to the charred, unrecognizable body of PFC Rossi as though he were waiting for the dead Marine to speak. He leaned into the coffin and moved his ear to within an inch of where the fallen Marine's lips would have been located, if his body had been intact. He paused as though waiting for some type of interaction. After a moment, Alan returned to his position of attention, repeated his salute, and closed the casket.

He returned to the pew and sat down beside Mrs. Rossi and took her hand. He looked deeply into her eyes. Jameson wondered what he saw reflected there.

Alan wasn't exactly sure what to say to the grieving woman but somehow the words just came to him. "Your son told me that he is well and wants you to be well. He loves you and wants you to honor his memory."

As Alan continued speaking to Mrs. Rossi in a soothing tone, Jameson saw him hand her the small rosary pouch. Mrs. Rossi wiped her eyes. She reached out her large arm and wrapped it around Alan's neck, nearly dragging him over. Alan embraced her and she thanked him for his kindness. The reverend returned to the back of the chapel, and Mrs. Rossi apologized to him for her earlier behavior.

The two Marines made their way back through the vestibule into the small parking area in front to await their military escort to the grave.

"I can't believe you gave her that pouch," Jameson said. "I thought that was from your childhood friend."

Alan nodded. "Yes, but it was time to give it to someone who really needed it. It helped me once, long ago, but today I saw someone else, someone in great despair, who needed it more than I."

"How'd you know it was time," Jameson asked, then paused, "to give the rosary away, I mean?"

Alan shook his head slowly from side to side. "I just knew."

Jameson sighed and chuckled softly. "I got to hand it to you, Corporal. I can't believe you got that woman calmed down. Where did you come up with that stuff you told her?"

"What do you mean?"

"Come on, Corporal," said Jameson. "You remember what you said. All that stuff about her son telling you that he was all right, that it was time for him to go on, and that she should try to move forward. But what really amazed me was how you got her to listen."

"Oh yeah," Alan asked calmly, "and how was that?"

"By speaking Italian to her. I didn't know you spoke Italian. What did it mean, what you said?" asked Jameson.

Alan looked genuinely puzzled. "Lance Corporal Jameson, what the hell are you babbling about? I don't speak Italian. I merely reiterated the same things the reverend had said. This was her son, I was very sorry for her loss, and everything would be fine. That's all I ever said to her."

"With all due respect, sir, you uttered a phrase. It sounded Italian to me. After you said it she listened to you as if you were her favorite high school teacher. She hung on your every word. You told her some wild story about how her son spoke to you. As though he had spoken to you from the grave and given you a message for his mother. I figured you were just trying to comfort her."

The two sat in silence for a moment. Then Jameson spoke again. "I say all of this out of respect. You have a real talent. I couldn't have made all that stuff up so quickly. You really made her think that you cared."

"How can you be so sure that I made that up?" Alan asked. "And I do care. But for the last time, I don't speak Italian, or for that matter any other language than the one we're using right now. Whatever you thought you heard, you didn't."

Jameson nodded his head. "Whatever you say, Corporal." He knew the conversation was over.

CHAPTER FOUR

"Destiny is not a matter of chance; but a matter
of choice. It is not a thing to be waited for;
it is a thing to be achieved."

—William Jennings Bryan

A LAN LOST TOUCH WITH JAMESON a few years after they both left the military. Jameson had moved to California to pursue a career as a mechanic with a major airline, a skill he'd acquired from the Marine Corps. Alan's experience earned him a successful career in law enforcement. After seven years of service he advanced to the rank of sergeant in the patrol division.

He was driving through an older neighborhood when the call came out for an accident with injuries on Highway 11 at the 304-mile marker. After seven years on the job Alan was no stranger to accidents with injuries. He flipped on the lights and siren, then accelerated to a speed that allowed him to enjoy a subtle adrenaline rush. As he rounded intersections and drove down the on-ramp to enter the highway, traffic ahead of him slowed and moved gradually to both sides.

He crested a small hill and caught sight of the scene. Thick, dark tire marks scorched the inside lane of the highway, drawing a line to the tractor-trailer blocking one lane of the road. The tractor portion was turned slightly inward, its front wheels buried in the grassy median. Smoke billowed from the front of the tractor. As he approached Alan caught a glimpse of the back of a smaller car near the tractor wheel well. *This isn't good*, he thought.

Positioning his car an adequate distance behind the trailer, Alan called dispatch to advise that he had arrived and needed more help. He got out and ran closer to the tractor where he could now see the entire car, or what was left of it. Its front end was compacted from the hood to the front door frames. The metal was sheared and smashed as if someone had shaved it off with a huge grinding wheel. The grill of the trailer was slightly bent toward the bottom, and the massive bumper was cracked. The driver's-side door of the tractor stood open.

Alan ran around the back of the car and approached the driver's-side door. A large man wearing jeans and a tattered, gray T-shirt was leaning through the driver's side window. His face was unshaved and sweat dripped from his balding head.

The man's voice was panic-stricken as he shouted, "Are you okay?" and reached in to shake the figure. Alan heard no response. "Come on, wake up! Are you okay?" the man in the T-shirt asked again. The figure in the car sat motionless.

Alan placed a hand on the man's shoulder. "Sir, let me help. Please step back."

The man took a few steps back, an expression of sheer horror on his face.

"She came across, I didn't see her! I tried…" He trailed off, tears streaming from his eyes.

The man doubled over. "It'll be okay," Alan said. "Sit here for a minute. We have an ambulance on the way."

The man sat down on the grass. In his mind, Alan knew that everything wouldn't be okay. But you do what you have to in order to quell the panic.

He turned his attention to the driver of the car. She was slumped forward with her face resting against the top portion of the steering wheel. Alan called to her. "Ma'am?"

No response.

He called once more. "Ma'am, can you hear me?" Again, no response.

Looking for a pulse, Alan placed two fingers on her neck. He repositioned his fingers two or three times but found nothing. In the distance he could hear others approaching. A siren had been gradually increasing in volume but had abruptly gone silent. He could hear the rush of footsteps coming closer. Alan found the door lock and forced it open. Then, grabbing the handle, he lifted with all his strength. It wouldn't budge. The mangled metal had twisted and crumpled together to form an impenetrable cage.

Alan noticed no seatbelt holding the driver in. She was an older woman with gray hair and a round face. Her nose was bleeding slightly but no other areas of her head appeared to be cut. He wondered whether he should try to pull her through the open window, but before he could act he felt a hand on his shoulder and turned to see a paramedic standing behind him.

"What do we got?" the paramedic asked, gesturing for Alan to step aside.

"Elderly lady, unresponsive, no pulse, slight nosebleed. Doesn't look like she was wearing a seatbelt. The door is jammed. I can't get it open."

Alan took a few steps back as the paramedic approached the motionless woman. He went through many of the same steps Alan had tried: attempting to rouse the woman, searching for a pulse, pulling on the door, all without success. Two more paramedics ran down to the car carrying a long, yellow backboard.

The first one yelled, "We need fire down here to get this door open." One of the paramedics ran back to radio for more help.

Alan looked around at the scene. He studied the path the car had taken as it left the road and crossed the grassy median where he was now standing. There were no skid marks on the pavement or in the grass, indicating that the driver had never attempted to brake.

He turned his focus to the distraught man sitting on the grass. "Sir, are you the driver of the truck?"

The man nodded and continued to sob.

"I need to get some information from you," said Alan in the most sympathetic tone he could muster. "Can you start by telling me your name?"

"Is she gonna be all right?" asked the man.

Alan didn't answer. "Why don't we come up this way and talk?" he suggested, motioning for the man to follow.

The truck driver stood and followed Alan up to the area near the tractor, where the door still stood ajar.

Another police officer ran around the back of the tractor-trailer and yelled to Alan. "Sergeant, where do you need me?"

"I need you out front on traffic control. Have Murphy stage about a half-mile down to slow cars as they crest that hill."

The officer nodded and ran to do his duty. Numerous fire department personnel were now carrying large pieces of equipment toward the car. He watched as they placed generators, hoses, and the "Jaws of Life" rescue tool near the door where the woman was trapped. Moments later he could hear the distinct screeching sound of metal being forced apart as if it were screaming in protest. It ended with a loud *pop*.

Alan refocused on the truck driver. "Sir, I need your name for the report."

The man wiped his eyes and peered down at the car, where two firefighters were yanking the last portion of the door from its hinges with what appeared to be two large grappling hooks. Alan waited a moment, letting the man deal with his shock.

"My name is Art, Art Rommus," he said at last. Alan scribbled the information down with the pen and pad he had pulled from his pocket.

"Mr. Rommus, do you have your driver's license on you?"

Art nodded and fumbled in his back pocket to retrieve a huge wallet crammed with numerous papers, cards, and receipts. As he opened the wallet, three cards fell out. Alan bent down to help him pick up the fallen items. One was his driver's license, another was an insurance card, and the last was a credit card.

Alan handed the credit card back to the man and said, "Here are your license and insurance card. Let me copy this information down and get it back to you in a minute."

As Alan scribbled down the information Art said, "I never saw her until she hit me. She came out of nowhere. I feel terrible." He began to sob once more. "Is she dead?"

"There were no skid marks from her vehicle on the other side of the highway. She clearly crossed over the median. She may have fallen asleep, had a heart attack, or somehow been rendered unconscious. I've seen it happen before. I assure you, sir, we'll investigate this and figure out what happened. Right now it seems like an accident. You couldn't have done anything to prevent it."

"I know," said the man. "I'm not worried about fault. I had a sister who was killed in a crash a few years back. It upsets me when I see someone die in an accident like this. She is dead, isn't she?"

His voice trailed off with the slightest trickle of hope until Alan replied, "Unfortunately, it appears so."

The man's shoulders slumped forward. He sat down on the grass, holding his head in both hands. "Her family will be so upset. My mother was in so much pain when she learned of my sister's death. Please tell them I'm sorry. Please tell them I…" He trailed off, shaking his head once more, as if he were out of words.

Alan placed his hand on the large man's shoulder and said in a compassionate voice, "I'll help them, Mr. Rommus, I promise."

Art nodded, seeming comforted for a moment. He placed his hands over his temples as if he were trying to rub the painful memories of his past out of his mind.

Over the radio, Alan called in the man's license number along with the license plates from the tractor-trailer and the car. The dispatcher informed him that Mr. Rommus and the two vehicles were on file and properly registered.

A fireman made his way up to Alan, carrying a small blue purse. "Found this on the passenger floorboard," said the fireman.

Alan opened the purse and found a decorative wallet inside. He pushed open the clasp and searched through it, scanning the contents for something that would reveal the identity of the woman. After a few seconds of thumbing through credit cards and coupons he finally found her driver's license. Anne Munsin, born in 1939. Sixty-eight years old.

He scribbled the name down, then called in the information to dispatch. Alan scanned the rest of the license. Her address was listed as 136 Carnac Lane, right here in the city.

The city of Riverston was small, about 13,000 people, with a police department composed of about thirty sworn officers. The center of the city was a large lake, surrounded by the most expensive, upscale homes in the region. In the summertime the lake was packed with boaters; in the winter it was a great place to ice skate. For the most part, it was a quiet community with peaceful residents. But although there was an illusion that nothing bad ever happened in Riverston, Alan knew differently. The city did enjoy good neighborhoods and friendly people, but it still had its share of problems. This wasn't the first fatal accident he had worked, nor was it the worst fatality he had seen. There had been two murders in seven years, as well as numerous suicides, rapes, and sexual assaults, not to mention the cases of child abuse and other disturbing child-neglect incidents he'd seen both personally and in reports.

No, Riverston wasn't perfect, Alan knew. But it was okay. It was different from the old neighborhood where he'd grown up, where a fight was almost inevitable every time he left the house. He remembered his father telling him, "Never start a fight, but if you're forced to fight, make sure you win." By the time he was fourteen years old he had broken his nose five times but had established "respect," which was key to survival.

The reality of the matter was that he hated to fight. He hated violence of any kind. As an adult he'd seen his fair share of it and often wondered why he'd chosen the career paths he had—soldier, police officer—certainly not professions where he'd be likely to avoid conflict. Perhaps if he'd gone into banking or sales he could have avoided this morbid environment where there was often little respect for life. Alan knew that helping people was ingrained in his core, that in many situations he could fulfill the needs of those in trouble for kindness and compassion. He knew that he was drawn to law enforcement for a reason, a purpose—perhaps the same purpose that Tommy McKelvy had spoken about after he died. He looked down at the badge on his chest. *That's who I am, no use in pretending differently*, he thought.

Alan glanced down toward the car and saw the firefighters and paramedics lifting the woman out of the wreckage. They placed a sheet over her body and placed her onto a stretcher. They then dragged the stretcher up to the road and loaded it into the back of the ambulance. The ambulance eased its way into traffic, slowed because of the accident, then disappeared down the road. A flatbed tow truck had arrived on the scene some time earlier, and the driver was now unraveling a long cable and tow hook.

Alan returned to his car and retrieved a camera. He photographed everything pertinent: the car, the tractor-trailer, and both sides of the road. Since the front end was no longer there, the tow truck driver affixed the hook to the rear of the car. He lifted the mangled door, torn off by the firefighters, and crammed it into the front seat of the demolished vehicle. Alan watched as the tow truck pulled back onto the road and sped away.

The scene was slowly starting to wind down; the fire trucks and other emergency equipment began pulling away. Alan radioed dispatch to tell them that he was leaving. As he pulled onto the roadway he saw another officer directing traffic. Alan rolled down his window and yelled, "We can all take off. Head down to the morgue and call the medical examiner. I'm sure they'll want to take a look at the body to determine what happened." The officer nodded once in acknowledgment and made his way back to his car.

Alan would have preferred to return to the station and begin writing up the report, but he knew that he had one last thing to do. He told Officer Murphy over the radio to meet him at 136 Carnac Lane.

CHAPTER FIVE

*"Life is mostly froth and bubble; two things
stand like stone: Kindness in another's
trouble, courage in your own."*

—Adam Lindsay Gordon

KAREN MUNSIN MADE HER WAY AROUND the back of her house to the flower garden that stretched along the side of the garage. It had been weeks since she'd tended to pulling the weeds and trimming back the various bushes and shrubs. She was kneeling down, attempting to level out the mulch, when she noticed two figures standing behind her. A bit taken aback, she jumped to her feet. Two police officers stood in front of her. One was a taller man in his midthirties with light brown hair; the other was a younger man, short and stocky, with a neat clean haircut. "Can I help you?" asked Karen.

The older officer spoke. "Ma'am, are you related to Anne Munsin?"

"Yes, she's my mother," Karen replied, her heart quickening. "Is she okay?"

"I'm Sergeant Crane and this is Officer Murphy," the first officer said. "Is there somewhere we could speak, perhaps inside?"

Karen took off her gardening gloves. "Uh…sure. This way." Her voice trembled as she hurried to a side door that led into a garage. Her mind raced. *Has Mom been hurt?*

Don't even think that, she told herself. Perhaps she had lost her purse —but why wouldn't the officers have told her that outside? Maybe she had done something wrong—speeding, running a stop sign? *Nah, Mom is a safe driver. Besides, two officers wouldn't show up at my house for that.* Her pace quickened. She could feel a vile burning in her stomach. It rose up through her throat and made it difficult to breathe. She led the two men through the garage and into the kitchen.

"Tell me what's going on!" She begged as her imagination began to consume her.

The older man, Sergeant Crane, stood close to her and placed his hand on her shoulder.

"There's been an accident. Your mother's car struck another vehicle out on the highway—"

"Is she all right?" Karen interrupted. "How bad is she?" Somewhere in the back of her mind something was telling her that her mother was gone, but she pushed this thought away, clinging to the last bit of hope she could muster.

"She didn't make it, ma'am. I'm very sorry," the sergeant said in a low, soothing voice.

"No!" Karen cried. "No, this can't be! She can't be dead!"

It was done. The fear she'd pushed to the back of her consciousness suddenly and violently resurfaced.

Trembling, the heartbroken woman pointed to various wrapped boxes sitting on the table. "No, this can't be…it's her birthday next week. Everyone's coming over, and look…look at all these presents. They're hers." She began to sob uncontrollably and fell to the floor.

Alan caught her as she fell, pulled her up, and embraced her. Murphy was looking at the floor, unable to make eye contact with either of them.

Karen caught her breath and screamed. "Why, why?"

After a moment she drew in a deep breath and steadied herself. Alan helped her over to one of the stools along the kitchen's center island. She sat down, and in a much calmer voice asked again, "Why did this happen?"

Murphy spoke up. "Well, ma'am, we're not sure. Your mother may have passed out, or she may have fallen asleep. Does she have any type of medical history?"

Alan cut him off by raising one hand and shaking his head slightly. "Is there anyone else we could call for you?" he asked. "Some close friends or family members who could help?"

"The Evanses, in the brown house. They knew my mother. They..." Karen trailed off, lost in thought.

Alan leaned over to Murphy and whispered, "Go inform the neighbors of the situation and see if they'll come over to comfort Ms. Munsin."

Murphy nodded and quickly made his way out the front door. Karen was now drying her eyes once more, using a box of tissues that Alan had pulled off a nearby counter. "I just don't understand why this happened," she said. "Why her?"

This was the unanswerable question survivors always asked. Alan found it best to remain silent during these times, giving his sympathy and offering practical help with whatever they needed.

"I moved her up here so she could live with me, so she could be safe. Her old neighborhood wasn't the best. Now she's gone—it makes no sense." She began to cry into her hands.

Moments later the front door opened and Murphy reappeared with two other people. One was a middle-aged woman who glanced around the room, spotted Karen, and ran to hug her. "I'm so sorry," she said through a sob.

The man with her wore a long, drawn face full of sympathy and grief. He walked over to Alan and said, "Thank you for being here to help Karen. The other officer told me it was an accident?" Alan nodded in confirmation. "We'll miss Anne. She was a nice, sweet woman. I can't believe she's gone."

Alan looked over to where the two women were still embracing and heard the neighbor asking who else she could call or what else she could do.

Alan reached into his wallet and pulled out a business card. "I'm going to leave you my card," he said, handing it to Mr. Evans. "If there's anything she or her family needs, please call me."

Mr. Evans took the card. "Thank you again. I'll let her know."

Alan glanced over at Murphy and motioned for him. They made their way to the front door. Once they were outside, Murphy said, "I hate doing these things. I never know what to say. I really hate when they ask why it happened. We're always at a loss, especially when we haven't had time to conduct an investigation. That lady may have fallen asleep, may have had a heart attack—who knows."

"That's not what she was asking," Alan said, shaking his head.

"What do you mean?"

"She wasn't asking *how* it happened, she was asking *why* it happened," Alan clarified. Murphy looked even more confused. "She wanted to know why her mother was chosen to die at that moment. She wanted to know why her mother was the one traveling down the road at that specific time and place, why her life ended there on the side of that highway. Why she wasn't injured, rushed to a hospital, and saved. Why her mother was never going to come home again. Why her mother won't be there for her birthday next week. She wanted to know why some people live and others die. Sometimes people want to argue for what's just, what's fair, who's deserving or not deserving."

Alan stopped and looked over at Murphy, whose mouth was slightly agape. He was a good police officer, but his eight months on the job still left him in the category of "having a lot to learn."

"Well they can't expect us to know all that," he said finally.

"They expect a great deal from us and *we* should have a high expectation of ourselves. I've thought those questions many times; in fact, every time someone dies. But there is no answer. The best you can do is say you're sorry and offer to help."

"I really struggle for the right words," Murphy said helplessly.

Alan nodded in agreement. "I know what you mean. It takes a while to get used to."

"Yeah, but it seems like you really know how to deal with it. I was at a loss when she started crying, but you handled it great. You knew when to talk, when to shut up, and when to leave."

"Thanks for the compliment," said Alan, "but don't be too hard on yourself. It will come with more time on the job. You have to feel real empathy for them."

"Sympathy?" asked Murphy.

"No, empathy," corrected Alan. "You need to put yourself in their place. Try to imagine their pain and embrace it. Then you can find the right things to say."

As he dropped his gaze to the ground, Murphy nodded. For a moment the two stood in silence. Then Alan asked, "Don't you ever wonder why it happens? Don't you ever try to put yourself in the place of the one who died? What really happened? Did they die quickly, or feel pain, or did they just fall asleep never to wake up? Was it their path or destiny? Why?"

"There's no reason. As far as putting myself in their place, well, as long as I go home at the end of the day, that's what's most important to me," Murphy replied.

"Going home is important," Alan agreed, though Murphy had clearly missed the point. "I'll catch you back at the station." They said good-bye and left in their separate cars.

Alan returned to the station and finished his paperwork. He briefed the next shift on the accident and other events of the day. As he drove home Alan realized how exhausted he really was. He was still thinking about everything that had happened throughout the day as he pulled up to his house. A smile came over his face at the calming thought of seeing his wife and daughter. He hurried inside.

CHAPTER SIX

"There's no vocabulary for love within a family,
love that's lived in but not looked at, love within the
light of which all else is seen, the love within which
all other love finds speech. This love is silent."

—T. S. Eliot

I**T WAS A COOL AUTUMN MORNING SIX YEARS AGO** when Alan had responded to a disturbance at a small French bakery on the south side of town. He arrived to find a burly man in a leather biker jacket with his arms raised above his head and a look of shock on his face. In front of him stood a petite woman with auburn hair, holding a large knife pointed directly at his chest. The butt of a revolver protruded from the man's belt, and Alan quickly drew his gun. Beads of sweat poured down the man's face as he said in a panicky voice, "I give up! Just tell her to put the knife down. I don't want the money anymore…just get me outta here!"

Alan quickly cuffed the man and called for backup. After additional officers arrived and the man was taken away, the woman told him how she'd thwarted the robbery. He marveled at her story. "I was going to give him the money, but then he pushed my father to the ground. That's when I grabbed the knife."

The woman's name was Alison and her father, Mr. Benedict La Pucelle, owned and ran the bakery. Alan was so impressed with Alison that he decided to come back the next day for lunch. The rest was history. They hit it off and were married a year and a half later. Alan still chuckled whenever he recalled the confession of the man who had attempted the robbery. "I went in to rob the place, yeah. I pushed the old man down and she moved so fast I didn't see it coming. Before I had time to even think of grabbing the gun, there was a knife pointed at the center of my chest. I've had people point guns and knives at me before, but I saw a rage in her face that convinced me that I was gonna die. When I looked at her, I saw no fear."

Alan had taken great pleasure in telling him, "Well in that case, you're welcome. I guess I saved your life by arresting you just in time."

Alan opened the door and entered his home to find Alison reading a magazine at the kitchen table, her hair tucked behind her ears. Beside the open magazine was the usual stack of junk mail from today's delivery.

"Hey, how was your day?" Alison asked, glancing up at him.

It was the same thing she asked every day and Alan gave his typical response. "Oh, it was okay. You know, the usual."

Having been married to a cop for six years, Alison could decipher a good day from a bad one from the way Alan spoke, the way he walked, the way he held his shoulders or focused his eyes. She waited a moment. She had great patience when it came to communicating. "So what happened today? You seem to have something on your mind."

Alan downplayed it, as he always did. "Nothing much. There was a bad accident on the highway and a woman died."

Alison waited and listened, knowing he would continue. She knew he wanted to discuss it, but she also knew that when discussing difficult situations at work Alan spoke slowly and methodically.

As if on cue, Alan continued. "A car crossed over the median and struck a tractor-trailer. I got there first and found the woman trapped. I think she was dead before I arrived. I couldn't find a pulse."

"Maybe she fell asleep?" Alison offered.

"Yeah, perhaps, or maybe it was a heart attack. She lived in the city with her daughter. I had to go by and tell the woman that her mother was dead," Alan said.

"And how did her daughter take it?"

"Not well, as expected," Alan replied. "But some of the neighbors came over to stay with her."

Alison put her arms around him and rubbed his back. She knew that this kind of thing bothered him, but to outwardly ask him would only bring a denial. Besides, he had already admitted it by burying his head in her shoulder.

"Missy's been asking for you," she said. "She's in her room playing."

Alan walked down the hallway to where a door stood open. He peered at his two-year-old daughter. She was playing with building blocks covered with large letters and animals. She turned to Alan with bright blue eyes and a huge smile appeared on her face as she squealed, "Hiya Dayee!" which translated to "Hi Daddy!"

Alan momentarily forgot about anything that had happened that day at work. Missy ran to him, giggling uncontrollably, her two pigtails bouncing. She grabbed a stuffed toy monkey lying near her bed and started to speak baby gibberish to it. Alan couldn't quite understand the conversation, but he listened intently to everything she had to say. She was trying hard to explain to Alan what she meant.

As she spoke, he gave her words of encouragement by saying, "Really? That's good," and, "Oh…that monkey." When she finished, Alan said, "I love you," and hugged her tight. Missy giggled once more, apparently pleased with herself for relaying her wonderful story.

Alan returned to the kitchen with Missy and the family sat down at the table to eat dinner. He turned to Missy in her highchair and said, "Let's say a prayer before we eat." Missy pressed her tiny hands together and spoke in baby language once again. Alan wasn't quite sure it was a prayer—she mentioned the "meenkee" at least twice. Nonetheless, when she finished Alan said, "Amen."

Alison's home-cooked meal of baked chicken, potatoes, and carrots was delicious; there were even apple crepes for dessert, made from the old La Pucelle family recipe. Alan ate until he was full, then got up and began to clear the table. As usual his wife told him to leave everything for her to clean up. Alan replied as he typically did, that since she'd cooked the meal after working all day, she deserved to rest. When the dishes were done he kissed his wife on the cheek and said, "I'm going to take a shower, be back out in a few."

He waited until the water was hot, then jumped in. As the water ran over his head and shoulders he reflected on his day. His mind slipped back to the scene at the highway, Anne Munsin's lifeless body behind the steering wheel. He wondered if he could have saved her had he shown up a bit sooner or whether he should have pulled her through the car window right away. Then he remembered his fingers on her neck, trying to find her pulse when he first arrived.

Perhaps she had fallen asleep. Perhaps a heart attack had overtaken her. Maybe she had dropped something and reached down to grab it when her car slid off the road. *I hope she didn't suffer*, he thought as the water streamed over his head. *I wonder what she would have said had she still been alive when I first got there. "Tell my daughter I love her, tell her not to worry." Who knows.* The thoughts lingered in his mind for a moment.

His thoughts shifted to the memory of Karen sobbing as she struggled to deal with the shock of her mother's death. He hoped he'd done enough to comfort her, attempting to make right a situation that could not be made right.

The warm water felt good on the knotted, twisted stress in his upper neck and shoulders. He turned off the shower and dried himself. *I did what I could*, he thought.

He decided not to dwell any longer on any of it. Feeling somewhat better, he put on a large blue bathrobe and made his way to the family room, where his wife was watching television.

After a short time, he and his wife led Missy to her room and tucked her into bed. Alison kissed him on the cheek and retired to the bedroom. He contemplated staying awake for a while and watching TV, but as he yawned and stretched he decided that he'd had enough for one day. It was Saturday and he was off tomorrow; he hoped to have a chance to relax and unwind. His head was spinning as he lay down. Alison was already fast asleep. *How does she do that*, he wondered, envying her ability to fall instantly into slumber. He lay awake and stared at the rotating blades of the ceiling fan. Eventually his eyes grew heavy and he drifted into sleep.

CHAPTER SEVEN

"The perfect church service would be one
we were almost unaware of. Our attention
would have to be on God."

—C. S. Lewis

SUNDAY MORNING ARRIVED, daylight drifting in through the bedroom window. Alan was still half asleep and couldn't understand why there was a monotonous tapping pressure on his head until he opened his eyes to see a tiny hand patting him on the forehead. "Dayee...up!"

He looked up to see the baby's face inches from his. She smiled, her blue eyes wide. "I'm up, I'm up," he said. She giggled with excitement.

It was 9:00. Alison had been up for a while. Alan rolled out of bed, stretched, and shook his head to get his senses about him. He made his way into the kitchen to pour himself some coffee. Sipping it slowly, he shed his sleepy state of mind. Missy was already wearing a sundress with white and pink stripes, two pink bows in her short pigtails. Alan pulled her onto his lap and sat at the table, grateful to be at home instead of at work.

Alison entered the room wearing a flowered sundress that left her shoulders exposed. As she walked past the bay window in the kitchen the sunlight highlighted her features. There was a warm glow about her. Suddenly Alan was conscious of how attractive she was to him and of the qualities he loved about her—strength and confidence, encompassed by a gentle, loving demeanor.

"What are you looking at?" she asked with a grin.

He smiled and told her in a soft voice, "Your eyes—they remind me of how much I love you."

She blushed, then kissed him. "I love you, too."

A tiny voice from down below said, "I love Dayee, Mommy." The two looked down to see Missy smiling and clinging to each of their legs.

"Come on," said Alison. "Let's go before we're late for church."

The morning sun streamed through the stained-glass windows of the church as Pastor Flynn arranged everything for the 10:30 service. Standing only five two made it difficult to light the candles alongside the altar. To compensate for his lack of height he had to stand on the tips of his toes while he lit the flame with the ornate brass lighting stick. After the candle began to glow, he stood down and wiped some of the sweat from the bald, shiny center of his head.

He'd had a long week, with a wedding service, weekly rounds to St. Mary's Hospital, a visit to a nearby preschool for a charity event, and the funeral of a parishioner who had died in an automobile accident. These activities, along with running the day-to-day operations of the church, had drained him, so the fact that the week was nearly over was something of a relief.

It had been a dreadful funeral. "Why? How can God let this happen?" *The survivors always ask the same questions*, the pastor thought. That poor family was made up of long-time members of the church. Pastor Flynn had listened intently as the daughter told him how it had taken her a great deal of time to convince her mother to move in with her. When it finally happened, the woman, Karen, had been elated and anxious to introduce him to her mother. He had first met her last Sunday. She seemed extremely happy to be with her daughter and son-in-law.

Her husband had died three years earlier, and when she spoke of his passing, Pastor Flynn could see the look of loss and despair in her eyes. The woman had gone on to explain how fearful she'd been to move from the home where she'd lived for over forty-five years, but that she had found new comfort in being close to her daughter again.

The pastor scratched his short, gray beard as he looked out over the empty church. He could recall the extreme pain on her daughter's face at the funeral as she asked for the second time, "Why did this happen?"

He had answered as he always did when these questions were posed. "God works in ways we do not understand. Your mother is at peace. Your faith and family will help you through this."

As people began to enter the church, Pastor Flynn made his way over to greet them. Everyone smiled as they passed, acknowledging him with nods, waves, or handshakes. A group of children on their way to catechism class ran past and yelled, "Hi, Father." When most of the congregation was inside, he made his way over to where the rest of the entrance procession had gathered.

Father Joseph Antonio was the one who would actually give the service; Pastor Flynn was merely assisting for the hour. Although he enjoyed conducting the mass, he likewise enjoyed assisting. It allowed him to observe the congregation. *It's funny what people will do when they don't think anyone is watching*, he thought. He often watched the facial expressions of his congregation to try to determine their thoughts. It helped him learn who they were as people. Sometimes he felt guilty, as if this were an invasion of privacy, but in the end he concluded that his frequent case studies allowed him to focus on those who were in greater need of moral direction or spiritual support.

The procession entered the church and everyone took their places. He scanned the room and fixed his gaze on a woman sitting with her husband and two small children. The woman kept looking over at her husband. She grabbed his hand and slid her arm over his shoulder.

Her husband wore a look of indifference. He allowed her to fidget with his hand and move his arm, though he would occasionally roll his eyes to indicate that her attentiveness was a bit overbearing. The only time the woman wasn't clutching him was when she turned to keep the kids entertained and quiet. *She's starved for attention,* Pastor Flynn thought to himself. He saw the man make a quick motion to peer at something he took from his belt. As Pastor Flynn looked closer he saw that it was a cellular phone. *And he's just checking the time, counting down the minutes until he gets out of here, probably thinking about the ballgame coming on at noon.*

Pastor Flynn turned his focus to a teenage girl who was looking down at her nails. She held her hand out in front of her as if she were testing the color against her clothing. After numerous glances, she finally went on to twirl her hair and stare blankly at the floor. *Sheer boredom,* he thought.

He focused his attention on a man in the front row who was kneeling with his hands folded tightly. He didn't recognize the man, but this wasn't uncommon since the congregation was so large and continued to expand each year. The man didn't seem to be following the service. He had his eyes closed and a look of concentration on his face. Occasionally the man muttered something, his head hanging over the railing in front of the pew.

Yes, Pastor Flynn thought. *That man is actually praying, trying to communicate. He has something to say or do. I must introduce myself after the service.*

After the service concluded, those present slowly filed out. The man who had been praying was still in one of the front pews. After almost everyone had left, he stood up and made his way over to an arrangement of candles on the eastern wall of the church. He was accompanied by a woman and toddler. After he lit one of the candles, he knelt down in front of the arrangement and began to pray once more. The woman whispered something and kissed him on the cheek. Then she and the child made their way to the back of the church.

Alan stared as the flame danced slightly from left to right. He prayed for the Munsin family. He prayed for them to be comforted and consoled. He prayed for Anne Munsin, hoping that she had not endured any suffering and was finally at peace, never to be harmed by anything again. As he finished his prayers he stood up to see a balding priest in front of him.

"Everything all right?" asked Pastor Flynn.

"Yes, Father, thanks for asking. I was just praying for someone who had died and their grieving family."

"It's always difficult to lose someone close to you. But God heals us over time. Faith can make the difference," said the pastor in an attempt to comfort Alan.

"I didn't really know her or her family. I was there when it happened. I saw the despair and grief on the faces of those she left behind."

The priest looked as if he understood somehow. He seemed to admire Alan for showing compassion for others he didn't even know. "I've found that in times of great despair there often comes a sense of clarity for what should be done, what is right."

Alan nodded in agreement. "Thank you, Father. I'm sure I'll see you next week. I hope you have a good day."

"And I hope your prayers are answered, Mister…?" The priest paused expectantly.

"Crane. Alan Crane," Alan said, as he extended his hand.

Pastor Flynn shook his hand, "Nice to meet you, Mr. Crane, and God bless you."

Alan nodded. He made his way to the back of the church and held out his hands to his wife and daughter. Together they left the church.

Chapter Eight

*"The only people without problems
are those in cemeteries."*

—Anthony Robbins

AFTER ALAN DROPPED ALISON AND MISSY OFF at home, he drove out through the back of his neighborhood onto a narrow road that eventually led to the entrance of a small cemetery. A white fence stretched along its border, separating the cemetery from the road and a bean field farther out. To the south was a large, open meadow with neatly cut grass; to the back was the tree line, creating a barrier that led to yet another field. Headstones lined the area behind the white fence near the main driveway that split the cemetery into two distinct portions.

The driveway wound through the cemetery, touching the edge of the bean field and the grassy meadow. Two buildings sat between the fields. The first was a large mausoleum containing numerous vaults, nineteen across and seven high. The walls were constructed of polished marble engraved with the names of those buried within. The other structure was a tiny chapel with a small viewing room and a single row of chairs.

As Alan approached the southern side of the mausoleum he stopped to observe the colorful displays on many of the vaults. Each had a small knob located in the upper corner of a marble stone faceplate; the knob was used to hold a plastic vase. Many of the vases were filled with flowers, projecting a wonderful collage of color that offset the dark, polished marble. Alan noticed numerous notes, keepsakes, flags, and other items, all left by the loved ones of those who had died. Each seemed to have a significant meaning and held a sense of love, grief, or remembrance.

One particular vault caught Alan's eye. Taped to the front of the marble was a piece of notebook paper. The weather had worn away some of the writing, but shiny, blue stickers of puppies and butterflies could be seen on the top and bottom. The words that were still legible were written in crayon and hard to decipher, but Alan could make out the message: "Daddy, I miss you and I made this for you. I don't know why you're gone, but I love you and will come back soon." He looked up at the engraving on the marble that read:

Bonner
Jason M. Elizabeth R.
1970–2000 1971–

Jason had been thirty years old when he died. Seeing this, Alan was momentarily overcome with a feeling of emptiness.

His eyes dropped to the ground. He saw a picture of a young boy directly below the paper. He picked it up and looked at the back where "Tanner, 2007" was written. He peeled back one of the butterfly stickers and used it to reattach the picture. Shaking his head, all he could think about was his daughter and the joy they brought to each other's lives— joy that Tanner and his father would no longer share.

He walked around to the eastern side of the building where a small overhang spanned from the roof of the mausoleum to the roof of the chapel. A small marble bench sat on the edge of the walkway that stretched around the mausoleum. Alan sat down on the bench and stared at the graves in the second row. The feelings of loss conveyed by all of the small trinkets strewn about the cemetery began to overwhelm him. He had seated himself across from the topmost grave in the second row. The engraving read:

Jonathan L. Crane
1984–2005

Alan looked around to make sure he was alone. After letting out a long sigh, he spoke quietly. "Well, I'm back. I had a long week. Work has been hell. Missy's getting bigger—she's got a real imagination. I wish you were here to see her. You'd really like her." He hung his head for a moment, consumed by a sharp pain that shot up through his chest and tightened his throat. As he fought back a tear, he continued, "Mom and Dad are doing really well. I know Mom doesn't come to visit much, but she took it really hard after you were gone. I hope you're happy— wherever you are." He turned his gaze back up to the vault and said, "I'll see you next time. Try to stay out of trouble."

His brother Jonathan had been ten years younger than he was. Jonathan was the personality of the family, the life of every party, and the one who brought humor to any situation. Alan was the serious one, the leader who had no time for jokes, perhaps because he was the oldest.

When Jonathan was eighteen years old he enlisted in the Navy and went south for basic training. Two weeks into training, during a run, Jonathan collapsed and was rushed to an area hospital. They believed he had suffered a brain aneurysm. The doctors performed emergency surgery and relieved the pressure in his head, ultimately saving his life. Jonathan returned home with a medical discharge, fully recovered. After a few months he began to get sick with frequent headaches and vomiting. He returned to a hospital where more tests were performed. Finally the doctors located an inoperable brain tumor. The doctors told all of them that Jonathan's condition was bleak. They said he had six months to live.

Three years later, Jonathan died. Family and friends gathered at the cemetery to pay their respects. Alan's fellow police officers showed up to comfort him and offer support. It was one of the worst days of Alan's life. He had found himself asking the question for which he thought he would never receive an answer: "Why? Why him, why now?"

Standing up, Alan walked between the headstones until he came to one in the back row near the white fence. His thoughts shifted from his family to his brothers and sisters in law enforcement as he ran his index finger over the etched police badge at the top of the large marble stone in front of him. A surreal feeling overwhelmed him; memories of flag-draped caskets filled his mind as the echoing of bagpipes and bugles momentarily engulfed him. *Police funerals are rough*, he thought as he stared down at the name engraved on the black headstone:

Officer James E. Travis
1981–2007
Bakersville Police Department

Alan remembered Jim Travis. He had worked for the neighboring community of Bakersville and had been on the job for about three years before he was killed. Travis's death had been senseless. He was conducting a traffic stop on a middle-aged man with a clean record. The motorist was a successful psychologist named Stewart Anderson, who was pulled over for running a stop sign. Travis had taken Anderson's driver's license and returned to his patrol car to check on the license status and vehicle registration.

Suddenly Anderson had jumped out of his car and produced a nickel-plated .45-caliber pistol. He fired at Travis through the front window of his patrol car. Two rounds caught Travis in the neck and one struck him on the left side of his skull. He died that evening at the hospital. Anderson was arrested and made an initial statement saying that he had believed that he had a warrant for his arrest for not paying a traffic ticket. He'd panicked because going to jail would ruin his professional career—*as though killing a cop was going to help it*, Alan thought. Anderson was later convicted of first-degree murder and sentenced to life without parole. Three days after he began serving his sentence, he hanged himself in his cell with a bed sheet.

The memories of James Travis's funeral faded from Alan's mind as the disturbing vision of a murder scene entered it. He backtracked toward the driveway once more and stopped at a headstone that bordered the road. There was a large tree just to the right of the grave. Numerous wind chimes hung from the branches. One of the chimes consisted of four crystal angels that glistened in the sunlight, projecting soft colors all around. The engraving on the headstone read:

Melissa A. Timmons
1975–1998

Small statuettes and decorations lined the headstone. Propped up against the lip was a small, engraved plaque that read:

Our loving daughter,
who was taken from us without warning.
We'll never know why.

A somber mood came over Alan as he looked at the tombstone. He recalled the pain on her parents' faces when they were told that their daughter had been murdered. Melissa Timmons was a hardworking college girl who held down two jobs while going to school for her nursing degree. She lived alone in an apartment in the eastern part of town. One evening, to get some fresh air, she had left a downstairs window open and gone to bed. A young man who was staying with some friends in the area had torn the screen and entered Melissa's apartment. In the morning she was found raped and strangled. The image of Melissa's lifeless body still stuck in Alan's mind. Her skin was pale white; the suspect had poured bleach over her, trying to destroy any DNA evidence. Alan remembered that day well. It was the day he had questioned his faith. *How could this be just? How can God let this happen?*

The murderer was eventually arrested and confessed to the crimes. He had been attempting to steal something in the house and was under the influence of several narcotics. He was later convicted of rape and first-degree murder.

As Alan made his way up the driveway with Melissa's murder still on his mind, he passed another headstone with a sculpture of an angel encompassing the outside. The angel's great wings wrapped around the border of the stone and her head was buried in her folded forearms as if she were weeping. In one of her hands she held a single, wilted rose. Alan pondered the symbolism and significance of the crying figure. *Perhaps God grieves alongside those who are in pain*, he thought, *those who are distraught, those who seek the answer to the mystery of death.*

He returned to his car and drove down the rest of the driveway, winding through the western half of the cemetery. As he gazed over the numerous headstones and plots, his mind wandered to all of those buried within. He wondered how each of them had died and who they had left behind. What was their story? Why were they chosen?

As he rounded the loop he saw a large statue of the Virgin Mary with her circular halo—twelve stars at the ends of twelve distinct beams radiating out. The black marble base of the statue was about two feet tall, with seven golden rods reaching to each of the hands, as if she were pulling light from the ground, pulling power from below, reaching out into the darkness and finding something good in a pool of despair.

Alan circled back around and headed up toward the entranceway. He pulled onto the roadway and drove back the way he had come.

Arriving home, he parked and went into the house. As he entered the kitchen he saw the Sunday paper on the counter. He glanced down at the headlines and read:

Woman Killed in Accident
Remains a Mystery

Alan moved his eyes below the caption to the article, which read:

Anne Munsin, sixty-eight years old, died Saturday afternoon when her car crossed over the median of Highway 11 near the 304-mile marker and struck a tractor-trailer. Ms. Munsin had been residing with her daughter in Riverston. Police, firefighters, and EMS responded to the scene to find Ms. Munsin dead behind the wheel. The driver of the tractor-trailer was unharmed. Emergency responders on the scene would not give definite conclusions as to how the accident occurred but stated that Ms. Munsin may have fallen asleep at the wheel or lost consciousness. The exact cause of Mrs. Munsin's death has not been determined; however, the Tri-County Medical Examiner's office will be conducting an autopsy soon. She is survived by her daughter, Ms. Karen Munsin, who stated that her mother had recently moved to Riverston and described her as a "sweet and caring woman." Ms. Munsin went on to say that her mother will be missed by all and she wished that she had more answers as to why this tragic incident had occurred.

CHAPTER NINE

"The ghosts you chase you never catch."

—John Malkovich

AFTER A RESTFUL WEEKEND, Alan returned to work and tied up all of the loose ends associated with the fatal accident report. The rest of the week was fairly uneventful, with only the typical calls involving property damage and minor thefts. On Friday he was sitting in his office reviewing some activity reports when his phone rang. It was Lisa, the receptionist for the police department.

"Alan, there's a gentleman at the front desk requesting to see you," she said.

"Did he give a name and reference?"

Lisa replied, "He didn't give me a name, but he said that he was from some federal agency, the National Crisis Intervention Bureau. He's dressed like someone from the federal government—suit and tie, you know the type. He wouldn't give me a reference, only that he needed to speak with you. The lieutenant is out with him right now; he may be able to tell you more."

"That's okay. I'll be up to meet him in a few minutes."

He straightened some things on his desk and cleared off a large stack of forms from one of the extra chairs in his office. He walked down a long hallway until he came to the main door leading to the lobby. As he swung the door open he observed a tall, official-looking man dressed in a dark suit with a neatly pressed white shirt and a dark red tie. His serious facial features looked like they were chiseled out of stone and his short, black hair was perfectly groomed. *Definitely a fed*, thought Alan. The man extended his hand and Alan shook it.

The man's voice was deep and serious. "Hello, Sergeant Crane. I'm Michael Simmons. Is there somewhere we can talk?"

"Sure," said Alan. "Follow me."

Alan led him inside the department and briefly stopped at the break area to offer Mr. Simmons a cup of coffee. Simmons politely refused. They continued down the hallway and into Alan's office. Mr. Simmons sat down in the chair that Alan had cleared off as Alan took a seat behind his desk.

"I'm sorry Mr. Simmons—what agency did you say you're with?"

"The National Crisis Intervention Bureau. We deal with law enforcement matters involving victims and survivors to help render aid to those who need it."

"Ah," said Alan. "I didn't know that branch of the federal government existed. So how can I help?"

"Well, your help is exactly what we're looking for. We're branching out and looking to form teams within each county. We're aware of how well you handle victims and survivors of fatal situations. Your talents have not gone unnoticed. You seem to have a real knack for showing compassion during times of grief."

Alan sat back, thinking. This whole encounter was odd. He was beginning to think that it was a well-mastered practical joke that some of the guys were playing on him. His thoughts raced back to Murphy, who had complimented him just last week on how good he was at handling Karen Munsin.

"By chance, do you know Officer Murphy?" asked Alan, watching

Simmons closely for some indication that this was all a setup. The man said nothing as Alan looked for a smile, a flinch, or some other flaw in his body language.

Simmons gave off no such signals.

Instead he looked rather confused and said, "No, I don't know any Officer Murphy." He went on. "We'd like you to be a member of our regional team for this area. I've already spoken with your lieutenant and your captain and cleared it with them. Since this is not a full-time commitment, it will not interfere with your other duties here. It will be on a case-by-case basis."

"What would I be required to do?" asked Alan.

"It's simple. You'll meet with victims and survivors to assist them through their difficult time, just as you've done many times in the past—like you did last weekend."

"You sure you don't know Murphy?"

"No, can't say I've ever met him. Why do you ask?"

Alan dismissed it, unsure now of his suspicions. "Oh, no reason in particular. I thought maybe he had talked to you about last weekend."

"I see. No, actually Ms. Munsin thought you did an excellent job. She was very complimentary regarding your kindness and concern when you broke the news of her mother's death to her."

Feeling somewhat stupid about his earlier paranoia, Alan shrugged. He wasn't overly anxious to spend even more time in those difficult situations involving grieving loved ones, distraught and upset. But the experience with a federal agency would look good on his resume, and he had no real excuse if his superiors had already given him permission. "Well, since my supervisors are okay with it, I guess I can help out. How do I get started and what do I have to do?"

"Well," Simmons began, "there's not much to do initially. Here are some credentials; you'll need them to identify yourself as part of our team." He handed a box over to Alan. "We'll contact you when we need to activate the team. I appreciate your time. Welcome aboard," said Simmons. He stood up and extended his hand to Alan.

"Thank you," replied Alan. "Do you know the way out?"

"Yes, I'll manage just fine." And with that he left the office.

Alan reached out and picked up the square box that Michael Simmons had left. Inside he found a gold-plated badge on a lanyard that he could slip over his head. Alan studied the badge closely. There were no markings on it.

Strange, he thought.

There was no organization name, no seal in the center, no department serial number of any sort. Underneath the badge was a plastic ID card that had a small photo of Alan, his name, date of birth, height, weight, and eye color. On the top of the card were the letters NCIB. Alan wondered how his photo had been obtained; they must have contacted the Division of Motor Vehicles and taken it from his driver's license, as it was the same picture. He stuffed the badge and ID card into his pocket.

His phone rang again. The receptionist said, "Hey, don't forget about this guy in the lobby."

"Already spoke with him and he's left."

Lisa's voice was confused. "Uh, he's still sitting here."

Alan wondered why Simmons was still in the lobby. Perhaps he had forgotten something. "Okay, be right there," he said as he got up and left his office for the second time.

He made his way back to the reception desk and approached Lisa. She motioned to an older man sitting in a chair at the other side of the room.

"I thought you meant Mr. Simmons was still here. Who is this guy?"

Lisa, normally fairly composed, looked completely bewildered. "Who's Mr. Simmons?"

Alan came a bit too close and knocked over a cup of pens. As they spilled across the desk Lisa scooped them up and put them back in the cup, aligning them just right so that all of them were perfectly upright and an equal distance from one another. She then placed the cup back in its proper position on the desk and lowered her gaze, as if she were measuring the distance between it and the stapler that sat to one side. Alan rolled his eyes, slightly annoyed by Lisa's obsessive behavior—or, as she would put it, her heightened attention to detail.

"Simmons, you know, the guy from the National Crisis Intervention Bureau." Alan tried to keep his impatience out of his tone.

Lisa screwed up her face in complete puzzlement. "The guy who was just here," Alan clarified. "The fed, the guy in the suit. He just left my office. *You* told me he was here, remember?"

"Alan…the only person who's arrived here today asking for you is that gentleman sitting in the chair over there. His name is Elmer Hollenhoff. He wants to file a complaint against Murphy."

Alan wanted to continue the debate about his visit from Mr. Simmons, but when Lisa had motioned to him, Mr. Hollenhoff had risen from his chair and was now walking over. Alan guessed him to be in his late seventies and noticed that his purple and blue plaid pants were pulled up nearly to his chest.

In a raspy voice he asked, "Are you the one in charge?" His breath smelled like a mixture of onions and stale coffee. Alan took a step back so as to avoid another pungent dose.

"I'm the sergeant on duty at this time."

"Good. I need to talk to you about a very serious matter. We must speak alone."

Grudgingly, Alan said, "Follow me."

He led Mr. Hollenhoff into the station and back to a small conference room. Both of them sat down and Alan said, "How may I help you?"

Mr. Hollenhoff took out a yellow piece of paper. Alan recognized it as a defendant's copy of a traffic ticket. "This Officer Murphy of yours. I have a real problem with him."

"What's the problem?"

"He's unprofessional and rude," barked Hollenhoff.

"And what did he do that was unprofessional and rude, Mr. Hollenhoff?"

"He gave me a ticket for speeding," said the old man in a thoroughly disgusted voice.

"And were you speeding?"

"Well, yes, but he could have cut me a break. Do you realize I've lived in this city for forty-two years and I've never been pulled over, not once?"

"Weren't you involved in an accident recently?" Alan asked, suddenly recognizing the man's name. "You ran a stop sign and struck another motorist."

"Yeah," said Hollenhoff indignantly, "but I was never *pulled over*. Like I said, I've lived here for forty-two years and I know everyone around town. I know the mayor and I know everyone on the city council."

"Sir," Alan interrupted, "you were pulled over for speeding and ticketed accordingly. You need to go to court and speak with the judge about this matter, not complain to me."

"You're no better than that Murphy cop. I can see why he has such a bad attitude. You probably trained him. I'm done with you. Who's your boss?"

"Oh, my boss?" asked Alan said with a grin. "That would be Lieutenant Mario Gaspero. If you'd like to speak to him, I can check to see if he's in."

"Show me where he is," ordered Hollenhoff.

Alan stood up. "Right this way."

Gaspero was sitting at his desk. He was a short man with a dark complexion, curly black hair, and a thin mustache. He was looking down at some reports when Alan knocked on the door and opened it.

Gaspero looked up. "Yes?" he asked.

"Lieutenant, there's a gentleman here who wants to complain about me and about Officer Murphy. He's upset with Officer Murphy because he issued Mr. Hollenhoff here," Alan paused to point at the old man standing next to him, "a summons for speeding. And he's upset with me because I didn't offer to void the ticket." Gaspero's lip began to curl slightly in annoyance. "The gentleman admits that he was speeding," Alan continued. "However, he's lived here for a long time and claims to know many important people in the city, including our mayor and elected officials."

Hollenhoff was halfway in the door and could hear everything. He pushed his way past Alan and strode into Lieutenant Gaspero's office.

If Alan could pinpoint one distinct weakness in Gaspero, it was an inability to restrain himself from expressing his thoughts and opinions.

"So," Gaspero drawled. "You're upset because Officer Murphy wrote you a ticket for speeding? Which, by your own admission, you were guilty of doing? And you're also upset at Sergeant Crane because he didn't offer to fix your ticket, which you admit you deserved. Is that accurate?"

"Yeah," said Hollenhoff. "I think that's unprofessional. I'm a taxpayer here, and I'm paying everyone's salary."

"Tell you what. You go back home and come back to waste my time when you're not acting like an idiot. Which in my opinion may never happen. If you want to complain to anyone above me you'll have to make an appointment, but until then, get out of here and work on grow-ing a brain—or borrow someone else's! Oh, and tell the mayor I said hi when you see him. We're old friends, go way back. Have a nice day." He paused and addressed Alan. "Show him out, Sergeant, unless he has some type of crime to report."

Hollenhoff's jaw was agape. He was speechless.

"Right this way, Mr. Hollenhoff," Alan said.

Hollenhoff followed Alan to the front door, growling something indiscernible under his breath. He walked past Alan as though he were in a trance. Alan closed the door behind him and returned to Gaspero's office. The lieutenant was still shaking his head, a disgusted look on his face.

"Hey, Lieutenant, I wanted to make sure that I'm clear to participate in the Crisis Intervention Program. I met with Mr. Simmons, the coordinator. He said that he'd cleared it with you."

"Don't know any Simmons," replied Gaspero. "But we did receive paperwork requesting your participation on that team. The captain said he liked the idea, so you're all ready to go. Let me know what you need so I can make the appropriate arrangements."

"You never spoke with Mr. Simmons?" Alan asked, perplexed. "He said that he'd spoken about the program with you and the captain."

"Nope," drawled Gaspero. "He must have seen the captain. I've never met him."

Alan thanked him and left.

As he drove off after work he decided to go by and check on Ms. Munsin to see how she and her family were doing. He pulled into the driveway at 136 Carnac Lane, got out of his car, and approached the door. Within a moment or so after he rang the bell, Karen Munsin came to the door and smiled as she saw him.

"Please come in," she said as she took a step back from the doorway.

"Hello, Ms. Munsin. I don't mean to intrude but I thought I would see how you and your family are doing."

"No intrusion at all, Sergeant. I wanted to thank you for your help that day. It's still difficult, but we're getting through it." She sighed heavily but gave him another brave smile.

"Ma'am," Alan began, "did someone from the National Crisis Intervention Bureau visit you in these past few days? Specifically an agent named Michael Simmons?"

She shook her head. "No, nobody like that has visited. Why do you ask?"

"No reason really," Alan said, thinking quickly. "Sometimes they do follow-up visits with victims or survivors of critical incidents. I was just wondering if they had made it by," he said, hoping this would not alarm her.

She seemed to dismiss it. "No, I haven't seen anyone yet, but that sounds like a wonderful program."

"Yes." Alan agreed. "Yes, it is. Well, I won't keep you. Just wanted to check to see how everyone was doing. If you need anything, don't hesitate to call."

"Thank you, Sergeant Crane," she said.

Alan backed out of the door and left. His curiosity was piqued now. He had the feeling that he was being deceived. He returned to the station and went to the receptionist desk where Lisa was talking on the phone. He waited until she hung up the receiver, then resumed the conversation they had not finished when Mr. Hollenhoff had interrupted.

"Okay. Once more from the top. You don't recall a man in a navy blue suit who asked to see me?"

"No," said Lisa with a bit of annoyance in her voice. "The older man with the complaint was the only person asking for you today."

"And you didn't see me walk out here and escort anyone in?"

"Just the grumpy old man," answered Lisa, somewhat indignantly, as if Alan was questioning her work ethic.

"Okay." Alan knew that the conversation was over.

He left the lobby and made his way into the communications center where he met with the supervisor. Angela was a middle-aged woman who had been a dispatcher for years. Her experience allowed her to multitask with ease; she listened to Alan as she was talking to someone else on the phone.

"Angela, I need to look at the security tape of the lobby from an hour ago."

Angela nodded, continued talking on the phone and began typing on her keyboard.

A small video screen on her computer changed to show the department lobby. The time and date were displayed in the lower right-hand corner. Alan could see Lisa sitting at her desk. The video went on for a while. Then Alan saw a shot of himself walking through the door, turning, and reentering the department. A few moments later Mr. Hollenhoff entered and approached the desk. Alan looked at his disgruntled face and imagined him barking his discontent at Lisa as she sat there and nodded politely.

"It's not there. Rewind it and play it again," Alan said quickly. Then, thinking that he may have come across somewhat rude, he added, "Please."

Angela played the scene over again.

"Nothing," said Alan out loud. "I can't believe it, he's not there." *Maybe I imagined it*, he thought. *Maybe I'm too stressed out.*

He reached into his pocket and pulled out the badge and ID card.

No, he concluded. *No way I imagined it. Maybe he was out of the cameras' viewing range when he entered the lobby.*

Alan made his way back down the hallway and turned to go back to his office.

Michael Simmons, Alan thought. *Lisa didn't see this guy. He's not on the camera. Neither Lieutenant Gaspero nor Karen Munsin spoke to him.*

Alan paused just outside his office, then turned and headed down the hallway toward the administrative offices instead. He approached an office door that held a placard to the right of it reading, CAPTAIN THOMAS FINCH, ASSISTANT CHIEF OF POLICE. He peered through the window in the center of the door and saw the captain sitting at his desk looking at a stack of papers. Alan knocked. The captain motioned for him to come in.

Captain Finch was a stocky man in his late fifties who had salt-and-pepper hair and a thick mustache. He was typically a pleasant person to talk to and had a fatherly demeanor toward Alan.

He looked up and said, "Hello, Alan. How is everything?"

"Good, Captain. I'm not interrupting you, am I?"

"Not at all. Come in and sit down. I don't get to talk to you guys enough. What can I do for you?"

Alan sat down. "Well, I was wondering if you had heard about the National Crisis Intervention Bureau asking for my assistance?"

"Yes, I did. Sounds like a great program. I know you'll be great at it. Our officers sometimes excel in specific areas because of the work they do on the job. Just so happens that you have a knack for the communication end, which in my opinion is the most critical of all skills."

"Thank you, Captain. I'm looking forward to it. Say—did a representative or special agent from the NCIB speak with you? Someone named Michael Simmons?"

"Yes, Mr. Simmons spoke with me this morning. I've spoken with him before; he's a real professional. You'll like working with him."

Relief washed over Alan, so much so that Finch gave him a concerned look. "Everything okay?"

"Oh, yes sir. Just wanted to make sure I had clearance to participate."

"Absolutely. If you need anything, you let me know."

"Thank you, Captain. I won't keep you any longer. I need to get back to some paperwork."

"Don't we all?" said Finch, gesturing at his own stack of forms. "I'll see you around."

Alan left Finch's office and headed back to his own. Relieved to know that he wasn't going crazy, he sat down in his chair and breathed deeply. He took the stack of reports from the corner of his desk and began to check them over. *Simmons must have avoided the camera in the lobby. But I wonder how he could have gotten by Lisa. She's so obsessive about exact details. I'll definitely have to tease her later about it,* Alan concluded with a half smile.

CHAPTER TEN

"To awake from death is to die in peace."

—Doug Horton

E VA KRATSON STOOD IN THE MIDDLE of her kitchen pouring apple filling into a newly formed piecrust. She finished, put the pie into the oven, and stirred a large pot of homemade soup on the stovetop. She wanted to get everything ready before her daughter Abby, her son-in-law, and their two children arrived for lunch. She and her husband, Andrew, were in their early seventies and both eagerly looked forward to seeing their family, especially their grandchildren. Lunch wasn't anything fancy today, just soup and sandwiches. She had cooked a ham the evening before and baked some bread from scratch. *Nothing like food made from scratch*, she thought, stirring happily. Besides the apple pie, she had already baked a cherry one, and even some chocolate chip cookies. The room was filled with the wonderful aroma of baking.

It was 12:15 already; there wasn't much time before everyone arrived. Andrew had been doing some work in the yard and was now upstairs taking a shower. Eva hoped he was hurrying. *I really need him to bring up those extra chairs*, she thought.

She took out a prescription bottle and opened it. How she hated these child-proof caps, so hard to open. But with grandkids around, you needed them. Andrew was forgetful at times and didn't remember to take his medication, but Eva was always on top of it. His blood pressure had really improved since he'd started taking this particular prescription.

The cuckoo clock on the wall read 12:28. *What's taking him so long?* she wondered. The soup on the stove began to simmer, so she placed the metal lid on top of the pot. Hurrying just a little, she went upstairs. Their townhouse was small, a one-bedroom with a bathroom upstairs and the kitchen, family room, and laundry room on the main floor. There was also a small basement for minimal storage space, but they didn't have many things to put down there. Outside there was a small porch with a tiny yard where they had planted a tree and a few bushes. Andrew loved working on the landscaping and the area was just big enough to keep his interest.

As Eva topped the stairs she could hear the sound of the water beating down on the base of the shower tub. She approached the door and knocked.

"Dear," she called, "are you almost done?" There was no response, but Andrew was somewhat hard of hearing. She called again, knocking louder this time. There was still no answer.

She returned downstairs quickly to check on the food. The soup was still simmering nicely and the pie needed to bake a little longer. Eva returned to the bathroom. This time she grabbed the doorknob and twisted it.

"I'm coming in," she called as she pushed the handle.

The door wouldn't budge. The doorknob turned, but the door wouldn't open. It felt blocked.

Her anxiety beginning to rise, Eva yelled, "Andrew, are you all right?" No response.

Panic set in. She hit the door with her hand and screamed, "Andrew, can you hear me?" Determination and fear giving her strength, she pushed her shoulder into the door, but it still would not open. She ran downstairs, grabbed the phone, and dialed 911.

Alan was finishing lunch in the department break room with Murphy when the dispatch came over the radio.

"Available units copy for a 'check the well-being' at 901 Shallow Meadows Court. Caller advises that her husband was in the shower and is concerned for his safety as he's not responding to her shouts through the door. Further advises that the door is stuck and her husband has a history of high blood pressure and heart problems."

Alan acknowledged the dispatcher and advised that they were en route. He requested an ambulance response to meet him there. Within a few moments they were approaching the parking lot in front of the townhouse complex, Alan's car pulling in just ahead of Murphy's. They hurried toward the front door. Mrs. Kratson appeared, still wearing her apron with a frantic look on her face.

"Please help! I can't get the door open."

"Where is it?" asked Alan. Mrs. Kratson led them through the kitchen and up the stairs.

"He's in there. He won't answer me and I can't get the door open. Please help me." Her voice was trembling.

"What's your husband's name, ma'am?"

"Andrew."

He knocked on the door loudly and yelled, "Andrew, can you hear me?"

He pushed with his hips as he twisted the knob. The door seemed to be jammed. As he heaved his shoulder into it, Alan felt it give way slightly. He could hear the water running and now could feel hot steam escaping from the crack in the doorway. Pushing even harder, he was able to force it back even more and reach one hand inside. Murphy lent his strength to pushing the door, and together they finally created a large enough opening so that Alan could peer into the bathroom.

He immediately saw the elderly man face down on the floor. His head was propped up against the door and his feet were braced against the tub, which explained why they'd had to push so hard to get in. Alan squeezed his shoulders through the opening, grabbed the man under the armpits, and lifted him away from the door enough so that Murphy could open it all the way. The bathroom was extremely small; Alan barely had any room to maneuver. He placed the man on his back, grabbed his hands, and pulled him out into the hallway.

"Go get the defibrillator out of your car," he ordered Murphy. "I don't think he's breathing and I don't feel a pulse."

Mrs. Kratson began sobbing uncontrollably. "No! No!"

Just then the doorbell rang and she darted downstairs behind Murphy. Alan took out a CPR pocket mask and placed it over Andrew Kratson's mouth. He tilted the head back. As he did, the man shook his head and opened his eyes.

"Sir, can you hear me?"

"Yes, I can."

Andrew sat up. As he rubbed his eyes, Alan could see a dark, red bruise on the right side of his forehead. He moaned. "I was taking a shower and slipped on a bar of soap in the tub. The next thing I knew you were leaning over me."

"Well, you gave us all a scare. But it looks like you're doing better now. Still, we want the paramedics to check you out. Did you have any chest pains before you fell?"

"Nope," replied Andrew. "It was all that blasted bar of soap."

As Alan helped Mr. Kratson to his feet, he looked up and saw someone ascending the stairs. It was Michael Simmons.

Alan shook his head in confusion. "What are you doing here?"

"I thought you might need a hand."

In a somewhat apprehensive tone, Alan said, "All is well here. Mr. Kratson took a tumble, but he's okay. How did you know about this call—how did you get here so quickly?"

"We monitor your radio traffic." Simmons turned, then asked, "Doing okay, Mr. Kratson?"

"Yes, indeed, thanks to this officer."

"Come on, I'll help you downstairs," said Simmons as he took Mr. Kratson by the arm.

"Be down in a minute," said Alan as he crumpled up the CPR mask and looked for a place to dispose of it. Simmons and Mr. Kratson descended the stairs together as he went back into the bathroom to find a trash can.

Where's Murphy? he wondered.

Murphy had run out to his car to grab the defibrillator and should have returned by now—they were parked just out front. Alan found the trash can. As he threw the mask away he heard someone breathing hard behind him.

"Giving up on him, boss?" asked Murphy.

"Giving up?" Alan was confused. He turned to see Murphy standing with the small, yellow, boxlike instrument in his hand. "What are you—"

He never finished the sentence. As he looked down at the lifeless body of Mr. Kratson lying on the floor in front of him, a cold sense of fear and anxiety gripped his throat and struck him in the center of his chest.

Alan scrambled back down to where Mr. Kratson lay motionless. "What the hell? He was awake! He was just up!"

Murphy was now on the floor hooking up the electrodes to the device. He placed them on Mr. Kratson's bare chest. Alan shook his head in confusion as he noticed the CPR mask on Mr. Kratson's face. *What is going on?* Murphy switched on the defibrillator. It ran a short diagnostic test as it warmed up, then set forth an audible voice signal. "Shock recommended," it said.

"Stand back, Sarge," said Murphy.

"I'm clear."

Murphy pressed the shock button and Mr. Kratson's body lurched. The device ran another diagnostic test, looking for a pulse. Then came the same audible voice signal: "Shock recommended."

Once more Murphy pushed the button and Mr. Kratson's body heaved in distress.

Alan's head was spinning. He was dizzy and wondered if he might pass out. *No*, he told himself. *I've been in worse situations. I need to pull it together and get this done.*

Once again, no pulse was found. The defibrillator recommended a third shock. Murphy obliged.

By this time two paramedics had come up the stairs. Alan moved back to give them room to assess Mr. Kratson. Mrs. Kratson was cowering in a corner of the hallway, apparently in shock. Alan walked over to her and, putting his arm around her, led her downstairs. She continued to sob as he led her into the kitchen.

A moment later four people walked through the open front door, a man and women with two small children. The woman ran up to Mrs. Kratson frantically. "Mom! What's wrong? What's happened?"

Mrs. Kratson replied, voice shaking. "Your father, I think he had a heart attack."

She sobbed as her daughter yelled, "No, this can't be! Where is he?"

Alan replied, "He's upstairs. The paramedics are trying to help him. You should stay here and help your mother."

She pushed Alan aside, seeming almost enraged.

"Abby, wait," said the man with her, but it was too late. She had already run up the stairs. Alan heard her scream hysterically. Both children began crying in fear.

Alan stood up. In a low voice he said, "Why don't we all go outside for a few minutes?"

The man nodded and put his arms around the kids, who were still crying. They all went out onto the front porch, and Alan felt them all take a collective breath.

"I know it was his heart," said Mrs. Kratson, "I just know it was. It's all my fault. I should have made him take his medicine this morning."

"Eva, it's not your fault," said the man. Alan guessed that he must be her son-in-law.

Mrs. Kratson turned and looked at Alan. "Do you know what happened? You saw him, you were up there."

"I think he slipped on a bar of soap and fell in the tub. He hit his head. I don't think he had a heart attack."

"How do you know that?" she asked. She stopped crying for a moment.

"Well," Alan began. "Well, he told me he had slipped. I guess he told me right before he…" Alan trailed off.

"Did he say anything else?" asked Mrs. Kratson.

"Well, yes. He said he felt fine."

A bittersweet smile came over Eva Kratson's face. *How can she believe what I'm telling her?* Alan wondered. He wasn't making it up, but he was having problems believing it himself. He knew things just weren't adding up.

"At least he wasn't in any pain," she said, sounding somewhat comforted.

"I don't believe so. He seemed to be happy…you know, before he was gone."

Mrs. Kratson nodded as if she accepted and approved of this thought. She choked back some more tears. "Good, that's good." She paused for a moment, thinking, then asked, "If he was awake and talking to you, then how did he die? If he felt fine, then what happened?"

Alan was wondering the same thing himself. With a blank stare on his face he replied softly, "I wish I knew. He was there one minute, then gone the next. I wish I knew."

He composed himself. "Ma'am, the medical examiner may want to do an autopsy to determine what happened. Perhaps that may give us some answers."

Mrs. Kratson said nothing. She hugged her son-in-law and grand-children tightly. Her daughter had stepped outside. She joined them, her face somber and dazed. Her husband embraced her as she cried on his chest. Inside the house, Alan heard footsteps descending the stairs and saw paramedics approaching the front door. They were bringing out their equipment. They stopped to speak to Mrs. Kratson.

In a soft, comforting tone, one of the paramedics said, "Ma'am, I know it's a very difficult time, but we need some information from you." Mrs. Kratson nodded and followed the paramedic into the parking lot where the ambulance was parked.

They both returned a short time later. Mrs. Kratson joined her other family members. The paramedic approached Alan and said, "We have everything we need. Thanks for the help."

"Same to you. We'll get it wrapped up here soon."

The paramedics jumped in the ambulance and left. Murphy came through the front door holding a clipboard and talking on a cell phone.

He hung up the phone and said to Alan in a low voice, "The medical examiner has someone on the way to take the body."

Alan nodded in confirmation, then approached Mrs. Kratson and the others. "The medical examiner's office is sending someone out to help. They will transport Mr. Kratson. If you can think of a funeral home you wish to use, let us know. I'll have those from the medical examiner's office explain more when they arrive."

Everyone nodded. Mrs. Kratson and Abby were still sobbing.

Alan motioned to Murphy and said, "Follow me."

Murphy followed Alan back into the house and up the stairs to where Mr. Kratson's body was lying lifeless on the floor.

"Murphy, listen to me. I have to tell you something. There was a man here named Michael Simmons. He works for the federal government on some type of victim's task force. He was here, right here, and he spoke with Mr. Kratson before he died."

Murphy looked utterly confused. "You mean he may have had something to do with this guy's death? How do you know he was here? You think he snuck up on the victim while he was taking a shower, or..."

"No, no. When you left to get the defibrillator, Simmons came up the stairs. The old man sat up and was talking to me. Simmons helped him up—took his arm and started walking him down the stairs. I went back into the bathroom to throw the mask away. That's when you reappeared and Kratson was lying on the floor like it had never happened."

Murphy shook his head. "There's no way someone passed me either in or out of the house. I was only gone about thirty seconds, and I ran the whole way. Mr. Kratson was in the same position as when I left... and...well, your CPR mask was still on his face when I got back up here."

Murphy paused, his expression saying clearly what he could not put into words: Alan must have been seeing things.

Sparing him the awkwardness, Alan said, "I'm just having a bad day. Not enough sleep last night, you know? Sometimes this job gets to you."

Relief flashed over Murphy's face as he accepted Alan's answer. "Yeah, tell me about it."

The thought briefly crossed Alan's mind to ask Mrs. Kratson or the others if they had seen Simmons, but he realized that the conversation would go extremely poorly. That question would lead to a great deal of other questions on their part, questions for which he had no answer.

They both heard the sound of a car door opening. Alan and Murphy returned outside to see a black minivan parked in front of the townhouse. Two men in suits were standing there speaking to the family.

One of them approached Alan and said, "We're here from the medical examiner's office. Where is the deceased?"

Alan motioned behind him. "Up the stairs."

The man returned to the minivan and opened the rear hatch. The other man helped him unload a stretcher. Mrs. Kratson and the other family members went back into the kitchen as the two men rolled the stretcher through the front door. Within fifteen minutes they had returned with Mr. Kratson zipped up in a black body bag. They loaded him into the minivan and left.

Alan went back into the house and handed his business card to Mrs. Kratson. He expressed his sympathy once more before he and Murphy departed.

His mind raced as he drove back to the station. He started doubting himself and what he had seen. Still dazed, he entered the station and sat down in his office. Anger came over him as he ripped open the center drawer in his desk and took out the badge and ID card that Simmons had given him. He searched around in frustration for a business card where he might find a contact number. He scanned both back and front of the ID card for any possible way to communicate with Simmons but found nothing. Disgusted, he threw both items back into his desk drawer and stood up to leave. As he grabbed the doorknob, his phone rang.

It was Lisa. "Hey, there's a Mr. Simmons here to see you."

Alan gritted his teeth. "Are you *sure* he's here?"

"Well, yeah. What are you talking about?"

Alan said, almost indignantly, "Mr. Simmons is actually here and wants to see me? You see him standing before you, is that correct?"

"That's what I said, he's right here." She sounded almost offended.

Alan snapped back, "Okay, send him back to my office right away."

Alan waited several moments, then redialed her extension. "Lisa, did you let Mr. Simmons in to see me?"

"Who?"

Alan choked back the urge to yell. "Mr. Simmons. Has anyone come through asking to see me today?"

"No, nobody all day."

"Okay. Thanks." Alan slammed down the phone.

CHAPTER ELEVEN

"To see the right and not to do it is cowardice."

—Confucius

SIMMONS APPROACHED THE OFFICE DOOR and reached for the handle. As his hand touched it, Alan flung the door open. "Get in here and sit down." Simmons walked over slowly and eased himself into a vacant chair. He looked up at Alan, crossed one leg over his knee, and sat with his hands folded in his lap, as if he were listening intently. He seemed neither surprised nor offended by Alan's demeanor.

Alan's anger continued to rise at the thought of being deceived. His jaw clenched as he said in an angry, accusatory tone, "I don't care who you are or where you're from or how important you think you are simply because you work for the government. I don't like the game you're playing. The one thing I can't stand is someone lying to me."

Simmons sat there with an understanding look on his face and continued to listen. It seemed as if he had been in this situation before, as if this weren't the first time someone had said such things to him. "Why are you so angry, Alan?" he asked pleasantly.

"Because you're lying to me!"

Simmons shook his head. "I've never lied to you."

"Lies come in many forms, Mr. Simmons. Omitting information is a type of lie. I'm confident that *you*," Alan pointed his finger, "aren't telling me everything." His voice rose simultaneously with his anger. "He was alive, I spoke to him. You"—once again he pointed a finger at Simmons—"led him down the stairs by the arm. I saw you. Do you deny it?"

Simmons replied calmly, "No, I don't deny it."

"Then how the hell do you explain—" Alan was yelling now. Looking through the window in his office door, he saw three officers in the squad room staring in his direction with some concern.

Alan took a deep breath. He waved and nodded to assure them that everything was all right. He lowered his voice and brought his face closer to Simmons's. The crease in his forehead became more prominent. "How do you explain how you got past all of those people at the Kratson house without anybody seeing you? And how did Mr. Kratson end up on the floor—dead? I should hold you for questioning and call the FBI. For all I know, you killed Mr. Kratson. Maybe you climbed out of a window so that nobody saw you."

"You know that didn't happen, Alan," Simmons said in a calm voice. "You *know* that Mr. Kratson slipped on a bar of soap and hit his head as he fell out of the tub. He told you what happened himself."

"I know what he told me," said Alan. "But I'm starting to think I imagined it. I'm starting to think that Mr. Kratson's body never moved at all. My CPR mask was still on him when Murphy returned to the room. I think I'm losing my mind—and it's pissing me off!"

"His body didn't move from its original location," Simmons confirmed.

Alan threw both of his arms up in the air and nodded his head in a mocking manner. "Oh, I see. Then I suppose I was speaking to his ghost. Are you trying to make me look like a nut?" Alan paused a moment to catch his breath, then rounded on Simmons again. "One of my officers already thinks I'm crazy and deluded. I tried to tell him what happened. You're undermining my credibility with my subordinates. I have to maintain a level of confidence so that I can do my job effectively. Do you understand that?"

"Yes," replied Simmons. "You'll need to use the utmost discretion when discussing certain things in these circumstances."

"These *circumstances*." Alan lowered his eyebrows and curled his upper lip. Simmons's subtle refusal to clarify and explain how everything had occurred was only further infuriating Alan. "Why don't you explain these circumstances? I'm a bit confused," he said with a sneer.

"I will in time. Right now I can't," Simmons said with a smile. "You did well for your first time. I think you're ready to join the team and do some real work for us. I'll be back next Monday at one o'clock for our first assignment; perhaps then you'll understand more. Make sure to bring your badge and ID card."

"I don't think I want to participate anymore," Alan told him. "As I said, I don't want to play your game."

"That's your choice," replied Simmons. "But just know: this isn't a game. What we do is extremely important and we need your assistance. If you decide that you still want to help, be here at one o'clock."

"You mean thirteen hundred hours," said Alan. He caught Simmons off guard and took pleasure in the momentary confusion on his face.

"Thirteen-hundred hours," Alan repeated. "Shouldn't a *federal agent* speak in military time?"

Simmons regained his composure quickly. "Thirteen-hundred hours. Or one o'clock in the afternoon," he said with a slight smile. "Whatever you like."

"Unless, perhaps," Alan mused, as though Simmons hadn't spoken, "you're not with the government after all."

Simmons smiled once again. "In due time you'll have some answers. See you Monday." Simmons stood up to leave and opened the office door.

"If I *were* to show up on Monday, what should I wear?"

"Business attire," replied Simmons.

"No gun? No body armor vest? No baton?"

Simmons shook his head. "No, you won't need any of that. Make sure you have your badge and ID." He walked through the door and left.

"Introduce yourself to Lisa in the front lobby," Alan yelled as Simmons crossed the open squad room. "I'll feel better if more people around here see you."

Simmons raised his eyebrows as if this were a silly request, but he nodded.

Alan couldn't focus for the rest of the day—especially after Lisa called him to tell him how charming Michael Simmons was. Simmons had gone out of his way to fulfill Alan's request, even gone a bit overboard. Lieutenant Gaspero caught Alan in the hallway to tell him that he'd received word that Alan was going to be assigned to work with the federal task force this coming Monday. Gaspero congratulated him and said that "Special Agent Simmons" had briefed him on how "important this was for national security." The praise made Alan want to scream.

The next day came and went, bringing news from the medical examiner's office. It was their professional preliminary opinion that Mr. Kratson had died from blunt force trauma to the head, causing an internal fracture and bleeding. Murphy was impressed with Alan's assessment at the scene; he'd been betting all along that Kratson had died of heart failure —especially since an automatic defibrillator will not shock someone who's heart has already stopped.

That night, Alan lay awake. He heard Kratson's voice say over and over again, *I was taking a shower and slipped on a bar of soap.* Then he heard himself say, *Well, you gave us all a scare.*

In the back of his mind Alan was afraid. He would never admit it to anyone, but it was there. He had never been a person to shy away from responsibility, especially when it involved helping other people. If Simmons were sincere about the need for Alan's skills with handling people in difficult situations, then he would commit to making a difference. But that night, lying in bed, he wondered, *Why me? Why did he—or whomever he works for—pick me?*

As soon as he asked the question, he knew the answer. Although this path in life was not appealing to him, Alan would grind his way forward if he believed it was the right thing to do. He saw this attribute, this loyalty to what was right, as both a strength and a weakness. He was confident that Michael Simmons had known this long before they met. Simmons had known, even before Alan admitted it to himself, that he would show up on Monday to go with the team. *That* was why he had been chosen to "play the game."

CHAPTER TWELVE

"The grave is but a covered
bridge leading from light to light,
through a brief darkness."

—Henry Wadsworth Longfellow

A LAN WAS UP EARLY ON MONDAY MORNING. He put on his dress pants, a white button-down shirt, a tie, and a jacket before heading off to the office. As he placed the badge and ID card Simmons had given him inside the breast pocket of his coat, he strapped a small .32-caliber pistol to his ankle. Simmons had told him that he wouldn't need a gun, but somehow he didn't have enough faith in Simmons to throw caution to the wind.

For most of the morning he reviewed reports, e-mail, and voicemail. At 11:00 he ate a sandwich and some potato chips he'd brought from home, as he was unsure whether lunch would be part of his upcoming duties. He suspected that their assignment might include visiting various people who had lost loved ones recently in an attempt to comfort and assist them through their trying time. This didn't really appeal to Alan, but Simmons had promised him some answers and he was still curious about what happened the day Mr. Kratson had died.

As the afternoon rolled around his phone rang and Lisa informed him that Mr. Simmons was in the lobby waiting for him. Alan made his way up, wondering why Simmons was here early. Simmons was dressed in his typical manner—navy blue suit, white shirt, burgundy tie.

Alan approached him. "I'm ready to go."

"Good," said Simmons. "I'll drive. I'm parked out front."

They walked to a black Ford Crown Victoria with tinted windows. The car definitely looked like a federal vehicle. Alan opened the passenger side door and got in. As they left the parking lot he scanned the interior of the car. No radio, no emergency equipment.

"Did you bring your badge?"

"Got it right here," Alan said, holding it up.

"Excellent. Hang it around your neck."

Alan looped the chain over his head. "How should I identify myself?"

Simmons tilted his head slightly and pressed his lips together as if he was thinking about the question. Alan tried to clarify. "I mean, when I approach people, who do I say I'm representing?"

"Don't worry about that." Simmons shook his head. "They'll know who you are."

This seemed like a very strange answer, but Alan decided to let it go. There were other questions he wanted answered, and he didn't want to exhaust all of Simmons's patience on this first point.

"So, where are we going?"

"A twenty-five-year-old woman died in a car accident. We're going to start with her."

"How long ago did she die?"

"She died today at twelve twenty-five," Simmons replied.

"Are there survivors or next of kin?"

"No."

Alan glanced at the dashboard for a moment, then turned toward Simmons with his mouth slightly agape. It was 12:22 PM. "Do you mean that she died this morning?"

Simmons's face was expressionless. "We're coming up on the scene of the accident."

Alan looked around but couldn't see anything that resembled a crash. They reached a fork in the road and Simmons pulled off to the side.

"Here we are," he said.

"Where are we?" Alan asked, thoroughly confused.

"At the scene of the accident."

Alan was extremely annoyed. "What accident? There's no accident here. There are no cars here. I thought that we were going to comfort the survivors." He paused. A streak of blue behind them caught his eye.

A dark blue Ford Mustang flew by at an incredible speed. As it came to the fork in the road it swerved from lane to lane. Alan saw the brake lights illuminate. The car attempted to turn to the left, but its speed forced its momentum forward. It catapulted into the air and crashed into a large oak tree between the two forks. The hood and front end buckled; the tree didn't budge.

"What the hell!" Alan gasped, leaping from the car. He ran to where the other vehicle was mashed up against the tree. Using his cell phone, he dialed 911 and requested an ambulance. Through what was left of the driver's-side window he saw a young woman pinned between the steering wheel and the driver's seat. Blood streaked down her hair from the open gash in her forehead. Her white T-shirt was drenched in a deep red stain that flowed over her tattered blue jeans. Alan reached in and pressed a finger to the woman's neck to find a pulse. Nothing. His hand began to tremble slightly as he repositioned his finger to check once more.

Simmons walked slowly over to where Alan was standing. Alan clenched his teeth. "How'd you know this was gonna happen? And if you knew, why didn't you tell me? We could have stopped this!"

"We couldn't have prevented this," Simmons said calmly.

"I could've tried if I'd had some advance notice," Alan barked back at him. "If I'd known that this car was going to go off the road here and now, I could've attempted to slow her down before she hit the tree." Frustration rose within him. He felt responsible for the young woman's death—a death he could have prevented, had Simmons told him what was about to happen.

"It doesn't work like that," Simmons said with the same expressionless face as before.

Emergency lights were approaching, and Alan heard the sound of a siren wailing. As they grew nearer he could make out the boxy form of an ambulance. It pulled up and stopped just ahead of a fire truck that was close behind. The scene of firefighters unloading equipment as they prepared to cut the woman out of the car was eerily familiar.

Alan grabbed Simmons by the arm and spun him around so that they were face-to-face. "Did you have something to do with this? Did you cause this to happen? How in the hell could you have known that she was going to do this here and now?"

"Just trust me," Simmons said. "Give me a few moments. Everything will be clarified in a little while."

The firefighters worked feverishly to cut the woman from the car. Slowly they dismantled the side, piece by piece, until they had made enough space to get the woman's body out. Alan watched as they placed her on a stretcher and made their way back to the ambulance. She was covered in a white sheet from head to toe.

Simmons placed a hand on Alan's shoulder and said, "Come on."

Sighing, Alan followed him to the ambulance as he watched the paramedics hoist the stretcher inside. Simmons then climbed into the back and motioned for Alan to join him. They both sat down on a small bench to the side of the stretcher. The paramedic who had been securing the stretcher now opened the rear doors, climbed out, and shut both doors behind him. Simmons pulled the white sheet down to reveal the woman's head. As Alan looked at her, he noticed that her face was not cut and torn as it had been in the car. There was no blood oozing from the wounds he'd seen a short time ago; the wounds themselves were no longer present.

The woman opened her eyes. Alan jumped back in shock, overwhelmed. His eyes grew large and his breathing became shallow.

The woman sat upright. "How do you feel, Leslie?" Simmons asked.

She replied with a smile. "Great. I feel great. Never felt better."

She was very young, in her early twenties, with blond hair that hung down just past her chin. Her eyes were a deep brown, and Alan couldn't help but notice a small stud earring protruding from the right corner of her lower lip.

Simmons drew closer. "How did this happen?"

"I was depressed because my boyfriend and I broke up. I got in my car and put the pedal to the metal—you know, to relieve my frustrations. I lost control of the car and hit the tree. I didn't mean to hit the tree, it just happened. Some people might try to say that I did it on purpose, but I didn't. You have to believe me!"

"I believe you," Simmons said. "We're glad to have you. If you're ready, we can get going."

Alan held up his hand and said, "Wait a minute. I need some explanation. This isn't happening."

"This *is* happening. I'll explain what we need to do along the way," replied Simmons. He took Leslie by the hand and helped her to her feet. He flung open the back doors of the ambulance and the three of them stepped out. To Alan's astonishment he was not outside. Instead he was standing in a dark hallway about ten feet wide and constructed of what appeared to be polished, black marble. No lights could be seen. The slick finish of the floor nearly made Alan slip. A musty smell like that of an old wine cellar filled his nostrils; wherever they were, it must be someplace very old. Alan reached down to feel for the butt of the gun still strapped to his ankle. Peering downward, he noticed that the badge hanging on his chest was now giving off light. It illuminated the hallway a short distance ahead of them.

"All right," yelled Alan, "enough! Where in the hell are we and where are we going? I'm starting to get concerned."

Obviously this was an understatement. He'd been "concerned" when the dead woman opened her eyes in the ambulance; now he was past anxiety and close to terror.

"We're in a hallway and we're going to help Leslie find her way to where she needs to go," replied Simmons.

They walked a great distance, until Alan saw a glimmer of light coming from the wall straight ahead of them. He grasped the badge and held it straight out so that they could see more clearly. As they drew closer, Alan saw that it wasn't a wall, but rather a large door. Small flickers of light poked through around the door frame.

"We're here," said Simmons. "This is where you need to go, Leslie."

The woman turned toward Alan and said, "Please make sure that nobody thinks I killed myself. I didn't *want* to die. I lost control of the car. I tried to stop."

Still holding the illuminated badge in front of him and looking at the door, Alan tried to take in everything that was happening. He managed to answer her. "I'll let people know," he promised.

Her smile soothed his anxiety. Her expression was one of gratitude. "Thank you, Illissia Alona," she said. "Until we meet again, I bid you farewell."

She reached down and turned a large brass handle. The door swung open and sunlight streamed through. Alan thought he smelled the fragrance of an open field beyond.

She was gone in an instant and the door closed. Alan reached up to grab the handle, but it was gone. It was dark once again in the hallway. He felt around to find the edges of the door frame but could not. It was now just a smooth wall of dark marble, seamless, cold to the touch.

He stared at it for a long time as though he were in a trance.

"This way, Alan," Simmons called.

They walked back the way they had come but no words were spoken. When they reached the beginning of the hallway there was an opening full of light. They stepped through it, and Alan found himself in the back of the ambulance once again. Leslie's lifeless body was still on the stretcher, covered in the wounds he remembered from his first glimpse of her.

As they opened the rear doors of the ambulance and stepped outside, Alan saw two sheriff's deputies from Greenville County Sheriff's Department looking at the car mashed against the tree. One of them spotted Alan, walked toward him, and said, "We found this in the car. We think this may have been a suicide."

He handed Alan a piece of notebook paper. It was a handwritten note that read:

Bobby,

I can't understand why you don't want to see me any longer. I love you dearly and don't think I can live without you. I'm going out for a drive to clear my head and try to deal with this, but the pain is so great I don't think I can take it. You told me that you didn't think our relationship was working out, but I don't understand why. You haven't given me a real answer as to why we can't be together. I moved down here to be with you and worked two jobs trying to support us. I really want us to get through this; I'll get another job if I need to. Just give me another chance. I know we can make it.

I love you,
Leslie

Alan read it, then said to the deputy, "No, it's not a suicide. She didn't mean to hit the tree. The skid marks show that she tried to apply her brakes but couldn't stop. Someone who wants to die wouldn't try to brake. I think she was going too fast and lost control of the car. Besides, the note sounds like she wanted to get through a tough spot, not escape from it."

The deputy considered Alan's theory and looked over at the thick black marks on the roadway. They led through the mangled grass and mud and ultimately to the tree.

"Yeah, I guess you're right; just a bad accident. We'll have someone reconstruct it. That will give us more information."

"You wouldn't happen to know who this boyfriend of hers is, this Bobby person?" Alan asked, gesturing to the note.

"It might be Bobby Hunter. He lives over on Forest Green Road," said the deputy. "Second trailer down on the left, rusted-out pickup in the front yard. He's a real dirtbag."

"Thanks." Alan frowned and shook his head. He turned to Simmons and asked, "Anything else I need to do?"

"No," replied Simmons. "We're done here."

The two of them made their way back to the car. Alan, much calmer than before, turned to face Simmons and said, "Wait, before you leave— you told me that you'd explain some things. Now it's time to answer some of my questions."

Simmons smiled. "What would you like to know?"

Alan drew a deep breath and said, "I'm just taking an educated guess when I say that I don't believe you're with the federal government."

Simmons smiled once again. "No, you're correct. I'm with…well, a larger organization."

"Good enough," said Alan, nodding. "I'm not actually ready to hear any more on that right now. Second," Alan continued, "Greenville County is a small rural county in the southern portion of the state. It's approximately an eight-hour drive from our station, yet we made it here in a manner of minutes."

"Yes," replied Simmons. "That's correct."

Alan raised his eyebrows and stared at him, waiting for a further explanation. Simmons, seeing that Alan wasn't satisfied, elaborated. "Let's just say that in my line of work, time and distance are no obstacle." He paused for a moment, then said, "Especially where I'm from."

Alan frowned, somewhat frustrated. "Well that's the whole crux of the matter, isn't it? Where you're from—maybe a different planet or something?"

Alan's voice was sarcastic, but Simmons seemed unaffected. He kept an upbeat expression on his face as he said, "Planet? No, not at all. Perhaps you could say a different existence, world, or realm."

"Okay," Alan said. He glanced away for a moment to collect himself. "Knew I shouldn't have asked that one. Let's continue. We're in a different county at the scene of a fatal accident with various emergency personnel who don't know us at all. We never identified ourselves and we aren't wearing anything that would tell them who we are, yet they approached us and treated us as if we belonged there. How'd you make that happen?"

"In my line of work we have ways to impose an aura of acceptance. It allows us to achieve our goals with greater ease; as you saw, we've accomplished what we set out to do. We led Leslie where she needed to go."

"Yes, indeed. Leslie," Alan said, turning back to look at Simmons. "Let's talk about Leslie. Where should I start?" He placed a finger over his pursed lips and tapped them as if to indicate that he was thinking about what to say. Simmons said nothing, but raised his eyebrows and smiled as if he were waiting for the next sarcastic remark.

Alan continued. "For one thing, she's dead, mangled up in a car that wrapped itself around an oak tree." Alan threw both hands up in the air, cocking his head to one side as he blurted out, "Oh, but that doesn't matter. Even though she's dead, we still walked out of the ambulance with her into some type of corridor and led her down to some strange door that leads to…" Alan paused and drew a deep breath, then continued with his voice raised. "Leads to…well, I don't know where the hell it leads to! All I know is that it leads to someplace sunny with the fresh smell of grass or wheat or something." He lowered his voice and let out another sigh of frustration, "Do you see where I'm going with this? Do you understand my frustration and apprehension?"

Alan stopped to catch his breath. Simmons nodded and spoke in a soothing manner. "Yes, I know this is a lot to take in, but you're doing well. I don't want to lay all of this on you at once. I want to explain this slowly so that you have time to accept what is—and what will be."

"Why do you keep saying that I'm doing well?" asked Alan. "I haven't done anything."

"Oh, but you have," replied Simmons enthusiastically. "In time you will see what you have accomplished. There is a reason. There is a purpose for these…"

Alan finished his sentence for him. "Deaths. Were you going to say that there is a reason for these deaths?"

"Yes."

"There's no good reason for death. Life is precious," Alan said, as if the concept repulsed him. "It seems to me that you know when these people are going to die."

"My knowledge of when they pass is very limited. But all will be explained in time," Simmons said calmly.

"Well, then why don't you tell me what else you know about this *purpose*," Alan suggested in a skeptical tone.

"I know that we're helping those who pass," said Simmons.

"Yeah, after they die—deaths that I still believe we could prevent," sneered Alan.

"As I said before, we have no control."

Alan cut him off again. "Yeah, yeah. Save it, you already said that. So how many people are we going to watch die—or should I say *help*, as you put it?"

"We're helping them find their way. What we do is important. Leading them to where they need to go is—"

"How many?" yelled Alan.

"Sixteen in all."

"Sixteen," said Alan. "Sixteen deaths on my conscience."

"Sixteen people who are needed very badly somewhere else," said Simmons. "All will be explained."

"I know. You're repeating yourself. All will be explained in time—I know."

Simmons put the car in drive and they pulled onto the street. There was silence between them. Alan stared out the window. After a moment he calmly asked, "The woman you called Leslie—she said something to me before she went through that door that I couldn't understand. She called me something, something like *Illus Ola*." Alan struggled to remember the exact pronunciation.

"She called you Illissia Alona," Simmons said, "but she was mistaken."

Exasperated by the limited explanation, Alan exclaimed, "Well, that's clear as mud! Care to clarify that a little more for me?"

"In my organization," Simmons explained, "we have various ranks, just as you have ranks in your organization. Illissia Alona is a certain rank, in a manner of speaking. However, you don't hold that rank."

Alan shook his head in confusion. "Oh," he said. "Do I hold any rank within your organization?"

"Not yet," replied Simmons. "After your training is completed you will have earned the first rank, Illissia Galau."

Alan wanted to ask more, but looking ahead he saw a street sign on the left. It read Forest Green Road.

"Turn here," he told Simmons, a feeling of apprehension rising inside him.

Simmons looked confused. "What do you mean?"

"Just turn here, I need to do something," Alan said.

Simmons turned the car and continued down the street. Alan pointed out the window and said, "Here, stop here."

Simmons pulled the car over. A rusted-out pickup truck sat on the front lawn of a small single-wide trailer. Alan got out of the car and Simmons followed him up to the front of the trailer, where Alan knocked on a rickety, metal screen door. When nobody answered, Alan knocked louder. Flakes of white paint fell off the door. Alan heard slow footsteps approaching from inside the trailer. Within a few seconds a man approached the door, staggering as he walked. He was wearing a stained and dirty white T-shirt. His eyes were glazed over, and Alan could smell the odor of stale beer on his breath and seeping from his pores.

"Yeah?" the man said rudely.

"I'm Sergeant Alan Crane. I'm a police officer. Are you Bobby Hunter?" asked Alan.

"Yeah, what do you want?" asked Bobby in a challenging tone.

"It's about your girlfriend, Leslie." Alan realized that he'd never gotten Leslie's full name. "She was killed in a car accident." There was no reaction on Bobby's face as Alan continued. "She left this note."

Alan took the note from his pocket and opened it. As he handed it to Bobby he heard more footsteps within the trailer. A blond girl in a tube top and skin-tight jean shorts stumbled over to where Bobby was standing. Alan guessed her to be between nineteen and twenty-one. She seemed to be extremely drunk. She wrapped her arms around Bobby and used him to balance herself.

"What do *they* want?" she asked in a slurred voice.

"Guess your stupid sister was in an accident and got herself killed," Bobby said as he glanced at the paper. He tossed it over his shoulder.

Alan could tell that he was also intoxicated, as he kept swaying from side to side. His eyelids drooped so low that Alan wondered if he could even see. The alcohol must have numbed his mind beyond comprehension of how serious the matter was; he looked directly at Alan and said, "Serves her right. She was an idiot. I'm glad she's dead. Now I don't have to listen to her stupid mouth telling me how she loves me. Besides, I'm with her sister now anyway."

"Yeah, that's right, baby!" yelled the woman. A mist of saliva sprayed the air around her like a splash of tainted rain. Her blatant insensitivity toward her sister's death made Alan believe that she was even more drunk than he'd first thought.

Alan looked at the woman and asked, "Are you old enough to drink?" She laughed and nearly fell over as she said, "Sure—whatever."

"Have any drugs in the house?" Alan asked as he turned to Bobby.

Bobby laughed and continued to sway as he replied, "Well, maybe I do, but I know that you can't come in unless you got a warrant—I know the system, so you—"

He nearly fell over, but at the last minute grabbed the inside of the door jam to steady himself.

"Yeah, I'll bet you do," replied Alan in a sarcastic tone. It seemed that Bobby knew enough about the law to know that Alan couldn't legally enter his home. That, mixed with the alcohol—or "liquid courage," as some called it—made reasoning with either of them impossible.

"Now, if you're done, you need to get the hell out of here. I hate cops and—"

Bobby never finished the sentence. Alan thrust his hands through the screen door and grabbed both sides of Bobby's shirt, forming a tight collar around his neck. He pulled Bobby's face through the screen until it was inches from his own and he could smell the stagnant mixture of marijuana and cigarettes. He glared into Bobby's eyes, which were now wide with fear. In a slow, methodical tone Alan said, "Perhaps you didn't appreciate what I said. This woman is *dead*, and the last thing she was thinking about before she died—unfortunately—was you!"

Simmons placed a hand on Alan's wrists. Alan slowly let go of Bobby. Simmons motioned to Alan to step back and said, "It's okay. Let me have a word with him."

Simmons, who was now very near to Bobby's face, said in a low and convincing voice, "Mr. Hunter, there may be a day very soon when you will find yourself walking a long and dark corridor leading nowhere. You will find yourself alone, wandering in an endless, drunken state as you do now. At that time you will feel the consuming grip of regret for not doing what was right. Search deep within yourself to remedy this tragic flaw, Mr. Hunter." He lowered his voice even more. "After you have passed from this life, I will remind you of our conversation." Alan noticed a white hot gleam of blazing light in Simmons's eyes. "Do you understand, Mr. Hunter?"

Bobby Hunter looked pale and frozen, unable to move, as if he were looking into the eyes of a beast rather than a man. Simmons said, "Excellent. Well then, good day."

Bobby stayed there for a few moments, staring blankly. Saying nothing, he turned and walked back inside the trailer, dragging the drunken girl with him.

"Let's go," Simmons suggested to Alan, who followed him back to the car. They left. After a few moments Alan said, "I'm sorry, I was wrong. I shouldn't have lost my temper like that."

Simmons replied, "Mistakes are more often judged by how you remedy them, rather than the act itself. In the future you will handle similar situations differently. No harm was done."

Alan sat in silence, still somewhat embarrassed by how he had reacted to Bobby Hunter. Within five minutes the car pulled off onto the exit for Riverston. As Simmons pulled into the police station he told Alan, "You've done well today. Go home and get some rest. We'll do this again on Friday; I'll meet you here at the same time as before." Alan looked at his watch. It was exactly 5:00 PM.

As he opened the door he turned to Simmons and asked, "What do I do with the ID card you gave me? I assume that the National Crisis Intervention Bureau isn't a real entity. It seems that nobody cares who we are when we…well, you know, when we do what we do."

"Yes," replied Simmons. "You can throw it away if you'd like. I only gave it to you to make you feel more comfortable."

Alan raised his eyebrows, then grinned as he replied, "Well, it's not working." He placed the ID back on the dashboard of the car.

Simmons smiled. "It will. You'll see in time how important all of this is. Be ready to go next Friday."

As Alan headed toward his car, his mind fixated on one thing: *Who were the sixteen people who were going to die?*

CHAPTER THIRTEEN

"The real problem is in the hearts and minds of men. It is easier to denature plutonium than to denature the evil spirit of man."

—Albert Einstein

I T WAS 6:30 AM WHEN RANDAL SWEENY entered the all-night Moto-Mart on Vine Street in Riverston. The clerk, a nineteen-year-old boy with long, stringy, blond hair, sat on a stool behind the counter reading a magazine, paying little attention to anything around him. Randal walked to the back of the store near the beer cooler and quickly pulled a black ski mask over his face. He was short and overweight, which made him struggle a bit while trying to pull the .38-caliber pistol from his belt. The palms of his small, pudgy hands were coated with sweat and the gun nearly slipped out onto the floor. He tightened his grip. His breathing grew shallow as he moved forward and pointed the gun at the clerk's shoulder.

"I need the money!" he yelled.

The clerk jumped up and raised his hands in front of him. "Don't—don't kill me," he begged.

"I won't, just give me the money, now!" Randal shouted.

The clerk frantically pressed buttons and banged on the cash register until it opened. Randal felt sweat pouring over his face underneath the mask. His hand was still shaking. The barrel of the gun bobbed up and down.

"Come on!" he screamed at the clerk. "Get it in a bag. Let's go!" The clerk shook violently as he dumped the money into a plastic bag, accidentally knocking over several cartons of cigarettes behind the counter.

Randal brushed against a gumball machine as he grabbed the bag out of the clerk's hands and headed for the door. The glass globe on the machine exploded, scattering an array of gumballs everywhere. Randal slipped and his legs gave way, sending him tumbling through the front door. He was uninjured, but a bit shaken as he steadied himself. He got to his feet and noticed that the clerk had ducked down behind the counter. Randal took the opportunity to make his escape.

Alan arrived at work at 6:45 AM. He was making his way into the station as three night-shift officers ran by him.

"What's going on?" he asked as they ran past.

One of them yelled, "Robbery at the Moto-Mart, just occurred."

Alan ran to his patrol car and jumped in. He was always somewhat groggy as he walked into the station in the morning, but as he started the car and flipped on the lights and siren his adrenaline started to flow. He heard the dispatcher saying, "Subject fled the scene in a dark-colored BMW, unknown direction of travel."

Alan was the last one out of the lot. He tailed the other three patrol cars by a few car lengths. They sped along, nearing a hundred miles per hour. The high-pitched whistle of the wind pushed through the light bar on the roof of Alan's car. The lights of the business district were coming into view; Alan could see the illuminated sign of the Moto-Mart ahead. Two of the police cars sped past the gas station to hunt for the suspect vehicle while Alan and another officer entered the parking lot, stopping a good distance away and positioning themselves parallel to the front corners of the building. Alan grabbed the shotgun from the rack next to him and chambered a shell.

He walked toward the corner of the building closest to him as the other officer approached from the opposite corner. Alan cautiously walked toward the front door and peered through the small window where customers could hand their payments through a pane of bullet-proof glass. He surveyed the store in an attempt to locate the clerk or anyone else who may have been inside, but all he could see were the shattered remains of a gumball machine.

Alan continued slowly toward the front door as the other officer approached from the opposite side with his pistol drawn and held at the ready. The two met on either side of the double glass entrance doors and paused. Alan gave a nod.

Together they pushed the doors open and cleared the door frame quickly, pointing their guns in opposite directions to cover the entire interior of the store. Alan approached the front counter as the other officer made his way to the refrigerated sections in the back of the store. Alan pointed the barrel of his gun over the front counter as he slowly walked around to see whether anyone was crouched down out of sight. He saw several packs of cigarettes on the ground as well as an empty cash register drawer. As he turned around he noticed a doorway leading to an office. He gripped the forearm of the shotgun tightly and pressed the butt against his shoulder as he looked through the doorway both left and right, but saw nothing. The other officer was now behind him and covering the rest of the store. He nodded at Alan, indicating that he should continue into the office.

Alan stepped toward the doorway. As he moved his right foot began to slip out from under him. He calmly steadied himself, then lifted his foot and felt it stick to the floor like a fork clinging to a plate covered in maple syrup. Reaching out with his left hand, he felt around the wall near the doorway until he located a light switch and flipped it on. Now he could see the dark crimson pool of blood around his foot. A drop of sweat formed on his forehead as he surveyed the room. His mouth was dry, and he tried to swallow as his eyes took in the gruesome scene before him. A young man lay facedown in the center of the blood pool. His shirt was shredded. Four large, gaping wounds protruded from his back, which continued to ooze blood onto the floor and stain his stringy, blond hair.

Alan yelled out to the other officer. "In here! I found the clerk. Call an ambulance, then get some crime-scene tape."

The other officer poked his head in, took one look at the body, and disappeared back through the doorway. Alan carefully made his way over to the boy and bent down to look for a pulse, knowing that there was little chance that the clerk was still alive. Failing to find any signs of life, he hung his head and closed his eyes. A sense of frustration came over him. He stood up and dialed the station on his cell phone. The dispatcher answered.

"We have a possible homicide out here," Alan said. "I need the bureau notified. We'll be securing the scene."

As he hung up the phone the other officer returned to the office holding two large rolls of yellow crime-scene tape.

Alan said, "Do two perimeters. Section off the front of the store for the inner, then tape off the entire parking lot for the outer. Post one officer at the front door and have him start a log of those entering. Post another at the parking lot entrance and have him start a log also. Nobody but the bureau on the inside. Let's back out."

They both made their way out of the store. Within moments the scene was taped off and officers were placed at the perimeter entrances. After a while two detectives showed up. Alan briefed them on the situation. The lead detective, Clint Rogers, told Alan that they would pull the surveillance tapes to see if they could come up with any quick leads.

As he was about to leave, an officer ran up to him and said, "Sergeant, there's some federal agent here who says he needs to talk to you. He's over there in that black vehicle."

The officer pointed to a black Ford Crown Victoria with mirrored windows. Alan approached the car. As Simmons rolled down the window, Alan noticed an unusual look on his face: concern.

"Get in for a moment," said Simmons.

Alan walked over to the passenger side of the car and got in. "Do we need to…help this person, or lead them…like we did the other day?"

"No," replied Simmons, "I already took care of that. His name was Nick Swanolski. I spoke with him and led him where he needed to go." Simmons paused, lowered his eyes, and rested his index finger over his lips, obviously frustrated, as if he were searching for an answer.

"You look upset," said Alan. "Did Nick say anything about who did this? Anything that might help us catch our suspect?"

"Not really. He said that a man came into the store and made his way to the back. He didn't see the man's face, nor did he pay much attention to him. The man returned to the counter wearing a ski mask, pointed a gun at Nick, and demanded the money. Nick gave him the money in the drawer and bent down behind the counter to dial 911, but as he did someone grabbed him from behind. He said he felt something tear at the skin on his back. Then everything went dark."

"I saw the body," said Alan. "He had four large wounds on his back."

Simmons raised an eyebrow. "Describe these wounds."

"They looked like some type of knife wound, very deep and wide and…" Alan paused.

"And what?" asked Simmons. He sounded more concerned.

"They were very dark, almost black—like the blood that oozed from them, black blood. Why do you ask? What does that mean?"

"I don't know," said Simmons.

Alan wanted to interrogate Simmons further about his concerns regarding Nick's wounds but concluded that no answers would be forthcoming. He decided to let it go for now.

"Did he say anything else?"

"No," replied Simmons, staring into the dashboard of the car as though lost in thought.

"Did you know about this? I mean, did you know that this was going to happen?"

Simmons placed his hand over his forehead and rubbed his temples. He looked even more disturbed then before as he said, "No, I didn't."

"I thought you knew about these things. I thought you could predict when these things were going to happen."

Simmons let out a deep sigh and said, "Yes, well, most of the time I can. Sometimes I'm unaware. But this one really bothers me."

Alan looked at him curiously. "Why's that?"

"Because I should've known about this one. I was able to lead him away. I should've known."

Simmons's eyes fixed on Alan as his voice became low and serious. "Listen to me. When you find who did this, I'll need to know right away. It's critical. Contact me as soon as possible."

"Well, that may be a little difficult, since you've never given me any type of contact number."

Simmons pulled out a pen and small white card, which Alan assumed was his business card. He wrote down a number, then handed it to Alan, "Here, use this number."

Alan took the card and looked at the number written on it. *Nothing unusual*, he thought. *Looks like a regular cell phone number*. He flipped the card over to see how Simmons had his business card arranged, only to find it completely blank.

Alan smiled. "Your organization really doesn't like to advertise, huh?" He held up the blank side of the card so that Simmons could see it.

"Yes, well, there's really no need to advertise. Sooner or later everyone comes to see us. Well, most everyone," Simmons said with a half smile. Alan sensed that he was attempting to make light of a bad situation —something that police officers did quite often to keep their sanity after enduring horrific situations. For the first time he felt a stab of pity for Mr. Simmons.

"Well," said Alan, "you actually tried to make a joke. Guess that proves you aren't with a federal agency. You have a sense of humor."

Simmons smiled, but the look of concern soon enveloped his face again. "Let me know as soon as you discover anything," he repeated.

"I'll notify you right away," replied Alan. He reached for the door handle and got out of the car. "We still on for Friday?"

"Yes, as planned. I'll be there. See you then." Alan nodded and closed the door.

As he sat down in his office to write the police report his mind wandered back and forth between the image of Nick Swanolski's body and the look of concern on Simmons's face. In the short time that he had been around Simmons, Alan had always known him to be confident and unwavering. Until today.

After he had written for about forty minutes, the phone on his desk rang. He picked it up and Clint Rogers's voice came over the line. "Hey, we found something on the tapes."

"Really?" Alan's voice had a tinge of excitement. "Whatcha got?"

"The tape shows our suspect in a ski mask pointing a gun at the clerk and the clerk emptying the cash register. The suspect then grabs the bag of money and runs toward the door, colliding with a gumball machine. The camera angle doesn't allow us to see the entire store. I'm not sure if he makes it out the door, but moments later the clerk bends down. Then the suspect runs back in and bends down behind the counter. The next thing we see is the clerk being dragged into the office by the suspect, who runs out again a few seconds later."

"Wait a minute," said Alan in a skeptical tone. "You're telling me that the suspect came *back in* to kill the clerk? Why the hell would he do that? It doesn't make any sense. He's already gone with the money—why wouldn't he just keep running?"

"Don't know," said Rogers. "Maybe he saw the clerk starting to dial the phone and figured he needed more of a head start to get away. Anyway, it was a sloppy escape job. His car was parked too close; we got a shot of the license plate from one of the outside cameras."

"Excellent," said Alan. "Who's it registered to?"

"A guy named Patrick Kent. He lives over in that ritzy subdivision, Winding Woods—you know, the one that borders the golf course. I'm heading over there now to speak to him. I'll call you back and let you know what I find out."

"Good," replied Alan. "I'll go brief the lieutenant. You let me know what you find out ASAP."

"Will do."

Alan arrived at Lieutenant Gaspero's office just as he was entering from the side door. Gaspero looked quite tired. "I'm here and the captain and the chief are on their way in," he said, rubbing his temple. "I'll need a full brief on what's happening. The press is already flooding us with calls."

Alan sat down and briefed Gaspero on everything he knew, except of course for the parts that involved Simmons. When he was finished, Gaspero looked pleased and said, "Good. Perhaps Rogers will come up with something that will lead to a quick arrest."

Alan returned to his office and worked on the report. At lunch time Rogers appeared at Alan's office door. Clint Rogers was about six feet tall with a short, flat-top haircut. He was slightly overweight, but hid it under an old, cheap suit jacket that still sported a jelly stain on the left cuff.

He threw a large sandwich on Alan's desk and said, "Here—Chief's ordered some food. Just got done speaking with the captain and lieutenant. Figured you'd want to know where we're at. Grab that sandwich and eat, and I'll bring you up to speed on what we know so far."

Alan unwrapped the sandwich and ate it. Rogers stuffed his face with a large sub and started talking through a mouthful of meat and cheese.

"Okay," he began as he swigged down a gulp of soda. "Got over to Patrick Kent's house and made contact with Mrs. Kent. She tells me that Patrick is out of town in DC on some business trip; he's some type of CPA working on government contracts. He's worth a small fortune— sounds like some rich jackass to me. Anyway, she says he's out of town and tells me that he left last Sunday. I asked if he drove and she said, 'No, his car is right out here.' She walks out to the driveway and freaks out when she sees that his car is gone, yelling and screaming—'Our car, someone must have stolen our car!' I knew better than to tell her that the car was used in connection with a homicide. She would've really gone over the edge. Anyway, she finally calms down and I ask her if there's any way I can contact her husband to clarify his whereabouts and safety. So, she gives me a phone number for a hotel in DC. I call the front desk and, sure enough, they have a Patrick Kent registered. They connect me to the room and he answers. So he isn't our guy."

Rogers paused to pile some more of the sandwich in his mouth and slurp down another drink of soda. Placing his fist in the center of his chest, he let out a large belch. Alan winced, hoping that Clint wouldn't cough any of the food back up. "So," Rogers continued, "I saw that our one lead is drying up and I decided to look around the driveway and yard where the car was last parked. And what did I find at the edge of the grass near the driveway? A *wallet*." A huge smile came over Rogers's face. "I'm so glad the IQ of the common dirtbag is low. I opened the wallet and found a driver's license for one Randal Sweeny. I ran his criminal history. He has a number of petty thefts and even a felony assault. He's been in and out of jail for the last eight years."

Rogers paused to belch once again, then continued. "So I run by his address and meet with his wife. She lets me in and I take a look around. Came up empty, just her and a twelve-year-old daughter. So, anyway, we got him entered in the computer as wanted and we'll pick him up when he surfaces."

Rogers wolfed down the last bit of sandwich, washed it down with some more of the soda, and got up to leave. "If we find him, I'll let you know."

"Thanks, Clint."

Alan picked up his phone and dialed the number that Simmons had given him. Simmons answered the phone, and Alan filled him in on the details of the case.

Simmons seemed pleased. "When you pick him up, call me."

"I thought perhaps you had some type of…well, *special* way to find him."

"Nope," replied Simmons. "Certain things I have control over and certain things I don't. Let me know when you locate him."

"Will do. I'll see you Friday."

As the phone disconnected, the last word he had spoken hung in Alan's mind: Friday.

Who will die on Friday? he wondered.

CHAPTER FOURTEEN

*"Most of our obstacles would melt away if,
instead of cowering before them, we should make up
our minds to walk boldly through them."*

—Orison Swett Marden

ANGIE KROFTS SAT IN HER ROOM, staring at the satin dress that hung in the doorframe of her closet. *It's beautiful and perfect,* she thought. Tomorrow was prom night.

She peered into the full-length mirror that hung on the wall next to her closet and looked at her image staring back. She was tall and thin with long, strawberry-blond hair and a flawless complexion. Her fingernails were perfectly manicured and polished a light red that matched her lipstick with impeccable accuracy.

She had it all, or so she was told constantly by her friends and parents. She was a straight-A student and had been chosen prom queen over three other girls who now envied and resented her for it. As head of the student council and captain of the cheerleading squad, she was awarded a higher status among the popular crowd. Two of the most popular boys in her school were fighting over who would accompany her tomorrow evening, which should have made her feel very satisfied. She had waited until the last minute to decide which one would turn the most heads on her special night. Angie had stepped on some toes to get where she was, but such was the competitive environment of being a teenager. Even her life after high school looked bright; she'd been accepted to two of the best universities in the state and a modeling agency had been calling her every week trying to get her signed.

Despite her good fortune she wondered why she felt so depressed and alone. Tears began to stream down her cheeks. Her makeup ran and dripped off the end of her chin. So many people told her how well off she was and how happy she must be. Thoughts raced through her mind, reminding her that every aspect of her life and character had to be perfect, or at least appear so. Leaving the house without her hair and makeup exquisitely done was completely unacceptable. The unwritten rules of popularity dictated that she must dress in the latest fashions and keep them updated as they changed. It was mandatory that she date the best-looking guy in school, have the highest grades in her class, and top the popularity poll in all other categories. She knew that if she didn't meet these standards of perfection, many of those who called themselves her friends would exploit her shortcomings.

Those so-called friends circled her like a school of sharks awaiting the first sign of blood. As she watched the edges of the circle close in, Angie knew that she had put herself in this position. She could feel it suffocating her, squeezing out her very identity. In the end she was destined to be crushed into an image of others' opinions and expectations. The thoughts danced through her mind like flames flickering from a thousand candles.

Blinded with despair, she ran over to a desk. From the center drawer she grabbed a pair of scissors, which she opened and grasped by one blade. She grabbed the dress and ran the other blade down the center. The fabric split and frayed. Sobbing uncontrollably, Angie stabbed at the dress as if it were a person she was trying to kill, a person she hated, a person from whom she was trying to escape. The scissors punctured the satin and lace, and even the closet door. As the fourth blow impacted the wood Angie's hand slid down the blade, slicing it open. A stream of blood ran down her arm to her elbow, dripping onto the gray carpet. The scissors dropped from her hand, which was now throbbing from the gash.

"This is too much," she whispered to herself. "I can't take it anymore. I need to get out. I need to escape. I don't want to be *me* anymore."

As she opened a side drawer in the wooden desk that stood at one end of the room, she focused on two prescription bottles. The first bottle contained diet pills. She remembered the first time her mother had given them to her. She had been twelve years old.

Her mother's words still echoed in her head. "You need to maintain your weight and stay thin if you want to have any chance of winning," she'd said. Her mother had just talked her into signing up for a preteen modeling contest and Angie had won second place. Although her mother had told her that she'd done well, she concentrated on the fact that she was *second* and not first—but that could be remedied if she were to exercise more, lose weight, and spend more time on her hair.

Two years later, after much exercise, dieting, and attention to her appearance, Angie won first place in a larger contest. A week before her victory her mother had told her that she noticed "terrible bags" under her eyes and that she needed to do something about them for fear of coming in second again. It was then that she handed Angie a bottle of sleeping pills.

Angie sobbed and poured the pills onto the desk. Reaching around the back, up near the wall, she grasped the neck of the vodka bottle she had taken from her parents' liquor cabinet. They never noticed that it was gone but Angie always wished they would have. They never seem to notice anything. She wondered how long it would take them to realize she was gone. She scooped up two handfuls of the pills and poured them into her mouth, then downed two gulps of the vodka, gagging as it burned the back of her throat. Taking out a pen and piece of notebook paper she began to write to the only person to whom she wanted to say good-bye: her younger brother, Sam.

Dear Sam,

You're the only one I want to talk to. I want to tell you that I will miss you and I'm sorry. I want to tell you that I do not want you to be like me. I don't like who I am. My life isn't great and wonderful, even though you will hear everyone else say how happy and proud I should have been. Last year, when I cut my hair short and everyone—Mom, Dad, my friends, everyone—said it was a big mistake and I should never have done it, you said that it didn't matter because I still looked like your sister. I know you're only eight years old but I wanted to tell you that you're smarter than any of the other people in my life. You can have all of my teddy bears and anything else in my room that you want. Make sure that you live your life for you and not everyone else. I will always be your big sister, and I will always watch over you.

I love you very much,

Angie

Tears flowed from her face and struck the paper, smearing the ink slightly. There was a terrible pain in her stomach, and her head was spinning as she lay down on the bed and drifted off.

When she awoke there was a man standing over her. As she looked over the edge of the bed, she could see vomit where she must have thrown up. The excruciating pain in her stomach was gone. Even though there was a stranger in her room she was not afraid—in fact, for some strange reason she felt at peace. The man wore a white, button-down shirt and a red tie. She assumed that he was a police officer, as he had a badge hanging from a chain around his neck.

"Well, guess it didn't work," she said as her eyes focused on the empty vodka bottle on the floor.

"I'm Alan Crane, and if you're referring to your suicide attempt, I'm afraid that you were successful."

Angie froze for a moment. Then realization came over her, and she knew that the man was telling the truth. As acceptance set in she felt fear at first. Then a deep surge of regret swelled from within.

Another man dressed in a navy blue suit entered the room and stood off in one corner.

"I see that you wrote a note to your brother," Alan said as he raised the note above his head. In a criticizing tone he said, "Do you know how much pain he's gonna be in when he learns that you're gone?"

Angie sat up and hung her head between her knees. Her bottom lip began to quiver. In a voice cracked and broken from her sobs she said, "I know, I was selfish. I don't want him to suffer. You need to take care of him. Please say you will—please comfort him."

Alan threw the note back down on the desk and shook his head in disgust. He let out a sigh. "I'll do my best. But now we need to take you with us."

Angie stood up on shaky knees and continued to cry. "I know I was wrong. I was scared and felt trapped, but I was wrong...I shouldn't have..."

"What's done is done," said Alan. He put his arm around her shoulder, his voice now calm and soothing. "Now come with us. We'll take you where you need to go."

Alan glanced at Simmons, wondering what to do next. Simmons, who had been standing in the corner, made his way over to the bedroom door and opened it. All three stepped through the door and found themselves in a dark hallway of marble. Angie stopped crying once she reached the hallway; it seemed that she had a sense of understanding.

She grabbed Alan's arm with both of her hands, as if a sudden sense of fear had come over her. "Don't leave me, no matter how long it takes or how hard it becomes. Please."

Alan turned to face her with a puzzled expression. "I won't leave you. We'll get you where you need to go."

He looked back at Simmons, who nodded. Alan wondered how far the hallway stretched. They had been walking for a while, but he could no longer see the entrance, nor could he see the other end.

After walking for forty-five minutes the end finally came into view. Alan breathed a sigh of relief as they continued to approach, but as they drew nearer he could see no signs of a door on the smooth marble wall. Alan held out his badge, which illuminated the hallway to reveal passages leading both left and right.

Confusion and concern in his voice, he looked at Simmons and asked, "Which way do we go?"

"I don't know. We'll have to try each way to determine the right path."

They started with the left hallway, which made a few brief turns before leading them to another dead end. Alan held up his badge in one hand as he felt the solid marble wall in front of him with the other.

"Dead end. No door." His voice was quick and anxious.

Angie's eyes widened as her grip on Alan's arm tightened. "Please—don't leave me. Please show me the right way to go."

"I promised you that I wouldn't leave you. We'll go back and find the right way," said Alan as he placed his hand on top of hers.

She forced a slight smile. Alan could feel her hand trembling. He recognized the inner conflict she was fighting—whether or not she should trust him. After all, she had been misled all of her life by those around her: her parents, her friends. Why should she trust two people she had just met?

They made their way back to the junction and headed off in the opposite direction. Fifteen minutes of walking down this passageway revealed yet another fork in their path. They chose the right passage and stopped at a solid wall about fifty feet in. Angie was breathing heavily, as if she were having an anxiety attack.

"We'll never get where we need to go!" she said, her voice thick with panic. "I need to go back. I'm sorry, I—"

Simmons reached out and grabbed her by the arm as she spun away from Alan. In a calm and soothing voice he said, "We'll be okay. We're very near the end. You'll be fine. Please trust us."

As Simmons's eyes met hers, a sense of acceptance seemed to fill her. She took Alan's hand once more. They walked back the way they'd come, found the second junction, then continued down the other passage. After five minutes Alan saw a glint of light illuminating an outline of a door. He reached for the handle. Angie breathed deeply, as though a huge burden had been lifted from her shoulders.

Hugging Alan, she said, "I will not forget you, Illissia Galau. I'll remain loyal and learn from my mistakes. Thank you for your patience and determination."

"You're welcome," replied Alan. He opened the door. Rays of sunlight filled the hallway. As Angie slipped through the doorway he thought he heard a stream of running water flowing over rocks. *How surreal must be the scene beyond that door*, he wondered.

As it closed, Simmons said, "Let me clarify some things we've experienced today."

Alan listened patiently as they walked.

"First and foremost, you need to know about the hallways. The length and difficulty of the hallways vary from person to person, depending upon how they've lived their lives. For those we accompany, the ones who are doing what's right—making good choices, showing compassion and kindness—they make our job easier. The hallway is not so long or confusing for them."

Alan nodded, still listening.

"You will learn more about the hallways over time, but we don't need to discuss those right now. As far as those we lead," Simmons continued, "never let them get out of your sight. *You* are the one guiding them. Some will get confused and frightened, especially if the journey is long and full of obstacles. Always keep them within close proximity. If they run and you cannot see them," he paused for a moment, "you'll lose them."

"Where do they go if we lose them?"

"All in good time," Simmons said. "All in good time."

Alan sighed in frustration, but said nothing. They continued walking in silence for some distance until Alan finally asked, "Before Angie went through the door she called me that name we discussed earlier. What language is it? What does it mean?"

Simmons nodded as if he had expected the question. "She called you Illissia Galau, which is, as I told you, a rank in my organization. And as I said before, you will attain that rank once you're on your own and your training is complete. The words are from the language we speak. It is our native tongue or national language, to put it in your terms. The translation in your language would be *light guide* or *guide to the light*, meaning one who takes you down the right path. In time you'll learn more about our language and translations."

"I see," replied Alan. "One more thing I wanted to ask you."

Simmons raised his eyebrows expectantly.

"She wasn't aware that she was dead at first. She seemed surprised when I told her. Why are some people aware while others aren't?"

"Good question," replied Simmons. "It depends on the person's acceptance or denial of their mortality. Some people accept that they are going to die eventually; others reject the concept and try to push it out of their minds. Those who deny it often need additional guidance to initiate awareness of their passing."

The doorway through which they had come was now visible. As Alan and Simmons stepped back through, they found themselves in Angie's bedroom once again. The door to the bedroom opened and a small boy appeared. His hair was light blond and stuck up in different directions as if he had just awakened. He wore blue pajamas and furry slippers that forced him to take big steps so he wouldn't trip. As he walked into the room and stared at the body of his sister lying motionless on the bed, he seemed to sense that something was wrong. He ran to the bedside, nearly tripping over his large, furry feet. His eyes opened wide and pools of tears began to well up as he reached for the hand that hung over the side of the bed.

The tears began to flow over his cheeks like an endless river. Alan picked him up and said, "We should go outside and talk."

"No," he wailed. "I want to see her, just let me hold her hand."

Alan set him down. The boy ran over and grabbed his sister's hand. He shook it as if he were trying to wake her up, but it flopped lifelessly.

"I suppose you're Sam?" Alan asked. The boy nodded and continued to cry as his grief and lack of understanding overwhelmed him. "Well, Sam, your sister wanted me to tell you something."

Sam stopped sobbing for a moment and looked up at him. He glared at Alan, clearly wondering if this was a trick. Alan continued, "She wanted you to know that she made some mistakes in her life. She wanted to make sure that you didn't make the same mistakes."

Sam looked as though he was about to start crying again, so Alan said, "And most important, she told me to tell you that she was safe and very happy and that she loved you."

Sam looked up at Alan and said, "She said she loves me? Does she love me best of all?"

Alan replied, "She said she loves you more than anyone else. She even wrote a note to tell you how much she loves you, just so you'll always know."

Sam stopped crying and took the note from the desk. "Did you help her?"

"Yes, I helped her and made sure she was safe and happy."

Sam ran to Alan and embraced his legs. He stared up at the badge that hung from Alan's neck. "Thank you, Mr. Policeman."

Alan hugged him back and patted him on the head.

As Alan and Simmons walked out of the room, two paramedics passed them. Angie's mother entered behind them, looking distraught. She was tall, with an elongated face and bony chin. Alan guessed her to be in her late thirties or forties, though her leathery, overtanned skin made her look older.

She made her way over to the bed and placed her hand over her mouth as if to stop herself from crying. "No. Oh, no..." Her eyes scanned the room and she saw the pills scattered across the desk. Her voice began to quiver. "She took all of these? She was only supposed to take...she shouldn't have..." Her words trailed off. She lifted the bottle of vodka and stared at it in shock. "I should've been here. I should've been here to stop her."

Alan stared at her with contempt, clenching his jaw, then said, "Yeah. You know what I want to know?" He paused a moment to make sure he had her attention, then continued. "How the hell does a seventeen-year-old girl get prescriptions for the medications that killed her? Would you happen to know why she was taking prescription diet and sleeping pills, Mrs. Krofts?"

The woman looked down and muttered, "Well, I don't really—"

Alan interrupted by holding up his index finger. He began to pace back and forth in front of her. "You know, I've seen cases like this before; in fact, I had a similar case where a twelve-year-old girl was taking diet pills to win a pre-teen beauty contest. And you know what the really disturbing part of the whole case was?"

Mrs. Krofts's eyes became wide as a look of guilt came over her. She hung her head.

Alan continued, "The most disturbing part was the fact that her *own mother* was the person who gave her the pills. Her mother was so absorbed in what she thought her daughter *should* be that she failed to see or appreciate who her daughter really *was*. Tragically, the case ended up like this one, another dead teen—because her life was run by the expectations of everyone else. Simply tragic." Alan paused again. "Of course, her mother's now in jail, having been charged with child endangerment and manslaughter. But that's the way it goes." Alan lowered his voice and said, "I'm sorry for your loss. Your son is in real need of comfort. I believe that I may be stopping by from time to time to check up on him. Until then, I hope all is well and your family is safe."

Mrs. Krofts was speechless. She continued to stare at the floor. Finally she sat down in a nearby chair. Alan and Simmons left the room and headed back to their car.

CHAPTER FIFTEEN

"Do the right thing. It will gratify some
people and astonish the rest."

—Mark Twain

THE WEEKEND CAME AND ALAN GRATEFULLY spent the time off with his family. As he went through his usual routine, his weekly trip to the cemetery yielded numerous deep thoughts. He passed by the headstones and wondered how had they died. *How long was their walk, and who led them to their door?*

As he returned home he saw the familiar black Crown Victoria parked in front. He approached the car and Simmons rolled down the window. Alan quickly held up both hands, "Hey, it's the weekend. I'm off. I'm not up for anything. I need to see my family."

"What time is it?" asked Simmons.

"It's twelve fifteen."

"I'll get you back by twelve sixteen. Can you spare a minute?"

"Yeah, I guess I can spare a minute. So you're using the time…thing, or whatever to…?"

"Yeah, that's right. I'll get you back at twelve sixteen," Simmons repeated.

Reluctantly, Alan lumbered into the house. He had really been looking forward to a relaxing day. He returned a moment later, got into the car, and looked at his watch. Laughing he said, "Well, guess I can't go. It's twelve nineteen. You're already late."

Simmons smiled. "Put your seat belt on. You'll be back by twelve sixteen, I promise."

Alan sat there for a moment, stunned, then said apprehensively, "You mean you can go back? It's already twelve nineteen, but you can bring me back earlier? I don't believe it." He was speechless.

"You *do* believe it. You know you do. After everything else, do you really doubt that it can be done?"

Alan sat and pondered this a moment, then said reluctantly, "Actually, no. You're right, I don't doubt that it can be done. It's just that it could open up so many possibilities." He considered the opportunities that opened up with the ability to disregard time and even manipulate it. Then, as if a light switch had been turned on in his head, he said, "You could go back. You could go back and undo things. You could stop the murder from happening at the gas station and—"

Simmons cut him off. "No, it doesn't work like that. Nothing can be altered. But I'll have you back as I said I would."

Alan was somewhat disappointed. He grabbed for his seat belt. As he engaged the buckle he asked, "So who are we going to see now?"

"We're going downtown to a shooting. A young man named Tyris Cotton."

Alan rolled his eyes upward, trying to remember something important. "Tyris Cotton. Why do I know that name?" Then the answer came to him. "Yes, Tyris Cotton. I know him. He's an inner-city gang member. He's been involved in selling drugs and other violent crimes."

"Yes, I know."

Alan shook his head and said in protest, "You know? What do you mean *you know*? We can't help this guy. We'll never find the right path for him. We'll be lost forever, especially if the hallways are set up based on how good or bad they've been."

"Things aren't always as they seem. Let's go and assess the situation. Besides, I have a concern with this one."

Alan looked at him curiously. "What's the concern?"

"I couldn't predict this one, either. Heard about it over the police scanner traffic—which reminds me, have you located Mr. Sweeny yet?"

"No, unfortunately we haven't," replied Alan.

Simmons looked frustrated. The car pulled into an apartment complex that Alan vaguely recognized as some portion of the Southside Projects. As they stopped in front of 5 Bennington Way, Alan saw two police cars and an ambulance parked near the curb. He and Simmons got out of the car and approached the building. The front window of the apartment was shattered and the front door was standing open, with a uniformed police officer just inside the entryway.

As they approached the officer Simmons asked, "Could we have a few moments to examine the deceased?"

The officer nodded and said to the others inside, "Feds are here. They need us to step out for a few."

Two police officers, two paramedics, and an older black lady left the apartment. The older lady, whom Alan assumed was Tyris's mother, was crying and holding onto the shoulder of one of the officers. Simmons and Alan stepped into the entryway where the body of a young black man was lying face down on the floor. He was of medium height and had a stocky build. His muscular arms displayed several tattoos from his shoulders to his wrists. Scattered over his back were several gunshot wounds. They looked like splotches of red paint spattered on the white, cotton, sleeveless T-shirt he wore. As Alan looked closer at Tyris's face he noticed a teardrop tattoo just below his right eye. The far wall across from the plate-glass window frame bore several other holes; Alan concluded that they were caused by the same weapon.

"Looks like a drive-by shooting," said Alan.

"That's what it was," Tyris said as he sat up. Alan nearly jumped out of his skin. "I was sitting right here on this couch and I heard it—*blam, blam, blam!* They came through that window and I felt heat on my back. Next thing I know, you guys show up."

Simmons asked, "Do you know who did this?"

Tyris nodded. "Oh, I bet I know who did this. Maybe not directly himself, but he put some people up to it. I know it was R.D."

"R.D.? Is that someone in your gang?" asked Alan.

"Hell, no," replied Tyris. "First of all, I'm not in no gang no more. That's probably why this happened. But I know R.D. had something to do with it. He was mad at me."

"What's R.D. look like?" Alan asked. "And how do you know him if you're not gang brothers?"

"Don't really know what he looks like," said Tyris. "He'd meet us late at night. It was someplace dark and he always wore this black, hooded sweatshirt. Would pull the hood over his head so you couldn't really see him, even in the summer when it was hot. But I do know something about him."

"And what would that be?"

"Well, I know he's a white dude. I saw his hand one time when we were meetin' with him."

"And why would you meet with him? What would take place at these meetings?" Alan asked, as if he already knew the answer.

"He'd want us to run some stuff—you know, run some drugs—and he'd want some of us to do some folks also."

Simmons gave Alan a confused look and Tyris clarified. "He wanted us to kill some folks."

"And did you ever do these things he wanted?" asked Alan.

"I sold some drugs, but I never did anyone. I told him I wasn't about all that—I wasn't into that kind of stuff. That's when I realized the gang wasn't for me. I got a job and tried to support my mom and little sister.

But R.D., he was mad. He told me that he wanted me to do this clerk in a little town out west."

"The Moto-Mart in Riverston?" asked Alan.

"Yeah, you know about that? Anyway, I told him that's not how I roll. I told him it wasn't right and I wasn't doing his monkey-ass work. Well, he didn't like that and said I'd regret it. That was the last I heard from him." Tyris shrugged. "That's all I know."

Alan nodded. "Okay, Tyris, thanks for the info. I guess it's time for us to go."

All three made their way over to the front door, where Alan found himself once again in the familiar black, marble hallway. As they began walking, Alan said to Tyris, "It took a lot of guts to stand up to him and the others. I admire that—though selling the drugs was wrong."

Tyris hung his head. "Yeah, I know. I messed up. I started thinking about that after I quit the gang. I started thinking, how would I feel if someone sold some to my little sister? I shouldn't have done it. But that's why I got out. I told myself I was going straight, didn't care what happened. Even if I died…and, well, guess what happened?"

Alan nodded his head as if he understood. "I have to admit that I misjudged you at first. In the end, you did what was right, even at the risk of losing your life, and I respect you for that."

"It's a tough neighborhood where I come from. Belonging to a gang—well, that's the thing to do."

They continued walking for about fifteen minutes. Then the hallway turned sharply to the right and Alan saw a door ahead. The walk had not taken long at all. As they approached the door Alan could make out its outline from the light shining through.

Simmons said, "No more rough neighborhoods now. I think you'll like the new area."

Tyris smiled. Alan extended his hand and Tyris shook it, "Thanks for walking with me. I'll see you soon."

Alan nodded back in agreement. "Yes, nice to have met you. I'll check up on your mom and sister when I get back."

Tyris smiled again and slipped through the door.

The remaining two men started to make their way back. "I guess I was wrong about him," Alan said. "His background and associations made me think that he would have a struggle finding his way."

"While among the living it's never too late to find the right path. It's never too late to invest in what's good, even if you've made mistakes." Simmons paused, then continued. "However, after you've passed—well, that's a different story."

"So basically being a good person determines how difficult the path is to the door. Does it affect anything else? I mean, *after* you go through the door?"

"Yes," replied Simmons. "It determines how strong you are in our world and many other things you'll come to know in time."

Alan thought for a moment. "What do you mean by strength? Is that physical strength?"

"Not necessarily physical strength, but those things relating to one's spirit, such as inner strength, willpower, fortitude, constitution, intellectual strength—all of that translates to power."

"Why would strength be important in your world?"

"It affects many things. For one, the stronger you are, the better you are in battle," replied Simmons.

Thoughts started racing through Alan's mind as he focused on the one word that Simmons had just revealed to him: *Battle.*

He stopped and turned to face Simmons. "You mean to tell me that in your world, beyond those doors, you *fight*? You battle?"

"Of course," replied Simmons. "Why would that surprise you?"

"Well, I just thought that your world—you know, where you come from—would be peaceful, without any fighting or conflict," Alan said, a hint of disillusionment in his voice.

Simmons picked up on the tone of his voice, "Don't despair. My world is extremely peaceful. We don't fight among ourselves like you do."

Alan wondered whether it might be time to end the conversation; the next question he wanted to ask unnerved him and he wasn't sure he really wanted to hear the answer. "So then who do you battle if it's not yourselves?"

"Alan, surely you must know that there are opposite forces in everything. We are among the light—that which is good, kind, compassionate, and focused on doing what's right. But there is an opposite force—that which is bad and cruel and takes the wrong path. The light battles the darkness. It's not that different among the living, is it? Look at your world. You have all of that among yourselves now."

Alan was silent. He knew it was time to stop the conversation. Simmons noticed the concerned look on Alan's face. "Don't dwell on it. You'll learn more later on."

Alan nodded. They reached the entrance to the hallway and reappeared in the entrance to Tyris's home. Alan and Simmons stopped to comfort the young man's mother and sister, who were extremely distraught. Mrs. Cotton was a large woman with scraggly, unkempt hair. Her face was drawn and tired; there were large bags under each of her eyes, now soaked from tears. Tyris's sister was a small girl of about seven years old with two long pigtails hanging from each side of her head. She wore a tattered sundress with a yellow bow tied in the back. She clung to her mother, obviously upset and confused by the recent events and all of the people in the house.

Alan told Mrs. Cotton about Tyris's courageous stand against his old gang. He told her that her son's goal had been to legitimately support her and his little sister.

His mother smiled tearfully. "I was so proud of him. I never had much to offer him, but I tried to teach him right. Even in this bad neighborhood. I always told him—just because others around you are doing wrong doesn't mean you need to be."

As Alan walked away he said, "I wish there was something else we could do to help her. They have nothing, no money."

"That won't be the case for long," said Simmons.

"What do you mean?"

"Tyris's little sister will be an extremely successful singer in her teenage years. They'll both be well off and she'll live a long time."

"You know all that?" exclaimed Alan.

"Sure. It's not completely absolute; sometimes the future may be altered. But I'm fairly confident."

"Well, do me a favor," said Alan. "Keep my future a secret. I'd rather not know."

"Of course."

They got into the car and Simmons pulled up onto the roadway. "Are you still concerned over this incident, this death?" Alan asked.

"Yeah I am. Someone killed him and I couldn't see it coming. Perhaps we'll know more in the future."

The car pulled up in front of Alan's house. He looked at the clock in the middle of the dashboard. Twelve sixteen. As he got out of the car he said, "I'll see you soon."

Simmons nodded and sped off down the street.

CHAPTER SIXTEEN

"You cannot escape the responsibility of
tomorrow by evading it today."

—Abraham Lincoln

BILLY COX SAT ON A PLUSH LEATHER stool inside the Locker Room Sports Bar and Grill. He had arrived there for happy hour; it was now 7:30. He finished his fourth beer. His girlfriend, Amy, had just entered. She made her way to the far corner of the bar where he was seated. He watched her as she approached, admiring her slender legs and long red hair, which she flipped to one side as she sat down. She was much younger than Billy, in her early thirties, and had a bubbly personality that made him forget that he'd just turned fifty. She smiled and ordered both of them a couple of shots of tequila. Billy grinned and drank down the shot, then wiped off his thin, gray mustache with a small drink napkin.

"What took you so long?"

She smiled as she said, "Trouble finding a babysitter."

"Ah. But you found one, I guess?"

"No, I just left Jenny in charge. She can handle it if we're not gone too long."

She wrapped her arm around his and drew closer to him.

116

The bartender came over and pointed to Billy. "You good or you need anything?"

Before he could answer, Amy said, "Yeah, whiskey straight up. Two." She held up two fingers.

Two, Billy thought. He had been dating Amy for about two months and had even met her two children, but could only vaguely remember them. Her youngest child, Tony, was in preschool. Amy's daughter, Jenny, was a little older; Amy had told him that she had problems picking Jenny up from school because of her work schedule. As he finished his drink, he noticed that Amy was clinging to his upper arm as if she were using it to hold herself up. She rested her face on his forearm and began to kiss it.

As she closed her eyes, Billy asked, "Did you drink anything before you got here?"

"I had a few with the girls after work, but just a few," she replied in a slurred voice.

"Seems like more than a few."

The bartender returned. He picked up Billy's glass and again pointed to both of them. "Everyone good here?"

Amy spoke up at once. "Yeah, we'll take two more—"

Billy interrupted quickly. "No, I'm good. No more for me."

The bartender nodded and poured another drink for Amy.

As Amy took the first sip, Billy asked, "So how's everything working out between Jenny's school and your work schedule—still having problems?"

"Oh, it's still a huge pain," said Amy. "And when she gets into middle school it'll be even worse because they get off earlier. I'll have no way to pick her up. She'll have to take the bus and wait at home for me. But that's still a few years away."

As she continued to sip her drink, Billy's mouth fell slightly open, "So Jenny is in elementary school?"

"Yeah," said Amy, her words still slurred. "Fairview Elementary School." She repositioned herself on her stool and nearly toppled over.

A feeling of disbelief, mixed with anxiety, began to rise in Billy's gut. He stood up and asked, with a slightly raised voice, "How old is Jenny?"

"Oh, she's six, but she'll be seven in a few months," replied Amy.

Disbelief filled Billy's mind, followed quickly by a rising anger. "Are you insane? You can't leave a six-year-old home alone with a preschooler!"

"It's only for a short time. Hey, I have a life, too!"

Her answer increased the rage within him. He grabbed the drink out of her hand and slammed it down on the counter. Throwing some money down beside it, he took her by the arm.

"Hey!" she said. "What are you doing?"

"We're leaving to go check on your kids!"

Standing, he realized that he might also have had too much to drink. He was so infuriated by Amy's lack of common sense, however, the thought quickly vanished. *How could she be so irresponsible?* he thought as he shook his head and clenched his teeth.

Amy protested, "No, I wanna stay. I'm not finished with my—"

"We're going!" Billy barked. He pulled her away from the bar.

She didn't protest; she was too busy trying to hang onto him to steady herself and keep from falling.

"Okay, but I'm driving," she said.

"Like hell," he replied. "You're too drunk to stand up, and I'm not much better off but we're going anyway—and *I'm* driving. Get in the car and shut up!"

He unlocked the passenger-side door of his car with one hand and propped her up against the rear door with the other. Once open, he helped her get in, which was not an easy feat, given that both of her legs went out from under her. She landed on the pavement. Billy pulled her back up far enough to push her into the seat and close the door, then hurried over to the driver's side and got in.

He threw the car in drive and tore out of the lot, heading in the direction of her apartment. The last drink he'd had was taking effect, numbing his fingers. He balled them into a fist to regain some feeling. He accelerated past a cluster of cars in the slow lane. His head was spinning slightly and his vision was somewhat doubled. He slammed on the brakes just in time to avoid another car that had cut him off from the opposite lane. For a moment all was clear as his fear and anger made him focus.

His voice was direct and stern as he asked, "Which turn is it?"

She did not answer.

He looked over and noticed that Amy was passed out in the passenger seat. Billy pursed his lips and began to grind his teeth. He grabbed her shoulder and began to shake her. Amy's head wobbled as he asked again, "Which turn is it to your apartment?"

"Umm, it's..." But it was no good. She had passed out again.

He slammed his left palm down on the steering wheel and shook her harder with his right hand as he yelled, "Where do I turn?"

Her long, red hair was now hanging over her face; some of it was matted to her mouth from the drool that was running down her chin. She blurted out, "Right, right, turn right," and flopped her head back down on the passenger side door with a loud thump.

Billy turned right down a narrow street, accelerating once more. Amy lifted her head up and said, "I don't feel well. My head is killing me."

Billy lowered his eyebrows and frowned in complete disgust, but said nothing. Amy leaned forward and rested her head on the dashboard, both hands clutching her temples.

They were fast approaching a large intersection. Billy asked, "Straight at the intersection?"

"Yeah, that's my parking lot, straight across the intersection."

Billy sped up and guided the car toward the crowded intersection. Amy continued to rub the sides of her head, which now hung between her legs. All at once she let out a huge groan and spewed vomit all over the floor.

"Damn it!" Billy yelled. He fumbled for the button to roll down the passenger-side window. Finding it, he rolled the window down the entire way and yelled to her, "Out the window, hang your head out the window!"

As they approached the intersection the light was still green. Billy continued forward, determined to make it to the parking lot before Amy threw up again. She raised her head up, flung it to her left, and began to vomit again, this time across the center console of the car. Billy attempted to move and avoid the splash, but could not. He felt the warm, vile liquid begin to soak into his pant leg.

This relationship is so over, he thought, grinding his teeth once again.

Amy continued to vomit. Her left hand reached up and caught hold of the steering wheel as she attempted to steady herself. She pulled down hard.

The car began to turn sharply. Billy, distracted, saw what was happening and grabbed the wheel in an attempt to right the car, but it was too late. They spun out of control. Billy had just enough time to see another car coming at him head-on.

The impact was tremendous, like a volcanic eruption of metal and glass shooting with an unmatched fury in all directions. Everything went black.

When Billy opened his eyes he saw a figure standing outside his window, which was now broken and scattered across the pavement.

He looked over and saw Amy sitting in the passenger seat. "Are you okay?" he asked.

"Yeah, I'm fine. What happened?"

She didn't seem to be intoxicated any longer. *A traumatic incident can sober you up quickly*, he thought.

"You don't remember? You were throwing up and grabbed the wheel. We crashed. I hope those other people are all right."

A hand on his left forearm caught his attention. He looked up and saw a figure with a police badge around his neck standing outside the car window.

"Come on out," the man said in a calm voice.

Billy nodded. As he got out of the car he could find no vomit strewn about, nor on his pant leg.

Strange, he thought as he reached for the door handle. To his amazement the door opened, even though it was mangled. As he exited, he saw Amy getting out of the other side. His heart raced as he saw the other car they had struck. He could make out two figures sitting in the front seat of the smashed wreck. The entire front end of the car was crushed into the front wheel wells and the windshield was shattered. Billy ran to the other car and saw two teenage girls sitting inside.

"Everybody okay?"

Both looked extremely frightened, but nodded.

Letting out a huge breath of relief, he turned back to the police detective and said, "I'll get my license and insurance card."

"No need for that. Just follow me."

Billy saw another figure in a suit approach and say something to the girls in the other car. The detective walked over to Amy and said, "Ma'am, you'll have to wait here for a few minutes. I'll be right back."

"Please, Officer," Billy said, "there are two young children in an apartment over there by themselves. Someone needs to check on them." He struggled to remember the right address, then turned and pointed to Amy, who said, "It's number 628."

The detective nodded and held up his hand to calm everyone down. "Yes," he said, "Tony and Jenny are fine. Your mother is with them. My partner checked on them a little while ago."

Billy wondered how the police knew that the kids had been there alone. *Perhaps a neighbor had called?* But at any rate, they were safe. *Now*, Billy thought, *to get this mess cleaned up*. His insurance company wouldn't be happy with him. He might even go to jail for driving under the influence. But at least nobody was hurt.

Wonder why this cop doesn't want my insurance card or license. Isn't that pretty much standard procedure? Maybe they're just taking me straight to jail, he thought.

The detective led Billy through the middle of the intersection, which was now crammed with fire trucks, police cars, and tow trucks.

They both stopped at an ambulance. The detective opened the back doors and said, "After you."

"Okay. I feel fine, though."

"Yeah, I know you do," said the detective with a slight nod and sympathetic smile.

Billy shrugged. He stepped through the doors and suddenly found himself standing in a dark hallway, rather than sitting in the back of an ambulance as he had naturally expected. The only illumination was coming from the badge the detective wore around his neck. The other man in the navy blue suit had also entered. Billy suddenly realized what had happened. He and the others had not survived the crash.

The detective said, "Let's get going. We may have quite a distance to cover."

Billy nodded. The three of them set off together.

Amy made her way over to the ambulance where she had seen Billy and the two men disappear. As she reached up to grab the handle the door swung open. The man dressed in the suit held out his hand to help her up.

"Thank you," she said. She grabbed his hand to pull herself upward through the doors.

Entering, she found herself in a dark hallway with the other man. The taller one with the glowing budge around his neck said, "Wow. Didn't think we'd ever find our way back from that last one. That was a long walk."

The man in the suit replied, "This one may be worse, we'll see."

To Amy he said, "Hello, Amy, I'm Alan Crane. This is Michael Simmons. I assume you know why we're here and what we have to do."

A feeling of enlightenment came over her as they spoke. "Yes, I understand."

Chapter Seventeen

*"Sometimes we stare so long at
a door that is closing that we see too late
the one that is open."*

—Alexander Graham Bell

THE THREE OF THEM BEGAN WALKING. AFTER about fifteen minutes the hallway split. Taking the right passage, Alan led everyone forward. The floor descended for a while before it began to level out once more as they came to a dead end.

"Let's go back," he said to the others with a tinge of disappointment in his voice. They all began the long walk back as Amy started to panic.

"I'm sorry. I've caused this. I've caused all of this," she said as she attempted to push past Alan.

He grabbed her arm, "It'll be okay. Just stick close." He loosened his grip and grabbed her hand instead.

"Let's check out the other way," suggested Simmons.

As they approached the place where the hallway had split Alan noticed that the opposite passage led upward. They began climbing. As the hallway ascended and the grade became rather steep their pace slowed. Once they reached the top of the slope the floor became level once again. They continued, slowing to catch their breath from the climb. The smooth, black surface of the marble walls reflected their distorted figures like a mirror that had been twisted and bent to alter its reflection. After about ten more minutes of walking, Alan could see the faint outline of a door reflected at the end.

"There. I told you we'd make it."

He glanced at Amy, who now wore a look of relief on her face.

Alan reached for the door handle. As he was about to open it, Simmons yelled, "No, don't open it!"

Alan's eyes widened. Simmons's reaction had somewhat startled him. He released the handle. "Why not?"

Without taking his gaze from the door, as if he were hypnotized, Simmons said, "Because it's not the right door." His voice was low and tense.

Alan, confused, shot Simmons a look of concern. "How can you tell?"

"If you recall, all the other doors we've encountered had a faint light outlining the door frame. This one doesn't. Hold your badge close to it and you'll see what I mean."

Alan grasped the badge around his neck and held it so that the illumination reflected toward the door. He noticed that the light emitting from the badge was being drawn into the space between the door and the frame—as if it were being *absorbed*.

"It's devouring the light."

"Yes." Simmons nodded as he continued to stare at the door. "The darkness is consuming the light. We need to leave."

Fear appeared on Amy's face. Alan felt a hollow pain in his stomach. They all walked backwards very slowly, then turned around once the door was no longer in sight.

"Simmons," whispered Alan, so that Amy couldn't hear, "we're out of options. There's nowhere else for us to go."

"There's always a way. We must have missed something."

They retraced their steps all the way back to the beginning and started once again. As they made their way back down the first hallway,

Simmons said, "Search each wall, high and low. We must have over-looked it."

Alan ran his hands along the smooth marble, attempting to feel something out of the ordinary, but there were no seams or breaks. It was one continuous, solid piece. They made their way back to the place where the hall had split. Simmons suggested once again searching the passageway to the right. Alan wondered what exactly the "wrong door" was, especially since he could still vividly recall the apprehension on Simmons's face and in his voice when they had discovered it.

They began the slow descent down the right hallway. Alan held his badge close to the wall, trying to catch a glimpse of anything that might reveal a doorway. Amy was clutching the back of Alan's shirt tightly. Every once in a while he could feel her tremble. They found their way back to the place where the hallway ceased its descent and the floor became level once again. It was at this point that Amy stopped walking and sat down with her back propped against the wall.

She sobbed and said, "I can't make it. You two have tried and I appreciate it, but we're not going to make it. I've neglected my kids. I drink too much. I've been a horrible person and—"

Alan bent down and grabbed both of her shoulders. "Look at me. Look at me!" He shook her slightly until she raised her eyes to meet his. "You *will* make it. You have to trust me. You have to have faith in me. I haven't walked this far to give up, and I won't tolerate this from you!"

His voice was stern, but she continued to wipe her eyes and shake her head from side to side, as if she had given in to defeat.

"Now," Alan said even more assertively. "You're going to get up and you're going to take my hand and we'll continue." He stood up and extended his hand. "Do you understand me?"

She raised her eyes slowly until she caught his gaze, now stern and commanding. She reached up slowly and grasped his hand. Alan pulled her to her feet and the three of them continued down the hallway as

Simmons surveyed both sides of the passage. As Alan watched, he wondered how Simmons could see so well in the dark. *Perhaps he knows the hallways from previous visits. But if that were the case then he never would have led us to the wrong door.*

The end of the hallway was drawing near. Alan gripped Amy's hand tightly. He had tried to sound confident when he told her that they were going to prevail, but the truth was that in spite of those words, doubt lingered in his mind. He buried his negative thoughts, knowing that if he showed any pause or lack of confidence she would dash off and be lost. The dead end was now very near, perhaps four feet in front of them. Alan started to feel around with one hand. His fingers ran high on the wall but felt only the familiar cold, smooth marble that existed throughout. His other hand was still clutching Amy's; he feared she might run if he released it. Failing to find any change, he bent down and ran his fingers lower on the wall.

His hand brushed over a seam of some kind. "I found something." Standing up, he looked at Amy. "I'm going to let go of your hand, but you *must* stay here."

She nodded. Alan saw Simmons position himself behind her as if to indicate that he would stop her if she tried to flee. Alan bent down and felt the edge of the line that ran horizontally along the floor. It was approximately four feet long. At each end he discovered two vertical lines running down, which then met another horizontal line, forming some type of square seam. Retracing the boundaries of the square twice to familiarize himself with the edges, Alan placed his palms on the square and pushed.

Nothing happened.

Alan repositioned his hands a bit farther apart, braced his feet against the floor and pushed with more strength, using his shoulders and hips. The marble square folded inward and down, as if there were a hinge at the bottom. Once the marble piece was all the way down, Alan noticed that it sat completely flush in the floor, as if a space had been cut there to hold it. Alan peered into the opening, about four feet tall and four feet wide. It was pitch black.

He stood up and looked at Simmons. "Guess we've found the way."

Amy looked at the opening and said in a fearful voice, "I can't. I can't go in there. I'm claustrophobic, I won't make it. I can't do it."

Simmons spoke to her this time. "To reach your goal you must conquer your fears. You've made mistakes in your life and you must think of those whom you've disappointed. Use them as your strength. Let their memory serve to push you onward into that which may frighten you. Once you breach these obstacles you'll know that you've helped them in the end. You won't be alone. We'll be with you."

Though trembling, she nodded her head and inhaled deeply. Alan got down on his knees and wrapped the chain of the badge tightly around his hand. Holding the badge outward into the small crawl space, he illuminated the space a few feet in front of him, but no more. He crawled forward several feet to allow the others to enter. Amy entered next and Simmons followed. After Simmons had crawled a few feet beyond where they had entered, Alan heard something snap shut and knew that it was the hinged piece of marble he'd pushed open at the entrance. Amy let out a gasp. Alan heard her breathing quicken.

Her mind was racing as she felt the cold marble on all sides pressing inward, crushing her. For a moment she thought that she might pass out. She had the impulsive desire to have a drink, the thing she had done so often in life that allowed her to escape the ever-closing walls of responsibility—an escape that had ruined everything and left her even more trapped in the end.

No! she thought. She pushed the urge to drown her fears in alcohol out of her thoughts.

Alan could not turn around to face Amy nor grab her hand, so he turned his head as far as it would go and said, "Just follow the light. We'll make it."

With that he took the badge in his hand and felt around for the clasp on the back. He undid it and fastened the badge to the right side of his belt, where it illuminated the right wall. He could hear Amy begin to breathe a bit more slowly as he continued onward into the complete darkness, all the time feeling with his hands. For another ten minutes they continued straight as the floor of the crawl space began to descend.

The grade was not overly steep, but enough to make their hands slip forward every once in a while. After the floor leveled out once again Alan stopped for a moment so that everyone could rest.

"Simmons, does it seem like we're going in the right direction?"

"Yes," Simmons replied. "We're fine. We must keep going."

The crawl space continued, but they now found themselves ascending and turning at the same time. As the narrow passage turned there seemed to be a little bit more room, but as it straightened and leveled out once again, the additional space diminished to the same as before. Alan continued forward on his hands and knees. He was tired and not paying much attention—until his head collided with the wall in front of him.

"Stop," he said to everyone. "There's a wall here—give me a minute."

He pushed as hard as he could and felt the marble wall start to give way. It folded outward and down, snapping into place as if on another tight hinge. He unhooked the badge from his belt and thrust it through the opening. Reaching out, he let his hands hang downward, but could not feel the floor. He turned over on his back and reached upward above the opening and could now feel what appeared to be the ceiling.

"We must be up near the top of the wall."

Rolling back onto his stomach once again, he moved himself farther out into the opening so that he could reach deeper in an attempt to find the floor below, but to no avail. The glow from the badge illuminated about a foot or so down, but the floor could not be seen. The crawl space was such that he could not maneuver his feet to go out first. If he were to drop, he would go down face first, which didn't appeal to him at all.

"Amy," Simmons said in a calm voice, "you're going to have to hold onto Alan's ankles so that he can lower himself down."

Amy's voice was cracked and apprehensive. "I'm not that strong. He must weigh over two hundred pounds. I'll never be able to hold him. You should do it."

"I can't. There's no room for me to pass you in this crawl space. You must do it. You must find a way to hold on. Do not let go," Simmons urged.

Alan was listening to the conversation. The thought of Amy holding his ankles while he lowered himself into a place where he couldn't see made his stomach tighten into a knot.

"I guess there's no other way?" he asked Simmons as a last appeal for a new plan.

"No. This is our only option. I'll try to steady her as she attempts to do the same for you."

Alan shook his head and wondered why he'd ever signed on to do this. The thought of dying had never crossed his mind before during any of these assignments, but now he wondered what would happen if he fell. Would he die? And if so, who would take care of his family, his daughter?

"Okay," he said reluctantly. "Don't let go. I have a wife and a daughter and I fully expect to see them again."

"I won't let go," replied Amy.

Alan sensed a newfound confidence in her voice that he hadn't heard until now. It was almost convincing. Alan unraveled the chain attached to his badge. He placed the chain between his teeth so that the badge hung down another foot or so beyond his face, allowing him to keep his hands free in case he needed them to brace his fall. He slowly moved himself forward until his waist was even with the edge of the opening. Amy's hands gripped his ankles tightly as he bent over the opening at the waist and placed his palms on the wall, attempting to ease his way down. The smooth marble surface was not well-suited for traction; he felt every joint in his wrists and fingers begin to flex and bend, burning with pain. Suddenly he remembered how much he feared heights. Sweat began to form on his palms, making them slide on the slick marble.

"Wait," he said, his voice betraying his discomfort. "Hold on a minute."

His face was nearly flush against the wall as he craned his neck and lifted his head in an attempt to see the floor. He could not. The pulsating feeling of blood rushing to his head made him queasy as he came to the realization that Amy would have to push him out the rest of the way and attempt to catch his ankles at the very edge of the opening. If the floor were more than a few feet down beyond that point, he was in real trouble because she would not have the strength to pull him back up—or even hold him for very long.

"Okay, Amy," he said with hesitation in his voice, "you're going to have to lower me down farther."

"I'm ready."

With determination Amy clenched her teeth tightly. *All my life I've failed. All my life I've let people down, let them fall. Not this time,* she thought.

Alan felt her pushing him forward. It was painful; his shins scraped over the hard edge of the opening and all at once he felt the weight of his body shift and fall as her hands loosened. Fear overwhelmed him, and he closed his eyes. Then he stopped abruptly. He felt her forearms wrap around both of his ankles in a bear hug.

A faint noise below made him open his eyes. He lifted his head once again and saw that the badge had struck the floor. Reaching out with both hands, he pushed off the floor to relieve Amy's grip on his ankles.

"I'm good!" he yelled up. He heard her take a deep breath as she let go.

Alan propped his legs against the wall, bent at the waist, and rolled into a sitting position. He stood and saw the opening above. He reached up and waited for Amy to descend. Grabbing her hands, he helped her down and looked up to see Simmons peering out of the opening for a moment. Then he disappeared.

"Hey, you coming down?"

In an instant he saw Simmons's feet protruding through the opening. At once he leaped down to the floor unassisted.

"How'd you turn around in that crawl space?" Alan asked. "And you jumped—how?"

"No matter. We need to keep going."

Alan pointed his finger at him. "You can go first next time."

Simmons ignored him. They all continued forward. This time the hallway was a bit steeper. As the grade ended and the hallway leveled out Alan saw a set of stairs leading up to an archway. He paused to look at it for a moment. He had never encountered anything like this. Cautiously he approached the top of the stairs. He glanced back at Simmons, who nodded. Alan peered through the archway.

There was no hallway beyond. What did lie beyond the archway must have been a larger room, since Alan could not see the walls to either side nor across to the other side. A strange, faint, methodical dripping sound, almost like the steady tick of a clock, came from the distance. Alan began walking to his left to see if he could locate a wall. Within five minutes he was successful. Backtracking, the others following, he walked in the opposite direction and found the other wall at an equal distance from the center, making the room approximately one hundred and fifty feet wide. The faint light of the badge was not enough to light up the whole room.

"Looks like we're going forward," he said to Amy and Simmons.

They both nodded and continued onward.

Suddenly Alan gasped as his foot slipped off a step and he nearly fell. He lowered the badge to illuminate a series of steps leading down. They descended at a cautious pace. Alan stopped when his shoe hit liquid. He felt a cool sensation as his sock filled with what felt like water. He angled the badge down toward his foot and saw that the steps continued into the large pool before them. The light from the badge glistened off the water, creating a wonderful display of colors. It didn't seem to penetrate past the surface. The water was quite cold; Alan's toes curled within his shoe in response to the initial shock. One step deeper and it rose above his calf. One more step and it rose beyond his knee. The next step took the water up past his thigh.

"I don't like this. I don't like this at all."

"Well, there's no going back," said Simmons. "Tell me, Amy, can you swim?"

She nodded. Alan held up the badge in an attempt to see how far the water stretched. He couldn't see the other side. He stepped forward two more steps to find the water up to his chest.

The water was nearly at Amy's chin. As it penetrated her clothing, the cold chill brought forth the image of her children sitting in her car on a cold, rainy October day. She had turned the engine off because she was running low on gas. She ran into the liquor store to get her fix, forgetting to close her car door. As she engaged in spirited conversation with the cashier, whom she knew well, the minutes flew by, longer than she'd expected. Returning to the car, she found her kids soaked and shivering, their cheeks bright red and their teeth chattering. She had smiled at them, started the car, and opened the bottle she had just purchased.

How could I have done that? What kind of monster was I? How could I be so numb to the ones who needed me most? The thought dissipated as some of the salty water entered her mouth. She wondered if they were in the ocean.

Alan looked around. "I guess we start swimming. Everyone stay close. You know, I would've dressed differently, had I known." He glanced back at Simmons, who gave him something of a smile and a nod.

The three of them entered the water and began to swim. Within a few moments Alan heard a dripping, which sounded very close. He looked up to see droplets of water falling from above, perhaps from the ceiling, too far overhead to see. The weight of his clothes dragged him down, but he kicked his feet and pulled with his arms as he continued forward. Within a few moments his foot hit something solid: the water level was decreasing and Alan could now see that the ceiling above met the water in front of him. "It looks like we need to swim down under the water if we want to continue," he said shaking his head reluctantly. Amy and Simmons met his eyes and nodded.

He took a deep breath and plunged his face into the cool water as the others did the same. At thirty-five seconds he began to panic and wondered if everyone, including himself, could hold their breath for much longer. At forty-five seconds he saw a faint light above him. Feeling as if his lungs were about to explode, he swam rapidly upward.

Finally he was able to raise his head out of the water, exhaling hard, spitting and gasping for air. Amy was right behind him. She also flung her head up, gasping much the same as Alan. Simmons surfaced shortly thereafter, but merely spat out some water and breathed normally. He wasn't even winded.

"You're a good swimmer," Alan said.

"Yes, lots of practice," replied Simmons. Alan knew that this was just a polite way of covering one more extraordinary secret that Simmons was keeping.

"Perhaps you have gills," teased Alan.

"Well, perhaps."

As he caught his breath, Alan turned and focused his attention straight ahead. The surface below his feet was slippery. The water level was decreasing as they continued on.

Once they were out of the water the distance between the walls grew wider. Straight ahead there was a set of ascending stone steps with an archway at the top. As before, the room beyond was very dark. Alan entered it with the same caution. The temperature had dropped dramatically; he could see his breath in front of his face and his wet clothes clung to his skin. He was chilled to the bone.

As he walked forward, he came to the edge of what looked like another set of steps that led downward. He put his foot forward but found that it was not a step at all. As he peered over the edge into the darkness he felt a cold breeze blowing from below. He withdrew his foot from the precipice and put his badge close to the edge so that he could see farther down. But the light only shone a couple of feet below the surface. He coughed from the cold chill, and he heard the echo from the emptiness below. He took a coin from his pocket and dropped it into the abyss, counting until he heard the sound of it striking the bottom.

There was no sound.

How were they going to get across?

"Okay," he said to Simmons, "I'm still in training and *you're* the trainer. What do we do next?"

"You find a way across."

"That's a big help, Simmons. I don't think I could've figured that one out myself. I'm sure glad you're here to mentor me," said Alan sarcastically.

"Follow the edge and examine it closely."

Fifty feet to their right he found an old, rickety bridge. It had no planks to walk on: it was made solely of rope, with a series of rungs like a ladder to walk on and two ropes on either side like handrails. The bridge was anchored by two huge eyehooks embedded in the marble wall behind them. Alan yanked on the ropes with all his weight to see if they were sturdy enough to hold him. They held firm.

Once again, Alan's fear of heights made him lightheaded. "Simmons, maybe you should go first this time."

"All right."

Simmons began to walk across the bridge, and Alan felt the ropes straining as his weight pressed down. As he disappeared out of sight, Alan prepared to follow.

He held out his hand to Amy. "Let's get this over with. You go in front of me so that I can grab you if you slip."

They began walking and the bridge began to sink lower with their added weight. They were now so far out that they couldn't see where they'd started. A cold wind blew. Alan squeezed his fists tightly to fight off the numbness. Simmons was now about ten feet ahead. He seemed to be walking on the wobbly bridge with little effort.

Suddenly, Alan felt the ropes begin to shift and he heard a loud snap. He felt the horrible sensation of freefall as he realized that the ropes connecting the bridge must have given way. For a moment he thought he saw Simmons falling below, but he didn't hear any sound. Fear gripped at his chest. They were falling fast. He clung to what remained of the bridge. "Hold on tight!" he yelled to Amy. As the slack was taken up by the ropes, he felt a sharp jerk that almost made him lose his grip and then they collided with the wall—his head, elbows, and knees struck the cold, marble rock far below the edge where they had started. Amy let out a scream from below as her body hit the wall. He wondered how badly she was injured. Closing his eyes until all motion ceased, he felt the cold emanating from the slick stone just inches from his face as he thought to himself...*is this the end of my life?*

Chapter Eighteen

"Look for the light in those times of darkness and allow your heart to guide your soul."

ALAN DREW A DEEP BREATH ATTEMPTING TO QUELL his anxiety, "Simmons, are you there?" he shouted.

There was no answer.

He yelled more loudly, "Simmons, can you hear me? Are you there?"

Again, there was no answer.

Looking down he saw that Amy had managed to wrap her arms around part of the ropes and was hanging on just below him. He estimated that they were about one hundred feet below the edge. He couldn't see the bottom below them. Or Simmons.

Amy was shaking in shock. The cold wall in front of her was black. As she stared at it she could see her reflection staring back, judging her, forcing her to look inside her soul where her true character was exposed. *Ugly, hollow,* she thought as she stared into her own eyes. The thought of letting go and plunging into the darkness crossed her mind. Then someone spoke her name.

"Amy!" Alan yelled down.

He began to climb down. Before long he was level with Amy's face, which was blank, staring straight ahead.

His breath was labored. "We need to get back to the top," he said.

"I can't make it," she mumbled as she stared at the black wall in front of them.

"Come on. We'll take it one rung at a time."

Slowly they both began to ascend the tattered ropes. Every two or three feet of climbing brought with it a horrible straining sound, as if the rope was about to break. Whenever Alan heard that sound he winced. If the ropes broke, there would be nothing to cling to on their way down—only smooth marble.

Somehow they reached the top and lay on the floor to catch their breath. A few moments later Alan began pulling up the remains of the ropes. They were light, which meant that Simmons was not clinging to them farther down. He must have fallen.

As Alan pulled the last bit of the bridge up, he noticed two eyebolts hooked to the ends of the ropes and realized that they must have come loose from the opposite side. He struggled to feel a sense of hope, wondering if they would ever get out of this desperate situation.

The pit is impassable, he thought. Then he remembered what Simmons had said earlier: There's always a way.

Amy began to cry. Alan put his arm around her and whispered, "Don't give up. There's always hope. We'll get through this." He had no idea how they were going to get through this, but some inner sense was telling him that their survival was linked to persistence and will.

As Alan sat there he heard the sound of someone coughing or clearing their throat. He looked over the edge, but it was too dark to make out anything.

"Hello? Can anyone hear me?"

Simmons's voice answered. "I'm here, about thirty feet down below you. There's a ledge and an opening."

Alan redirected his gaze straight down over the edge trying to locate Simmons through the enveloping darkness as he yelled, "Lucky you hit that ledge."

"Actually, I didn't. I fell a great deal farther and had to climb back up. I found this ledge along the way."

"That's impossible," replied Alan. "These walls are made of smooth marble—there's no way you could've climbed them, or even caught yourself, for that matter."

"We can discuss my acrobatic talents later," said Simmons. "Right now we need to get you two down here."

Who are you Michael Simmons—or for that matter WHAT are you? The thought danced around in Alan's head. "You're right," he said aloud, focusing on the challenge at hand. "It's way too far to jump. If we try to lower each other down we'll never make it. Hang on a moment."

He picked up the heap of rope piled on the floor—the remnants of the rope bridge.

"Simmons, I'm going to try to throw you what's left of the bridge. You'll need to catch it and hang on so that we can climb down."

"Understood. I'm ready when you are."

Alan held onto one end of the rope, then pushed the remnants over the edge and heard the two eyebolts clang off the wall below. He began to swing the rope in the direction of Simmons's voice. On the fifth swing the ropes went taut. "Okay, got it," Simmons yelled.

"Okay," Alan shouted back. "We're coming down."

He had Amy go first and watched her descend slowly. When Alan could no longer see her, Amy finally yelled up, "I'm down! Your turn."

He breathed a sigh of relief and then began his own descent. He slowly lowered himself, carefully testing each rope rung as he went, all the time hoping that the eyebolts on this side were sturdier than their failed counterparts. Finally he saw Simmons and Amy standing a few feet below.

He joined them on the narrow ledge that was perhaps only two feet wide. The ledge spanned the perimeter of the room allowing them to slowly make their way to the other side where the bridge had broken free. Once there, Alan found himself walking up yet another steep flight of stairs, noticing a faint glow emitting from the top.

Finally they reached the top, where they found themselves in a hot, humid room. The walls were circular and dripping with condensation. In the center of the room there was a shallow, circular basin filled with about three inches of water.

In the center of the basin stood a statue of two small children sitting on a bench with their heads hung low. As Alan looked closer he thought he could see tears running down the children's faces. Then he realized that the humidity from the room was causing the drops of water to fall from the ceiling onto their faces and then into the basin. From there, the water gradually seeped through a crack in the bottom of the basin. The scene was lit by a dull light.

"What's this? What does this mean?" He shook his head and looked at Simmons, who didn't reply.

Then Amy caught sight of the statues. She knelt down and cried hysterically.

"Those are my kids," she said. Memories began to flood her mind. She remembered seeing this look on the faces of her kids many times before. Because she was so self-absorbed she had always had the ability to tune it out. This time there was no looking away, no shutting it out, no denial. The image was there, and all she could do was stare at it in regret. "I'm sorry," she said out loud. She ran up to the statues and knelt down in the warm water as she added her own tears to the basin. "I'm sorry. I wish I could ask them to forgive me," she cried through uncontrollable sobs.

A strong sense of understanding came over Alan as he realized where the water in the basin was going. He recalled the vast pool they had passed through and remembered seeing the water dripping from above.

"Yes," said Simmons, sensing her thoughts. "It seems that you've swum in a sea of tears to get here. The good news is that you've made it and will now be at peace. Use this image to serve as a reminder that the journey is long and hard for those who don't choose to do what's right and just and good. Come here."

Amy got up and walked behind the statues to where Simmons was standing near a large door, which was outlined in a golden, glowing light. Alan joined them. As the door opened, a bright flash of sunlight lit the room as the statues turned to face them. Alan noticed that the light had dried the water that once ran down their faces, and both figures were sitting upright with glowing smiles.

Amy looked at both Alan and Simmons, smiling, "I won't forget either of you."

She slipped through the door, and it closed behind her.

Alan drew a deep breath, "I'm not going back the way we came. You'd better figure something else out."

Simmons smiled, "No, our path is much easier than hers."

With that, he pointed to a far corner of the room where another archway had appeared. They walked through it and found themselves back in the original hallway where they had begun.

"What will become of her children?" asked Alan.

"Amy's mother will raise them. They'll be taken care of. I checked on them earlier and they're doing fine. Sometimes children have a greater understanding of death than adults do. The purity of their hearts allows them to accept things that adults find hard to cope with."

As they walked toward the entranceway Alan stopped, "I want to ask you about that first door."

"Yes—what did you want to know?"

"Where did it lead? I saw the apprehension on your face."

"It led to another path. It led to the darkness, which she could have chosen. It was the easier of the two paths, but she persevered with your guidance and she overcame her fears and inadequacies to be amongst the light."

Alan nodded as they continued back to the entrance.

As they reached the door, Alan said, "I'm glad that's over—I need a break."

"We're not done yet," Simmons replied. "We have a couple more to take care of."

Chapter Nineteen

"The day is done, and the darkness
falls from wings of night, as a feather is wafted
downward from an eagle in his flight."

—Henry Wadsworth Longfellow

A S THEY STEPPED BACK OUT OF THE AMBULANCE, Alan realized
that they were just in time. Everything was still in place. Billy's and
Amy's bodies were still seated in the mangled remains of their car.

"Let's speak to these two over there," Simmons said.

He led Alan over to the other car, and they peered inside to see two
teenage girls seated inside. Alan guessed they were sixteen or seven-
teen years old and noticed that they looked alike. Both had light brown
hair and wore blue jeans and pink T-shirts with the words "Gardenview
High School, Class of 2010" on the front.

"You two are sisters, I take it?"

The driver replied in a shaken tone, "Yes sir, this is my sister Melissa."

"And your name?"

"I'm Emma Bornhopp."

"Okay, Emma. Why don't you come with us and we'll come back to
speak with your sister in a few minutes? Everything is going to be fine,"
said Alan.

The girl in the passenger seat was holding a pink cell phone in her hands and frantically pressing some buttons. She began to cry. "It won't go through," she said hysterically. "I'm trying to send a text, but it won't go through."

Emma's hands were still gripping the steering wheel. "Please sir, I'm very scared. I didn't see that car at all. I would've stopped if I'd seen it. I hope those other people are all right."

"The other people are just fine," Alan said. "We just finished speaking to them. Both of you need to know that this was not your fault. We're going to take care of you."

Both girls, pale and trembling, still appeared shaken from what had happened.

Emma spoke again. "My dad is going to be so angry that we wrecked his car. Even if it isn't our fault, he won't understand." Melissa dropped the phone and began to cry even harder.

"He won't be angry with you," Alan said, speaking to them both. "I'll speak to him and make him understand what happened."

Alan thought of their father's reaction and knew that it would not be anger—at least, not anger directed at them.

"I know he'll be angry because he'll be scared."

Alan was a bit confused by her statement. "Scared?"

"Yes," she replied and paused to wipe a tear that ran down her cheek. "My older brother was killed six months ago in a motorcycle accident. Melissa and I are the only two children left in the family. My father will be extremely frightened that we could've been killed. And my mother... well, I don't know how she's going to take it. She hasn't left the house since my brother died. My dad keeps telling us that we should wear our seat belts. We have to call once we arrive wherever we're going just so he knows that we're safe. He's overprotective because he's scared after what happened to my brother. We all cried for days after that accident. I still remember how bad it was when we all found out, when that police officer showed up at our house and told us what had happened. When you talk to my dad you need to let him and my mom know right away that everything is okay, please. Let them know quickly so they won't worry."

Alan knelt down on the pavement and hung his head below the door. He said nothing for the longest time. The grief was overwhelming. He shook his head. The hollow, empty feeling in the deepest part of his soul was back. He could imagine the reaction from the girls' mother and father when they heard the news that their two remaining children had been killed in an accident. Would the fact that it wasn't their fault comfort them? He thought not. Would anything he could tell them be enough? Again, he thought not. His silence continued as he rubbed his hand against his forehead, as though this would somehow make the situation better.

Emma broke the dark, ominous sensation that was smothering him. "Will you tell my dad that we're all right?"

Alan couldn't look up, but managed to mumble, "Yes, I'll tell your parents that you're fine."

He stood up. "Wait here a minute. I need to speak with my partner. I'll be back shortly."

He turned and motioned for Simmons to walk with him so that they were out of earshot. Once a good distance away Alan remarked, "Do you realize the pain and grief that their parents are going to go through because of this?"

"Yes," said Simmons in a sympathetic tone.

Anger swelled in Alan's voice. "Yes? That's all you have to say—*yes*?"

He turned away from Simmons for a moment, then rounded on him infuriated. "Well I'm not buying it. I've had enough. Their parents are going to be devastated, and they're going to want some answers, but in the back of their minds they're going to know that there *are* no answers. They'll want to know why their kids are dead, why they have to go through this pain right after losing their first child. They'll want to know why this is happening to them, how this is fair, and what they can do to make it better. And there will be *no answer* to those questions."

Alan paused to catch his breath. "But what they *don't* know is that there *is* an answer. And since you probably won't be talking to them, I'm going to ask the questions that I know you can answer."

He looked Simmons in the eye as if he could burn a hole through the center of his head with the fiery rage that stirred within him. "So I want to know: Why them? Why now? Do you have a good reason as to why their children are gone? And it had better be good!" Alan was so mad that he could barely see straight.

Simmons put up both of his hands in an attempt to calm him down. "They were chosen because of their talents, so to speak. They are strong. Most of all, the girls are needed to help us fight."

Alan interrupted, "Yes, yes, yes, the fight…the light, the darkness. You said it before, but it doesn't make any sense to me. You need two teenage girls? If you need people to fight, there are many able-bodied adults around the world who could serve. Look at all those killed in combat—or my fellow police officers who have fallen. Certainly they would be better suited to fight than two teens."

"It doesn't work like that," Simmons explained. "The attributes you hold as high qualities for those who would persevere in a fist fight aren't the attributes needed in this kind of battle." Alan remained silent. "Soon you'll know what I'm talking about. It isn't enough for me to explain it. You'll need to see it. Then you'll realize why this happens."

Alan looked around. He kicked a small pebble lying near his feet.

"Come on," said Simmons. "Let's help them get where they need to go. I promise you the place they're destined for is far greater than any-thing they, or you, have ever seen or experienced."

Alan nodded his head and slowly walked back to the car where the girls were still sitting. Alan looked inside and said, "Don't worry, girls. I'll take care of your parents." Both girls looked relieved. "Emma, come with me," Alan said gently. "I need to speak with you and make sure you're okay."

As Emma got out of the car, Simmons said to Melissa, "We'll be right back."

Melissa nodded and dabbed her eyes with the end of her shirt.

Emma, Alan, and Simmons entered the back of the ambulance and stepped into the marble hallway beyond. This time the hallway was very short. Alan could see the glowing door at the end almost as soon as they stepped inside. Emma's demeanor had changed as they entered: she seemed a bit more cheerful. She realized at once what had happened and acted as though she knew that her destination lay beyond the door. She told Alan of wonderful times she had shared with her sister and family.

She asked Alan, "Will my sister come, too?"

Alan could not answer. He stopped and looked at Simmons.

"Yes, she will. You'll see her soon," said Simmons.

Emma smiled, then stopped once more and asked excitedly, "Does this also mean I'll be able to see my brother?"

Alan once again stopped, tilted his chin up, and raised his eyebrows as if to indicate to Simmons that he very much wanted to know the answer to this question also.

"Well, yes. I believe that there is a very good chance that you'll see your brother. In fact, he has been with us for some time now. I spoke with him very recently."

Emma's entire face lit up with joy. She smiled as she hugged both of them. "Oh, thank you. Thank you both so much!"

"You're very welcome, Emma," replied Simmons. "However, you must realize that we really haven't done anything. You are the one who made this possible. The person you are, your kindness and compassion, your sense of goodness and all that is right."

They arrived at the door and Alan opened it for Emma. She waved and slipped through as the sunlight poured out. The door closed, and they began to walk back.

Alan said, "Well, she certainly did seem happy."

"Yes. You'll understand when you see the destination for yourself."

"Hey, I have a family to look after. If you know something about when I'll have to go—"

Simmons cut him off. "No, no, I didn't mean when you die. There will be a time when you'll need to see where they go and in a sense…visit… our world."

Alan was somewhat relieved. "Oh, okay. I thought you were implying that I was going to…"

"Not at all, Alan. I need you here. We do need to complete your training, which should be done soon. You're progressing very well. Soon you'll be doing this without me, but you'll need to visit our world in order to get an understanding of why your job is so critical."

As they made their way back to the car where Melissa was still seated, Alan noticed that she was writing something down on a piece of paper. He walked over to the passenger's door as Simmons stood on the opposite side of the car.

"What are you writing?"

She paused for a moment and said, "I'm writing a note to my parents to help them through all of this."

"Oh," replied Alan. "You think they'll still be scared because of the accident."

She looked at him and said, "I *know*."

Alan once again looked confused and asked, "You know?"

"I know I'm not going home. I know I'm dead. As soon as my sister passed through that door I knew instantly what was going on; we're very close, you know. We share a common bond and have a sense for what the other is feeling. We're only a year apart. From the time we were little we've always coexisted. We have always communicated to each other from very early on in our lives. She said that she would see me soon and that we would get to see Stephen, our brother. She said she was in a beautiful valley walking toward a running stream and that I'd be joining her soon."

Alan was amazed by what she had just told him. He stood there for a moment until finally he said, "And what are you going to tell your parents?"

"The truth. I'll tell them the truth."

Alan did not interrupt her. After a few moments he saw her sign her name and put down the pen. She glanced over it and said, "Let me read it to you, since you'll be the one to give it to them."

"I'm listening."

She began to read aloud:

Mom and Dad,

I first and foremost want you two to know that Emma and I love you very much. I'm writing this to tell you what happened and try to convince you that we're okay. We were riding down Monroe Street and went through the intersection at Monroe and Pine where we were hit by another car. We were wearing our seat belts and Emma had a green light. That isn't important. As you are reading this letter you will know that Emma and I are no longer living in this world. The important thing you need to know is that we're okay. I will be joining Emma soon in a wonderful place and we'll be joining Stephen.

When you read this you may not believe that it is actually me writing this note. To prove it, I want you to look in the bottom of my jewelry box, in the back of my closet, under my old sleeping bag. When you remove the bottom drawer there will be a picture hidden under the drawer of Emma, Stephen, and myself. The picture was taken when we were all very young and were on vacation at the beach. It's stained orange from some juice I spilled on it. You had thrown it away, but I took it out of the trash when you weren't looking and have kept it ever since.

I assume that one of your greatest fears will be that you won't see any of us again, but I want to assure you that this isn't true. There will be a day when we are all together, but before then you should know that we are around from time to time if you listen and watch closely. We will visit you on our birthdays and perhaps other times as well. You will know it's us by the subtlest things, things that often go unnoticed. Just remember us when you feel the warm sunlight on your face or see the wind gently moving in the trees or smell the fresh smell of the spring flowers. That will be us. All you will need to do is stop and savor these moments when they arise.

We love you and will see you soon,
Melissa

She finished reading and folded up the letter into a small square. She handed it to Alan. "You will make sure this gets to them?"

He nodded his head. "Absolutely."

She smiled and got out of the car. The three of them made their way to the ambulance and entered. They walked into the hallway and Alan noticed that it seemed to be the same length as the one he had walked through with Emma.

As they approached the door Melissa said, "The two people in the other car—I do hope they made it to this place."

Alan replied, "Yes, they did. Their path was not so easy as yours, but they did make it."

Nodding, she said to Alan, "Don't despair over these things. We're needed badly in this other world. You'll know in time how great the need is."

Alan was somewhat taken aback by her comments. "You seem very wise and much more mature than a person of your age."

She smiled and said, "You will see that age and other things that have such emphasis among the world of the living are of no relevance in this world. Only those things that are vitally important affect us here. Those are the things that lead us to the light."

Alan looked at her with a sense of perplexed respect. "I'm astounded by your sense of understanding."

"It seems that death is a great teacher. As my destiny grows near, the clarity of these things becomes almost second nature."

She opened the door and said with a sincere tone, "Thank you both. I'll see you soon." Then she slipped into the sunlight beyond.

Alan and Simmons drove over to contact the girls' parents. They approached the house, rang the doorbell, and watched as a man and a woman came to the front door. Alan and Simmons introduced themselves, and the girls' parents did likewise: Betty and Max. Betty was a petite woman with gray hair; Max was a stocky, gruff-looking man with short hair shaved on the sides and a Navy tattoo on his right arm. As Alan told them the news they were as devastated as he had expected. He handed Melissa's note to their father who read it through tear-filled eyes rubbing a huge hand over his unshaven chin.

"Is this true? All of these things she says…she says she wrote this after she was dead. Is this true?"

"I was there. It's all true."

Max handed the note to Betty, who began reading. He disappeared down a hallway off to the left and quickly returned holding something in his hand.

"Betty," he cried. "Look at this."

Finishing the letter, she glanced up at a picture he held in his hand. As Melissa had described, there were three children seated on a beach towel with sand all around. The picture had an orange tint and was somewhat blurred.

Betty put her hands over her mouth and began to cry. "I can't believe it—it's true!"

Max turned back to Alan and said, "You saw them and they were—" he paused for a moment, then said—"at peace?"

"I was there. They were extremely happy, and they were ready to find Stephen."

"Please," said Betty, fighting back more tears, "I would very much like it if you would come to the funerals."

"Certainly. Just let us know the time and place and we'll be there."

He glanced back at Simmons, who nodded, then scratched down a number on the back of one of his business cards. "Here is my phone number," he offered.

Betty forced a smile and said, "Thank you," embracing each of them.

Max nodded his head, also fighting off tears. "Yes, thank you." He extended his massive hand to each of them.

Two days later Alan, his wife, and daughter were in the car on the way to the Bornhopps' funeral service. Alison slid her hand over to grasp Alan's as she said, "It's so sad. I don't know how people cope with such a tragedy."

Alan shook his head. "It must be very hard," he said as he pulled the car to the side of the small roadway behind a long line of other vehicles.

"Those poor girls," murmured Alison.

Alan wasn't paying much attention. He caught only a portion of Alison's words, but what he heard made him freeze. "…She'll have quite a long walk."

For a moment he was silent as his mind rewound to the images of the seemingly endless obstacles when he and Simmons walked with Amy Lansing, the woman who had left her children home alone and died in the crash. The image of the large room with the pool and the narrow tunnel through which they'd had to crawl flashed before him. *Does she know?* he asked himself. *Does she know about the walk or the doorways?*

Perhaps Simmons had told her. Confused, he could only say, "What...
a walk?"

Alison half smiled and said, "You're not listening to me. I said I hope
it isn't far to the grave site for Missy's sake. She'll have quite a long walk.
If so, we'll need to carry her." Alison pointed out the window at several
people making their way up a hill between the hundreds of grave plots.

"Oh," said Alan with some relief. "No problem, I'll carry her." As he
unbuckled Missy from her car seat and carried her around to the other
side of the car, he suddenly felt guilty about keeping his experiences
secret from Alison. He toyed with the idea of telling her, but decided
that he needed to know more before he did so.

They met Michael Simmons a short distance up the hill, and the four
of them began walking. Alan introduced his wife and daughter to Simmons, and pleasantries were exchanged. As they walked to the top of
the hill where the Bornhopp family and friends were gathered over the
two caskets, Alan's gaze rested on Betty who was standing in the front
row opposite them. He noticed something unusual about her. She wasn't
hanging her head or looking at the minister like everyone else. Instead
she had her eyes closed and her chin tilted up. Alan thought that this
looked quite strange—she didn't look at all grief-stricken—and then he
saw what she was actually doing. She had turned her face so that the
sunlight was beating down on her. The breeze blew through her short
hair, and as it did she actually smiled.

Then Alan looked at Max, who was standing beside her and looking
in the opposite direction. His eyes were fixed on something across the
cemetery, and Alan followed his line of sight to see what it was. A good
distance away from them stood a tall headstone topped with two statues
of angels holding hands and facing each other. As Alan looked closer at
the statues, he noticed that there were two large birds perched on top
of the headstone. He stepped back slightly so that he could get a better
view. As he did so he realized what they were.

"Eagles," he whispered to himself, "two huge eagles."

This was extremely strange. Eagles weren't native to this part of the country, nor had he ever seen one anywhere close to where they were.

"Simmons," he whispered. "There are two huge eagles sitting on that headstone over there."

Without even turning his head, Simmons replied in a whisper, "Yes, I know."

Alan continued to watch them. At once they took off. Their wings were enormous. As Alan watched them rise and take flight he saw that they flew upward and off into the morning sun. A lone feather floated slowly to the ground and landed exactly in front of Max, who picked it up. He placed it in the inner pocket of his jacket, then looked upward and said, "Thank you."

Alan and Max were the only ones who had seen the two birds; everyone else was looking down with their heads hanging low. But as they flew off he felt a soft tug at his pant leg and looked down to see his daughter smiling up at him as she said, "Birdie, birdie," pointing a small finger to the sky.

Alan smiled at her and she giggled. He looked up and refocused on Max, who smiled and nodded as their gazes met. Although no words were spoken, Alan knew what his thoughts were and nodded back in confirmation. Max took his wife's hand and looked down at the caskets. Alan saw a look of peace come over his face.

CHAPTER TWENTY

"Every gift from a friend is a wish for your happiness."

—Richard Bach

THE NEXT DAY SIMMONS MET ALAN AT the police station. As he entered Alan's office he shut the door. Alan noticed that he was carrying a box about eight inches wide and two feet long. Handing the box to Alan he said, "Here, a gift for all your hard work."

Alan opened the box and found a sheathed dagger.

"Uh, thanks," replied Alan, trying to seem grateful. "But what is it?"

"It's very old," said Simmons. "It's one of our weapons. One of the tools we use in battle."

Alan examined it more closely. The knife had an ornately carved hilt that appeared to be of gold. The cross guard was two silver wings that covered his hand when he gripped it. The sheath was also gold. Alan picked up the dagger. It was extremely light. He placed one hand on the hilt and one on the sheath, then drew out the blade, which was bone white in color and seemed to be made of a polished stone.

"So," Alan said slowly, "you use these to fight?"

"Yes, it's one of the weapons we use," replied Simmons. He could see that Alan was wondering the point of this conversation. "You seem surprised at this."

"Well, I figured you were more advanced. I mean if we had a war here…well, we use guns and such, as I'm sure you know. It just seems a bit, well…archaic. Don't you think?"

Simmons smiled. "You should keep it with you when we're helping others on their way."

"Look, there's something I haven't told you. Ever since we started doing this I've had a gun strapped to my ankle. If we had any trouble, it would've been much more effective than this knife."

"Actually, the gun would be useless. The weapons of your world do nothing in ours. They don't affect those who have passed. The battle is between the light and the darkness, as I've said before. Keep the dagger close. You may need it."

"Yes," said Alan as he raised his eyebrows and took a deep breath, "and that leads me to my next question. Why would I need it? Is there some threat I need to know about?"

"There could be. As I've told you, conflict exists and you may encounter it, so be vigilant."

Alan worried that he might have sounded unappreciative. "It's a very interesting gift. Thank you. It won't exactly fit in my pocket, so I'll have to figure out where to keep it so that it's out of sight."

Simmons picked up the box and drew out a long, silver rope.

"Use this."

The cord had some type of clip on the end. Simmons attached the dagger to it and then draped one end over Alan's shoulder. The opposite end with the dagger attached rested at his waist, the cord stretching across his chest.

"Won't it flap around?"

Simmons smiled and said, "Yes, like this it will. Grip the hilt."

As Alan grasped the hilt of the dagger the cord tightened and flattened out like a piece of steel, fitting exactly against his chest and attaching itself tightly to his belt.

Alan jumped, slightly startled, "This *does* come off, doesn't it?"

"Of course, just take it off."

As he placed his fingers around what now felt like flat metal, the cord re-formed and hung down loosely.

"What makes it change like that?"

"You do," replied Simmons. "When you're ready to take it off, it responds to your will."

Alan stood looking at the dagger for a few moments, then set it on his desk.

"So, you were saying something about our weapons being archaic?"

"Maybe I misspoke." Alan wondered what the dagger was actually capable of.

Simmons smiled. "Well, I've got to go. Until next time, have a good day and I'll see you later."

"Thanks again for the gift. I'll see you soon," Alan said, still bewildered.

As Simmons left, Alan sat back in his chair and examined the dagger. *I'll have to keep this at the office—I don't know how I would explain it to Alison if she happened to find it at home*, he thought. Once again he felt guilty for keeping this secret from his wife, and once again he contemplated whether he should tell her or not. He knew that she would support him no matter what, even if she didn't believe him, but as before, he concluded that he needed to understand more about his experiences before he told her.

As he ran his finger over the smooth blade, his mind quickly returned to the purpose of the gift. The thought of a weapon concerned him, and the fact that Simmons had given him one meant that there might be a time when he would have to defend himself. Simmons was, as usual, unclear as to what the "conflict" might be. Alan went over the possibilities of where a fight or threat could occur, his thoughts racing back to the door that shed no light, the door that had startled Simmons, the "wrong door" he had nearly opened. He could still picture it in his mind—the light being absorbed by the space between the door and the frame. It was eerie; whatever was on the other side, he didn't want to confront it, especially with a dagger.

Walking over to the detective bureau, he poked his head inside to see Clint Rogers hunched over some paperwork.

"Anything new on Randal Sweeny or his whereabouts?"

Clint looked up toward the ceiling as if he were trying hard to remember. "Sweeny, Sweeny."

"Randal Sweeny—the one who murdered the Moto-Mart clerk in the robbery. Our homicide suspect?"

"Oh, yeah. Randal Sweeny," said Clint, as he nodded his head and pointed his index finger toward Alan. "Nothing really. We've been watching the house and keeping in contact with his wife, but she claims that she hasn't seen him in days. Their daughter apparently has a serious degenerative illness, which might bring Randal back soon. Hopefully we'll catch a break. The higher-ups are really breathing down my neck on this one. If I come up with anything, I'll call you right away."

"Thanks, Clint. I appreciate it. I really want this guy."

"You're telling me. He's already out the door with the money and comes back in to stab that poor kid in the back four times—What kind of person does that to another human being? He must be a real animal."

"That's a good question," Alan said as he dropped his gaze to the floor. "That's a really good question." His thoughts continued to dwell on Clint's last word: *Animal.*

CHAPTER TWENTY-ONE

"Avoid popularity if you would have peace."

—Abraham Lincoln

Ross McDonald knew that his parents wouldn't be back for days and relished the fact that he had the run of the house. It was Saturday and he had made dozens of phone calls to his friends, calculating that he was going to set a record for the number of people he'd have at his house party. He was a junior in high school and really wanted to impress some of his older peers. *This party is my ticket to getting recognized, perhaps even respected. What I wouldn't give to be one of the in-crowd*, he thought to himself. This was definitely his night, and even though he wasn't one of the popular kids at school, he expected everyone to show up. He knew they couldn't resist an opportunity to drink and let loose.

It was 6:00 PM. He wanted to make sure everything was set. Some of his friends were bringing over a couple of kegs, and he had already picked the lock on the liquor cabinet so that he could get to all the good stuff. His parents would be furious if they discovered that he'd taken their liquor, if only because it would prevent them from partying after they returned from their trip. *Can't keep them from their booze*, he thought. His plan was to save the bottles, then replace the liquor with cheaper stuff tomorrow. *They'll never know.*

Everyone was expected to start arriving around seven or seven-thirty. Ross wanted to get a head start and be the center of attention right from the beginning. His typical weekend consisted of downing a twelve-pack on Saturday night, so the first few beers his dad had left in the fridge had very little effect. Ross knew that since he hadn't eaten all day, the hard liquor would hit him more quickly.

After a few shots of whiskey he sat down on the couch. His head started spinning slightly and he thought, *This is great. I wonder how many girls will show up tonight? I know they'll be here. They won't pass up a party.* He wandered into the bedroom and looked at himself in the mirror. He was tall and slim, with brown hair and a large nose. *Maybe I'm not the best-looking guy in school, but there's no reason I can't hang with the popular crowd. I drink with them—that should count for something,* he thought as he tried flattening down the piece of hair that always stuck out in the back. The volleyball team consisted of the best-looking girls in school. Hosting a party might be all he needed to get a chance to talk to them; they completely ignored him otherwise.

At 7:00 PM he opened a bottle of vodka and started drinking it from a plastic cup. His eyes were fixed on the front door, waiting for the first people to arrive. At 7:10 PM the doorbell rang and Ross made his way to the foyer with the cup in his hand. As he opened the door he saw his friends Jimmy and Fred carrying two kegs of beer. Jimmy was a lanky redhead with tons of freckles all over his face. He struggled as he bear-hugged the large metal barrel. Fred was stockier, which allowed him to carry his keg over one shoulder. Jimmy clanged the keg down on the floor and tried to catch his breath.

"You're pathetic, Jimmy. You need to lift some weights with me so you won't be such a wimp," said Fred, placing his keg down gently.

"Close your fat pie-hole, Fred. Tall guys like me have problems lifting things. But you wouldn't know that because you're a midget."

Jimmy caught sight of the cup in Ross's hand and laughed. "Man, what are you doing, drinking already?"

"Yeah," replied Ross with a level of satisfaction. "I wanna get a head start on everyone."

"Cool," replied Fred. "So where do we go with these?" He pointed at the two half barrels on the floor.

Ross opened the door that led into the garage and hit the opener pad on the wall. The garage door rose slowly. Jimmy struggled and strained as he lumbered into the garage, dragging the beer behind him. Fred lifted his with one arm and placed it in one of the large buckets of ice that Ross had set up, then grabbed Jimmy's barrel and did the same. Ross downed the rest of the vodka and refilled his glass with beer.

"Man, you'd better slow down or you might miss your own party," said Jimmy.

"Nah, I'll be fine."

At 8:00 PM, twenty-five people had shown up at the house, and half an hour later there were about fifty more. By 9:00 PM there were well over a hundred people, and Ross's head was spinning. He felt numb all over. He stumbled up the stairs, sat down at the kitchen table, and joined the three girls and two boys who were seated there.

One of the boys stood up, "Hey, here's Ross! Great party, man. You did good, and for having us all over, we got you a present."

Ross smiled and slurred, "Oh yeah? And what's that?"

Out of a bag, the boy took an extra-large funnel with a long piece of hose attached to the end.

"Beer bong, man. Let's see if you can handle it."

The girls all smiled as Ross sat down. "No problem. Let's do it."

Ross looked at the boy's face and could only vaguely recall him. He knew his name was Scott and he'd been in Ross's American history class last year. They both sat toward the back of the classroom since the front was reserved for the popular clique. *An outcast like me*, Ross thought to himself. *Guess he's just trying to make a name for himself like I am. Well, not at my party!*

Scott handed Ross the hose end, and Ross plugged it up with his thumb. Another boy at the table started pouring beers into the funnel.

Ross counted them as each beer went in. "One, two, three…"

"Five beers, man. Think you can do it?" Scott asked in a challenging tone.

"Of course! I'm ready."

Scott lifted the funnel into the air, and Ross put the hose in his mouth as he released his thumb. The beer flowed down the clear tube and Ross heard everyone chanting his name. He gulped the alcohol as fast as he could. Suddenly, his mouth and throat were so full of beer that he gagged and pulled the hose out of his mouth. The remaining contents spilled over the table and onto the floor. One of the girls jumped up to avoid the splash. *So close, so very close*, Ross thought.

"Ah, Ross, I knew you couldn't do it!" yelled Scott, holding the funnel.

"I can do it," Ross said, wiping away some of the beer that had poured through his nose.

"Whatever," taunted Scott. "You choked. Face it, you can't handle it." It was almost as if he were prodding him to have another go at it.

Ross stood up on shaky legs and yelled, "Yeah I can, fill it up again! I'll show you."

"That's what I like to hear. Let's see if you can do it—but I'll bet not." The challenge had been issued once again.

As Ross sat back down, Scott began to fill the funnel. Ross started drinking but only made it about halfway this time before he spit it out.

"I knew you were a lightweight. You can't handle it. Maybe you need to drink with the girls," said Scott in a jeering tone.

A couple of the girls seated at the table giggled.

Ross stood once again and nearly fell backward. "Oh yeah? Well, just hold that thing right there. I'll show you who's a lightweight."

He staggered over to the kitchen counter and grabbed two bottles of hard liquor.

"Set that thing back up," he said as he placed his thumb over the hose once more.

Scott held up the funnel and Ross handed him one of the bottles. "Pour this in," he said.

The boy drained the half-full whiskey bottle. Ross handed him the other bottle, which contained a clear liquid.

"This one, too," he ordered.

One of the girls sitting at the table stood up. "Ross, this isn't a good idea—half a bottle of whiskey and half a bottle of rum? The last one is over 160 proof. I don't think…"

"Shut up," Ross babbled. "Just watch."

He moved his thumb and closed his mouth over the hose. The liquor began to run down.

No matter what, I'm not going to stop. I won't gag this time, he thought.

The alcohol hit his mouth and throat. It felt like he'd just swallowed a blowtorch. He could feel the burning sensation lighting his insides on fire but he kept concentrating, determined not to stop. A few seconds later the last drop had run out into his mouth. He threw his hands up in the air as Scott gave a loud yell of encouragement.

"I was wrong. You're the man!"

Scott and the other boy stood up and left the room. Ross could barely focus; his head was spinning horribly. The girl who had spoken to him was now standing beside him with a look of concern on her face. She was cute, with black hair, dark brown eyes, and a nice tan. Ross remembered her from school—her name was Emily Jacobs and she played on the girls' varsity softball team. As she drew closer he noticed the sweet smell of her perfume. He wondered if perhaps she was showing some interest in him.

He began to sway back and forth. He felt her shoulder underneath his armpit as she tried to support him.

"Ross, this way," she said.

She led him out onto the deck. A few other people were standing there off to the side. Ross thought, *I've hit it big now. She likes me. This party was the best idea I've ever had.*

"You need to get some air."

He began to slip slightly and realized that she was holding him up. She now had both of her arms under his armpits trying to support him as she braced herself against the railing of the deck. Ross leaned forward to kiss her.

She was repulsed and turned her head, "What are you doing? Stop that!" She pushed his face away with one hand.

Ross felt hugely embarrassed. A burst of rage came over him. Without thinking, he forced his hands up onto her shoulders and drove her backward as hard as he could. She screamed. Before Ross could react he watched in horror as she toppled over the rail.

Ross heard someone else on the deck yell, "What the hell—what are you doing?" Suddenly someone grabbed him by the head and threw him facedown on the deck. Everything went black. He heard several of the others below the deck gathering around Emily. A girl screamed, "She's bleeding! Call 911!"

Alan and Simmons had to park a good distance away from the house; there were many cars lining both sides of the street. As they approached, some of the teenagers were scrambling into their vehicles trying to drive away as fast as they could. Alan and Simmons walked up the driveway where they saw the rest of the teens pouring out of the front door, trying to leave. Three marked police cars and two ambulances sat in the street with their lights on as a police officer ran out to intercept them.

Two more police cars arrived. An officer standing by the front porch yelled, "Nobody leaves until we're able to talk to everyone."

The officers started escorting the teens back to the house, all the time keeping a watch out for stragglers attempting to flee. As Alan and Simmons approached the front door, the officer nodded to let them pass. There was barely enough room to walk. Both sides of the entryway were lined with people. As they pushed their way up the stairs to the main level, Alan looked at the faces of the teenagers. There was a wide gamut of emotions. Some were truly afraid. Some indifferent. And some were too drunk to be aware of anything that was happening.

They made their way through the crowd. Alan could smell the beer and cigarette smoke. They finally found their way out onto the deck where a teenage boy was lying on his back with two paramedics beside him, strapping him on a backboard and then lifting him onto a stretcher as they yelled, "Clear the way, coming through." The crowd inside the house parted to make a path for them.

Peering over the railing, Alan saw three paramedics down below looking at another body sprawled out on the brick patio.

Alan heard one of the kids below, "She fell and hit her head on the corner of this grill." A large gas grill stood to the right of the girl's body.

He turned to one of the teenage boys on the deck, "What happened?"

"Ross was drunk." The boy motioned in the direction of the kid who had just been wheeled out on the stretcher. "He tried to kiss Emily. She pushed him back. She was just trying to help him up, and I guess he was so drunk that he thought she was coming on to him…you know. Anyway, he got mad when she pushed him, so he grabbed her and pushed her back. And she fell." The boy pointed toward the deck railing.

Another officer on the deck near them began scribbling notes. Alan turned to him and asked, "The boy who was just wheeled off—do you know his condition?"

The officer looked around and stepped back to distance himself from anyone who may have been listening. He said in a low voice, "I couldn't get a pulse. I think he's dead. Paramedics ran a strip already and couldn't bring him back. I think it's alcohol poisoning."

Alan nodded. "Thanks."

The officer returned to the boy. "Can you tell me who this belongs to?" he asked as he reached down and grabbed a funnel with a long hose attached to it.

The boy replied, "I think that's Scott's. I saw him with it in the kitchen earlier this evening."

The officer nodded. "Yes, we have others who said that they saw Ross drinking from it. Two bottles of hard liquor and a good quantity of beer. Did you happen to see that?"

"No, sir," replied the boy. "I was out here most of the time. I grabbed Ross and threw him down as soon as I saw him push Emily, but it was too late. She had already fallen."

"Okay, that's all I need," said the officer as he finished scribbling.

Alan turned to Simmons. "So who do you want to see first?"

Simmons thought for a moment then replied, "Let's go check on Ross and see how he's doing."

Alan thought that this was a silly response from Simmons, as he knew that Ross was doing anything but well. The kid had to be dead. If he wasn't, there'd be no reason for them to be here. They shoved their way back through the crowd and out onto the driveway as they approached one of the ambulances. They climbed into the back. As they sat down, Ross sat up.

As Alan looked at Ross's face he recognized him immediately. "I know you. I've arrested you before, haven't I?"

"I don't know. Maybe."

"Yeah, I'm sure of it. I've arrested you before for driving under the influence and possession of alcohol, since you're too young to drink. In fact, I think other members of our police department have arrested you for the same thing."

"Yeah, whatever. I don't get along with cops."

"So, Ross, how'd your party go?" Alan asked in a sarcastic and condescending tone.

Ross didn't answer for a moment, then finally said, "Bad."

Alan nodded, "Perhaps you're not as stupid as you look. And how much did you drink?"

Ross hung his head between his knees. "Way too much. I felt that hard liquor burning my throat and I remember being...well, kind of remember being outside, and sort of getting mad. Then everything went dark, I guess."

"I see," replied Alan in a critical tone. "Let me ask you a question, Ross. How can you *kind of* be outside, and how can you *sort of* be mad? And how is it that you can only guess about everything going dark?"

Ross didn't answer or make eye contact, so Alan continued. "You see, you can't be *kind of* outside or *sort of* mad. You're either outside or you're not; you're either mad or you're not. And as far as *guessing* at everything going dark, well, I'm *guessing* that's not the truth, now is it?"

Alan sat down beside Ross, who turned his head in the opposite direction so that he didn't have to face him.

"You see," Alan continued, "I think you do remember. I think you do remember getting mad and pushing Emily. I think you remember her face as she fell. But I wonder if you saw her when she hit the ground. Did you know that her head smashed into that gas grill on your patio? Did you know she was lying on the ground bleeding?"

Ross put one hand over his eyes and asked in a low whisper, "Is she dead?"

Alan replied in a completely unsympathetic voice, "Yeah, Ross, I believe she is. Now do you remember any of that? Perhaps you'd like to explain to her parents how this happened?" His voice rose a bit, and he said accusingly, "Perhaps you should see her mother and father crying when they find out their daughter's dead because you wanted to have a good time. Perhaps you should stare into their grief-stricken faces! Do you think you could do that? Do you think you could handle the guilt?" Alan exhaled, pausing to see if he was getting a response.

"I'm not saying anything," Ross said. "Shouldn't I talk to a lawyer or something? Don't I have the right to talk to a lawyer?"

Alan paused a moment, fearing that he would completely lose his temper, then finally said, "No, Ross. You don't have a right to talk to a lawyer, not now. You would if you were alive, but you're not. You see," he paused to make sure the next two words out of his mouth were crystal clear, "you're *dead*." He spoke them in a low and deliberate whisper, dragging out the word "dead" so that it lingered in Ross's mind.

Ross's hands began to tremble dramatically. "You're trying to trick me into telling you something," he screamed. "I'm not dead! I'm not! You're trying to get me to…"

Ross stood up and ran to the rear doors of the ambulance, flinging them open and darting through. Alan sat there for a moment and listened to his footsteps beating down on the hard marble floor.

Simmons stood up at once. "Let's go, before he gets too far."

"No. Screw him. Let him fall. He's a little worm. He deserves it."

Simmons said in a very certain tone, "That may be, but it's not for us to decide."

Alan reluctantly stood up and they started off down the hallway. They continued straight for about twenty minutes until they came to an archway.

Alan stopped, turned toward Simmons, and said, "I'm not jumping off cliffs for this kid. If he doesn't want help, I'm not going to stick my neck out."

"Let's just see what lies ahead," replied Simmons.

They both stepped through the archway, and Alan held up his badge to illuminate their surroundings. The lighting in this room was better than most. Alan glanced around the square area in which they stood. There were ten archways on each wall except the one they had just come through. He saw Ross kneeling and sobbing in the very center of the room.

"Ross," yelled Alan, "come over here."

Ross didn't move, so Alan repeated himself in a more calming voice. "Look, Ross, it can be dangerous around here. I'm sure by now you know what you have to do; we're here to help you. Come over here and we'll start figuring it out."

Ross stood up slowly and walked back to where Simmons and Alan were standing.

He looked up at Alan. "I'm sorry, you were right. I usually don't drink that much—I usually only have about a twelve-pack or so on the weekends. I did get mad and push Emily. I lost my temper. I didn't mean for her to fall. I feel terrible about her..." He almost couldn't say the words, but finally whispered, "...her death."

Alan nodded. "Did your parents know about your drinking?"

"Yeah, they've actually bought me beer in the past. They were okay with it as long as I didn't drive, and as long as I didn't drink their stuff."

Alan shook his head. He began to see the bigger picture that had led to Ross's tragic end. Many times in his career Alan had seen irresponsible parenting add to the already complicated problems of youth. Accountability had to be passed around to all involved. He was determined that, along with his sympathy, he would also voice his concerns to Ross's parents when he met them.

Alan let out a sigh. "We need to focus on getting you where you need to go, so stick close to us. First we need to decide which of these thirty archways we'll go down." Alan turned to Simmons. "I guess we're going to have to walk down each of them and see which one contains the door."

Simmons replied, "That may not be as easy as it looks," and pointed upward.

Alan looked up and realized that the room had multiple levels. The center of the room was completely open and stretched upward far beyond where Alan could see. Each level had a narrow walkway surrounded by a black iron banister around the edge, which overlooked the open center area. Stairs on the left and right side of the room gave access to the floor above. As Alan peered at the next level he could see ten more archways, just like the room they were in. Looking through the archways, he discovered that each led to a small, ten-by-ten-foot room. As they moved up to the next level, they found that those also led to dead ends, as did the third and fourth levels. As they arrived at the fifth level, Alan decided they should to go all the way up to the top and work their way down.

Simmons nodded, and they began climbing the stairwells. As they stepped onto level twenty-four, they stopped for a rest. Alan, breathing heavily, said to Simmons, "You ever seen anything like this?"

"No, but most of these situations are unique."

Alan peered down over the banister and then looked up, still unable to see the top. He wondered how high they would have to climb. As they reached level forty-five they stopped once again for a break and Alan sat down.

"So was this the first party you ever had?" he asked Ross.

"Yeah," replied Ross. "As I think about it now, it was stupid. I thought it would make me popular and people would like me more. I was very excited about it. I wanted to see how many people would come; as you saw, it was quite a few. In fact, I counted, just so I could brag about it at school on Monday. It was the biggest party of the year—a hundred and two people from school, and that beat Jeremy Sudgin's party last month where eighty-eight people showed up."

Alan nodded and said, "Yeah, I remember being a teenager. I had the same thoughts as you, but I never could get my parents to leave the house long enough for me to have a party." Alan laughed a bit in an attempt to make Ross feel better.

Ross shook his head. "Be glad your parents never left. This was the worst mistake of my life, and I regret it deeply. I was a real idiot. I don't deserve your help."

Alan couldn't help but feel sympathy for him. "We'll make it. Just stick close."

Two more hours passed, and Alan had long ago stopped counting levels. As they reached the next one he sat down, panting, and rubbing his legs. Simmons stood nearby; as usual, he wasn't even winded.

Alan shook his head. "How do you do that? How do you walk up..." he paused to try to come up with the number of the level they were now on.

Simmons finished his sentence for him. "...walk up eighty-nine levels?"

"Eighty-nine!" exclaimed Alan. "We've come up eighty-nine levels?"

"Yes. We have."

Alan looked over at Ross, who was rubbing his calves and wiping sweat from his forehead.

Through labored breathing Alan asked Simmons, "Can you see the top?"

Simmons stuck his head over the banister and looked up. "Yes. It's not too far."

"Okay, we'll move on in a few," replied Alan.

After about fifteen minutes they all began climbing once again. Wearily they pressed onward. Within another twenty minutes they reached the top level. Alan's lungs were on fire and he lay flat on the floor, trying to catch his breath.

"How many floors was that, Michael?" he gasped.

"One hundred and two, to be exact," replied Simmons.

"Great. Guess you counted right, Ross. A hundred and two—same number of people you had over tonight."

After a few moments, when Alan and Ross could finally stand again, they peered over the banister and looked upward. They could see the ceiling now. It was a large, dome shape. There was a small, stone platform suspended by four enormous chains, which were attached to the dome. A long, stone stairwell extended from the ledge down to an opening cut into the banister, not far from where they were standing. As they made their way over and peered up the stairs, Alan could see the very top of a door on the ledge. The familiar golden glow shimmered around its frame, and he knew that they had found what they were looking for at last. As Alan looked at the stairwell, he noticed that it was narrow with no railings or wall on either side to prevent one from falling. They'd have to climb it in single file.

Ross started to climb first, crawling on his hands and knees so as not to fall. Alan was ten or fifteen feet behind him, and Simmons followed about the same distance away. Suddenly Alan stopped, thinking he had heard something. It had sounded like someone was moving around above them on the ledge near the doorway.

"Ross," he whispered. "Ross, stop—I think someone's up there."

But Ross was about thirty feet in front of him and could not hear. As Ross got within five feet of the top of the ledge Alan could hear a terrible crunching sound overhead. One of the great chains had come loose and was falling toward the stairs where they stood. As it fell, the ledge shifted without support, and the part of the stairs where Ross was kneeling fell away. He let out a yell and grabbed onto the huge chain with both hands. Fortunately, the chain was large enough for him to fit his whole hand through one of its links.

"Hang on Ross, just hang on!" Alan screamed.

He motioned for Simmons to back up. As the two tried to back down, Alan noticed that someone had tripped above them and was falling. After colliding with Ross, who instinctively held out his hand, the figure grabbed onto it and Ross looked down to see that it was Emily hanging onto his arm, causing him to strain to balance both of them. She wrapped her legs around his, and to keep his balance, Ross grasped the huge chain again by pushing his arm through the massive link right up to his elbow.

Emily was screaming hysterically, "Ross! Don't drop me! Please don't let go, please!"

"I can't hold on much longer."

Alan thought of climbing down the stairs to see if he could find something they could throw to Ross and pull him back, but he knew now that there would be no time to do it.

"Look," said Simmons as he motioned toward the floor.

Alan looked down and saw a black mist rising from below.

"What the hell is that?

"The floor must have given way. There's no floor…the mist rises from the depths."

"What does that mean, Michael—what in the hell does that mean? The floor is gone?"

"It means there *is* no floor. Below lies the darkness. If they fall…"

Alan didn't hear Simmons's last words. He knew that falling into the darkness was not something he'd wish on anyone.

The situation was now dire. He climbed back to the end of the stairs and leaned over with his hands extended. It was no good—the two teens were about ten feet beyond his fingertips.

Ross surveyed his bleak situation, knowing that if both his hands were free, he could climb up the chain to the doorway. His shoulder burned from the strain, and his fingers started to pull apart. As he looked down into Emily's face he saw the fear in her eyes and he clenched his teeth. *I'm not letting go, not this time. It's not about me this time*, he thought. He started rocking back and forth, swinging the chain to gain momentum. His arms were completely numb but he kept rocking. Once he had reached the point where they were very near the stairwell, Ross flung

Emily toward Alan. As she hurtled forward, Alan caught her hands and held on just as Ross's legs slipped from the chain link and he plummeted downward. On his descent he saw the levels that they had climbed rushing past him and a cold, dark mist began to burn his face.

He knew he was going to fall into the darkness. It was closing in on him....

CHAPTER TWENTY-TWO

*"A journey is best measured in
friends rather than miles."*

—Tim Cahill

R OSS FELT HIS BODY COLLIDE WITH one of the banisters. He looked up to see Simmons dragging him back over one of the railings. They were about fifteen levels below the top. Ross wondered how he had covered so much distance so quickly. Badly shaken, he and Simmons made their way back up and met the others near the archway.

"I'm sorry," Ross said to Emily, "I'm sorry for everything."

"Thank you for saving me," she replied. "You didn't let me fall the second time. You did the right thing. Thank you."

Alan looked up the stairwell. "I don't think we'll be able to get either of you up to that door."

Emily replied, "There's another way. Follow me."

They all followed her through an archway that led to another set of stairs. As they reached the top of this staircase they came to a tiny, round room. Located directly in the center of the room was a small square opening in the floor, just large enough for an average size person to crawl through. Fastened to an eyebolt in one of the walls, there was a rope that dangled down through the opening. As Alan began pulling the rope up, he noticed that he was now standing directly above the ledge that had been suspended by the chains. As he drew the last of the rope to the top, he looked back at Michael who gave him a nod of reassurance to continue. Alan tied the rope around Ross's waist and told Ross to grip it with both hands. They began to lower him down slowly until he reached the ledge below.

Once there, Ross untied the rope. "Thank you!" he said as he opened the door and slipped through.

Alan pulled the rope back up. "Okay, Emily, your turn," but as he turned around he saw that she was not there.

With confusion and concern, he turned to Simmons. "What happened—where'd she go?"

Simmons replied, "Only one door per person. This wasn't her passageway."

"Tell me there's an easier way down rather than walking a hundred levels?"

"There is," said Simmons. He grabbed Alan by the arm and dragged both of them through the hole in the floor.

They plummeted quickly. "What the hell have you done?" yelled Alan as fear gripped his heart. He closed his eyes and felt a slight impact as his feet hit the bottom of the ambulance floor and he fell back in a seated position on one of the benches.

He glared at Simmons, "Thanks. Next time I'll walk down. Got it?"

Simmons smiled as Alan flung open the rear doors of the ambulance. He was still shaking from the fear of the fall. They made their way to the house and walked to the back where two of the paramedics were lifting Emily onto a stretcher. Alan and Simmons followed them to another ambulance as she was loaded into the back. One of the paramedics got in while the other jumped into the cab.

They both climbed into the back of the ambulance with the paramedic.

"You guys coming along?" he asked, surprised.

Alan wasn't sure what to say, "Yeah, we're coming with you." Emily's head was wrapped in a gauze bandage and traces of blood had run down over her face. Alan sat down on the bench in the corner with Simmons. The ambulance started to move, and he wondered when they were going to help Emily down her hallway. The paramedic continued working on her, adjusting the various IV tubes in her arm. Ten minutes later the ambulance came to a stop, and the paramedic quickly jumped out.

Assuming that the time had come, Alan placed a hand on her forehead. "Emily, can you hear me?" She didn't respond. Alan said once again, "Emily, can you hear me? We have to get going. Are you ready to go?"

Once more, Emily didn't respond. The paramedic returned with some hospital staff and they began to unload the stretcher. They worked quickly and wheeled her through the sliding glass door into the emergency room.

Alan was confused. He turned to Simmons. "What's going on?"

Simmons said nothing. He exited the ambulance and entered the hospital. Alan followed and saw Emily being rushed into another room, apparently for emergency surgery.

Alan turned to Simmons. "She's not dead, is she?"

"No."

Alan continued, "And she's going to make it. She's not going to die, is she?"

"I don't believe she will."

"I want to wait, if it's okay with you," requested Alan.

"Of course."

The two of them walked into the waiting room and sat down.

About twenty minutes passed. Suddenly a man and a woman rushed into the waiting room. Alan knew immediately by the frantic looks on their faces that these were Emily's parents.

A nurse came out to meet them, and Alan overheard her telling them, "She's in surgery right now. It will be a little while before she's out. We won't know anything until then."

The man put his arm around the woman and they both sat down in nearby chairs. The woman began crying as Alan slowly made his way over to the couple. He bent down and introduced himself to them.

"Your daughter's going to be fine. She'll make it."

The man asked, "How do you know? The nurse said they wouldn't know anything for a while."

Alan looked straight into his eyes. "You need to trust me. I know. I've seen many instances of…well, similar situations, and I know your daughter will be okay."

The man nodded and said, "I hope you're right. I really want to believe you."

"You'll see, she'll be fine."

About forty-five minutes later a doctor came into the waiting room and summoned Emily's parents. He spoke to them briefly and Alan could see that they looked relieved.

Emily's father walked back to Alan. "You were right. Thank you for everything. They said she's weak and needs to rest but should fully recover."

Alan smiled and nodded. "Glad to hear it."

The man paused, then asked, "You said you were at the party. What happened to the boy who pushed her?"

Alan dropped his gaze. "He died. Alcohol poisoning, I believe."

For a moment Alan expected the man to show some anger toward Ross, perhaps even say that he was glad Ross was dead. Instead he said, "I'm sorry to hear that. What was his name?"

"Ross McDonald," replied Alan.

The man shook his head as if he were trying to recall who Ross was. "I don't recognize the name. I'd like to send some flowers to the funeral.

Would you happen to know the details of where he'll be laid out—perhaps the funeral home?"

"Regretfully I don't, but I'll find out and contact you with the information if you like," replied Alan as he took out a pen and pad.

"Thank you," replied the man. He gave Alan a phone number.

Alan found a new level of respect for Emily's father. "I admire you for being concerned over Ross's death and the kindness you're showing toward his family."

"Losing a child is a devastating thing to deal with. I wouldn't wish it on anyone," replied the man.

"I'm very sorry that this happened. Your daughter may have a long road to recovery and there will be lots of physical and emotional obstacles, but I'm so glad she's alive," said Alan as he smiled.

The man smiled back, "As long as there's hope, I'm grateful. Thank you for all that you've done." He shook Alan's hand as Emily's mother came over and hugged Alan. They departed down the hallway while Simmons and Alan left through the ER doors. As they left, Alan asked Simmons, "Did you know she was going to make it? Did you know all along?"

"No."

"Are you happy that she made it, that she lived? You don't seem overly excited about it," said Alan.

"She'll have to walk her own hallway eventually, when the time is right and the need is great. But I'm glad her parents were spared the grief of her death."

As they departed the hospital Alan struggled to count the number of people who had died. Anne Munsin, the elderly woman in the car accident. Andrew Kratson, who slipped on the bar of soap. Leslie Wallace whose car smashed into the tree. Nick Swanolski, the murdered store clerk. Angie Krofts, the troubled teen suicide. Tyris Cotton, the former gang member who did the right thing in the end. Billy Cox and Amy

Lansing, who crashed into the Bornhopp sisters, Emma and Melissa. And finally Ross McDonald, the teen who drank himself to death. *Eleven in all*, thought Alan.

Eleven deaths, all tragic in their own way, all unrelated—or so it seemed.

He tried to focus on how these incidents could be linked, but couldn't reach a conclusion. Exhausted from concentration, Alan shook the images out of his mind. He moved his thoughts to the future. *Five more to go. Who will it be?*

Chapter Twenty-Three

"Life is either a daring adventure or nothing.
To keep our faces toward change and
behave like free spirits in the presence of fate
is strength undefeatable."

—Helen Keller

MADDIE KLINSTROM RAN HER FINGERS through her short, dark, curly hair and appreciated the fact that she had it once again. Three years ago she'd been diagnosed with breast cancer and had fought her way back. She was only twenty-nine years old and had two small children—Nancy, five, and Zach, four. Her husband had left her right after Zach was born and she'd raised her two children on her own. Her sister, Barb, had taken care of her when she became ill.

They had talked about Barb taking the children should anything happen to her. Years ago, when she had first become sick, the doctors had told her that she would not live more than six months. But Maddie refused to accept their opinion and decided that she would not die. Her motivation stemmed from her need to save more money to make sure her kids could go on if she was not around. Determined to ensure that her children would be able to stay in the same home to which they were accustomed, and that they would have the chance to go to college one day, she made up her mind to survive and beat the odds. And she did, as well as defeating the sense of hopelessness to which she could have easily fallen victim.

Although she painted a picture of enormous courage and the will to live, the doctors had stuck to their medical opinion that she would die soon. A year after their initial diagnosis, their opinions changed when her condition took a turn for the better. But now things had changed again. Six months ago at one of her visits to the hospital she was told that the cancer was back and her health had deteriorated. She was in a great deal of pain, bedridden, and her sister was once again taking care of her and the kids.

On this morning, with the sun shining brightly through the bedroom window, she decided that this was the day she would start her recovery.

She opened her eyes and thought, *I've beaten this before. I will do it again.*

The night before she had been so weak that it was hard to move, but this morning she fought through the pain and fatigue, determined to overcome the disease she knew so well. She started by opening her eyes, then attempted to move her right hand. Concentrating hard, she lifted her hand over her body and with a great effort tried to grab the bedrail. Determined, she concentrated harder and tried to move one of her feet. The pain was almost unbearable, and she couldn't move even her little toe. Thinking of her children, she became angry at the pain and disease, which she blamed for taking her away from everything she loved.

She gritted her teeth and tried harder. To her utter astonishment, she swung both feet around and hung them over the bed. As she stood up and stretched her arms high, the word "miracle" flashed through her mind. Walking with ease across the room, she made her way down the stairs and into the kitchen. The pain had lifted entirely!

She heard Barbara, her sister talking to someone on the phone. Barb's voice was broken and distraught. "She fought hard, but she finally lost her battle."

This isn't right, Maddie thought. *I feel great. I've won.*

Without alerting her sister, she went upstairs to her daughter's bedroom where Zach and Nancy were playing. Running over to them, she knelt down and they smiled and hugged her tightly. She told them that she loved them and would always be with them. Nancy pulled at her long blond hair, giggling, while Zach beamed a huge smile, his gleaming green eyes wide with joy.

Maddie didn't fully understand why her sister was acting as though she were gone. She felt a hand on her shoulder and turned to see two men standing in the room, and she began to accept what was happening to her.

She looked at the taller man, with a badge hanging around his neck. "How's this possible? My children can see me. They can hug me—they recognize that I'm still here."

The taller man looked as though he didn't have an answer. The shorter man in the navy blue suit spoke up. "Yes, they can see you and touch you. They understand and they believe everything you say. You've told them that you will watch over them, which is the truth. But you know that you must come with us."

She nodded. "I will, but I need to tell them something before we go."

The shorter man nodded back. Speaking to her children she said, "Listen carefully. I want you to know that I love you very much. I also want you to know that you're going to hear many grown-ups saying that I lost my battle with cancer. That's how they will say it, but I want you two to know that I didn't lose. I won, and I want you two to remember that you can win anything as long as you have faith. I hope you understand this. Can you both remember what I've told you?"

The children nodded and smiled. She spoke once again. "I won't say good-bye because that would mean that I'd be leaving and you wouldn't see me anymore. You *will* see me again. I promise." She kissed each of them, and they hugged her once more.

As she stood up and walked through the door, both children began playing and laughing. Alan thought this was strange. He had assumed that there would be more despair and sadness; but, to the contrary, all of them seemed happy. As they walked from the room, Maddie said to Alan and Simmons, "Follow me."

Without disturbing Barbara, who was still on the phone, they all walked out of the house and into the backyard. One of several oak trees had a swing hanging from two ropes, which were draped over a large branch.

Maddie sat down and began swinging. "This is where I was sitting when Nancy took her first steps." She pointed to the ground in front of her. "I remember it as if it was only yesterday."

She smiled, then stood up and ran farther into the yard to a small bird feeder on a short pole. "This is where Zach and I used to come to feed the birds. He was only two years old, and some of them would eat right out of his hand. He loved it; he would giggle hysterically when they pecked the seeds out of his tiny palm."

She smiled and looked up at the gleaming rays of sun that pierced the treetops and warmed her face. "Yes, I'll always remember these places. Well, I guess you need me, don't you, Michael?"

Simmons smiled, "Yes, we need you."

Alan was surprised. "Do you two know each other?"

"In a manner of speaking, I know everyone who passes to the next world. Their level of awareness regarding their role in their new life determines whether they know me or not."

Maddie laughed and said, "That makes it sound so confusing Michael. But don't be alarmed, Alan. I know you as well."

Alan was even more surprised at this. "You know me, too? Then you must also know where we're going."

"Of course I know—to the hallway and through the door. Then I shall take my place helping the others. I know my rank, and I'll fight hard for what's right and good."

Alan was even more puzzled. Maddie raised an eyebrow.

"Ah, I see that you only understand portions of what I said. Why haven't you filled him in on what's behind the doors, Michael?"

"We're working our way up to that," Simmons replied.

"I see. Well, then I won't spoil your surprise." She walked farther into the yard and said, "This way."

They approached a small white shed at the back of the yard.

"You see, Alan, I've been close to death a few times, so I've been educated on what I need to do."

She opened the doors to the shed and all three stepped through into the marble hallway. Alan noticed that the hallway was a bit brighter than usual. They walked for only about ten minutes before he could see the door in front of them.

She stopped and turned toward Alan. "Remember," she said to him, "I didn't lose my battle with cancer—I won. I was victorious. I want you to tell everyone who says differently that they're wrong. Tell them that it no longer afflicts me, and it can no longer hurt me in any way."

Alan nodded. "I'll tell them."

"Now I'm off to the next battle—where I'll be just as victorious."

Alan opened the door and she slipped through.

As the two men walked back down the hallway, Alan questioned Simmons. "So, you plan on filling me in on this ranking thing? She said she had some type of rank, and she would be fighting the battle. I'm somewhat confused."

"Yes, you'll know in time. I'll show you the ranks and structures of those who fight for what is right and good."

Alan sighed and said, "You know, I'm tired of hearing the same old thing from you about how I'll know in time. It's getting old, if you know what I mean. And another thing—do you own any other clothes than that suit you wear? You never change it. You should try something else."

Simmons was taken aback; Alan thought that he might even have been slightly insulted by this last comment.

"You don't like it?" asked Simmons.

"No, I don't like being kept in the dark. I need to know—"

Simmons cut him off. "No, I mean you don't like my suit?"

"Oh," Alan said, now sure that he had somehow offended him. "Uh, no—I mean yes. I mean…I think the suit is fine. It's just that you wear it all the time. You might try changing the color of your tie perhaps… it's not a big deal—Honestly I could care less about your wardrobe. I just said it because I'm frustrated by your lack of answers and your expressionless reactions. I guess I'm just trying to get some type of emotion out of you—even if it's a negative emotion."

Simmons nodded and no longer looked insulted. They both slipped back through the small metal doors of the shed.

CHAPTER TWENTY-FOUR

*"All cruelty springs from
hardheartedness and weakness."*

—Seneca

MARY CHELSEY ANGRILY PARKED HER CAR on the curb outside the rundown apartment she frequently visited. She swept her greasy, blond hair back from her forehead as she stared down at the numerous needle marks on her arm. Glancing up at the rearview mirror, she caught a glimpse of the large, black circles under her eyes accenting the deeply sunken face that exposed her cheekbones and bony chin. *Monster*, she thought to herself. That was what the little girl in the grocery store had called her on seeing her face. She looked away from the mirror. The little girl's voice still echoed in her mind, infuriating her even more.

Her twin four-year-old sons, Gregory and David, sat in the backseat. She opened the car door and Gregory asked, "Mommy, where are you going?"

"Shut up and don't get out of this car—I mean it," she yelled.

Gregory flinched back and lowered his head, expecting her fist to strike him. He found that it was better to get hit on the top of the head than in the face where it hurt more. The bruise under his eye was still healing as was the cut on David's cheek. David's injury had come from Mom's boyfriend, Johnny. David had spilled his milk at the table last week while Johnny was over for dinner. The milk had run off the end of the table and spilled on Johnny's pants. He'd slapped David across the face, knocking him out of his chair. Johnny's ring—which David and Gregory had named the devil ring, since the face was that of a large skull with red rhinestone eyes and fangs—had sliced David's cheek. Within a moment it had begun to bleed. Mary had been sitting across the table when it occurred. Her goal in life was to please Johnny. When he became angry about something, so did she. She knew he didn't like kids, and stuff like this would just drive him further away, so she jumped up, grabbed David by his hair, and screamed at him. "You need to be more careful—take your ass to your room!"

David ran off down the hall, crying. Later on, Gregory made his way down to their room and brought his brother a wet napkin that he had run under the bathroom faucet. There was blood streaming down the side of his brother's face. Gregory put the napkin over it.

David yelled, "It hurts!"

Gregory replied, "I know, but this is what they do at school when I fall down and hurt my knee. It will help. You'll see."

The bleeding eventually stopped, leaving David with a large scab that ran from just below his eye down to his jawbone.

David and Gregory watched their mother get out of the car and run up to the door of the apartment. Gregory knew that this was Johnny's house, as they had done this many other times, but he still felt the need to ask his mother what she was doing. He was hoping that she wouldn't be in there as long as she was the last time—four hours. The car had grown so hot that Gregory eventually opened the door. His mother beat him when she returned, since she had told them not to get out. However, it didn't feel as bad as the heat that had nearly made him and his brother vomit.

Her hand shaking, Mary knocked on the door of the apartment. A tall man with thin, oily, black hair, unshaven and shirtless, answered the door.

"Didn't I tell you not to come over here?" he sneered.

"I'm hurting, Johnny. You have to help me, please."

A young girl, perhaps fifteen years old, appeared from behind him. "Johnny, who is it? I'm feeling good—like I'm a feather. Come on... come back to bed. I love you." The girl put her arms around Johnny as she staggered and attempted to keep her balance. Mary saw the track marks on her arms. Instantly, she was enraged.

She pushed her way into the house and slapped the girl, who fell backward. "Get away from my man!" she exclaimed.

The girl steadied herself and lunged back at Mary, but Johnny caught her and said, "Go back upstairs. I'll be there soon."

The girl turned and disappeared. Johnny grabbed Mary by the throat and yelled, "I told you not to come over here!"

Mary broke down and began to cry. "I thought I was the one you loved. I thought we were going to move in together."

Johnny looked frustrated, but quickly gained his composure as he focused on the possibility of making some money from a quick deal. Not wanting to lose one of his best customers, he released his grip and put his arm around her. He walked her over to the couch and sat her down. A small wooden box rested on the middle of the coffee table in front of the couch. Mary pulled out a twenty-dollar bill.

Johnny rolled his eyes and she said, "Please, it's all I have."

Johnny opened the box and handed her a baggie containing a couple of small chunks of methamphetamine, or crystal meth, as she called it. Johnny was a master at making meth but could also get his hands on any other type of drug she wanted—as long as she had the money. She wished she could afford to buy some heroine, as she hadn't shot up in over a week, but for now she had to settle for what she could get. *I'll bet that's what he's giving that little whore he has upstairs. He always starts them off on the good stuff,* she thought.

Mary wiped the tears from her cheeks. "Thanks. We'll move in together someday, won't we?"

"You know I don't like kids."

Mary began to sob once more. Johnny stood up, took her hand, and helped her to her feet. "You have to go. I have to meet with someone soon, business meeting—you know."

Mary nodded, indicating she understood. She made her way to the front door. Johnny followed her outside and gave her a hug. Slowly, she made her way down to her car and got in. Johnny's focus shifted from her to the backseat of her vehicle where the two kids sat. A look of disgust appeared on his face. Mary turned the key, shifted into drive, and began to pull away from the curb. Looking back, she saw Johnny getting into a BMW that had pulled up behind her. She knew that Johnny's "business meeting" was his monthly visit from his drug supplier. She continued to sob as she drove away.

"What's wrong, Mommy?" asked Gregory.

Mary didn't answer, but thought, *Everything. My whole life. I can never get what I want. Why did I ever have kids? They screw up everything.*

She was thirty-two years old and had never married. Her father had beaten her mother for years until finally one day, while he was in a drunken rage, he struck her mother in the head with a glass vase. She died later that evening at the hospital. Mary's father went to jail for manslaughter, and that was the last she ever saw of him. She was placed in several foster homes, but she would always run away.

Then one day, when she was eighteen years old, she met a man named Benny who gave her a place to stay and food to eat. Benny introduced her to the world of drugs and frequently had her deliver "packages" to his multiple "clients," as he called them. Benny was good to her; he only beat her a few times—much less often than she'd been beaten when she lived with her father.

After five years she found herself alone once again when Benny was killed in a bar fight. She stayed in his apartment until they evicted her, then moved into a government housing complex and applied for government aid. She became pregnant with the twins after a one-night stand with a man she'd picked up at a bar who had given her some marijuana. She had never even asked him his name. He had disappeared the next morning, never to be heard from again. A couple of years ago she had landed a part-time job as a clerk at the Fast Track Gas Station near her home. She was only making minimum wage, but the part-time hours allowed her to work while the kids were at school.

The job wasn't glamorous, but at least one positive thing came out of working there. It was where she met Johnny. He would come in for gas and beer nearly every other day. Each time he saw her he would flirt by offering her a cigarette. Mary would always plan her breaks around the time when he'd come in. After several social smoking sessions with him, he invited her over to his house for a party. The party turned out to be a four-day, drug-induced experience, during which she left her two sons at home alone. Mary hadn't even remembered them until Johnny had driven her back to her house. She came in to find them scraping the last small portions of peanut butter out of the jar with their hands because they were so hungry. She looked at them and actually said, "I'm sorry." The boys had smiled; it was the only time they could recall her ever apologizing to them.

She thought, *Damn how I hate my life. If only I didn't have these kids dragging me down. It's not like I planned on having them! If it weren't for them, I'd be with Johnny right now. If their father hadn't disappeared, then at least I'd be getting some money for child support...no-good bastard, leaves me all alone to raise two kids—two kids I don't even want.*

The car accelerated and swiftly rounded the corner.

After a few moments of silence, David asked, "Where are we going now, Mommy?"

"Home."

David said, "I'm hungry, can we eat?"

"I'm out of money. You two are draining me."

For fear that she would become even angrier, neither of the children spoke again until they arrived home. As they pulled into the driveway of the small, rundown house, Mary reached for the baggie and stuffed it into her pocket. Everyone got out of the car and went into the house. It was extremely small, consisting of two small bedrooms and a kitchen. There were holes in the walls and the roof leaked near the entryway. As the two boys sat down at the kitchen table, Mary opened the pantry door and found a few pieces of bread. She took out two plates and put a piece of bread on each. Opening the cupboard, she found a jar of peanut butter and unscrewed the cap. Empty.

"Damn!" she exclaimed. The boys lurched back in fear.

After slamming the jar into the overflowing trash can she opened the refrigerator door and took out a white tub of margarine. She scraped the mold from the top portion and threw it away, then began to spread the margarine onto the bread.

When she was finished she slid the two plates in front of the boys and said, "You two will have to drink water, 'cause I'm out of milk."

She came back with two glasses of water and set them in front of the kids. They began to eat and drink in silence.

Mary turned to them and said, "You two go play in your room when you're done."

"Okay," said Gregory. David just nodded.

Mary made her way into her bedroom and sat down on the bed. She took out the baggie and attached one of the chunks to the small metal pipe she kept in her nightstand. As she lit the pipe and inhaled, the drugs intoxicated her. A calming sensation came over her mind. Her head became clearer and she felt wonderful, or so she thought. Energy surged through her body and she felt reborn—alive. Her thoughts wandered back to Johnny and the life they could have together, never having to worry about money or her next fix. Everything would be heavenly.

She was awakened by a loud crash from the other room. The noise startled her. She stood up and staggered her way to the kids' bedroom. She opened the door to see that a lamp had been knocked over and broken. Looking down, she saw Gregory and David trying feverishly to clean up the mess. Their gaze met hers, and a look of panic and fear came over both of their faces.

She flew into a rage and screamed, "What were you two doing?"

"It was an accident, Mommy," said David. "I was trying to get my truck and it just fell."

David ducked his head as if he expected to be struck. Mary was so enraged that she slammed the door and ran back down the hallway.

"I'll fix this," she said to herself. "I'll fix this right now."

Running into the garage, she grabbed a half-filled can of gasoline that she kept for the lawnmower. She ran back into the hallway and began pouring the gas onto the floor, making a quick pass into her room and through the kitchen, then finally up to the front door.

The boys' bedroom door began to open. Mary screamed, "Stay in that room!" The door slammed shut.

She pulled a matchbook from her pocket. As she was about to strike it, she remembered that she had left her drugs in her bedroom. *Can't leave those*, she thought. Running to her nightstand, Mary grabbed the baggie and stuffed it into her pocket.

Standing near the front door, she struck the match and dropped it. Before the match hit, an explosion of flame and heat knocked her out of the door and onto the lawn. Coming to her senses, she felt her eyebrows. They were now singed and brittle from the fire. She made her way to her feet, panting and gasping, then fumbled for the car keys in her pocket as she staggered up to the car door. Pausing a moment, she watched as the smoke began to billow out of the windows and roof, then caught sight of flames licking the corners of the tiny home. She got into her car and drove off.

Gregory noticed smoke coming from under the door of their bedroom and asked his brother, "What's going on?"

David replied, "Let's go out the window."

The two tried to push open the window, but it was locked and neither was tall enough to reach the latch. Both began to cry and yell. "Mommy, help us!"

David looked over at the door. More smoke was pouring into the room, filling it and making it hard to see. The room became very hot.

Just then the door was thrown off its hinges and landed flat. A man in a navy blue suit entered the room and spoke to the two boys. "It's okay, everything will be all right."

David asked, with a panicky voice, "Are you a fireman?"

The man looked at him and replied, "Not exactly. But I'm going to get you two out of here. Take my hand."

Each grabbed a hand. As they did the smoke cleared the room. They walked back into the hallway. The walls were scorched and burned, but it was now cool. As they made their way to the front door, the boys noticed another man. He was taller and had a bright badge that hung around his neck.

The tall man spoke to them. "You boys are going to be fine. Nobody will ever hurt you again, I promise."

Both boys smiled and Gregory said, "Where are we going now?"

The man in the suit bent down, "Someplace wonderful. Don't you know, Gregory?"

Gregory thought for a moment. Then a look appeared on his face, as though someone had turned on a light in his head. "Of course, I do! You need our help, don't you?"

"Very much so," replied the man as he smiled at them.

David looked at him and smiled back. "And we're very strong. We'll fight for you and help people—just as you've helped us."

"I know you will," said the man.

The taller man looked down at the two, "Well, I guess we'll have to get you guys where you need to go."

Gregory looked up at him, "No need, Alan. We're only beyond this door. We'll see you soon."

David entered first, then Gregory. Light poured through as the door opened, illuminating the entire room. Once the boys were gone, Simmons and Alan stepped outside to view the burnt remains of the home.

"There will be a criminal investigation of this incident. Is there any information I need?" asked Alan.

"Their mother's name is Mary Chelsey. Look for her. You'll find gasoline poured throughout the house. Find her and you should have your suspect."

"I'm going to try to locate her now," said Alan. "I'll catch up to you later."

Simmons nodded and made his way back to his car. Alan, who had driven himself, got into his car and called the station to find Mary's license plate number. Within minutes Alan had the information he needed on Mary Chelsey. At least, as a drug addict, she wasn't hard to find. He drove off toward the address where she was known to frequent: the home of *one* Johnny Barnes.

CHAPTER TWENTY-FIVE

*"People with no conscience
often have no soul."*

MARY RAN UP TO THE FRONT OF Johnny's shabby apartment. Pulling at the heavy door, she was amazed to find it unlocked; Johnny was always paranoid about the cops raiding his place for drugs. *Strange*, she thought. Perhaps she should have knocked, but the excitement of her new life with Johnny overwhelmed her. She flung open the door and made her way into the living room.

"Johnny!" she called out in a gleeful tone.

No answer.

Peering into the kitchen, she tried to determine whether the young girl who had been there previously was still in the apartment. She looked down at the kitchen table, where she found a scribbled note in nearly illegible handwriting.

Johnny,

My buzz is wearing off and I didn't want to wake you up. I'm heading up to the gas station to get some beer. I borrowed some money and I have your car. Be back soon.

Love, Tabby

Stupid little whore, Mary thought. *She didn't even lock the door on the way out. Johnny's going to be mad at her when I tell him.*

She continued her search. "Johnny," she called again. As before, there was no answer.

Making her way down a short hallway to the bedroom, she entered and saw Johnny lying in bed under a large blanket.

A huge smile came over her face as she said, "We can finally be together. I've fixed everything. I love you so much."

When he didn't respond, she walked over to the side of his bed so she could face him. "Are you listening to me? I said we can—" She stopped in midsentence, horrified, and stared into Johnny's black, lifeless eyes. She placed both of her trembling hands over her mouth and took two steps backward. A cold fear rose within her. From behind, she felt a presence. Something cold. Something empty. Something evil.

CHAPTER TWENTY-SIX

"There has to be evil
so that good can prove its
purity above it."

—Buddha

A S ALAN PULLED UP in front of the rundown apartment he noticed a beat-up Chevy parked out front. Calling in the plates, he confirmed that it was indeed Mary's car. He approached the front door and was about to knock when he discovered that it was slightly ajar.

He pushed it open and called out, "Hello, anyone here?"

No response.

He called in once again, "Police officer, anyone here? Everyone okay?"

Again, no response.

Drawing his gun, he held it down at his side and stepped through the threshold of the doorway. His heart began to pound faster. He peered around the corner into a small living room where he saw a couch, a TV, and a coffee table littered with food, beer cans, and newspaper. As he moved closer he noticed remnants of a burnt, crystallized substance in an ashtray, along with a syringe and a clear glass tube with a charred end. He made his way into the kitchen, which was in the same state of disarray as the living room. He turned and entered a small hallway. Pointing his gun straight in front of him, he once again called out, "Police officer, anyone here?"

There was no reply.

He headed to the end of the hallway, where a bedroom door stood open. Alan entered and observed a man and woman lying on the bed.

"Hello," he called out to them. "Police officer. Is everyone okay?"

Neither of them moved nor responded. He made his way over to the woman and placed two fingers on her neck to locate a pulse. As his fingers made contact with her skin, he drew his hand back quickly. Her neck felt like a block of ice. He once again attempted to find a pulse, shocked by how cold her body was. Unable to locate any signs of life, he quickly turned his attention to the man's body. His skin was freezing also.

Alan's adrenaline rose. *Something's wrong*, he thought. "Something's *very* wrong," he said aloud.

Moving his hand over to the man's eyelids, he carefully opened one of his eyes. He jumped back in a near state of panic. The man's pupils were completely black and dilated, covering the entire white portion of his eyes. With trembling hands, he dialed the phone. His first calls should have been to the department, the crime scene unit; and then the bureau; however, the circumstances of the scene were unlike anything he had ever experienced. There was only one person to call.

Simmons answered. "Hello?"

"It's me. Something's wrong. I'm here with Mary Chelsey and Johnny Barnes—or what's left of them." He paused to catch his breath, panic rising. "They're cold, Michael, like blocks of ice. And their eyes—they're black, all black. Bodies don't get this cold; the apartment's not cold. Pupils don't turn that—"

Simmons cut him off. "Get out of there and wait for me in your car."

Alan could sense the urgency in Simmons's voice. He closed the phone. He backed out of the room with his gun still drawn. As he backed down the hallway and into the living room, something scurried between his legs from behind him. Clenching his teeth, Alan gripped his gun tightly, pointing in the direction of his attacker.

It was a large gray cat. Alan breathed a sigh of relief and ran through the front door and down to his car. Closing the car door and putting his gun down on the seat, he placed both hands over his face. Cold sweat poured through his fingers, and he tried to stop his hands from shaking.

A knock on the window startled him. He grabbed his gun and pointed it in the direction of the noise only to find Simmons standing outside with a concerned look on his face. The two said nothing as they entered the apartment.

Simmons stood looking down at the bodies. Finally Alan asked, "Why didn't you know about this? Do we need to walk these two down their hall?"

"No."

"No what? No, we don't need to walk them or no, you don't know why you weren't aware of this?"

Simmons drew a heavy breath. In a low voice he said, "No to both."

"This is bad, isn't it?" asked Alan.

"Yeah, this is bad."

Simmons turned toward Alan. "Call your people. They'll discover that these two died of drug overdoses."

Alan didn't move for a moment. "But there's more to this picture than a simple drug overdose, isn't there?"

"Yeah. But it won't be of concern to your department or your investigation."

"Yeah, but *I* should be concerned, right?" asked Alan; he knew there were more to Simmons's words.

"We should all be concerned."

Simmons made his way out of the bedroom and back into the hallway. Alan followed and noticed that he was looking up at the ceiling and along the walls.

"What are you looking for?"

"A doorway."

Alan walked back to the bedroom door, took out his phone, and began to dial the department. He was nearly finished when he promptly stopped and put the phone away before the call went through.

"*Michael*," his voice was a cold, icy whisper. "Michael, they're gone. They're both gone."

Simmons ran back into the bedroom and stared at the empty bed for a moment.

"It appears that I should've been looking in here."

Simmons flung the closet door open. The room dimmed as if the light in it were being sucked inside. As the two peered in, Alan saw the outline of a figure standing just beyond the doorway. The figure's back was to the door, but it turned slowly, as if it felt the light from the room pouring through. Alan felt a large, dry lump in his throat and a bead of sweat fell from his brow. Although it was dark, he could see the outline of the figure. It appeared to be a man in a hooded cape.

The figure took a step forward and spoke. "Michael. I see you have a new whelp."

The voice was low and deep. Alan wondered who or *what* it was. He could now see that the figure was clad in some type of black armor, like that of the obsidian walls of the hallways they frequented.

Simmons spoke. "Tiberius. I see you've been busy."

The figure cackled. "Yes, I have my job to do, as do you. Perhaps you care to dance?"

In a flash the figure produced a large dagger with a curved blade. The light from the room began to form into tiny, thin strands, which were drawn into the blade. The figure took another step forward. Alan drew his gun and fired twice into the figure's chest.

The rounds seemed to disappear into the armor, obviously ineffective. The figure laughed. "I see you haven't taught this one everything,

Michael. You better see fit to make him ready for battle."

"I will not be baited to fight in there. Maybe you'd like to step out and we can settle this?"

The figure stepped back and sheathed the knife.

"That's what I thought," said Simmons.

The figure sneered. "There will be a day when we meet for the inevitable. You know that. I'll see you—and your little friend—very soon."

"We'll be ready," assured Simmons.

"Let's hope so," replied the figure as it turned and disappeared into the darkness.

Alan's hands were trembling horribly as he holstered his gun.

"It's explanation time, Michael. Who or what was that?" he asked in the calmest voice he could muster.

"I know him as Tiberius. He does what we do—but for the other side."

"Yeah. The other side. We haven't spoken much of them. You wanna fill me in?"

"As you know, we fight for all that is good and right against all that is bad, evil, and wrong," Simmons said. "Tiberius leads those who fight for that which is bad, that which is cruel and wrong. He leads them to fight for the darkness and against all for which we stand."

"Okay," said Alan, catching his breath as he sat down on the bed. "Now tell me…*what* is he?"

"Well—" Michael paused. "He's a man. Perhaps living, perhaps not."

Alan said in a quick, somewhat angry voice, "No. He's no man. I shot him in the chest—*twice*. I know I hit him, but it didn't even faze him. He *laughed* when the rounds struck him. He's no man."

"As I've said before, weapons from your world don't affect our world in the same way. Did you see the armor he was wearing?"

"Yeah, I was getting to that. But first tell me that he wasn't some demon, some devil."

"The world of the living has many misconceptions, Alan. Evil and darkness don't need horns and fangs or batlike wings to fight. Those things only represent *images* of fear conjured by those in your world."

"Okay," Alan drew a deep breath, taking it all in. "The armor, tell me about the armor. It was black—the light was being absorbed."

"Yeah, it's what they use in battle. It absorbs and consumes the light, as they attempt to absorb and consume all that is good and right. Nothing from your world would even scratch it. Only our weapons will be effective."

"So the dagger you gave me, it would work? That would be effective?" asked Alan.

"It could penetrate if struck hard enough. In the hands of an experienced warrior, or soldier, as you like to call them, it would work."

Alan detected a word of caution in Simmons's voice and responded, "I think, you're trying to say that I'm not a warrior. So even *with* that weapon I couldn't necessarily defeat that thing?"

"No, you probably couldn't. Like any weapon, it takes training and discipline to work well."

Alan nodded, indicating that he understood. "Why didn't you fight him, then?"

"It's unwise to fight any enemy within their own territory. He wanted me to step into his. Within that hallway he would have had the distinct advantage, so I refused. When we do battle with agents of evil like Tiberius, they're at a disadvantage if they fight us within our realm. I offered him a neutral fight out in this world, which he declined."

"But they still attempt to fight you within your world?" asked Alan.

"Yeah, but we have the advantage when we're among the light. Sometimes they're successful, but many times they're not."

Alan nodded once again. "Do you know any more about him—his background?"

"No, but I doubt that it is his real name. He's what we call in our language the Balliste Galau, the guide to the darkness, if translated in your world. I know nothing further."

Alan sat for a moment then blurted out: "Amy Lansing."

Simmons looked at him and nodded in confirmation.

"Amy Lansing, the woman involved in the car accident, the one who left her young children at home alone. The one we had to guide a very long way. Early on we came across another door. I remember the light being consumed from the edges of the doorway and the look on your face when we came across it." Alan paused for a moment. "She could have been recruited by the other side. She could've been easily taken to fight for the other side."

"Yes." Simmons nodded. "But we have her now."

Alan rubbed the sides of his head while attempting to absorb the unbelievable events that had just occurred. "Let's get outta here."

As Simmons stood up to leave, Alan noticed that he clenched his jaw as if he were angry and determined, like a professional athlete who had just been challenged to a game—like a soldier who had just come face-to-face with his enemy. It was a side of Simmons that Alan hadn't seen before, but it was something with which he was very familiar from his days in the military and with the police. It was an aspect of leadership and command. It was a sense of duty, commitment, and honor to reach an ultimate goal: Victory.

CHAPTER TWENTY-SEVEN

*"We can only appreciate the miracle
of a sunrise if we have waited
in the darkness."*

NATASHA MALANIKOV SMILED as her husband Ivan came through
the door and kissed her on the cheek. She sat down at the table
with him to eat dinner and peered over at their four-month-old daughter, Anna, asleep in her baby swing.

Eight years ago the couple had emigrated from Russia to live with
Anna's mother in the small Midwestern city of Riverston. Anna's mother
had moved to the city many years back and had told Anna how peaceful it was, begging her to come live there. After Ivan and Natasha were
married they began working toward making the move, and within three
years they were on their way to America. A couple years after they
arrived, Anna's mother passed away and the two continued to live in
her rundown apartment. Ivan worked at a local grocery store, and Natasha had worked as a florist for a few years until she became pregnant
with Anna. Money had been extremely tight; they were barely able to
afford the bleak lifestyle as time slipped by. However, Ivan had recently
received a promotion and the two had been talking about moving into

something more comfortable because their simple apartment had so many problems—the roof leaked, the furnace was always going out, and occasionally a rat would appear, scurrying about.

Natasha couldn't wait to move and had been asking Ivan every week when this was going to happen since he was the one who budgeted all of their money. Ivan always answered, "Soon. Very soon."

One Saturday morning Ivan looked over at Natasha and said, "This will be the weekend that we look for a new home."

Natasha couldn't stop smiling. "I can't wait to get out of here."

As she lowered her gaze to Anna, she saw that she had started to stir in her swing. She caressed the baby's soft, red hair, which resembled hers. Picking her up, she kissed her on the cheek before resting her on her shoulder.

"It's time for bed. You're very tired," she said softly.

She carried Anna into the bedroom, laid her in the crib, and watched her sleep for a moment before she rejoined Ivan in the kitchen.

Alan was still in his office when a young patrol officer poked his head through the door. "Fire department is responding to a gas leak over on Maple Street."

Alan looked at his watch and noticed that it was nearly time to go home. Still, duty called. He nodded to the officer, stood up, and made his way out to his car to respond to the call. As he pulled up in front of the apartment he noticed several fire trucks and an ambulance out front.

As he approached the front door he saw several firemen trying to open it. The door splintered as it broke free, and Alan entered with the others. Three firefighters headed into the kitchen and two down the hallway. Alan followed down the hall and entered the first bedroom where he saw a crib in the back corner of the room. Running over to it, he saw an infant swaddled in a pink and yellow blanket, and his heart began to race. He reached down to touch the baby's face. She was warm to the touch, but she wasn't moving. A feeling of nausea came over him. He felt light-headed, as if he might pass out. Shaking his head from side to side, he tried to regain equilibrium as he placed two fingers on the baby's neck trying to find a pulse. Nothing.

Grabbing her up in his arms he held her, but her tiny body fell limp. He put the palm of his hand on her chest in an attempt to determine if she were breathing, but there was no movement. Placing her on a nearby bed, he started infant CPR. As he breathed into her mouth and compressed her tiny chest, he felt his own breathing increase. Anxiety flowed through his body.

Breathe, he willed. *Please breathe.*

He continued to blow short, controlled breaths into her mouth, his pulse quickening in time with the chest compressions.

"Come on," he said aloud. "*Breathe,* please!"

As he continued, the baby's limp body hung in his arms like a wet towel. Pressing her soft cheek to his face, a tear ran down the bridge of his nose. He had been in this situation before. All of those horrible memories flooded back into his mind. A few years back he'd had a call for a baby not breathing. When he arrived at the house he realized that it belonged to a friend of his from high school; his friend's three-month-old son had stopped breathing. Alan had scooped the baby up and initiated CPR. Although he tried to breathe life back into the infant, it had been to no avail. The overwhelming feeling of defeat had consumed him. Although everyone had told him that there was nothing more he could have done, it provided him no comfort. The face of his grief-stricken friend was burned in his mind to this day. He had cried for most of the night as he held his own daughter, who was only five months old at the time. He remembered how the lifeless body of the baby felt in his arms—so small, so helpless. Now he had to relive this situation again. A flood of emotion came over him, a sense of extreme grief and hopelessness. There was nothing he could do. But as he began to think about the recent experiences he'd had with death, a new emotion began to rise within him: anger. He looked into the face of the baby girl and his own daughter came into his mind. Then, as in many instances when someone has died, he looked for someone to blame.

He felt a hand on his shoulder and a familiar voice said, "She's gone."

Simmons stood behind him and kept a hand on Alan's shoulder. Alan gently set the baby down on the bed, ever so carefully, as if she might still awaken. He clenched his fists and closed his eyes tightly.

"No," he said.

Simmons seemed confused by his words.

"No," Alan said once more. This time it was in a low and bitter whisper. He felt a rage surge up from his chest and burn his throat and then rise to the very top of his head, through his arms, and down into his clenched fists.

"Alan, I know this is hard. I know this is—"

Alan rounded on Simmons and grabbed his wrist. "No, this won't happen—not again."

Alan was now staring straight into Simmons's eyes, glaring with a rage as though he could burn a hole through his very soul.

Simmons began to speak once again. "You know I can't—"

Before the last words were out of his mouth Alan pressed the barrel of his gun to Simmons's forehead. He did not appear frightened, but dropped his gaze as if he were disappointed, and yet sympathetic.

Alan recognized this emotion and nodded. "Ah, I see…I'd almost forgotten. I guess this gun won't do anything to you, will it? Yes, I remember now."

The words were pouring out of his mouth in a snakelike whisper. Everything became a blur. The thoughts of the dead babies made him lose control of his actions; he behaved as if he had truly been pushed past his breaking point—as if someone had killed his own daughter. He threw the gun across the room. Before Simmons had time to say or do anything, Alan brought out the white-bladed dagger and held it to Simmons' throat. Now he saw a glint of fear in Simmons's eyes; the other man's mood had suddenly changed.

In a cold, methodical voice Alan said, "Now that I have your attention, you need to listen to me very carefully. You are going to bring this one back or I'm going to run this blade across your neck. Do you understand me?"

Simmons said nothing, but nodded slowly.

Alan spoke once more. "Do you believe me? I will kill you if I have to. Or, if you can't die, we'll just see what happens when this blade pierces through you."

Simmons's eyes were wide. For the first time ever, Alan thought he saw a bead of sweat trickle down the normally impassive face.

Simmons spoke very slowly. "I believe you, and I understand what you're saying, but you will have to strike me down with the blade because I can't bring her back. I would ask one thing of you before you strike."

Alan drew a deep breath. "What's that?"

"Look at Anna."

Alan looked confused. "What."

"Please. Look down at Anna. The baby, her name is Anna."

Alan kept the blade pressed close to Simmons's neck and glanced over at the baby, whose eyes were now open. He lowered the dagger and scooped her up in his arms. She squirmed and nestled to him, full of life.

Alan rounded back on Simmons and said, "It's comforting, but I know better. She's still dead. I'm not going to face her parents with all their pain. This little façade is nice, but back in the *real* world, in *my* world, there will be two grieving parents who have just lost a baby. They won't get to see her like this!"

He grabbed the dagger once again and pushed it forward toward Simmons's throat. A slender, soft hand reached out and touched him on the wrist. Alan turned and saw a red-haired woman standing next to him.

She spoke. "We *will* get to see her, Alan. I'm Natasha and this is my husband Ivan." She motioned to the blond man standing next to her. "We're Anna's parents."

Alan lowered the dagger and handed the baby to the woman, who smiled and kissed her on the cheek.

"You did it. You did bring her back. You did it."

A sense of relief fell over him, but Simmons quickly said, "No, Alan. I didn't."

Alan was confused and rebutted, "No. You did it. Her parents, they do get to hold her again—alive."

"No. There was a carbon monoxide leak in the basement of this building. Anna and her parents have all passed together, peacefully."

Alan placed both of his hands over his face and squatted down on the floor as the horrible realization set in. All of them are dead. *That's even worse*, he thought. It was bad enough that the baby had died, but her parents also. … *How is this just? How is this right?* Alan wasn't sure how he should feel now—anger, grief, confusion? Everyone in the house was dead, and he had just attacked Simmons. *Would I really have killed him? Would I have done it? My God, what have I become? I'm a monster*, he thought. The emotion that finally came over him was extreme regret. He turned toward Simmons. "I attacked you. I don't know what to say. I don't expect you to forgive me."

"I forgive you," said Simmons in a sincere tone.

"I don't want you to forgive me. I'm not sure I can forgive myself."

Natasha gently placed her hand on Alan's back. "All is well, Alan. We're all at peace."

"I'm sorry that all of you have died."

Natasha and Ivan smiled at him. "Don't worry. We'll see you soon."

Alan turned toward Simmons and said, "I don't think I can do this any longer." The other man put his hand up as if to prevent Alan from saying anymore.

"No. It's mostly my fault. I should've shown you this earlier. I should've given you more of the picture. I try not to reveal too much to those I train, so that they are able to comprehend the full meaning of what we do rather than being overwhelmed by confusion and disbelief. You, however, caught on very quickly and have a good sense of acceptance. I should've accommodated for that."

"You haven't revealed very much about yourself, but I've picked up a lot from your mannerisms and demeanor. I've come to know these traits in others. It's the perks of being a cop," Alan said, attempting to make a joke. "I know what you are."

Simmons looked as if he were curious to see whether his new student was correct in his assumptions. "So what am I?"

"You're a soldier—a peacemaker. I know this well. Those are the roles I've played in my own life. From what I've learned recently, death and peace go hand-in-hand. I know *what* you are but I don't know *who* you are. So I'll ask the question: who are you, Michael Simmons?

"You're very perceptive. I was once a man just like you, a very long time ago. My background is large, vast, and unimportant. But what *is* important is what we must do. Our mission, our objective   that's what matters now."

Alan smiled. "Spoken like a true soldier."

Simmons smiled back. "Stay here. I'll be right back."

Alan nodded and sank onto the bed. As Simmons opened the bed-room door, he and Ivan stepped through. Natasha followed, carrying tiny Anna in her loving arms.

CHAPTER TWENTY-EIGHT

"Has this world been so kind to you that
you should leave with regret? There are better
things ahead than any we leave behind."

—C. S. Lewis

M OMENTS LATER SIMMONS RETURNED, "Okay, let's go."
Alan rose to his feet as Simmons opened the door once more and a blinding flash of light poured through.

"What's going on?" asked Alan, somewhat startled.

"I'm going to show you what's beyond the hallways and doors."

Alan hesitated. "But I won't be…dead…will I?"

Simmons smiled. "No, not at all. Everything will be all right. You'll be back soon. Please, follow me."

As the two stepped through the door, fear and excitement overwhelmed Alan. The blinding light gave way to sunbeams streaming down from far above and he realized that they were walking in a narrow rift valley that seemed to go on forever. The sides of the valley were deep and intimidating, and Alan tried to fight off the anxiety rising inside him. As they walked along Alan noticed that Simmons was no longer wearing a suit but was dressed in a white shirt and pants under a long, white cloak that was trimmed with gold, and he was carrying a white marble walking staff in his right hand.

Simmons paused for a moment to let Alan catch up and walk beside him. After some distance, the chasm began to grow wider, and Alan noticed that the sides changed gradually from a rocky surface to that of a wooded terrain.

"What is this place?"

"It's been called many things. The bridge, the path, the valley."

The valley, Alan thought. "The valley," he said it out loud. "The valley of death?"

Simmons stopped and looked at him. "The valley of death?" Alan repeated, sounding curious.

"Yes, the valley of death. You know—*Yea, though I walk through the valley of the shadow of death, I will fear no evil, for Thou art with me.* It's true—this is what they spoke of!" Alan said excitedly.

"Yes, others have spoken of this place." Simmons nodded.

They continued on for a great distance farther, but they never seemed to tire. As they came to the end of the valley, the path began to ascend. Alan noticed a structure on the horizon a long distance away. They had now been walking along the grassy path of a great meadow. A gentle breeze blew through the knee-high grass, and a leaf glided by before drifting off into the distance. The rays of sun kept the atmosphere at a perfect temperature, neither too hot nor too cold. *Peace*, thought Alan. *This is what peace looks like.*

Simmons said, "I know you'll have many questions, so I have made arrangements for you to meet an advisor, and in many ways he will be your teacher." Alan nodded, and the two continued onward.

As they moved forward, the building Alan had seen in the distance began to take shape and it was beginning to look familiar. They continued out of the meadow and joined the path on the other side, which was now very wide, twenty or twenty-five feet across. It was no longer made of dirt, but appeared to be a road constructed out of polished, square stones. Alan marveled at the smooth pathway, but his eyes were fixed on the structure they were slowly approaching. He stopped in his tracks in awe as he gasped at the huge building, which now resembled an enormous multileveled arena. His gaze drifted over to a huge stone archway that was the main entryway, which had two small openings on either side. His mind raced back to an ancient history course he'd been forced to take in college to satisfy an elective requirement. *I've seen this before*, he thought.

As they drew closer Alan could make out carvings on the front and sides of the monument—people, animals. And the columns, those columns...

Simmons noticed his reaction and stopped.

As if a lightbulb had been switched on in his head, Alan exclaimed, "It's Rome...it's ancient Rome! I remember; I studied this in college. I can't believe it—that's the Coliseum. And over there, that's the Arch of Constantine. You've re-created ancient Rome!"

"Well, no, we haven't."

Alan was utterly confused. "But all of this...I *recognize* it."

"Everything you see was *here* first. I guess you could say that the ancient Romans re-created this place."

Alan was in complete amazement. "How did they know about this place to replicate it?"

"There have been others who came here, just as you have. They were able to duplicate what they saw."

Alan marveled at the various structures. They were all made of a polished, white material like marble or stone. He surveyed the exterior. Unlike those of ancient Rome, there were no walls surrounding it. As they entered the city, Alan noticed people moving about. Everyone was clad in white or gold robes that very much resembled those of the ancient world. He remembered this from his old college textbooks. Passersby waved or smiled as if they knew both Alan and Simmons.

They made their way down the road and approached the Coliseum. Alan gazed up at its enormous walls and beautiful arches.

He shook his head. "I've seen pictures of the Coliseum in our world, but I've never seen it intact. The one we have is damaged; large parts are missing."

"Yes, I know. Years ago a man named Vespasian visited here and spent many days studying this building."

"The Roman emperor Vespasian?" asked Alan.

"Yes, that's the one."

They approached a building about four hundred feet wide and one hundred feet tall. Large marble steps led up to a huge entrance also fronted by enormous columns. They passed through the main entryway. More rows of columns now stood before them, forming a walkway that led into another impressive building.

Simmons paused, "In ancient Rome, they called this structure the Temple of Venus and Roma. Its actual name is Illissia Vensilla, which translates in your language to the "caretaker" or "mother" of light. The Romans associated this with their goddess Venus, who represented love, beauty, and fertility. The Greeks believed that this was a representation of their goddess Aphrodite."

Alan stood gazing at the enormous columns for a moment, then asked, "Who was right?"

Simmons turned toward him with a confused look. "I don't understand."

"Who was right? Is it Venus or Aphrodite? Which does this represent?"

"They're both right. Each had their own interpretation. Different people among your world see things in different ways. All of them are correct when they interpret anything with regard to what is right and good, and represents kindness and compassion."

Alan thought for a moment, "And those who associate or justify their actions with what's wrong, with what's evil? That which isn't compassionate or kind?"

"Many of those among the living would use their faith, their beliefs and values, to justify their feelings of hatred or carry out acts of evil, that which is inconsiderate and cruel—all based on a proclamation of acting on behalf of the light. However, they act in the name of darkness and all that's wrong. They act in concert with those whom we fight." Simmons paused briefly, then continued. "Some of those who occupied this city in your world fell onto the wrong path and came to serve the darkness."

"Every society has people who are good and bad," Alan said with a serious look on his face.

"Correct."

Alan noticed that Simmons's face looked drawn, as if the bad part of society made him sad. He quickly changed the subject. "There aren't any walls around the city, like those in our ancient Rome."

"No, we've no need for them. We're a good distance from any battle that might take place. It's quite safe here."

"Is this your main city, your capital?"

Simmons chuckled. "Oh, no, this is a small city. As you would say, it's on the outskirts of our realm."

Alan tried to imagine what a *bigger* city would look like, if this were a small one. He wanted to take everything in and remember it. He took out a pen and pad and began to scribble some notes, something that was second nature to him as a police officer. *I must remember this*, he thought. *It's fantastic—beyond belief.* His thoughts raced ahead to his daughter and how one day he would sit her on his knee and tell her the story of how he saw the great city, how he saw paradise, how he visited heaven.

As they entered the temple area, Simmons motioned to him. "Follow me. There's someone I want you to meet. He'll teach you more about this place and other things you'll need to know. Listen carefully to him, Alan, for knowledge is the key to power over the darkness."

Chapter Twenty-Nine

*"Love is missing someone
whenever you're apart, but somehow
feeling warm inside because
you're close in heart."*

—Kay Knudsen

A S THEY CAME TO THE CENTER OF THE temple, they approached an older man who looked vaguely familiar. He was as tall as Alan, with a thin face, short, gray hair, and a trim, white beard. His appearance reminded Alan of a history professor he'd had in college because he radiated both wisdom and patience. Looking into his eyes, Alan felt a sense of calmness surrounded by an aura of kindness—a person truly at peace.

Simmons turned to Alan. "I believe you two have met before. You knew him as Mr. Andrew Kratson." Simmons motioned to the man, who extended his hand.

Alan shook his hand and fought hard to remember. *Kratson*, he thought. "I recall the name, but forgive me, I can't remember from where."

Mr. Kratson smiled, "You were at my house. I owe you a debt of gratitude, first for trying to save my life, but most of all for the kindness you showed my wife and family."

Recognition washed over Alan as he recalled that Mr. Kratson was the man he had attempted to resuscitate after his fall in the bathroom.

"I thought at first that you'd had a heart attack, but actually you were in the bathroom and had fallen—you slipped on a bar of soap. I couldn't get the door open. You sat up and spoke to me. I thought you were okay, but you were really—" he paused, and Andrew Kratson finished the sentence for him.

"Dead. Yes, the truth was that I'd passed on. I walked downstairs with Michael and he showed me to the hallway, which led me here."

Alan dropped his gaze to the floor and said, "I'm sorry."

"For what? Don't be sorry; you did well. And you helped my family, which I appreciate very much. Besides, you should've seen the look on your face when you saw my body lying on the floor after having just spoken to me! I thought you were going to jump out of your skin." Andrew had a grin on his face. Alan nodded, and a smile came over his face also.

"Well, it was my first experience with the whole…you know, walking -and-talking-dead-people thing. It was quite disturbing."

"Indeed, but enough about that. There are many things you'll need to learn. We'll get started tomorrow morning."

"Morning? So I'm staying overnight?" Alan asked. A slight anxiety came over him, and his mind began to race. He was fascinated by this new world and the chance to see things that most people had only dreamed of in life, but he wasn't sure he wanted to stay for any length of time; after all, he had responsibilities back in his world. His thoughts turned to his family and the worry that his wife and daughter would feel if he didn't come home. The thought of not seeing his wife and not tucking Missy into bed, as he did every night, made him feel a bit homesick.

"I'm concerned for my family," he admitted. "If I don't return home they'll be worried."

Andrew smiled. "You've always made your family your first priority —a very admirable trait, Alan Crane. Don't despair. As you may already know, time is of no consequence between here and where you exist. You'll not lose even a moment with your family."

"And they'll be safe?"

"I assure you, they'll be fine," Andrew replied with confidence.

Feeling somewhat comforted, Alan turned his attention toward another question he had wanted to ask since he'd been told that he was to stay overnight. "Does night actually fall here? I was under the impression that it was light all the time."

"Light and dark refer to the surroundings of good and evil, of what is right and what is wrong, rather than physical illumination. Yes, it does become night here. We have a sun and a moon, just like your realm."

"So your sun and moon are just like ours?"

"Your sun and moon are replicas of ours," replied Andrew.

Alan nodded and remembered what Simmons had told him about everything being original to this world.

Simmons said, "I'll leave you two for now, but I'll check in soon." He left the temple.

Alan asked, "So shall I call you Andrew or Mr. Kratson?"

"Andrew will be fine. However, I am known as Illissia Artone here."

"That's your name here?"

"No. That is what I do. It's my rank, or job. It literally translates in your language to *light advisor* or *teacher*."

"Yes, my language. Michael told me briefly about your language here. He mentioned some of the words, or ranks, as he put it."

"Correct. Our language is not necessarily a language as you would think of it. It's rather a universal understanding. Those who come here are from every part of your world and speak every earthly language, but here they can communicate freely. We call it Illissia Disenution, which literally translates as *the language of the divine*. Some from your world have described it as enlightenment, and others have referred to it as speaking in tongues."

As he walked behind Andrew through the temple, Alan slowly tried to take in everything his new mentor was saying.

"Once I had an experience where I spoke to a woman who had just lost her son," Alan began. "I was in the Marine Corps and assigned to help the family of a young Marine killed by friendly fire. A young Marine who was present with me said that I spoke to the Marine's mother in a different language. But I couldn't remember any of it."

"Yes. I know of the occasion of which you speak. You were speaking to Mrs. Grace Rossi, who'd just lost her son."

Alan's jaw dropped. He was speechless.

"You know about that?" he asked in amazement. "I said something to her. I guess it was something that made her listen. I can't remember, though."

"You said *Dio mi ha detto cosi*…it's Italian, as is she. It means *God has told me so*."

They stopped in front of a white, polished-stone table surrounded by eight matching chairs. Alan's mind was still trying to grasp what Andrew had just told him. He noticed that the table was lavishly decorated with ruby-red place settings and what appeared to be marble plates. It contained a wide variety of food, including various meats, fruits, and vegetables. There was silverware next to each plate and large crystal goblets were placed to one side.

"Please, sit down and eat."

Alan thought this strange and asked, "Will you be joining me?"

"Sure, if that will make you feel more comfortable."

Alan sat down, thinking that Andrew's answer was somewhat obscure. "Do you have to eat here? I was under the impression that everything would be perfect here, that there would be no need for food or drink, nor a need to perform any other bodily tasks."

Andrew sat down. "Mostly, you're correct. To answer your question, no, we don't need to eat here, but you do. As you would in your world, you still need to eat and sleep and so forth. We don't need to eat, but I'll do so if it'll make you feel more at ease."

"So you don't ever get hungry or tired?"

"No. Only the consequences of battle affect everyone here. We'll discuss that more tomorrow."

Alan nodded as he fixed his plate. "So why do I need to eat and sleep while I'm here?"

"Because you're still among the living."

Alan paused. Andrew looked upward as if he were gathering thoughts to expand his explanation. "You're mortal, as many from your world put it."

Alan nodded as if this made the matter clearer, but in fact he was still confused about a great many things. How could he be here in the afterlife when he was still alive? How could Andrew Kratson eat if he wasn't flesh and bone? And who had cooked this meal? Alan chuckled a bit from this last thought, then took a bite of the food. It was unlike anything he had ever eaten before. Everything was the perfect flavor, the perfect temperature, and it all appealed so distinctly to his sense of taste and smell that it eased the tension of the last hours completely.

Andrew ate with him. After they were finished, the two left the table. Andrew led him out of the temple and down a long street lit by metal torches on either side. It was nighttime now and all was dark. Overhead Alan saw a bright, glowing moon and it did indeed look like the moon from his world. They stopped in front of another large structure, this one resembling a small palace, and entered a great foyer with a row of winding stone stairs, which they began to ascend. At the top of the stairs Alan saw a door that resembled many of the doors to which he and Simmons had led people, doors that linked the world of the living to this world.

"You can sleep in here. I'll see you in the morning."

"So is this heaven?"

Andrew raised his eyebrows and smiled once again. "Many have called it that. Others have called it different things. It's the realm of light, the place that contains all things that are good, all the aspects of your world that you would deem right."

Alan nodded again. Andrew turned and descended the stairs. Once he was gone, Alan entered the room. It was a large bedroom, elaborately constructed of the same polished white stone found throughout the city. A bed sat in the middle of the room. Many decorations were hung on the walls, mostly large tapestries depicting great battles. The two sides of the battles were distinctly apparent—each army was clad in white or black armor.

Alan took off his shoes and lay down on the bed. It was very rare that he slept away from home. His mind wandered back to his wife and daughter on a rainy Saturday morning when Missy had been eleven months old and had taken her first steps. Alan had been overjoyed that it happened on the weekend when he was home to see it. *Not a moment of time—Andrew promised I wouldn't miss a moment of time*, he thought. *Guess I'll have to trust him.*

As he fell asleep he wondered whether this whole experience was no more than just a dream. *In the morning I'll know for sure*, he thought. Then sleep overtook him.

CHAPTER THIRTY

"A teacher affects eternity.
He can never tell where his influence stops."

Henry Brooks Adams

MORNING CAME AND LIGHT SHONE through an enormous arched window at the far end of the bedroom. Alan rose feeling extremely well and noticed that he didn't labor from his usual morning backache. He left the room and descended the stairwell to an open dining area where he found a stone table and chairs in the middle of the room that mimicked those from the dining room where he'd eaten the evening before. The table was already set with fruits and meats and two place settings that were made up at one end. He sat down and began eating.

Moments later Andrew joined him. "Did you sleep well, Alan?"

"Yes. Very well."

"Good! When you're finished we will begin your education in the basics of all that we do here."

Alan finished his meal. The two departed the small palace and Andrew led him down a long road out of town and into an open meadow. The air was fresh and the temperature was perfect. Alan noticed a great mountain far off in the distance. As they drew closer, more of the mountain's features came into view. It was bigger than any other mountain Alan had ever seen. The base was bare rock, but forty feet up he could make out a good number of fir trees that colored the middle portion a dark green.

Another thirty minutes or so of walking brought them closer. The size of the mountain triggered a looming, ominous feeling in Alan. They were very close now, but still not at the base. The upper part of the mountain was hidden under a thick blanket of white clouds. White streaks of snow streamed down the visible areas near the top.

Finally they came to the base. Andrew stopped. He turned toward Alan, "Can you see it, the great mountain? Can you see it in its entirety?"

"Well, no. It's too large and we're too close."

"Precisely," said Andrew. He turned back around and continued walking.

Alan found this strange; he'd expected Andrew to say something else to help clarify the situation. They finally came to a set of stone stairs carved into the side of the rock wall. The stairs spiraled upward and out of sight.

"This mountain, it's bigger than anything I've ever seen in my world," Alan said.

"That's because it is larger than anything you have in your world."

"What do you call it? Does it have a name?" asked Alan.

"Well, that depends. Some have called it the mountain of the heavens and others who were here, the Greeks I believe, once called it Mount Olympus. Its name isn't important. You may call it what you like."

"Mount Olympus," said Alan, astonished. "The Mount Olympus of Greek mythology? The place where the Greek gods made their home? So it really exists."

"I guess it exists to some. It's a matter of interpretation as are many things in this world."

Alan's memory flashed back to the painful walk he'd made with Ross and Simmons, up one hundred and two floors. He cringed and reached down to massage his calves and then took a deep breath as he prepared for the rigorous climb.

"Ready?"

"Yes, I guess so," replied Alan, not really feeling very ready at all, but determined to go on.

They started up the stairs. Alan wondered how many there were—hundreds, perhaps thousands. They were narrow, allowing only one person to ascend at a time. The steps were polished and shiny and Alan was cautious, fearing that he might slip and fall. Along the open side of the stairs were metal posts with a circular metal brazier on top of each. The tiny braziers were around eight inches in diameter and illuminated by a steady, blue flame that lit the pathway, causing a wild, reflective design against the smooth, polished wall on the other side of the stairs. It was mesmerizing and beautiful.

Alan soon became aware that he wasn't tired after the long walk up the mountain. He seemed to have an unlimited supply of energy but, as they continued up the steps, he began to feel differently.

After approximately thirty minutes of walking he asked Andrew if they could take a break.

"Of course, we can."

The older man wasn't even winded, nor did he show any signs of stress or perspiration.

Catching his breath, Alan said, "You're in good shape."

Andrew smiled, "Best shape of my life—or should I say after my life." He ended with a booming laugh.

"Good to see that humor exists up here," Alan commented.

"As it should. It adds to all our good spirits." After a few minutes the two continued on. The clouds were now perhaps only fifteen feet overhead. As they entered the cloudbank, Alan felt cool droplets of water on his face. The swirling white mist danced around him, and it was difficult to see even the steps as they continued to ascend. Within a few moments they cleared the top of the clouds, and Alan let out a sigh of frustration. The mountain continued so high up that the peak was *still* invisible.

Andrew noticed his discontent. "Not too much farther. We're not going all the way to the top."

Somewhat relieved, Alan pushed on. As the stairs curved around the massive rock wall, he saw something jutting out from a ledge above them, and as they drew nearer he noticed that it was some type of bridge. They stopped when they reached it, and Alan noticed that it protruded straight out from the ledge and was almost a hundred feet wide. Alan strained to see where it went, but couldn't see the other side.

"This way," said Andrew as he began to walk across.

Alan marveled at the ornate construction. It was dark gray and made of the familiar marble. Massive pillars lined each side and carved statues depicting battle scenes decorated the spaces in between them. They reminded him of the scenes in the tapestries he had seen in his bedchamber—several figures on foot and horseback armed with swords, lances, and bows. The battle scenes clearly showed both sides of the fight; some statues were white marble while others were black. At the center of the battle, Alan stopped to look at one statue that towered above the rest. It was a huge, armor-clad male figure with a long, flowing cloak draped over his back. The figure was holding a massive hammer.

"Wow," said Alan as he continued to gaze up at the statue.

"It is breathtaking when you see these things for the first time," agreed Andrew.

At last, in the distance Alan saw what the bridge connected to on the other side. It looked like a huge castle made of the same gray marble and it had an entrance three times the width of the bridge. An enormous archway with a silvery-white stone portcullis stood open before them.

They passed through the gate and entered a great hall with hundreds of doors on each side. The doors were too large for one person to open and seemed to be made of some type of dark wood. Each was over twenty-five feet wide and thirty feet tall, and had a massive handle about fifteen feet above the ground. The sight was so overwhelming that he had to stop for a moment to marvel at it. He wondered how anyone would be able to reach the handle, but then his thoughts wandered back to the massive statue outside. *Giants*, he thought. *Perhaps they are giants.* He shook his head as if to deny the idea because it was so farfetched, but with all that he had seen recently, the possibility lingered in his mind. The sides of the hall were lined with wooden benches. Behind the benches stood suits of mail armor, and along the walls were various weapons—spears, swords, and bows. As he peered up to the ceiling, about one hundred feet above him, he saw tiny glints of glittering gold.

Andrew noticed Alan peering upward. "Shields."

"Shields?" Alan asked, shaking his head in confusion.

"The tiny glints on the ceiling are shields. They were once used in battle, but now decorate the hall."

Alan continued to look up in amazement.

Andrew continued, "This place has been called many things."

Alan was now used to hearing this.

"The Norsemen labeled this great hall Vallhalla. Others who have visited have called the entranceway the gates of heaven, or as some say, the pearly gates. This is, however, a place where we learn—perhaps more like a school or library from your world."

"Tell me about the Norsemen who were here," requested Alan.

"As you know, we need people from your world to assist from time to time with guiding those who have passed. The Norsemen we recruited were brought here, where they stayed to learn what they must do. They would meet with those who had passed, and we would set out a great feast on their first evening here. It made them feel more comfortable. Of course, those with whom they met, those who had passed on into this realm, did not need to eat, but they did so out of courtesy and respect.

So those Norsemen whom we recruited as Illissia Galau went back to tell the others the story of how they had met the heroes of their past and had eaten with them at a great feast in the hall of Valhalla. They told of the great hall whose walls were lined with weapons and armor from the warriors of their past and whose roof was thatched with golden shields. They told of the great hall that their chief god, Odin, had built himself, and how it contained five hundred massive doors—doors that would release eight hundred warriors who would fight in Ragnarok."

"Ragnarok. I'm a little rusty on my mythology."

"Ragnarok, a great battle that the Norse believed to be the predestined death of their gods."

Alan nodded as he took in the information. "Come this way," said Andrew. They crossed the great hall and exited through one of the massive doors at the back that stood open, then entered another room, not quite as large, but with a circular pool with multiple stone-carved benches surrounding it in the center.

"Now for some basics," Andrew started.

Alan looked at the pool and noticed the water swirling in small circles in different areas. "Look at the pool. You'll see that on this end is the light."

Andrew pointed to one end of the pool. The water there suddenly transformed into the familiar white marble rock, creating a miniature replica of this world. "And on the other side you will see the darkness." Andrew motioned to the other end of the pool, where polished, black obsidian rock formed from the water in jagged pieces.

"The realm of the darkness, it appears smaller."

"Yes, very observant. It is smaller," confirmed Andrew.

Andrew walked to the side of the pool and positioned himself between the two lands. "I'll need you to come closer." Alan obliged and moved closer to the edge of the pool. Andrew pointed to the center, "And here is your world, the world of the living."

Alan couldn't see anything. He waited a moment for something to rise up from the water. Finally he said, "I'm sorry Andrew. I can't see it."

Andrew smiled. "Look closer."

Alan strained hard at the swirling water. "I can't see it. Can you point to it?"

Andrew extended his hand and pointed at the middle of the pool. "It's not *in* the water; just above it."

Alan strained his eyes, trying to see where Andrew was directing him.

"I'm sorry, I just don't see it," Alan repeated, feeling foolish and frustrated.

"Allow me to point it out it for you." Andrew passed his hand across the pool. Then Alan could see a faint, glowing speck of gold near the center of the pool.

"There's a speck…a piece of dust perhaps, a grain of sand. What is this I'm looking at again? I forgot what you said."

"This is your world, the world of the living."

"What?" exclaimed Alan. "That *speck—that* represents our world? It's insignificant compared to the others."

"It has much significance and value. I merely wanted to show you the comparisons in scale of the different realms. The living realms are but a speck compared to the two others, but do not devalue them. They are of great importance."

"Living realms? As in, more than one? So we're not the only—"

Andrew interrupted with a slight chuckle. "No! Did you think that your world, your planet, was the only place among the living? Here, let me show you the others."

He waved his hand back and forth slowly in front of the pool. Alan was stunned as thousands of tiny specks began to appear before him.

"All of those?" he whispered. "All of those are out there?"

"Why, yes. It seems you are beginning to understand the basics of *what* exists. Now perhaps we can move to some basics of *why*."

Alan nodded and waited for him to speak further. "You see before you the position of the living realms between the light and the darkness. They are, in fact, neutral ground, a halfway point."

The word rolled out of Alan's mouth. "Purgatory?"

"Some have described it in such a way."

"But purgatory is a place where you go to after you die if your soul is trapped between heaven and hell. How can purgatory exist while you're alive in our world?"

"Who said that the trapped souls were among the living? Do you not think it possible that there are those from your world who have passed from the living and are trapped in your world—those who are never led one way or another?" asked Andrew as a teacher would quiz his student to spark intuitive thought.

"Well…I guess if I didn't think that possible before, I do now."

"Indeed. So you see, the worlds of the living exist to feed the light and the darkness."

"I never realized that all of this existed, that all of this is as you say it is."

Andrew nodded his head. "Yes, but you must realize that as much as I tell you and show you, there is an infinite amount that you haven't seen, nor could ever understand. There are things that I myself haven't seen nor understood, nor ever will."

On this note, Alan grew somewhat confused. "I don't completely follow you."

"Do you remember when we reached the base of the mountain?"

"Yes."

"And if you were to press your nose against the cold rock of the mountain, could you see how grand and large and significant it was?"

"Well, no."

"And why not?" asked Andrew.

"Well, I couldn't see the entire mountain once we got close to it. If I had my nose pressed against it, I certainly wouldn't be able to see any of it—it's too large."

"Exactly. So it is in this world. The things that occur here and in your world all feed into the Illissia Finistonus."

"The what?"

"Illissia Finistonus, which you could perhaps translate to *way of the light* or *a master plan*. It's our mission and vision, the path we all take. It's why we exist and what drives everything we do," said Andrew.

"So in my world, in our small speck of dust, understanding is limited because the scope is so great?"

"Precisely. You know this is true. How many have you spoken to in your world who've grieved over the death of a loved one? How many have asked you why, why has this happened? How many times have you struggled for an answer and felt despair because you didn't have one? The only thing you could've concluded was that there was no answer. To those among your world, this thing you call death seems so meaningless. Sometimes it seems like a waste. Or perhaps it's too large to see the entire picture—the entire mountain."

Alan felt himself go pale as he contemplated these thoughts. He could relate to every word that Andrew was saying. This was quickly becoming the most important conversation of his life.

He looked down at the floor and continued to listen. Andrew went on. "Now you understand a little more than those who grieve. Now you know a bit more, a very small piece of the puzzle. You now possess a small portion of understanding about what some have called an unbiased, invisible pattern: Death."

"Invisible pattern?" Alan repeated.

"Yes. From the perspective of those among the living in your world, death takes no specific path or course. It shows no bias. It cares not what significance or insignificance you have within your world. It takes souls at random and is unseen. However, you are starting to see that this isn't true. You are starting to see that there are reasons. Death is purposeful. You'll know much more by the time you go back to your world."

"But what of human suffering? There is much suffering in our world associated with death—pain, grief. Is that planned?

"No," Andrew shook his head. "The light is everything that is compassionate, kind, and good. The light is there to comfort and make right. Death is a mere passageway to a new life, a new responsibility, a sense of endless hope. Sometimes grief is caused by a lack of understanding, but suffering and hopelessness only exist because of the darkness. Circumstances are created, based on choices made by the living, that sometimes lead to pain and hurt."

Alan shook his head. "I understand, but shouldn't the light intervene to prevent those things from happening and stop the horrible atrocities of life that occur?"

Andrew looked at Alan with sympathy. "The light bestows the gift of choice upon the living as an act of love, kindness, and compassion. Limiting such a gift would not be right. I'm sure you've heard of the term *free will,* but with this gift comes the possibility of pain and grief. However, you must remember that when those horrible things occur, the light is there to console, to heal, to help make right."

Andrew paused. "I think that's enough for you to absorb for one day. You'll stay here tonight. If you go back into the great hall there will be food, and you'll be directed to a place where you can rest."

"How can you know all of this? You died only a few months ago?" Alan looked at Andrew inquisitively.

"I've been studying this for over one hundred years. Time here is not related to time among the living. A few months ago in your world could be centuries here."

"One more question. Who made the Illissia Finistonus, the master plan?"

"The light, of course."

"The light? So the light is God, I assume—and God is the leader here? He is the light?"

"There have been many names for the light, and no one name is incorrect. The light is neither male nor female. It is a supremely divine entity that is all-knowing and all-loving, and composed of all that is good and right. The light, or God, as you say, created the Illissia Finistonus and can see and understand all; it knows the entire mountain in all its greatness and size."

Alan nodded in agreement. "And the darkness—I suppose the darkness has a leader?"

"Yes," replied Andrew in a depressed voice. "Unfortunately it does. Many have cast names such as Satan or the devil to describe it. The way we refer to their leader is what I've said before—the darkness, the dark one. Their leader is the mirror opposite of the light—all that is bad and wrong. But remember this: the light is stronger than the darkness, because the darkness was once among the light."

Alan nodded. He was done asking questions; he'd had all he could handle for one day.

Andrew seemed to notice this as he said, "Go get something to eat, then rest. Tomorrow we will go over our basic structure here, our ranking systems and duties. You'll need to understand them before we get into the actual concepts of battle."

Alan walked from the room back into the great hall, where he found the familiar stone table with the variety of assorted, freshly prepared food. A woman appeared at his table. He thought she looked somewhat familiar. "Do I know you?" he asked.

"Yes. I'm Natasha Malanikov. I teach here, as Andrew does."

Alan then remembered her from the recent gas leak when she, her husband, and their daughter had died from carbon monoxide poisoning in their home.

"Oh yes. Good to see you again. Is your husband here also?"

"Yes—he's teaching here, too."

"And how is your baby?"

"Oh, very well. You'll meet her soon."

The statement seemed odd to Alan, who remembered holding her baby daughter in his arms only a few days ago. Nevertheless, he ignored the comment and finished his meal. When he was done, Natasha directed him to one of the massive doors. It swung open on its own, the three enormous hinges on the left side of the frame creaking from the weight. Alan followed a winding staircase to a bedroom that resembled the one from the night before. As he lay in bed staring at the ceiling, visions of the things he had seen raced through his mind. The long walk up to the great mountain, or Mount Olympus, as the Greeks and Romans might say. He imagined the Norsemen sitting at the stone tables in the halls of Valhalla, speaking to their fallen heroes as they anticipated pouring forth from the great doors, the hordes of heroes who would defend the gods. His mind wandered to the room with the pool and the thousands of specks of light that represented various worlds. He then turned his final thoughts to the way of the light, the master plan, the light and his adversary, the darkness. He reflected on the concepts of battle that would soon be described to him. As all of this filled his mind, he eventually drifted off to sleep and dreamed of what was most dear to him: his wife and daughter.

CHAPTER THIRTY-ONE

*"If you know the enemy and know yourself,
you need not fear the results of
a hundred battles."*

—Sun Tzu

T HE NEXT MORNING CAME QUICKLY. Alan awoke feeling as refreshed as he had after the first night. He wandered down to the table where he had eaten dinner and found it set for breakfast. He ate it quickly. Andrew appeared, sat down next to him, and sipped on a cup of tea. Once they were finished, Andrew led him back to the room with the pool to continue his lessons.

"We'll begin today with some fundamentals. As you've probably heard, we use various ranks and titles for different duties here. I assume you are already familiar with some of them?" Andrew paused as he saw the blank look on Alan's face. "Then again, perhaps you could use a review. Let's start with you: Illissia Galau, meaning light guide, or the one who leads others to the light. This is your rank—your position." Andrew waited to see Alan's reaction.

Alan nodded his head, "Yes, I've heard those words before. *That* at least does make sense."

"Good. My position is called Illissia Artone, which means light advisor, or teacher. I educate those who are here, and occasionally some from your realm, about our mission and duties."

"I see."

"There are many other positions, duties, and such. But right now I want to concentrate on the ranks related to our soldiers, as these will be important to the concepts of battle, which we'll go over tomorrow." Andrew watched Alan to make sure he was understanding what he was saying.

"The basic unit of battle is called a Seristrum, which is composed of eighteen warriors of different rank and skill," he continued. "The first basic rank is called Illissia Elosa, which is like a foot soldier. Illissia Elosa, or *light foot soldiers* if translated literally, makes up the majority of the Seristrum. We assign eight to the unit. They have the lowest level of battle skill and power, but they're a crucial portion of the Seristrum, as they provide the front-line protection and are among the first to engage the enemy. Each foot soldier is armed with a shield and short blade for close combat.

"Next we have two Illissia Helios, who are skilled archers armed with bows that we craft specifically for battle with those of the dark forces. They engage the enemies from a distance in an attempt to repel them from advancing on the higher ranks. Their tactics include long, straight-line shots and the arrows must strike the enemy squarely in order to have any effect. Any shot that does not hit straight on will fail. These archers possess a higher degree of battle skill and power than the foot soldiers.

"After the archers we have the Illissia Equine, our horsemen. Two horsemen are assigned to the Seristrum. These very skilled riders are equipped with a heavy lance. They drive back whatever forces overtake the light foot soldiers in close combat and make their way through the volleys of arrows from the opposing archers. Their maneuverability allows them to attack quickly and from various angles as they sweep down on the enemy. The horsemen possess greater battle skills and power than the archers.

"The fourth rank within the Seristrum is called the Illissia Strengos. They are the heavy warriors who wield huge swords. They're extremely skilled and agile in combat and typically stay back in the field of battle to guard the upper ranks of the Seristrum; but, if needed, they can move very quickly against the enemy. They possess greater battle skill and power even than the horsemen, composing as they do a segment of the upper portion of the unit.

"The second-highest rank within the Seristrum is called the Illissia Arcana, the battle master. This rank is the most skilled in combat. He or she is equipped with two blades and is deadly with each. The battle masters can quickly cover large areas of ground and close in on enemies from any angle, making them the most effective warrior on the field of battle. Their battle skills and power far exceed the others within the Seristrum."

Noticing that Alan was rubbing his temples, Andrew paused.

"So if the battle master is the most skilled and powerful within the unit, then why is that not the highest rank?"

"Ah, good question," said Andrew. "The highest rank within the Seristrum is called the Illissia Alona, or the light bringer. The light bringer holds the power of the light that feeds the rest of the unit energy or *spirit*, as some might call it. Without the Illissia Alona the rest of the Seristrum will fail. Without the light bringer, the unit will fall."

Andrew stopped for a moment then continued, "The light bringer holds the highest rank in the Seristrum and doesn't engage in battle unless there's an extremely dire need."

Andrew stopped and faced Alan and, as any good teacher would do, paused for a quick review. "What are the ranks of the Seristrum?"

Alan drew a deep breath and smiled. "I wasn't aware there'd be a test at the end." Andrew smiled as Alan continued.

"Here goes: Eight Illissia Elosa, the light footmen, compose the front line of defense. Two Illissia Helios, the archers, help keep the enemy at a distance and thin their numbers. There are two horsemen, the Illissia Equine, who wield heavy lances to close on the faster-moving enemy forces. The Illissia Strengos, the heavy warriors, provide the last line of defense and stay toward the back of the battle until needed. Behind them all we have the Illissia Arcana, our battle master, who because of their extreme skill and power can move to any portion of the battle when needed. Finally, we have the light bringer, the Illissia Alona, who provides the unit with energy or *spirit*."

Alan looked toward Andrew as if to check to see if he was right. "Correct. The light bringer holds the light and supports the entire Seristrum. Very well done! Most people can't remember all the ranks, especially their first time through. You did extremely well."

"Thank you. But I have another question. You said that the Seristrum was composed of eighteen positions, but you've only named sixteen. What are the other two?"

"The other two do not engage in battle, though they are crucial to the Seristrum. They are the first two I described, the Illissia Galau and the Illissia Artone—you and I."

It took a few moments for the words to sink in. When they did, Alan said, "So we're part of this unit?"

"Yes. Tomorrow we'll go and meet them so that you can see how they function." Andrew proceeded to go over the ranks in more detail, occasionally quizzing Alan on what he'd learned.

It was getting to be around midday when Alan started to feel hungry. "Are we eating lunch anytime soon?"

"Of course—forgive me for pushing you for so long without a break. When you return, we'll go over the basic ranks and units of the other side."

"The other side?" repeated Alan.

"Yes. Those who fight for the darkness also have a rank and structure that you'll need to know. Go eat and return when you're finished."

After Alan was done with lunch, he returned to the same room. Andrew wasn't there yet, so he sat down on a stone bench and tried to recall all of the things he'd heard earlier today. It was all very overwhelming; he tried to convince himself that he wasn't dreaming.

After a few moments, Andrew came back into the room. "Ready?"

"Sure, why not?" Alan replied as he half smiled and shrugged.

"The enemy unit is a mirror image of ours. Their ranks are as follows: Balliste Galau, Balliste Artone, Balliste Elosa, Balliste Helios, Balliste Equine, Balliste Strengos, Balliste Arcana, and Balliste Alona. As you probably noticed, their ranks are similarly named except for the prefix of Balliste, which translates to *dark* or *darkness*. Their ranks are of the same order and are structured according to skill and power almost exactly as ours are."

Alan interrupted. "You keep mentioning skill and power. I'm not sure that I'm following you. The stronger or higher ranks are more 'battle-ready' and possess a greater 'skill' or proficiency with their weapons?"

Andrew replied, "It's hard for me to describe such things. The demonstration tomorrow will prove more effective, I believe. For right now," he paused, trying to derive a suitable explanation, "I guess you could say that battle skill and power among our warriors is more related to their effectiveness in defeating the enemy. Physical size isn't as much a factor as the power that is derived from the light. Tomorrow you'll understand what I mean."

"Okay," Alan replied, dropping the subject. His mind was too full with all of the other topics that had been covered this day.

Andrew spent the rest of the day reviewing everything they had learned and showed Alan some of the armor and weapons used in battle. Alan's eyelids drooped at last, and Andrew must have noticed his fatigue. "Maybe we should stop for today," he said. "Tomorrow we'll go to the training grounds and observe our Seristrum as they ready themselves for battle. I'll meet you here in the morning."

"I'll see you then," replied Alan wearily.

As he lumbered out of the room his eyes came to rest on a suit of armor that stood just outside the doorway to the great hall. One tattered helmet sat on top of an assortment of armor; a large gash ran down its side. Alan tried to imagine what type of force would have been necessary to do such damage. The sight made him wonder if the blow had been fatal—or, for that matter, what was "fatal" here, since everyone here was already dead. Running his finger over the hole in the helmet, he found that the stone from which it was made must have been very sharp as he cut his finger and a drop of blood trickled down and splashed onto the white, marble breastplate. *I wonder if they bleed*, Alan thought. Many questions from the day hung in his mind, but he found himself exhausted from too much thinking, so he continued into the great hall where he knew dinner was waiting for him.

CHAPTER THIRTY-TWO

"Knowing others is intelligence;
knowing yourself is true wisdom.
Mastering others is strength;
mastering yourself is true power."

—Lao Tzu

WHEN DAYLIGHT CAME THROUGH THE WINDOW, Alan quickly dressed and made his way down to the dining hall, as he now called it. He thought to himself, *Well, I've made it to day four—or is it day three?* He was starting to forget how long he'd been away. His thoughts bounced back to his family, and he felt uneasy.

"Ready to go?" asked Andrew, walking into the hall.

"Sure. I'll skip breakfast today."

Andrew noticed the troubled look on Alan's face. "Everything okay?"

"I think I'm losing track of time. To be honest with you, I really miss my family."

Andrew nodded. "You'll see them soon. But I understand. I once had to take a trip out of town that kept me away for a month. I was so homesick that I wrote letters to my family every night—no e-mail back in those days."

Alan gave a slight smile. "What did you do for a living?"

"I sold vacuum cleaners. I'd often go out of town to negotiate large sales contracts, and I'd always tell my wife, 'Don't worry, honey. I'm sure I'm going to clean up on this deal,'" said Andrew with another boisterous laugh.

Alan rolled his eyes. "That's gotta be one of the worst jokes I've ever heard, Andrew."

"I know," replied the old man, still grinning from ear to ear.

"Let's get going before you attempt any more humor."

"Well then, follow me." They proceeded out of the great hall and began descending the mountain. Once they had cleared the cloudbank, Alan asked, "Where exactly do they train?"

"In the great arena, back in the city. The place you called the Coliseum."

"Ah, that would make sense."

By the time they reached the entrance to the Coliseum the sun was overhead and shining down on the magnificent arcs of the enormous structure. Alan marveled at the intricately carved stone of the huge archway as they passed through into the main arena. Andrew turned to the right and went up a set of stairs that led to a raised tier of stone benches. Sitting down in the first row, he motioned for Alan to join him.

Eight people gradually emerged out of one of the openings on the arena floor, all clad in white armor that reflected the sunlight as if it had a mirrored coating. The armor seemed to be the same white marblelike material as the suit of armor he had cut his finger on in the great hall. All eight carried small shields and short, white blades. They were sparring with the eight other people clad in dark mail shirts and greaves.

"There," said Andrew, pointing toward the eight. "The Illissia Elosa, our light foot soldiers." The eight were all different height and size. However, despite the differences in size and height, Alan noticed that each of them seemed to be equally matched in skill with their swordplay. As they parried, blocked, wove, and thrust, Alan came to the conclusion that all eight were very good at fencing and seemed skillful at fighting. The opponents in the dark mail were also extremely fast and agile, using a dark staff to throw flurries of attacks toward the white, armor-clad fighters. Occasionally, one would land a blow on the shoulder or side of the small skullcap helmet worn by the eight, but most of the blows were warded off by a quick block with a shield and a rapid counterblow of their blade that scraped across the dark mail shirts.

"Impressive," said Alan.

"That's nothing," replied Andrew. He pointed to the other end of the arena floor.

A good distance away, Alan saw two people approaching, both clad in light mail. Both carried great, white, curved bows in their hands with a large quiver draped across their backs. Each put arrows into their bows and aimed at small, black, square slabs fixed to a short column at the other end of the arena. Alan estimated the distance at over one hundred yards and wondered if the two archers could even see the tiny, one-by-one-foot square targets. As the two archers released the arrows Alan saw two streaks of white light impacting as they exploded in a white-hot shower of gleaming blue sparks. Once the archers had released the first two arrows, they backed up ten or so yards, and continued to back up after each shot. They were accurate each time, each shot exploding within the center of the square.

"Yes," said Andrew, "these are our archers, our Illissia Helios. And there at the other side," he pointed to two magnificent metal-clad horses and riders emerging from another entryway, "are our Illissia Equine, our horseman."

Alan watched as the two horsemen lined up on the opposite side of the arena floor and took turns charging two other horsemen, all equipped with lances. The two Illissia Equine were very skilled; they knocked the other riders off their mounts without breaking stride.

As Alan watched the jousting match, he felt Andrew grab his shoulder. "Look, down there—you see the two on the other side, those two? Illissia Strengos, our heavy warriors."

Alan looked in the direction and noticed two figures clad in heavy, white armor equipped with full-shielded helmets, each carrying a gleaming white sword. The two stood back-to-back as ten opponents circled them and closed in. Alan was astonished as he watched the two fighters swing the great swords with ease, striking multiple attackers and hurling them to the ground. *The weight of their armor and swords must not encumber them at all*, he thought. *They move as if they were wearing regular clothing and were swinging nothing heavier than a broomstick.*

"They must be incredibly strong," said Alan.

"Well, yes. They're skilled and powerful."

Alan was mesmerized by the combat from all of the fighters on the floor. He failed to notice the numerous dark figures gathered near the very center of the arena to whom Andrew now redirected his attention. Alan turned and looked, counting eighteen opponents in total, each carrying long, dark sticks made of a dark marble, much like that he had seen in the hallways.

"What are they doing?"

"Preparing." Andrew pointed to another corner of the arena where a short figure had appeared from another entryway. As the figure drew nearer, Alan could see that he was clad in white armor, lighter than the heavy warriors' armor yet heavier than that of the light footman. The helmet covered the entire back of the head, sides of the face, and bridge of the nose; two archlike openings on each side allowed for the eyes and chin to be exposed.

"The Illissia Arcana," said Andrew. "The battle master."

As the figure approached the eighteen opponents in the center of the arena, he drew two thin, curved swords from his back. The battle master walked into the midst of the attackers, who formed a huge circle around him. The circle began to close in as the dark sticks started swinging toward the small figure. In an instant, seven opponents were toppled from their feet as the battle master moved at blinding speed. At one point it seemed that he danced over the heads of his opponents. Alan saw the dark sticks being flung high into the air and landing several feet from those who had wielded them. Within moments the battle master had systematically disarmed and subdued the entire circle. Alan sat in awe at the sheer speed.

As the battle master ran around the group of eighteen, now lying on the ground, one of the horsemen attempted to catch up to him.

"It's unbelievable," commented Alan. "He outran that horse. Nobody can move that fast—it's impossible. I'd love to meet him."

"Certainly. But first I need to introduce you to someone else."

Two men were walking up the stone stairs. One of them Alan recognized—it was Simmons, who greeted him with a nod. The other was a tall, blond man dressed in a white tunic, pants, and a long cloak. Alan noticed a thin chain belt around his waist with a short sheath and handle fixed at his side.

"Alan," said Andrew, "this is Darion—Illissia Alona—the light bringer."

Alan shook the man's hand, "Nice to meet you."

"Nice to finally meet you. If I may, I want to extend my sincere appreciation for a job well done. You've equipped me with a fine Seristrum."

Alan paused for a moment and seemed a bit confused. Darion picked up on his bewilderment. "Come, let me introduce you to some of them so that you may further understand."

The four of them walked down the stairs and entered the arena floor, where they approached a few of the light foot soldiers standing nearby.

As Alan drew close, one of them said, "Alan! Or should I say Officer Crane? I wanted to thank you again for helping me." Alan looked at the face and thought that he recognized him. He was younger than Alan expected, but familiar. "It's me—maybe you don't remember? It's me, Ross McDonald."

Alan raised his eyebrows and was taken aback. "Ross—you're the kid from the party, the one who drank too much. You died. Yes, I remember. We led you—" Alan paused for a moment, then concluded, "—I guess we led you here."

"Yes, you did, and I appreciate it. The others are here as well."

Alan looked at another figure who had taken off his helmet and was standing next to Ross. He looked at the face and realized who it was.

"Billy?" said Alan. "Billy Cox from the accident?"

"Yes. Amy's here also." Amy Lansing turned around and greeted Alan.

"What about the girls, the two who were also involved in the accident? I can't recall their names—are they here?"

"Yes, we're here," said a voice from behind him. As he turned around, he saw the two girls sitting on top of the two armored horses. "Melissa, and my sister Emma Bornhopp," said the girl as a reminder.

"I'm sorry, it's been a while and—"

"No need for apologies," said Emma. "You helped all of us get where we needed to go."

Dumbfounded, Alan continued to look around. He was speechless as the two heavily armored warriors approached. They both removed their full helmets to reveal two younger men Alan didn't recognize at all. As he was about to speak, the battle master began to approach the group.

He refocused on him and said to Darion, "I don't know who trained him, but he defeated eighteen opponents and can move faster than anything I've ever seen. He's an incredible fighter." The small figure stood in front of him and let out a laugh. As the half-helmet was lifted, long locks of red hair fell down across her small face; Alan now saw that the battle master was a woman.

"My deepest apologies, ma'am," Alan said to her. "I shouldn't have assumed—"

"No apology is necessary, Alan. Like all the others, you helped me get here."

The battle master smiled, "I see that you don't recognize some of us—the twins back there in the heavy armor, don't you recall? Gregory and David?"

"The little boys who died in the fire, Gregory and David Chelsey. But you were only four years old!"

David spoke. "Time is not the same between the realm of the living and here."

"I know, I know," said Alan, nodding his head. "I've heard that many times." He focused his gaze again on the red-haired woman in front of him.

"You still don't recognize me, do you Alan?"

"I'm sorry, I don't."

She smiled once again. "Think hard. You've met me before. You brought me here—you carried me."

As the last words rolled off her lips Alan realized who she was. *You carried me here.* The words stuck in his head. His jaw dropped open as he whispered, "Anna—is that you? Anna Malanikov? You were the baby, the baby who died. I can't believe it."

"Yes, and now you see that everything has turned out very well. I'm no longer a frail infant. I owe you a great deal of thanks for your compassion and concern. You protected me and carried me here."

"You're very welcome," Alan said, looking down, almost shy before this great hero—a hero he had once carried in his arms as a babe. It was too much to take in.

"Look at me, Alan," she said. He raised his eyes to look at her face. "Everything's okay. Do you understand more now than you did at my death?"

"I'm beginning to understand. I have a feeling, though, that there is much more to come."

As Alan looked around him, he began to recognize the other faces. Tyris Cotton and Maddie Klinstrom each held great bows in their hands. He saw Angie Krofts, the teen who had been depressed and taken her life, and Nick Swanolski, the clerk from the gas station who had been murdered. He also recognized Leslie Wallace, who had died when her car struck a tree.

One of the foot soldiers approached. "Mr. Crane, you probably don't recognize me. Simmons actually led me here. I'm Randal Sweeny."

Alan paused for a moment to think, then replied, "Yes, I remember your name. We suspected that you had killed Nick at the gas station during the robbery."

Nick Swanolski spoke up. "Randal didn't do it. It was someone else. I couldn't see his face. Randal made some mistakes, but he didn't kill me. I'm glad he made it here to help us."

"We're still looking for the one who did it," said Alan. "Anything else you remember about the person who took your life, Nick?"

Nick thought for a moment, then said, "He stabbed me. The blade was cold and dark, like those used by the Balliste."

Alan looked around for some more clarification. "Andrew, can you translate?"

"Balliste," said Andrew. "The enemy—remember, we discussed it yesterday? The darkness uses weapons similar to ours. Their weapons are made of darkness. Black stone. Nick thinks that it may have been a blade of theirs. I'm unsure what this means."

Alan turned toward Randal. "How'd you die, Randal?"

"I was pushed off a bridge. My body ended up in the river, but no one's found it yet. I robbed the gas station because I needed money for my daughter's medicine. I'd do anything to make her better. I'd do anything—even die." For a moment all were silent. Then Randal continued. "I knew I was wrong in what I'd done, but I never killed anyone. I've told Nick that I'm sorry for my actions that night at the gas station."

Alan replied, "Well, you obviously must have done some things right or you wouldn't have ended up here. But I don't envy the one who had to walk you through the hallways."

"It was indeed a very long walk," Simmons said. Randal nodded in agreement.

"You hadn't told me about Randal," said Alan to Simmons.

"He only arrived two days ago," replied Simmons.

Alan asked, "Do you know who pushed you off the bridge, Randal?"

"No. I was on the walkway attempting to keep my face hidden because cars were passing by. Someone came up behind me and before I could react, I was falling."

Alan dropped his gaze. "I'm sorry about your daughter's condition, Randal."

"No worries. She'll be with us soon. When she arrives, she'll be a skilled, battle-ready addition to our ranks. But I do miss her."

Alan decided to lighten the mood. He turned to Nick and said, "I watched you fight today. Very impressive. If you keep practicing, perhaps someday you will be on a horse or clad in that heavy armor with one of these huge blades."

Nick laughed, as did many of the others. Alan was surprised. "Did I say something wrong?"

"No," replied Simmons. "It's just that you don't understand how power and skill work here."

"Okay. Well, could someone explain it to me?"

"Unlike where you're from," started Andrew, "practice will not improve your skill or power here. Practice will keep you ready for battle in your current rank, but nobody here moves up in rank. The foot soldiers will never be of higher rank, skill, or power."

Alan pondered this for a moment. "I'm not following you. If practice doesn't raise skill or power, then how does one achieve a specific rank? How did Anna become the battle master, and how were the others placed where they now are?"

"That's determined before you die," clarified Andrew. "It depends on how you live your life, how you choose to do right or wrong while you're alive, and what kind of person you are before you die."

Simmons chimed in. "Gregory and David were two four-year-old boys who were victimized their whole lives and were ultimately killed because of a cruel world, because of selfishness and evil. They were totally innocent and because of that, they have great power and skill here. Anna was a mere baby. She didn't have a chance to be anything but good, so her skill and power here are extraordinary."

Alan thought about these words for a moment. "So the innocent are vindicated in death. They're rewarded for enduring injustice. And what about those who try to make peace? I remember the sayings—*Blessed are the meek, the humble, and the peacemakers.* I guess those sayings are true?"

Simmons nodded his head. "Yes, I suppose they are."

Alan thought about all the victims he'd seen who had lost their lives unjustly. He thought about all those who had taken the lives of others and had slithered out of payment for their crimes. He breathed deeply as he reveled in the place where justice was truly real.

Everyone was silent for a moment. Finally Andrew said to Alan, "It has been a long day for you. You should rest. Tomorrow I'll show you the field of battle." Alan said nothing but nodded his head and followed Andrew back through the great arched entryway that led out of the arena.

As Alan and Andrew made the long walk back up the mountain and into the great hall, Alan grew tired and hungry. He welcomed the smell and sight of the full table of food that had been prepared at the hall before their arrival. As Alan sat down he noticed an older, bearded man sitting at the next table. He watched as the man stood up and made his way toward him, then sat down across the table from him. It was then that Alan realized who he was.

"Pastor Flynn?"

The man smiled and replied as if he knew him. "Yes. How are you, Alan?"

Alan stumbled over his words, "Good. I'm good. I remember you from church. I didn't know that you had—well—had died. How'd it happen?"

Pastor Flynn laughed and said, "I haven't died, Alan."

Alan said nothing.

Pastor Flynn smiled. "Are you dead?"

"Uh—well, no. I'm just visiting, I guess."

"Yes, I know. I was informed that you were to be one of the new guides. Congratulations."

"So you're also one—I mean, a guide like me?"

Pastor Flynn nodded. "Yes, I've led many here."

"So when you saw me in church, you knew who I was?"

"Yes."

"I was thinking about the Munsin family," Alan said as he recalled that day in church. "I remember that you asked me if everything was okay. You told me that in times of great despair there comes great clarity of purpose clarity in what to do and which path to take. You knew all along that those who'd passed were coming here."

"You're right," said the pastor.

"Why didn't you tell me?"

Pastor Flynn smiled once again. "Do you think you'd have believed me at that time if I'd told you, Alan?"

Alan thought about this for a moment. "Probably not." He paused. "I met my Seristrum today. I know now that it matters very little what you do once you get here. Your destiny, your rank, your mission are all set based on how you lived your life—the choices you made when you were alive, what type of person you were. Whether or not you chose to do what was right, whether you chose to be a kind and compassionate person."

"Yes, you do understand now."

"Well, I don't understand why we can't simply tell those who are alive that they need to be all of these things. We need to tell them to be kind and considerate. We need to tell them to do the right thing. We need to tell them that they need to love—"

Pastor Flynn cut him off. "Love thy neighbor as thyself?"

Realizing what the priest was saying, Alan fell silent. Pastor Flynn nodded. "You are beginning to understand. We *do* tell those who live with us among the living all of those things. But some of those among the living are too blind to see or too deaf to hear. Some of them are overcome by their arrogance. After all, some of those in our world think they're very important. But you know better, don't you?"

"Yes." Alan nodded his head as he said it.

"You remember the room with the pool—the tiny speck that represented our world. Do you remember approaching the huge mountain and your inability to see its greatness and size? You know, then, that some of those in the world of the living are blind in the same manner —unable to see or understand the importance of doing what's right. Do you know why some within our world make a choice *not* to be kind, considerate, or compassionate? Do you know why some of those among us refuse to do what's right—to love thy neighbor?"

Alan, anticipating an answer, said nothing.

Pastor Flynn continued, "Because many in our world frequently ask, what's in it for me? What's the upside of being good and nice? What do I get if I do what's right—after all, doing what's wrong seems to be easier. Why take the high road—what's the payoff?"

Pastor Flynn paused for a moment. He could see that Alan had a dreadful look on his face, as if he were reluctant to accept the truth of these words. "Of course, none of them know what we do. None of them have seen what we have. You see, Alan, I watch those who venture into church every Sunday. I watch them and can tell what they're thinking. Many of them are watching the clock, just going through the motions. Many don't listen, don't speak to God, don't get anything from the hour they spend sitting there every week. They just come because they were told years ago that they had to. They aren't necessarily bad people, but they don't look beyond their own surroundings." The pastor paused once again. "Yet there *are* those who understand. There are those who do not take their good fortunes for granted, those who believe that there is an upside to doing what's right, showing compassion, kindness, and forgiveness, those who thank God for what they have and ask for continual guidance. Luckily, we have those people in our world. They're the ones who benefit once they get here. They're the strong and wise and powerful after they pass from our world."

Alan absorbed what the pastor was saying. "I wonder how I stack up?" he said aloud. "I wonder how I've lived my life? I've made mistakes. I haven't always been a kind person."

The pastor smiled. "None of us have *always* done what's right; all of us have made mistakes. But you've shown compassion for others. You've tried to comfort those who grieve, even when you didn't have to, even when it wasn't required."

Alan nodded.

"You're a police officer, Alan. If you do your job right, you're already a step ahead. After all, as you've said earlier today: blessed are the peacemakers."

Alan looked up at him, "How'd you know I said that today?"

"It doesn't matter. Just keep doing what you do in the manner you do it and you'll be fine."

"Okay," said Alan as he stood up to leave.

The pastor stood up also. As he was walking away he said, "I'll see you at church on Sunday."

"You bet," replied Alan.

Chapter Thirty-Three

"There's no honorable way to kill,
no gentle way to destroy. There is nothing
good in war. Except its ending."

THE NEXT DAY, ALAN, SIMMONS, and Darion made their way down
the mountain and out onto a roadway that led away from the city.
They walked for a long distance until the entire view of the great mountain stood far behind them. After a while the road turned into a narrow
dirt path that led up to a grassy hill, which eventually turned into a
large, open valley. The valley was surrounded by trees on either side
leading up to a gentle rise around its edges. Alan couldn't see the other
end of the valley—it seemed to go on forever.

Simmons and Darion stopped. Alan looked a few feet ahead of them
at a dark spot of grass roughly the size of a dinner plate. As he gazed
across the valley he noticed more and more of the same dark grass circles. Running his foot across the spot closest to him, he discovered that
it was not a patch of grass at all, but rather a hole. He bent down to get a
closer look and felt a soft gust of cold air rising from the hole. As he ran
his hand over the top to feel the cold breeze, he tried to see how deep it

was, and although it did not appear deep at first glance, he could not see the bottom. It was a completely black chasm as far as he could see. Alan moved his body to allow some sunlight to shine into it, but it remained dark. He realized that the light was being consumed by the chasm.

"What is it?" asked Alan, stepping back quickly.

"It's the darkness," replied Darion. "The darkness always tries to consume the light. This is the way they invade our realm to engage in battle. As time goes on, these voids will become larger and eventually will serve as a passageway from their world to ours. Once that happens, they use the passage as a means to place their warriors here for battle."

Alan looked around and counted a total of sixteen spots.

"This is the valley our Seristrum is assigned to defend," said Darion.

"How long will it be until they arrive?"

"Ten more passages of light, maybe twelve," said Darion.

"Ten to twelve more days," Simmons clarified.

"How do their warriors stack up against ours?"

"Since we're in our realm, we're always stronger," answered Darion. "We feed off the power of the light, and they feed off the darkness that pours forth from the voids you see on the ground. The voids are collected and held by their unit leader. Our forces are always stronger because here we have a great abundance of light. The light weakens their forces. But there is one who has given us trouble, one who seems to be unaffected by the effects of our realm."

"Who's that?" asked Alan.

"The leader of their Seristrum. Their Balliste Alona or *dark keeper*, Tiberius. He is the most cunning in battle."

"Tiberius!" exclaimed Alan. "Is that the same one?" He turned to Simmons.

"Yes," Simmons confirmed. "Unfortunately, we've already encountered him."

"You have?" asked Darion with a bit of surprise in his voice.

"Yes," replied Simmons. "There were two deaths not too long ago. He was there, obviously recruiting."

Darion shook his head from side to side and seemed somewhat troubled by these words.

"I thought he was merely a guide. I wasn't aware that he led an entire unit," said Alan.

"He fulfills dual roles," replied Darion, "which allows him to hand-pick his soldiers."

"So how is the battle fought?"

"The two sides engage," Darion explained. "The footmen for both sides strike first, followed by the archers. Our horsemen attack soon after. The heavy warriors will eventually join the battle, as will the battle master, but the latter three will also protect the light bringer, or in their case, their dark keeper. The battle can be won in two ways. The first is if the other side's forces are eliminated. The second way to victory is if the light bringer or dark keeper falls. If either of those two fall, then the entire unit falls."

"I've been wondering about this. What happens if they fall—do they die?"

"No," replied Simmons. "None are among the living, so death isn't possible. They fall into the other realm and are captured," he said with a solemn look. He dropped his gaze.

"What happens if they're captured?" asked Alan hesitantly. "Do they ever escape?"

"Sometimes," replied Simmons, "but very seldom does this occur. It's very difficult to leave on one's own. Once you enter the other realm, the forces at work there weaken you. You do not have the energy to escape."

After a few seconds of silence Alan asked, "So how do we win the war?"

Neither Simmons nor Darion spoke for a moment. Anticipating an answer, Alan turned and looked at both of them. Finally Darion spoke. "What do you mean?"

"How do we win the war?" he repeated. "How do you conquer their forces so that you don't have to fight anymore? How do you end it?"

Both Simmons and Darion seemed confounded by this concept.

Simmons finally spoke. "End it? It never ends. The war between good and evil, the battle between the light and the darkness, never ends. Battle victories are gained but the war is never won."

Alan said nothing. This dreadful fact did make sense. He stared out at the open valley and wondered how many warriors had fallen into the darkness, never to be rescued or released.

After a few moments Simmons said, "Come on, let's walk back. It's been five days. You'll rest tomorrow, then return to your world."

The three turned and began the long walk back down the dirt path toward the great mountain as Simmons's words lingered in Alan's mind. *The war is never over.*

CHAPTER THIRTY-FOUR

"Someone who trusts can never be
betrayed, only mistaken."

ALAN AWOKE IN HIS OWN BED AND found that everything was as Andrew and Simmons had told him. He had not missed a moment in time; his family had no idea that he'd been gone for a week. Alison was still sleeping. He kissed her on the cheek and hugged her tightly.

She woke to his touch. "Good morning," she said.

"I missed you so much," said Alan instinctively, then thought perhaps he shouldn't have.

She smiled. "You missed me overnight—while we were sleeping?" she teased.

Alan nodded, but also searched his mind for a way to further explain. "Have you ever had a crazy dream where you've lost track of time—where you think you've been away for a long time, but you really haven't?"

She struggled to understand the feeling he was describing. "No, not that I can remember." She paused. "So what else did you dream about?"

"I dreamed about some people who recently died. About what they were doing now."

"Well, that's only natural," she replied. "You're a very kindhearted person. I know how much it affects you when you have to deal with death. You're very compassionate; that's one of the reasons I love you." She kissed him on the cheek, then got up and made her way into the bathroom.

Alan sat there for a moment feeling somewhat guilty for not telling her the entire truth. *I trust her more than anyone in the world*, he thought. *I should tell her.*

Walking into the bathroom, he said, "I have something to tell you. You may think I'm crazy, but I'm going to tell you anyway."

She stopped brushing her hair and turned toward him with an inquisitive look. As Alan was about to begin explaining, his attention was drawn to the door of the linen closet behind her. The image of the door reminded him of the door where he and Simmons had encountered the dark figure of Tiberius. He looked down at his finger, now scabbed over from where he'd cut it on the damaged helm in the great hall. *What if Tiberius were to show up here? What if telling her would put them in danger? I don't know enough about how all of this works yet; I can't put my family in harm's way*, he thought.

Alison brought him back to the present. "You were saying?"

"I love you," he said.

She laughed and said, "Yeah, I *do* think you're crazy—and I love you, too." She kissed him and went back to brushing her hair.

Alan left the bathroom and made his way to Missy's room. The baby was still fast asleep, curled up in her bed with her stuffed monkey under her arm. Alan kissed her on the cheek. A tear began to well up in his eye. *Above all else,* he thought, *I need to protect them.*

He dressed quickly and headed into work as he typically did. As he made his way into his office, Clint poked his head into the doorway.

"Hey, don't know if you heard yet about the bodies we found yesterday," said Clint.

"No, I haven't heard anything."

"Fisherman found them. Looks like they had been partying. We found a good amount of needle marks on their arms and suspect that they both OD'd on something. Guess we'll find out today after the autopsies."

Alan nodded his head. "Who are they—you have them identified yet?"

Clint opened a manila file folder and thumbed through some papers. "Yeah, Johnny Barnes and a female named Mary Chelsey. I thought you might want to know since she was a suspect in your homicide/arson case with her two sons."

Alan jumped up from his desk. "You found their bodies?"

"Yep."

"Where?"

"Washed up on the river bank. They must not have been in the river long, or at all. They were fairly normal and preserved, not like the usual floaters."

"Anything else unusual about them?" asked Alan with a bit of hesitancy.

"Not really, but we'll know more after the autopsy."

"Clint, would you mind if I came along?"

"Sure, no problem, you can ride with me. But we'll have to get going." Alan stood up, straightened his uniform, and locked his office. They arrived at the medical examiner's office soon after and were led by a receptionist to an examining room containing several medical tables, overhead surgical lights, trays with various scalpels, and other tools used to conduct autopsies. Two bodies covered by white sheets were set up on two tables. Within a few moments a woman dressed in medical scrubs entered the room. She was middle-aged, with a thin face, a narrow, pointed nose, and a defined chin that made her look very clinical and serious.

"I'm Andrea Catanick, the county medical examiner. We've already collected preliminary trace evidence and both have been weighed, so we can begin. Which one do we want to start with?"

"Whichever," replied Clint.

Andrea walked over to one of the tables and removed the sheet to reveal the body of Johnny Barnes.

"I'm sorry," said Alan, "can we start with the woman? Her name is Mary Chelsey, and she was my suspect in the double homicide of her two sons. I suspect a drug overdose."

"Sure, no problem," replied Andrea. She replaced the sheet on Johnny Barnes and removed the one covering Mary. She switched on the light above the table and positioned it to illuminate the center of the body. She activated a tape recorder and began to speak. "April 10, 2008. Subject: Mary Chelsey. White female, approximately thirty one years of age, blue eyes, brown hair. Preliminary assessment."

She turned and picked up a scalpel, then began to scan the body. She appeared ready to make an incision in the chest area, but stopped and peered at something on the side of the body instead, as though it had caught her attention.

"Clint, can you help me?" asked Andrea. "I need to look at her back."

Clint slowly and reluctantly walked over to a countertop and put on some latex gloves. The two rolled Mary's corpse onto her side. "Okay, hold her there," Andrea said.

Alan stepped closer to the table to see what Andrea was examining and immediately saw the three large, black marks across her back. They resembled deep bruises.

"What's that?" asked Alan.

"Hmm, don't exactly know yet. You two said that you suspect an overdose?"

"Just a guess," replied Clint.

"Looks like some type of deep bruise. There's some kind of blistering on the surface. Let me get a closer look." She positioned the scalpel and slowly made a shallow pass over one of the marks.

The flesh separated and widened to show a deep, black gash. Andrea turned and grabbed a small penlight sitting on the tray next to the table.

She directed the beam down into the open wound and drew her head closer in an attempt to further examine it.

She shook her head. "Looks like a burn, cauterized perhaps. It's very deep."

"So it was something hot, something that burned her?" asked Alan.

"No. It was something cold—very cold, almost like frostbite. Like it crystallized and deadened the tissue. I've never seen anything like this."

She moved the flashlight closer so that the end was only half an inch away from the surface of the gash. Alan peered over her shoulder and saw something that made him gasp. The beam of light streaming from the bulb was being absorbed—as if it were being sucked into a vacuum.

As he stared at the wound, it began to become more familiar to him. He knew where he had seen something similar. The battleground in the valley—the dark voids on the ground. They absorbed the light. This was the same, he knew.

He ran over to the other table and pulled the sheet off Johnny's body. Grabbing one arm, he lifted it to look at the corpse's back and stood in shock at what he saw: three more dark wounds, sucking away the light.

Andrea noticed him and said, "Hey, be careful over there. I'll get to him in a minute." Before she could join Alan by Johnny's body, a man entered the room.

Alan looked over and recognized Michael Simmons. Andrea stood upright, "Can I help you?"

"FBI," replied Simmons, displaying federal credentials.

"Michael?" said Alan.

"Hello, Officer Crane," he replied.

Alan nodded and Clint said, "Hey, I recognize you. You two have been working together on that task force or whatever it is."

Simmons nodded and said, "Correct, but I'm here in reference to these two."

Andrea walked around the table and stood in front of Simmons and Alan.

Clint slowly lowered Mary's body back down onto the table. A disgusted look came over his face from having to touch her waxy, discolored skin.

"I was doing some preliminary assessments on this first body and came across some strange bruising or old wounds on the back. They're like nothing I've ever seen before," said Andrea.

"Yes," Simmons said nodding his head as if he recognized what Andrea was saying. "We're tracking a suspect we believe has committed several murders nationwide. He stabs his victims and uses a chemical agent to destroy any trace evidence in or around the wound."

"Chemical?" said Andrea, pondering this possibility. "What kind of chemical could do this? It's like he has frostbite or the flesh was blistered and frozen. I can't imagine how he would do that."

"Liquid nitrogen perhaps? Nasty stuff, burns horribly. We don't know for sure yet," replied Simmons.

"Liquid nitrogen!" exclaimed Andrea. "But how would he transport it? It's a little bit harder to lug around than a tube of mace."

"We don't have any positive ID yet, but we've speculated from other crime scenes and victims that the guy we're looking for may be some type of chemist," replied Simmons. "That would explain his proficiency with using such a tricky material."

"Well," Andrea mumbled as she shook her head and looked back down at Mary's body, "he must be a real sicko."

Simmons turned and looked at Alan as he replied, "Yeah, we suspect he's a very dark individual."

Alan could see the concern on Simmons's face and knew that the story he was relaying to Andrea and Clint wasn't entirely true.

"There are similar marks on this body also," Alan pointed out, keeping eye contact with Simmons.

"As we expected," replied Simmons.

"Well, I guess we'll be working another double homicide," said Clint. He let out a long sigh. "I'm never going to get through all this paperwork."

"As a matter of fact, Detective Rogers, this has become a federal case. As far as paperwork goes, you're off the hook; I'll be taking over from here," Simmons said.

Clint gave Simmons a huge grin. "Hey, thanks. Don't mind if you do."

Simmons looked over toward Alan. "Alan, I need a word with you, if you've got a minute."

Alan replied, "Okay," then followed him out of the examination room into the office.

"Something very bad has happened. I need your help, but I can't discuss it here for obvious reasons," said Simmons. "Be prepared to accompany me back to our realm tomorrow. I'll meet you at work after you finish."

"I'll be ready."

Simmons left the office, and Alan returned to the examination room to finish the autopsy. Alan looked on as Andrea continued to examine the dark holes in Mary Chelsey's back and wondered, *What bad news does Michael have now?*

CHAPTER THIRTY-FIVE

"The greatest accomplishment is not in never falling,
but in rising again after you fall."

—Vince Lombardi

THE NEXT DAY AFTER ALAN FINISHED WORK, Simmons met him in the police department parking lot.

"Ready?"

"Sure," replied Alan, opening the passenger door and getting in.

They drove into town and pulled into the parking lot of the local library. "The library?" asked Alan.

"Yep," replied Simmons as he got out of the car.

Alan followed him up to a rear entrance and the two stepped through. At once Alan looked around at the familiar deep valley through which he and Michael had recently walked. "You said that something bad happened?"

"It's Darion. He's gone."

"Gone?" Alan was astonished. "What do you mean, he's gone? Did he leave?"

"Not by his own will. Let's meet Andrew and the others and we'll get more information."

The two continued up the valley and into the city, where they entered the large arena. Andrew and the rest of the Seristrum were standing off to one side near one of the large arched entryways. As they approached the others Alan noticed the despair on all of their faces.

Andrew looked up and said, "Ah, Alan, thank you for coming."

"Michael told me that Darion's gone. What happened?"

Nick Swanolski spoke up. "We were in the valley of battle, attempting to assess the time frame for the upcoming attack. Darion had walked up to the eastern ridge and was standing near the tree line. I was a good distance away, but I saw someone grab him from behind and drag him into the trees. We all ran to the spot but couldn't find him."

Alan asked, "Did anyone get a good look at who grabbed him?"

No one spoke for a moment. Then Randal Sweeny said, "Yeah, I saw him. It was one of them, the dark armor with a full helmet. It was one of them. It was their keeper, Tiberius."

Andrew spoke. "But this doesn't make sense; it just doesn't add up. They couldn't have overpowered him."

"Why not?" asked Alan.

"Because," replied Andrew, "they derive their power from the voids in the valley. As the battle grows near, the voids grow bigger and act as doorways that link to their realm. But Darion was taken yesterday and the voids were not nearly large enough to sustain any of them long enough to have overpowered him; no way. It may have been possible for one of them to transport himself there, but that person would have been so weak that he couldn't have stood upright for any length of time. Like I said, it just doesn't make sense."

"I thought that if Darion fell, then the rest of you would fall as well?"

"Only in battle. They've abducted Darion and taken the coward's way out. If he were to have fallen in battle, then the rest of the Seristrum would have fallen also. However, this does cripple us."

"How so?" asked Alan.

Simmons spoke. "The voids are nearly ready to transport them here to fight, perhaps two days from now. Without a light bringer this unit will fail."

"What can we do?" Alan asked.

Simmons replied, "That's why I've asked you here. We must find Darion and bring him back."

"Okay, any ideas where we'll find him?"

"Oh, yes," replied Simmons. "I think I know where he is, but I'll need you to accompany me."

"I'll help in whatever way I can. Where do you think he is?"

Simmons looked at Alan, "He's captured. He's in their realm. Among the darkness."

As Alan realized what they must do, dread and fear came over him.

Chapter Thirty-Six

"It is easy to go down into Hell;
night and day, the gates of dark Death stand wide;
but to climb back again, to retrace one's steps to
the upper air—there's the rub, the task."

—Virgil

A S ALAN AND SIMMONS BEGAN TO WALK back to the valley leading out into the world of the living, Alan said, "I have to tell you, I'm not really happy about going into the darkness, or hell, or whatever it's called."

Simmons let out a sigh. "I know, but I can't do this without you. It's critical that we do this, but you're not obligated to go."

Alan noticed the look of despair on his face. "I'll do it. I'm just saying that I'm not looking *forward* to it."

"I understand."

They continued a great distance until they reached the door that had led them to the valley. As they passed through the door and back to the parking lot behind the library, Alan asked, "So how do we get there? How do we reach the darkness?"

"We'll need to find a doorway."

"And how do we do that? Can you open one?"

Simmons shook his head. "No, I can't. We'll need to have one of them open the doorway, and then we'll follow them in."

"How the hell are we gonna do that? How do we know where to find them?" Alan asked anxiously.

"We'll need to find the person that killed Mary Chelsey and Johnny Barnes. That should lead us to a door."

"You know as well as I do that Tiberius killed those two—remember the wounds? I saw how the light was being sucked into them as if they were hollow, black voids. That wasn't caused by anything in my world. So how are we going to find him?" snapped Alan.

"He didn't kill them. Those who've passed into our realm can't kill the living. There would be grave consequences. If Tiberius had killed them, they would've come to us. That would've been a favor to us; he would've added to our numbers. He didn't do it. There must be someone working for him here. That's who we have to find."

For a moment, Alan sat and contemplated what he was saying. Then Simmons spoke once again. "Time is very short in our realm. The battle will fall upon us soon. Your Seristrum is in a key position to our defenses."

Alan pulled open his cell phone and dialed a number. Clint Rogers answered on the other end.

"Clint, it's Alan. I know it hasn't been very long, but did we get anything else back on the Barnes/Chelsey homicide—anything from the medical examiner?"

"Drug overdose, as we suspected," replied Clint. "Those weird bruises on their backs didn't have anything to do with their deaths. The ME still can't figure out what they were. She said it could have been a chemical burn, but she couldn't find anything."

Alan shook his head. "All right. Anything else?"

"Since the ME is classifying this as an accidental death due to a drug overdose, we've downgraded the priority. But I still did a little checking around and spoke to an older lady who lives next to Barnes's apartment. She frequently saw Chelsey hanging out with Barnes and suspected that both of them were drug users—not much of a surprise there—but she also mentioned that she noticed a dark BMW arriving every month around the same time. It could have been Barnes's supplier. But no matter now; the case is closed on our end and your buddy Simmons gets to deal with it now. I'm turning everything over to the Feds, but I'll keep you posted if anything else pops up."

"Okay, thanks Clint." Alan snapped the phone closed and placed it back in his pocket. "Let's head over toward Barnes's apartment," he told Simmons.

As the car approached the entrance to the apartments where Johnny Barnes once lived, Alan noticed a Fast Track gas station on the corner.

"Here, pull in here," he said to Simmons.

Simmons veered into the lot and parked in front as Alan got out of the car and surveyed the pump area of the gas station. As he and Simmons entered the station he saw a teenage boy standing behind the counter. He had greasy, black hair and wore a Fast Track shirt with several stains on the sleeves. Alan flashed his badge. "You have video surveillance here?"

"Uh, yeah, at the pumps."

"How long does the video cycle?"

"About thirty days or so, then records over."

"Okay. I need to see that tape—right away."

The kid had a blank look on his face but replied, "Uh, okay. Follow me."

Alan noticed another attendant at the other end of the counter, a girl who was younger and staring at him and Simmons, probably wondering what was going on. The boy stopped in front of her and said, "I'll be right back. I have to show the cops the video. Can you watch everything?"

The girl's eyes grew wide. She said nothing, but nodded. The boy led Simmons and Alan to a back office, which was just a bit larger than a broom closet. He sat down at the computer on the small desk and began typing as he gazed at the flat-screen monitor.

"Okay, sir. This is the last thirty days. You can advance it like this if you need to," he said as he moved the computer mouse.

Alan watched numerous cars pulling up to the pumps, then driving away. Alan sat down and began to activate the fast-forward function, occasionally stopping to look closely at the screen, trying to make out a car that might have matched his search. After twenty minutes of looking he froze the screen, showing a new, black BMW.

Alan turned to the attendant and asked, "You recognize this car?"

"Oh, yeah. Cool car, it comes in every once in a while."

"What's the driver look like?"

"Uh, well…he's about average height, maybe five eleven or so. Always dressed up—like in a tie and sometimes a suit. Comes in and buys gas."

Alan took out a small notepad and began writing. After he had completed his last note he asked, "You wouldn't happen to have a name on this guy, would you?"

"Uh, no. Can't say that I remember. But I could do this." He moved the mouse and advanced the screen to show the front view of the car. A few more clicks and the license plate of the car had been enlarged enough so that Alan could read it. He quickly scratched it down on the notepad and thanked the clerk. He and Simmons left the gas station and got back into the car.

"Where to now?" asked Simmons.

"Don't know yet. I need to make a call."

Alan opened his cell phone and dialed the number to dispatch. After the dispatcher answered he said, "Hey, it's Sergeant Crane. I need you to run a plate for me. ITL-182—that's Ida-Tom-Lincoln-one-eight-two. It's a 2009 issue." A few moments passed, and Alan scratched some more notes down on the notepad. "Okay, thanks," he said as he closed the phone and placed it back into his pocket. "It's starting to make sense now. I know this guy."

"Who is it?" asked Simmons.

"His name's Patrick Kent."

Chapter Thirty-Seven

*"Light thinks it travels faster than
anything but it is wrong. No matter how fast
light travels, it finds the darkness has always
got there first and is waiting for it."*

—Terry Pratchett

SIMMONS PULLED THE CAR into the entrance of the Winding Woods subdivision and parked a few houses down from Patrick Kent's residence. The house was entirely built with brick and decorative stone, and had a large fountain in the front and a long, narrow driveway leading to a side garage.

"So what now?" asked Alan. "Should we make contact?"

"No. Kent must be recruiting for Tiberius. I don't want to tip him off. We'll need to wait until we can follow him; hopefully he'll lead us to a door."

Alan nodded. "Kent's car was the one Randal used to rob the gas station, or so we thought. Our detective, Clint Rogers, found Randal's wallet in Kent's driveway, and Kent's wife believed the car had been stolen. I wonder if Kent was actually out of town, or if he somehow planted that wallet there." Alan glanced up at the clock on the dashboard of the car: 10:38 PM.

They continued to watch the house for movement or signs that someone was home, but couldn't see any. A few hours later, as Alan had nearly drifted off to sleep, he was awakened by Simmons's voice. "There's the car."

Alan shook his head, trying to refocus his eyes as he made out the taillights that had just passed and pulled into the garage. He watched as the garage door closed.

"Well, maybe he's home for the evening. Do we stay or come back tomorrow?" asked Alan.

"Let's give him a few minutes."

Alan nodded. They continued to watch the house as lights illuminated from within, starting in the foyer, then up through what must have been a central stairwell and eventually to an upstairs room. After a few moments the lights went out in the same order and the garage door opened once again. The black BMW pulled out onto the street, heading back toward them. To avoid being seen, Alan and Simmons slumped down in their seats and waited for the headlights to pass.

Once the car had traveled a good distance away they began to follow it. They watched the BMW travel through town and out onto the docks that bordered the river. Simmons pulled into a large parking area that serviced the dock warehouse. The BMW parked close to the rear entrance of the warehouse. Simmons and Alan watched a man get out of the driver's seat and walk to the passenger side. He opened the door to help a woman out of the car. Alan strained to make out their features, but they were too far away to see any specific details. The man said something to her briefly and then opened the warehouse door. Together they stepped inside.

"This could be it," said Simmons, his voice untypically anxious. "We must go quickly, before the door closes."

He got out of the car, popped open the trunk and removed something large. As he walked back to the front of the car, Alan saw that he was pushing a wheelchair.

"What's that for?" asked Alan, thoroughly confused.

"No time to explain. You'll see soon enough. Let's get through that door. We'll need to move quickly but we must be quiet," said Simmons, running over to the warehouse door and pushing the wheelchair in front of him.

He placed one hand on the heavy, metallic door and slowly pulled it open. Alan peered inside to see a dark hallway. He put the glowing badge around his neck and ran his thumb over the hilt of the dagger strapped to his waist. Simmons stepped in first and quietly pulled the wheelchair into the hallway. Alan stepped in right behind him.

"I think they're already through," whispered Simmons, "and I think this is a short hallway."

Alan squinted to see the end of the hall and thought he could make out a doorway in front of them. The two began to move forward slowly. As they reached the door, Alan felt his heart racing as if it were about to explode. Simmons placed one hand on the doorknob, turned it slowly, then pulled. A cold breeze rushed across Alan's face, and they stepped through the door. It slammed shut behind them.

CHAPTER THIRTY-EIGHT

"To him that waits all things reveal themselves,
provided that he has the courage not
to deny, in the darkness, what
he has seen in the light."

—Coventry Patmore

ALAN HAD CLOSED HIS EYES for a moment and was somewhat frightened to open them again. He feared that he would see a horrible sight of fire and lava, demons and evil everywhere. Breathing deeply, he forced his eyes to open up and saw that they were standing in what appeared to be a musty alleyway that smelled like a moldy attic. A fat, black rat scurried from one side to the other, and Alan flinched. As he scanned his surroundings, he looked down and saw that Simmons had collapsed on the ground. He bent down quickly and said, "Michael, what's wrong? Are you okay?"

Simmons's voice was weak. "Help me into the chair."

Alan grabbed his arm. It was old and withered. He helped Simmons into the chair. As he sat him back, he recoiled at the sight of Simmons's decrepit, wrinkled face. It was that of ninety-year-old man. Simmons was slumped forward and his hands shook uncontrollably; Alan realized that he had lost all of his coordination.

"Michael," said Alan in a whisper. "What happened to you? I don't understand."

Simmons replied in a raspy voice, as though he were gasping for air. "As strong as I am in my own realm, I am equally weak here. This is how it is. You understand now why I could not do this alone? Now you see."

"Yes. I understand, but why am I not affected?"

"You are among the living; it doesn't affect you. You maintain your current age and physical being in all realms, as you would in your world."

Alan noticed how labored Simmons's speech was. He decided to save his questions for later. "Shall we go on?"

"One moment. Before we continue, I'll need to fill you in on some things. We must not let on that you are not from this realm. When people see me they will see the light within and notice my physical weakness, thus identifying me as the enemy. You must tell them that I'm your prisoner and you're taking me to confinement. You *must not* let on that you are in any way associated with our realm or yours. Do you understand?"

"I think so, but won't they recognize that I'm not from here?"

"No. You are among the living. They won't be able to recognize that you're not one of their kind. They can only discover your identity through your actions or words."

Alan began to push the wheelchair down the alley. He looked around and noticed tall brick walls to either side. After a hundred feet or so Alan saw the end of the alleyway, which opened onto what appeared to be a normal city street.

As they approached it he said to Simmons, "This is the darkness? It looks similar to an alleyway on a common street. It's not that intimidating at all."

"Yes. There are many common misconceptions about the realm of darkness."

Alan surveyed the barren street. *Nobody here*, he thought to himself, *not a soul—but perhaps that's a good thing.* It appeared as if it had just rained; the blacktop surface of the road was damp, and a trickle of dirty water ran down the gutter and into a storm sewer. *Storm sewers in hell*, Alan thought, shaking his head as a slight smile came over his face. *Never would have guessed that.* As they left the alleyway, Alan looked around and noticed storefronts to the left and right. He continued to gaze at the brick and cobblestone sidewalks and above them several old-fashioned gas streetlamps. They were wrought-iron and black, and the flicker of small flames danced inside the glass housings, illuminating the way. The scene was very surreal and inviting, perhaps even peaceful, but worst of all, it was like home. *It can't be…this can't be the darkness*, Alan thought.

He stood there for a moment in utter confusion. "I don't understand. This place looks familiar. It looks like our old-town district back home. If I recall, there should be a bookstore a short way down this street." He glanced around and spotted what he had predicted: about four storefronts down, a small sign displayed the words "Best Bet Bookstore."

"See," said Alan, "there it is!"

"Yes, I know. Many things may look familiar to you."

"So I guess our world has duplicated things in this realm also—correct?"

"No," replied Simmons. "Everything you see here is copied from your world."

"Why?"

"To make this realm more appealing to those who come here. To fool those who follow the darkness. To make them believe that everything is normal and okay."

Alan continued to look around. "Well, I can certainly see why one would feel at home. What about the light here—I mean, it's somewhat overcast and the street lights are on, but I envisioned complete darkness with little illumination. But that's not so."

Simmons coughed and gasped for air. "The darkness refers to the *spirit* of this realm. It may look like your world and even be illuminated—there is day and night here—but the *spirit* of this place is all that is wrong and vile and evil."

"How does this place differ from our world among the living? It looks the same," asked Alan.

"Don't be fooled. This realm differs greatly. You see, the realm of the living is composed of both light *and* dark, good *and* evil. Many times they balance each other out. This realm doesn't contain anything good or right or just. Those qualities such as love, compassion, kindness, caring, and so forth don't exist here."

"I noticed that there aren't any people moving about. Do you know where we need to go?"

"Not exactly," replied Simmons as he coughed into his hand, "but it should be a home or house in close proximity to this door."

Alan looked across the street and saw some type of asphalt driveway with two large statues of gargoyles standing to either side of the entrance.

Alan pointed, "Maybe that driveway?"

Simmons nodded. "Could be."

Alan noticed that there were no cars traveling on the street. As they were about to cross, he heard a noise to his left. He turned to see someone in uniform resembling a police officer. He was standing over another figure on the ground. As Alan watched, he noticed that the uniform appeared more like that of a security or prison guard and that the person on the ground was an elderly woman. It appeared, at first, that the guard was trying to help the woman up, but, as he continued to watch, Alan saw the guard kick the woman violently in the ribs and abdomen. She screamed in pain. Alan felt a surge of disbelief and horror. His emotions quickly changed to rage as he said to Simmons, "Stay here, I'll be right back."

As Alan began to step forward, he felt an old, bony hand grab his wrist. "No, leave it alone. We'll be discovered. He'll know that you're not from here. Nobody here would help anyone else. As I said, there is neither kindness nor compassion here."

Alan slowly pulled away from his feeble grasp. "I only plan on being kind to one of them."

Alan walked briskly up to where the two were standing. As he closed in, the guard stopped and glared at him, then turned back to the old woman on the ground and began kicking her once again. Once Alan was directly behind the uniformed figure, he quickly flung his forearm around the guard's neck so that his throat was pressed against the inside of Alan's elbow. The guard seemed confused as Alan pushed his head forward, constricting both sides of his neck. As he drove his elbow down into the man's chest, the man began to thrash and kick. Finally the man lost consciousness. Alan dragged him back into the alley from where they had just come. He found a downspout secured to one of the buildings surrounding the alley and took out the handcuffs from the guard's utility belt.

After he cuffed the man to the downspout, he returned to the woman, who was moaning and crying. He carefully picked her up and carried her back into the alley, where he noticed that she was cut, bleeding, and appeared to have several broken ribs. As he reached the back of the alley, he opened the door and put the woman inside. A flash of light poured down on top of her as she stood up, seemingly healed. She was no longer old and frail but young and strong.

"Bless you," she said. "I knew you weren't from this horrible place. I fell in a battle recently, and I thought I was destined to be here forever."

"Go quickly—run straight down this hallway and back to the light," Alan said. He closed the door.

A look of fear came over Simmons's face when he saw a uniformed man coming out of the alley and walking directly toward him. As he drew closer, Simmons breathed a sigh of relief when he realized it was Alan.

"Ready?" asked Alan.

"Yes," replied Simmons, "but you gave me quite a scare."

"Sorry, but I didn't want to blow my cover, so I decided to borrow his uniform. Guess I should have told you what I was up to before I did it, but I needed to act fast. After I choked him out, I carried the woman to the hallway. She was bleeding and in terrible pain from her broken ribs. I really didn't think physical injury would affect you once you had passed."

"Those who pass into the light are not affected by physical injuries. There is no pain in our realm. Here there is pain. Physical injury is possible and those who reside here take pleasure in inflicting it," replied Simmons. He began to cough again.

"So you can die here, even if you've passed from the world of the living, my world?" asked Alan.

"No. Those who have passed once can never die again. In this realm you can bleed and be cut and lose consciousness. You may feel pain for days or months or longer, but eventually you'll heal. You'll never die here. You just heal to be beaten or stabbed or abused again."

As Simmons spoke Alan began to realize why this realm was so dark and evil. He began to understand the difference between the world of the living and the realm of darkness. He pushed the wheelchair across the street to the long drive that led upward into a wooded lot. As he continued, he grew tired and noticed that his energy was significantly less than when he was in the realm of the light.

After about ten minutes of walking he noticed a large mansion at the top of the driveway. At the front was a huge porch with two massive oak doors. The mansion was three stories high and there was a smaller detached garage where an overhead door stood open to reveal a black BMW.

"This is it!"

"Yes," said Simmons. "This is where they're holding Darion. We must find a way in. Let's look around back. Make a wide circle, so we can't be spotted."

Alan steered the wheelchair onto the lawn and proceeded to make his way around the back of the mansion. The chair bounced over the grass causing Simmons to nearly fall out. As they rounded the back of the garage, he spotted a door, which he found unlocked. Opening it slowly, he peered in to see if anyone was there. Inside was an enormous kitchen, well-equipped with stoves, food preparation tables, and cooking utensils. He quickly grabbed the handles on the wheelchair, and pushed Simmons across the room.

Before they got to the other side of the kitchen, a door opened opposite to where they stood and a voice yelled, "What the hell are you doing in here? You're supposed to use the side entrance, you idiot."

Alan froze and, without thinking, he turned and ran toward a man who was dressed in a chef's white apron and hat. Surprised, the chef took a step back, but Alan closed in, grabbed him by the neck, and lifted him off the ground. Alan could see fear welling up in his eyes.

"I was bringing in this prisoner and I got hungry. You got a problem with that?"

The man's voice quivered. "No. No, not at all—not at all!"

"I was just transferred here—I'm not familiar with the layout. You're gonna lead me down to the holding area or I'm going to stuff your head into that brick oven over there, got it?"

The man was trembling so hard that he could barely stand as Alan placed him back on the floor.

"Not a problem. Just follow me," simpered the chef. He stopped in front of a table containing a variety of pastries. "You want something to eat? You said you were hungry." The chef tried to force a smile.

Alan didn't think that eating something in the realm of darkness was very wise. "I'm too angry to eat now. Show me where to go and shut your mouth," he shouted.

The chef said nothing, but walked toward the door Alan had come through. Pushing the wheelchair, Alan followed. The man led them through a long hallway to a staircase with steps leading down. "Here you go," said the chef. "Just throw him down the stairs. They usually tumble all the way down, but if not, you can kick him when he gets stuck. You'll find the holding areas at the bottom."

The man held the door and waited for Alan to throw Simmons down the stairs. Alan knew that the chef would surely know he wasn't from this realm if he showed any type of concern for his "captive." He reached out and grabbed the chef around the throat. "I'm not going to expend my efforts kicking this scum down the stairs. *You're* going to carry him the entire way—and if you drop him, I will kick *you* the rest of the way down."

He released the chef, who was trembling again and he hoisted Simmons onto his back and began the descent. Alan followed with the wheelchair and cringed at the spots of blood splattered over each step as he went along. He wondered how many people had been tossed and kicked the entire way. The bottom of the steps ended in an underground tunnel. Alan glared down at the tiny chef, who was panting for breath as he placed Simmons back into the chair. "Now get the hell out of here and wait for me in the kitchen. I may be hungry when I return," barked Alan.

As he focused his gaze down the dark corridor he noticed several metal cages on either side—dungeons, holding cells. As he reached around to the back of the utility belt he'd taken from the guard, he found a small flashlight, which he turned on. The first few cells were completely empty. He continued further down, checking on either side for any sign of Darion, until he came to a holding cell with a man sleeping on a stone bench, covered with a tattered, woolen blanket.

"Darion, is that you?"

The figure began to stir and slowly stood up. His face was severely bruised and beaten. There was a long, bloody gash over the top of his head. Alan wondered if his skull had been cracked. The figure staggered slowly up to the bars, but Alan didn't recognize him.

He estimated the man to be about seventy or eighty years old. In a gravelly, broken voice he said, "It's me. I can't believe you two found me—thank you."

"Any idea where the keys to these cells are?" asked Alan.

"Each guard has a set. Check your belt," replied Darion.

Alan scanned the utility belt and found a set of keys in a small pouch near the left side. He removed them and opened the cell.

Looking at the bloody wound on Darion's head he said, "My God, your head…it looks like your skull is cracked. What did they do to you?"

"They beat me for several days. Every bone in my body was broken but it is now starting to heal. It's what they typically do to prisoners once they arrive—they beat you for a few weeks until you can't move, then wait for you to heal, then do it again."

"But you only disappeared a couple of days ago. How could you have been here for that short a time and have your bones heal after being broken?" asked Alan.

"Remember," said Darion as he coughed up some blood into his hand, "time between the realms works differently. It's of no essence from one to another. You know this from your training."

Alan nodded. A great sense of sadness and empathy came over him as he continued to gaze at Darion's horrible injuries.

"Okay," said Simmons, "let's get out of here."

"No, wait," said Darion, "there's someone else we must take three cells down."

Alan walked down three cells and peered inside. "This cell is empty." Darion staggered, slowly and with great effort, to where Alan was standing.

"Open the cell," he said. Alan opened it and walked in. He swung the flashlight from side to side, but saw nothing.

"See. Nobody here. Perhaps they moved him."

"Over here," said Darion. "This brick in the corner, remove it." Alan bent down and pulled on the brick Darion had indicated. It loosened, then eventually came all the way out.

"Reach in and grab the vial," said Darion. Alan put his hand into the wall and felt a smooth glass cylinder. As he brought the tube out, he examined it and noticed that there was a tiny speck of dust glowing inside.

"How did you know this was here?" asked Alan as he continued to gaze at the gold speck.

"I can see the light in the darkness—an ability granted to every light bringer." Darion coughed violently, then through a labored voice said, "In this place where there is overwhelming evil, I can spot the smallest sense of goodness. Now quickly, take it, and let's get going. We must leave now."

Alan placed the tube in his pocket and put his shoulder under one of Darion's armpits. Together they quickly made their way back to Simmons. Darion held onto Alan's shoulder while Alan pushed the wheelchair back to the stairwell. Once they reached the bottom of the stairs, Alan walked up and opened the door to see if the chef was still in the kitchen. Must have gotten scared and took off, Alan thought as he scanned the empty room. Hope he hasn't told anyone I'm here. With that thought, he hurried to the bottom of the stairs and hoisted Darion onto his shoulders.

When he reached the top, he set Darion on his feet in the hallway, then returned to Simmons and hauled the chair up the stairs backward, one step at a time. As he reached the top, he ran out of breath and had to stop for a minute. Then he turned the wheelchair around, positioned Darion to the side so that he could brace him on his shoulder, and began walking toward the kitchen door.

All three of them entered the kitchen and crossed to the exit. When they arrived at the door, Alan reached for the handle and pulled it open. But as he did a figure stepped through and peered at Alan face-to-face. Alan immediately knew who he was: Patrick Kent.

Patrick paused for a moment. As he realized who Alan was, a look of rage came over his face, and his hand darted into his coat. Before Patrick could remove his hand, Alan grabbed a pan from a nearby table and swung it violently, smashing him across the face. His chin split open and blood spilled out onto the marble tile below. Patrick fell to the side and rolled around on the floor, dazed and in pain. Alan quickly pushed Simmons through the doorway with Darion clinging to his shoulder. He plowed through the yard, pausing frequently to pull Simmons back onto the seat as the chair bounced over branches, roots, and twigs. Darion fell twice; Alan helped him up as they ran. They raced down the long driveway, and by the time they reached the street he could hear Darion breathing frantically. He turned to see that his face was pale and he was shaking violently.

"Don't stop," said Darion with labored breath. "Keep going."

Alan draped one of Darion's arms around his neck and grasped his forearm. With his other hand he pushed the wheelchair across the street. As they entered the alley he heard a voice behind him yell from a distance, "Stupid whelp, did you think you could beat me? I'm coming for all of you."

He turned to see a figure clad in dark armor coming toward them from across the street. The figure drew a large dagger with a black obsidian blade. Alan began to run, dragging Darion and pushing the wheelchair with all his might. They gained momentum, but he heard the footsteps behind him getting closer and closer.

He aimed the wheelchair for the door, which stood closed. With his last ounce of energy Alan pushed all of them through it. The impact of the chair made a terrible sound of crashing metal against wood. Alan sensed the figure right behind him. He envisioned the cold blade of the dagger plunging into his back at any moment.

The door gave way. As the three of them tumbled into the hallway, it swung closed again, sending the chair end over end. Simmons was thrown to the floor, but quickly stood up and pulled out the white-stone staff. It cast a brilliant light all around them. Darion had also fallen, but had not yet gotten to his feet.

The door swung open again, and Tiberius stood on the other side holding the dagger. Simmons took a step forward; Tiberius held his ground. Alan grabbed Darion's hand and dragged him back behind Simmons as he reached down and drew the white-bladed dagger from his belt.

Tiberius said, "You, Illissia Galau—you have entered my home, struck down my servant, and stolen from me. Prepare to battle and fall. I will be upon you soon." With that he slammed the door shut.

The three of them made their way back down the hallway and through the door leading back into the realm of light. Alan fell on the ground in the great valley and breathed deeply. He stood up, stretched, and found that energy was returning to him quickly. Simmons, completely revived, was bending over Darion, who appeared to be regaining his youthful qualities.

"Why's he still weak?" asked Alan.

"He was down there too long. He'll recover fully, but not right away." Simmons helped Darion to his feet and led him over to sit on a large stone.

"Alan, do you still have the vial?" Simmons asked. Alan reached into his pocket and pulled it out. "Quickly," said Simmons, "open it."

Alan pulled the stopper out of the end. An intense flow of overpowering light shot straight up in the air. Alan dropped the tube. He watched as the light continued to pour out with great force, blinding them all. After a few seconds the stream became smaller, then finally stopped.

Alan rubbed his eyes and squinted. As he did so he noticed something standing in front of him.

Jumping back, he marveled at the figure before him. It was enormous, over twelve feet tall and clad in what appeared to be ancient Roman armor. Its arms were huge and muscular, its legs were as big around as large oak trees, and its hands could wrap entirely around a full-grown man. The figure had human features, but its skin was bronze with a hint of gold. As Alan continued to gaze up at the giant, he noticed the most astonishing feature, which had not caught his attention at first: two huge wings protruding from its back. They were dark gray and ran the entire length of its body, from shoulders to feet.

It spoke in a deep, methodical voice as it looked down with two huge eyes. "Thank you, Alan Crane. You have freed me so that I may fight again."

Alan was finally able to get some words out. "You—you're an angel?"

The figure let out a laugh and said, "Well, yes, I have been called that before. But those among the living often depict us as frail; in fact, we are fierce and battle-tested, elite warriors."

"Do you have a name?" asked Alan.

The great figure looked down and replied, "Allisor."

"How long had you been imprisoned?"

"Five hundred and twenty-three years in your time. Too long. I've built up quite a thirst for battle in that time."

"But you were just a speck, a gold fleck in a vial…."

A huge smile came over Allisor's chiseled face. "Indeed, Alan Crane. But you now realize even more that what is powerful in one realm is not in the other."

"Well, nice to meet you, Allisor, and welcome back," concluded Alan.

"Thank you again, Alan. You have returned me to the light. Perhaps someday I'll be able to return the favor. For now, I must depart. Farewell." Allisor spread his massive wings; then, with one definitive motion, he shot straight into the air with incredible speed.

Alan watched as he continued to rise. Within seconds he had disappeared from sight. Simmons drew him back from his mesmerized gaze, saying, "Come, Alan—help me with Darion. The battle will be upon us soon, and we have much to do."

Chapter Thirty-Nine

*"I do not love the bright sword for
its sharpness, nor the arrow for its swiftness,
nor the warrior for his glory. I love only
that which they defend."*

—J.R.R. Tolkien

DARION WAS PLACED IN A BEDROOM off the west side of the great hall. His injuries were healing, but he couldn't stand. Simmons and Alan were standing over him as Andrew entered the room.

"I've just returned from the field of battle and the news isn't good. The voids are full. The enemy will be upon us by tomorrow morning."

Simmons let out a long sigh. "This is what I feared. Darion can't fight. This Seristrum is vital to our defense."

"I'm gathering the others in the great hall. We'll await you there." Andrew hung his head, then disappeared through the doorway.

Alan said, "You know, since I've been here I've never asked you where you fit in. I mean, what's your rank, your role? What's your role in all of this?"

Michael nodded, "My official rank is Illissia Alontis; it translates to the *light guardian*. I oversee what is known as a Grand Seristrum, a unit composed of twelve Seristra." Alan remembered the sense of leadership he'd felt before from Simmons and understood why he was suited to lead a Grand Seristrum. "Come and join me. I must address the others."

They left the room and made their way back down to the great hall. The other members of Alan's Seristrum were gathered near a large table.

"Darion won't be ready for battle tomorrow," Simmons said, breaking the bad news right away. "You'll be without a light bringer, so you won't be able to fight. We'll have to hope that others can close off the defenses to prevent Tiberius from advancing on our city. He'll be attacking through the eastern edge."

Anna interrupted. "No, Michael, that's too risky. He'll be able to clear a path to this city! Once here, you know how many will fall, plunging into the darkness to be captured, beaten, and tortured. There *is* another way."

"No," Simmons said sternly. "There's no other way. I know what you're suggesting and it is *not* an option. There's no other way. We'll have to make do."

Anna continued to protest. "Listen to reason, Michael. You haven't even made the offer and you assume that the answer will be no."

Simmons quickly rebutted, "I can't make that offer. I can't ask any more than I already have."

Alan, who was standing in the background feeling a bit left out, asked, "What's the other option? We should at least consider it as a team."

Anna looked at him. "Michael must tell you."

Simmons said softly, "I won't speak of it."

Alan turned and faced him. "Look, I don't quite understand all of this, but I think you can trust me enough to tell me what's going on. After all, I just helped you out, didn't I? I just ventured into what I consider hell and helped you retrieve Darion—and Allisor."

As he said the name, the others eyes' widened.

"My word," said Andrew, "you retrieved one of the divine from our enemy! You have done us a great service."

"Well, it wasn't really me," said Alan. "Darion knew where he was. I just carried him out in my pocket." He smiled briefly. "It wasn't that difficult—unlike backing a wheelchair up a flight of stone stairs and trying to push it through an alleyway before a maniac with a dagger stabbed me in the back!" As he spoke, he turned and glared at Simmons.

Simmons dropped his gaze. With a look of resignation on his face, he said in a low voice, "It's you."

"Excuse me. I don't follow you," said Alan looking confused. Simmons let out another long sigh. "It's you. *You* are the other option. You could lead this Seristrum into battle. You could carry the light and empower them with its spirit."

Alan said nothing. He stared down at the floor.

Simmons continued. "I can't encourage you to do this. You're right, I do trust you. You've done us a great service."

"I'll do it."

"Wait," said Simmons quickly. "Before you commit, I want you to be aware of everything that is involved. As you know, when we fall in battle we're captured by the enemy and sent to their realm. But if you fall, it would be different."

"How so?"

"You're among the living. If you fall in battle, you'll die, never to return to the world of the living. You'll fall into the darkness and be among the captured as we would, but you'd also lose your life."

Alan took a deep breath. Thoughts of his wife and daughter flashed through his mind. He thought of his friends, other members of his family, and his fellow officers at the department. He looked up, catching sight of Anna. As he looked into her eyes he imagined the baby he had recently held in his arms, the one he had wanted to return to his world, the one who became a fierce and powerful soldier for all that was right and just. She looked somber and guilty, as if she were sorry that she had pressured Simmons into giving Alan this choice.

After a long silence Alan said, "I won't have to worry about that."

Simmons, confused, asked, "What do you mean?"

"I won't have to worry about death or capture," said Alan as he looked into the eyes of each of those who stood around him.

"I'm not sure I understand what you're saying."

Alan stared everyone in the eyes until he had come full circle around the table. At the end he found himself staring at Michael Simmons.

"I don't have to worry about that, Michael, because I *will not* fall."

As Alan spoke, everyone stood upright; all concentrating on his every move. "I remember the walks we took to get all of you here. I remember how you fought to be in this realm, to be within the light. I've seen all of you fight. I know that I won't fall. I trust you, each and every one of you—even with my life."

Anna was the first to draw both of her swords. She went down on one knee. The others followed suit, the entire Seristrum kneeling before Alan.

Anna spoke. "You're right, Alan Crane. We won't let you fall."

Michael nodded, now seeming reassured. "Then kneel before me, Illissia Galau."

Alan knelt. Michael withdrew the glowing white staff. He raised it and said in a deep and serious tone, "You've come before us, Alan Crane, and have done us a great service. We now ask of you that which may cost you everything you know and love. Your courage and devotion are among the highest within the world of the living. Let this lead you to great victory. By virtue of my authority as Illissia Alontis, I deem you empowered to be filled with the spirit of the light." Michael touched each of Alan's shoulders with the staff and said, "Arise, Light Bringer."

Alan stood. Michael said, "Andrew will prepare you for battle. I must prepare the other Seristra. *Errondai,* or as they say among your world, Godspeed."

Alan nodded. Michael turned and left the great hall. He turned back to Andrew and said, "Let's get started."

CHAPTER FORTY

*"In preparing for battle I have always found that plans
are useless, but planning is indispensable."*

—Dwight David Eisenhower

ALAN FOLLOWED ANDREW back to the room where they had trained during Alan's first visit to the realm.

Andrew said, "You'll need a basic understanding of our responsibility and strategic location. We fight along the eastern edge of our realm. This city serves as one of the strongholds to protect the borders within this region. It's critical that we hold our position and fend off our attackers."

Andrew waved his hand over an illuminated map. "You see our valley here," he said as he pointed to a small sliver that glowed on the right side of the map. "Our Seristrum will fight there to seal off any advancement on this city." He waved his hand over the map, which enlarged to show the location of the valley in relation to the location of the city. Illuminated dots blocked off the mouth of the valley. "The other areas of the battle," said Andrew as he waved his hand over the map once again, "will be set to our west. You see the other Seristra in our battle group located here."

The map zoomed out and Alan saw several other glowing points over the western ridge of the valley.

"'That's all you need to know for now. I'll have to show you the rest when we get to the valley and field of battle. Go and rest. We must be on post before the rise of the light, or as you say, sunrise."

Alan retired to the bedroom. He tried to sleep, but it was no use. Images of his family and friends kept racing through his mind. After hours of tossing and turning, his eyes began to close—just to be reopened by the sound of someone entering his room. Andrew stood in the doorway and held something in his arms. "It's time. Here's your attire."

Alan jumped out of bed, took the white tunic and pants from Andrew, and put them on. When he finished, Andrew handed him a hooded cloak of white and gold cloth that hung down to his ankles.

"Anything else?"

"Yes." said Andrew. He handed Alan a thin, silver belt with a short dagger. The dagger was similar to the one Michael had given Alan before, but this one was more ornately decorated and had a longer, straighter blade compared to the other.

As Alan pulled the dagger from the sheath, it glowed with a brilliant white light. Alan nodded as he placed the dagger back in its sheath. "Okay, let's go."

"One more thing." Andrew took out a small, square stone box and handed it to Alan. As Alan opened the box, it emitted a strong light. Inside, he saw an amulet made of a pure white stone with a clear stone in its center. As Alan put the amulet around his neck he was filled instantly with energy. He no longer felt tired or anxious.

Andrew nodded. "Okay, let's get going. The others will meet us there."

As the two departed the city and headed toward the battleground, Alan placed his hand over the warm, glowing stone that hung around his neck. Its energy poured through him, sharpening his senses, warming his heart, and strengthening his very soul.

CHAPTER FORTY-ONE

"'Tis best to weigh the enemy more
mighty than he seems."

—William Shakespeare

THE OTHER MEMBERS OF THE SERISTRUM stood at the edge of the valley, ready to fight. All of them were clad in white-stone armor and carried their weapons. A soft glow rose in the distance.

Andrew said, "We haven't much time. Unlike your world, you must know that battle is very regimented here. There is a set way to fight; both sides adhere to it as it has been determined to be the most effective manner to engage in combat. Our eight footmen will advance and engage the eight enemy footmen first. They will assemble in the front. Then our archers will follow, attempting to thin the numbers of their front troops. Our horsemen will attack with lances, driving the rest back, as our heavy warriors and battle master stay by you in the back for protection until all are safe; then they may advance. If everyone on our side falls, you'll need to fight with all that you have. Remember that you are the source of power for the group. You carry the spirit of the light around your neck. If you fall, we all fall."

Alan nodded and said, "I have a question. While I was in the realm of darkness I saw how weak Michael and Darion were. How are the enemy warriors able to fight here? Won't they be very weak?"

Andrew shook his head. "The voids feed power to their troops; as the voids weaken, so do their warriors. The voids are a piece of their world that they bring here. This allows them to temporarily hold as much power as they do in their own realm. The warriors of the darkness fight quickly so they can maintain their maximum amount of power before the voids begin to fade. Don't be misled into thinking that they are easily defeated because they are here among the light. Don't underestimate their skill and power."

Alan nodded as Andrew continued, "As you know, our opponent is a dark keeper named Tiberius. He's had success in the past, and for some unknown reason seems to be stronger than our previous opponents."

Alan stood and waited. The sun began to rise and the first ray of light gleamed over the far edge of the valley. As it did, a dark mist filled the valley floor and Alan saw the dark armor rising from the ground. Alan's footmen walked forward to take their positions and engage the enemy. Alan quickly surveyed all of his opponents until his eyes came to rest on the figure in the back clad in black, full plated armor. Alan stared at him, watching his every movement. As the dark keeper turned to speak to one of his heavy-clad warriors Alan spotted something on his opponent.

In a moment of clarity Alan understood what he had to do. He called out to all of his troops, "Fall back and regroup here!"

All eyes from his Seristrum were now upon him, awaiting his command. "I've seen this method before. I can't believe I didn't recognize it earlier. It's a game of chess! All the pieces even match."

Andrew spoke, "Actually the game of chess was—"

Alan cut him off, "Yes, yes, I know—the game of chess was created from these battles. You were here first and the game was created from watching you fight."

Andrew nodded. Alan turned to the group and announced, "The battle plan has changed. Here's what we're going to do."

After Alan finished briefing them on the new plan, Andrew protested. "This won't work. You don't understand. Those of our realm and theirs don't deviate from the ways of battle. It's not like your world. Ego doesn't play into the strategy."

Alan turned to Andrew. "Trust me. In great moments of despair, there comes great clarity."

CHAPTER FORTY-TWO

*"Let your plans be dark and
as impenetrable as night, and when you
move, fall like a thunderbolt."*

—Sun Tzu

A S HE EAGERLY AWAITED THE ADVANCEMENT from his enemy, Tiberius stood on the floor of the valley and commanded his soldiers into position. Suddenly he saw something that confused him. A lone figure approached and a hooded cloak covered his face from view. He continued to watch as the figure walked to within ten yards of the front of his soldiers and stopped. The illumination of an amulet around the figure's neck caught Tiberius's eye; this was indeed the light bringer. He laughed to himself. *How easy, how easy he makes it for me,* he thought. *I guess he has given in. I knew Darion would be too weak to fight so soon after his rescue.*

Tiberius's soldiers were confused and turned to receive orders. He gave the signal to advance on the light bringer, but as they drew their swords, the cloaked figure called out, "So the great keeper Tiberius is seen in battle as a coward, standing in the back, protected—and weak."

Tiberius's troops were now very close, and the light bringer continued to speak. "Run from me, coward. Run from me, whelp."

Tiberius shouted a command to his advancing fighters and they stopped. *That isn't Darion's voice*, he thought. "Make way," called Tiberius as he moved through the ranks with two heavily armored warriors and his battle master following close behind him.

Alan looked out beyond his hooded cloak and watched as Tiberius and three others approached. As they grew closer, Alan could see that Tiberius's battle master was a woman, and he realized at once who she was: Mary Chelsey. As they moved closer to Alan, Mary drew forth two curved, black-bladed swords from her back and whispered something to Tiberius.

Tiberius looked at her and shook his head. "No. I'll deal with this."

Alan moved forward to close the gap between himself and Tiberius so that he was now face-to-face with the full-plated helmet of his enemy. "So you think you can best me, Light Bringer?" sneered Tiberius as he drew a long black dagger from his belt.

Alan lowered his hood. "I've done it before." He swung his fist upward under the plated helmet and into the slightly exposed chin of his enemy.

Tiberius's body lurched and his knees buckled. A stream of blood poured down over the black armor, as if an old wound had been reopened. Alan grabbed him as he fell and spun him around, unsheathing his dagger and holding it up under Tiberius's throat. Mary Chelsey took a step forward, positioning herself to strike. The others readied themselves as well.

All at once flashes of light flew by and struck two of Tiberius's footmen squarely in the chest. They fell to the ground. From behind the dark forces, a thundering noise could be heard as two white horses rumbled down and struck both of Tiberius's archers with their lances. Tiberius's soldiers were utterly confused as Alan's forces closed in from the rear and sides. Alan dragged Tiberius farther back and watched the battle unfold before him. Distancing himself farther from the conflict, Alan saw one of the opposition's heavy warriors fall to Anna, who was in the thick of the skirmish. As the large, heavy-plated figure hit the ground his helmet fell off to reveal his true identity: Johnny Barnes.

Johnny quickly got to his feet and swung his huge black sword, which glanced off Anna's shoulder. She rolled onto the ground, but recovered swiftly and was upon him again, sending a flurry of lightning-fast blows from all directions. Johnny attempted to parry, but she was too much for him. He fell to his knees as two quick slices of her swords pierced both sides of his armor.

Alan stopped for a moment and let go of Tiberius, who seemed to be unconscious. As Alan tried to catch his breath, he felt the cold sensation of something hard across his throat and saw the black, curved blade out of the corner of his eye. Mary Chelsey whispered, "Now it ends. You've lost."

Alan felt the blade move and fall forward. He felt her grip loosen. Mary fell to the ground, and Alan turned to see the twins, Gregory and David Chelsey, standing over her. He watched as Mary began to wither, the dark spirit draining from her. She curled up into a ball and aged instantly. The twins removed their heavy-plated helmets and bent down until they were very close to her face.

Gregory Chelsey spoke first. "Sorry, Mother. This is for all the years you abused us. You neglected us and eventually sent us to our deaths."

David Chelsey chimed in. "But still…you're our mother and we'll forgive you. You'll remain here with us, feeble and crippled, old and withered, but we'll take care of you."

The twins gently lifted her and carried her away from the battle. They draped a light blanket over her, then returned to where Alan stood over Tiberius. The remainder of Tiberius's soldiers fell quickly and Alan's troops gathered around him.

Anna said to Alan, "Destroy him so that he may fall and be captured among us."

"No," Alan said, shaking his head, "that won't work."

Andrew spoke up. "Alan's right—look at his forearm."

As Alan dragged him back, one of Tiberius's plated gloves had fallen off, exposing his hand and arm. On the back of his arm there was a black, diamond-shaped mark. "He has a Balliste argonis. It's a way of creating a void or passage after one has fallen in battle. If we strike him down, he could slip away back to the darkness. He would fall into the void that appeared automatically below him."

Alan said, "I wasn't aware of that, but there's something else that all of you need to know." Sure now that he had their attention, Alan went on. "When we first arrived here I surveyed all of our enemies, especially Tiberius. I can't explain how I could see as far as I could, but for some reason I could make out every detail of everyone who stood on the field of battle."

"Yes," Andrew clarified, "the power of the light bringer enhances vision and brings guidance in battle."

Alan nodded and continued. "As I studied Tiberius, I noticed something that didn't make sense to me: a dark, brownish-red flaw in his armor just below his helmet and neck. I thought at first that this was the sunlight reflecting off his chest plate at a strange angle, but then I realized that it was something else—blood. But not the blood of his enemies. That wouldn't make sense, since I was told that you don't bleed when you're struck down." He turned to Andrew for confirmation.

Andrew nodded. "Correct."

"I didn't think it could be his own blood, because he was such a powerful being in his own realm. It would take someone extremely fierce to inflict such damage. But as I studied him further, I noticed this."

Alan pointed to the lower portions of Tiberius's jaw, which was just visible below the edges of the heavy black helmet. Alan grasped both sides of the helmet and pulled it off. The face of the man below was covered in swelling scrapes and bruises along his chin and cheekbones.

"You see," said Alan, "I had already struck this person not long ago."

The man began to turn his head, trying to revive himself. A few seconds later he opened his eyes.

"Hello, Patrick," said Alan.

Patrick Kent glared up at Alan and the others.

"Patrick's from my realm. I struck him with a pan as I was escaping with Michael and Darion. I was told that Tiberius wasn't affected by the lack of the voids in this realm; that's because he is among the living. I knew that his arrogance couldn't take a challenge. I knew that his ego would dominate his actions."

Patrick spat out some blood. "Go ahead, Crane—kill me. Do it!"

"And send you back to your dark realm so that you can attain the power that's awaiting you? I don't think so," replied Alan.

Andrew concurred. "Yes, good thing we didn't strike him down. I don't know how he obtained that mark on his arm, but it would've taken him back. He must have done some great service for our enemies. Someone of great power among the darkness would've granted him that."

Alan looked down at Patrick and asked, "So how did you get that mark? What did you have to do, Patrick? What promises did you have to make? Sell your soul?"

Patrick Kent began to laugh. "Oh, I think you'll find out very soon."

At that moment Alan heard something. It started out as a low rumbling sound off in the distance, coming from the other end of the valley.

Anna perked up. "I think we should go see what that is." She and the two horsemen made their way across the valley and disappeared from sight.

Within a few moments they returned with great speed, Anna outrunning the horses. Upset, she blurted out, "The battle course is turning! They're coming, and fast."

Alan asked, "Who's coming, Anna? What is it?"

"The front, the wedge—they mean to make this the place of the breach."

Alan shook his head in confusion, but Andrew's eyes grew wide in comprehension. "The dark forces used Tiberius's unit as an initial attack to create an open pathway. They intend to breach the front of our forces, make their way to the city, and encircle our other troops. They must have had great confidence in Tiberius; that's why he was granted that mark."

Patrick Kent continued to laugh. "Very good, old man, very good. But too late."

All at once there was a thunderous roar of horses and footsteps rapidly approaching. Alan began to count. "One hundred…two hundred… three hundred," he continued. His heart began to pound.

Hordes of black-armored troops began to pour into the valley from all sides, like roaches closing in on food. Within minutes the dark army was everywhere, entirely surrounding Alan and the others. Anna and the rest of Alan's soldiers drew their weapons and stood around Alan defensively. Patrick Kent laughed as another dark keeper stepped forward with a dagger drawn. Anna whispered to Alan, "I don't know how many I can destroy, but we'll soon find out. I made you a promise and I'll fight to the end."

"No, we can't win this," Alan whispered back. "Today I join you and the others who've passed."

"Good-bye, Alan Crane," cackled Patrick Kent. "Good—"

An explosion interrupted his words. The eruption sent blinding shards of light everywhere and shook the ground, knocking Alan down.

When his vision began to return, he staggered to his feet and saw that the closest members of the enemy forces were also lying on the ground. Alan shook his head in order to focus. As he did, he noticed a large figure standing next to him.

A deep, melodic voice said, "You will not join the dead today, Alan Crane."

He looked up to see Allisor standing over them. From his impos-
ing stature he peered down at the members of the dark army, his great
wings spread in an intimidating stance. Alan sized up the war hammer
Allisor carried and estimated that the head of the hammer was the size
of a compact car. His great Roman armor gleamed gold in the sunlight.
As he readied the hammer, Alan saw the enemy soldiers' apprehension
heighten as they backed up slowly.

Within a few moments there was more commotion overhead. Seven
more columns of light struck the ground as seven more angels stood
over them. Three of them had hammers, while two more had huge
claymore-style swords with eight-foot blades. The last two were clad in
ornate white robes.

Allisor and the others with the hammers stepped forward. The enemy
archers released black, streaking arrows. Twenty or more arrows struck
Allisor in the legs and abdomen. He seemed to flinch, but didn't fall.
Beams of brilliant light shot from the fingers of the robed angels, which
seemed to heal the arrow wounds on Allisor as he pulled them from his
torso. The four with hammers raised their weapons above their heads.

As the hammers struck, the ground shook with great force like an
earthquake. Several large, thick cracks opened from the impact. Alan
watched in astonishment as the cracks began to widen and branch out
like a huge spider web, swallowing up the enemy soldiers. The other
two angels began to swing their great swords, and with each enormous
sweep cleared out ten or twelve enemies who fell to the ground frail,
weakened, and defeated. Alan and the others backed up as the eight
angels fought their way through the three hundred foes before them. As
the dark army's losses increased Alan sensed that they were on the verge
of retreat. Anna and the rest of Alan's soldiers finished off those few
remaining adversaries who had trickled through the assault.

Within a short period of time, all of the opposing army was driven
out of the valley. Allisor and the other seven returned to join Alan where

he was standing. As the giant warriors loomed overhead Alan thought that he would never again perceive an angel as some small, fairylike creature with tiny wings.

Allisor bowed his head. "Farewell, Light Bringer."

Alan returned the gesture. "Thank you, my friend."

The eight shot straight into the air like rockets, leaving a stream of brilliant light. After a few moments Alan spotted more soldiers of light from the western ridge of the valley approaching them. Michael was leading them and called out to Alan as he came close.

"You're victorious, Alan! I'm in your debt."

As Michael drew closer and stood in front of Alan, Patrick Kent looked up in defeat.

Alan looked at Patrick. "And what of our friend here?"

Michael had a look of disgust on his face as he stared at Patrick. "On his belt you'll find a dagger. It will link him to the murder of Nick Swanolski. Within his home you'll find an automatic rifle that will link him to Tyris Cotton's death."

Patrick Kent yelled, "I won't admit to anything! I have rights! I don't have to talk!"

Michael knelt down so that his face was very close to Patrick. "Not here," he said. "You have no rights here. Here you'll have to tell the truth. Here you'll tell Alan Crane everything. You may be able to lie among the darkness, but you are now among the light, which reveals all. I'm afraid that you'll live for a long time, Mr. Kent, locked in a cage among the living."

Michael stood once again and turned toward Alan. "He'll give you a full confession and will be unable to lie about any of the murders he committed. The light you wear around your neck has granted you extreme clarity; his deception will show through very clearly."

Alan nodded and dragged Patrick to his feet.

As they walked back, an archer approached from one of Michael's Seris-tra. He came up beside Alan, "Good fighting today—congratulations."

Alan handed Patrick Kent off to Anna, who told him to keep walk-ing. Alan replied to the archer, "Yes, thank you. How did you fare?"

"Quite well. I was wondering if perhaps we could talk for a bit? I wanted to ask you some things."

Alan nodded. "Certainly, ask away."

"How are Mom and Dad?"

Alan stopped in his tracks and turned toward the man. He looked into his face and realized that he recognized him. More than recognized him—knew him like a brother.

"*Jonathan*, is that you?" asked Alan, his voice quickening with excitement.

The man laughed. "Didn't even recognize your own brother! Has it been that long?"

Alan laughed and the two embraced. Tears streaming down his face, Alan said, "I can't believe it's you. I thought I'd..."

"Never see me again? Surely you knew better than that."

"Yes, I suppose I did know better. Come on—I can take a little time before I return. Let's eat. I'll meet you in the great hall and catch you up on all that you've missed."

Jonathan smiled. Together they walked off toward the great moun-tain. Once inside the great hall, Alan sat down and began to eat.

"I've learned so much since I've been here. So much about death and its purpose."

Jonathan replied, "Yes, those among the living know so little. Trying to tell them is like speaking to the deaf. But there are those among the living like you, those who know the answer, those who know the truth."

"Your cancer had spread all over your brain and you were in extreme agony," Alan said, remembering that time with sadness. "And pain—I remember how sick you were and then one morning I got a call from

Mom, who told me you were gone. I'll never forget that day—August 12, 1996, one of the worst days of my life. I came over to the house and ran to the bed where you were lying. You were still warm; I was going to do CPR to try to bring you back, but Mom stopped me. She told me that you had suffered enough." Alan trailed off as a tear rolled down his face.

Jonathan grabbed his brother's hand. "That was a great day Alan—that was the day I came here. Look at me. I can walk and talk—not like when I was sick and weak." Jonathan paused, then said, "Alan, I want you to tell Mom and Dad that you saw me and that I'm doing fine. I want you to tell them that they can go on with their lives and that someday I'll see them here. Tell them how happy I am. Please, tell them."

Alan wiped a tear from the corner of his eye and nodded his head. "They won't believe me, you know that."

"I know you'll find the words to make them believe you."

"Okay Jon, I'll find the words. I'll let them know."

"Good. And you can tell Dad that it was me who shredded his favorite tie."

"What?" asked Alan. "What are you talking about?"

"Dad's tie—remember that hideous paisley tie? I shredded it."

Alan began to smile. "We found it all mangled in the dryer and Dad was furious. What happened?"

"Well," said Jonathan, as if he were still embarrassed, "I put the tie on because I wanted to dress like Dad—I was only twelve at the time."

"Stop making excuses," Alan said with a laugh. "How'd you kill the tie?"

"I forgot I had it on and went to make a shake in the blender. The tie was too long and, well, you can guess what happened after that."

Alan laughed hysterically and Jonathan did likewise.

After both of them had caught their breath, Alan asked, "Who led you here? Who brought you through the door?"

Jonathan opened his mouth to answer, but before he could a voice spoke up from behind Alan. "I did."

The voice sounded familiar. Alan looked at a man seated at a nearby table, and everything started to make sense.

His thoughts flashed back to the day when he'd first met Michael Simmons and his frustration as he attempted to confirm Michael's visit with his receptionist. Lisa had denied seeing Michael that day. Alan's memory flashed back to the videotape that failed to show Michael in the lobby when he arrived, and Lieutenant Gaspero, who also said he had never met Michael—even after Michael had told Alan that he'd spoken with the lieutenant. Even Mrs. Munsin, the lady who had lost her mother in the car accident, had not remembered meeting Michael. Only one person that day had said that they'd met Michael Simmons. Alan stared at his salt-and-pepper hair while the man rubbed a finger across his thick, gray mustache.

"Captain?" asked Alan in astonishment. "Captain Finch, is that you?"

Thomas Finch came over to where Alan and Jonathan were seated and lowered himself into a chair. Looking over at Alan, who still appeared to be stunned, he said, "Yes, it's me. I was the one who led your brother here when he passed."

Alan sat for a few seconds in utter shock. "Then it was you—it was you who recommended me for this whole thing—to help Michael, to help lead those who have died?"

"Yes. I watched how you handled those who grieved for the loss of their loved ones. I saw that you honestly believed that being compassionate and caring was important and that doing right was a priority. I knew you would excel at the position of Illissia Galau—and I was right."

Alan nodded, "I suppose you were."

Thomas Finch stood up. "You've done well. I'll see you back at work soon, Officer Crane."

"Thank you, Captain."

Thomas Finch smiled. "No—thank you, Light Bringer."

CHAPTER FORTY-THREE

"Truth fears no question."

A LAN FOUND HIMSELF ONCE AGAIN back in his own world. He realized now how much more he understood about life and death. This was his first day back on the job and he was still thinking about the wonderful two days off he'd had with his wife and daughter. He pulled his squad car up in front of an older white house with a large wraparound porch. Two other police units sat in the driveway.

As he got out of his car he was met in the driveway by Officer Jeffrey Murphy, who said, "This guy is dead, probably a heart attack. He had a condition and was on medication for a long time. You may want to talk to the wife. She's all crying and breaking down."

Alan nodded. "Where is she?"

"In the kitchen. We finally convinced her to sit down in a chair."

"What's her name?"

"Emily Doogan," replied Murphy.

Alan followed Murphy into the house and saw another officer helping the EMS personnel load an older man onto a backboard. He entered the kitchen, where an older woman sat in a chair, sobbing uncontrollably.

He pulled up a chair next to her, "Emily, I'm Sergeant Crane."

The woman looked up, "I can't believe he's gone. We were married for fifty-two years. I don't know what I'll do now. I knew he had a condition, but he was doing fine. He was actually getting better! I don't understand. Why did this happen? Why now?"

She began sobbing again and Alan said, "Your husband was a very special person. He was needed somewhere else very badly. Because of his talents and the great deeds that he accomplished during his lifetime, only he could fulfill the role that he's now called to do."

Emily stopped crying, "What are you talking about? What great acts and accomplishments? He was a very loving and considerate person. He was kind and caring and a great husband; I loved him very much, but nobody recognized any great accomplishments at any point in his life. He didn't stand out."

In a calm, soothing voice, Alan said to her, "He didn't stand out here, but where he's going, those acts of kindness, caring, and love actually count for something. Where he's going, *those* things make you great."

Emily nodded her head as if she agreed with him. She seemed to be comforted. Alan smiled. "We'll all join him one day. Hopefully we'll measure up to the traits he had that made him so exemplary. This world doesn't typically reward those who try to do what's right, but the next one does."

Emily sat there for a moment, then wiped some remaining tears from her cheek. "I hope I can figure out how to go on until I see him again."

"You will. Remember: in times of great despair, there often comes great clarity in what to do."

Emily stood up as the paramedics wheeled the stretcher toward the front door. "I hope they take care of him," she said.

"You have my word. I will make sure he gets where he needs to go."

Emily hugged him. "Thank you," she said. A young woman with dark brown hair entered the room and ran to Emily.

"This is my daughter, Nikki," Emily said with a slight smile. The two embraced and sat down at the table. Alan knew that it was time to leave. He said good-bye and slipped out the front door.

No time elapsed as he walked Frank Doogan through the familiar stone hallway up to the door that led to the next world. As Alan got out of the back of the ambulance, Murphy approached him in the driveway.

"Hey. Looked like you really calmed her down."

Alan nodded. "She'll be fine."

"Looks like it's almost quitting time," said Murphy. "I have to get out of here on time. I have to meet Janine at seven and Alice at ten."

Alan thought about this for a moment, then cocked his head to one side. "I thought you and Janine were engaged?"

"Uh, well no—we actually got married last weekend down at the courthouse."

"Then who the hell is Alice?" asked Alan.

"Oh—well, I met her a few days ago. I can't meet her until ten because her husband doesn't leave for work until nine-thirty, and besides I have to have dinner with Janine at seven," said Murphy as if he had everything organized.

Alan shook his head. "So let me recap this. You got married last weekend and you're eating dinner with your wife at seven—and then meeting another woman three hours later after her husband goes to work?"

"Yeah, pretty much, that's it," said Murphy.

"And you don't think that this is going to blow up in your face?"

"Nah, I'll be fine. It's not like it's the first time."

Alan took a deep breath. "Murphy, can I ask you a personal question?"

"Sure, Sarge, go ahead."

"Do you believe in God?"

"Yeah, you bet."

"So you probably believe in heaven, right?"

"Oh, sure I do, Sarge. Watta ya getting at?" asked Murphy.

"Don't misunderstand me. I'm not saying that you won't *make* it to heaven, but I believe that when you die, Murphy, you may have a really *long* walk to get there. Are you following me?"

Murphy began to laugh. "Not really, but I know you're just looking out for me, and I appreciate it."

"What I'm trying to say is that you're heading for trouble, Murphy. Why did you marry Janine?"

"Well, I love her. I really do. I mean it."

"Then why are you seeing this other woman? Don't you think it's wrong?"

Murphy hung his head as if he were ashamed. "Yeah, it's wrong. I know it. I need to end it with Alice. I'll do it face-to-face when I see her tonight; owe her that much at least."

"And what about Janine?"

"What about her?" replied Murphy.

"Will you tell her what happened?"

"No way! That'd be crazy. She'd flip out. She could divorce me; no way I could tell her. Why, do you think I should?" asked Murphy.

"I can't answer that for you, Murphy. Doing what's right is always difficult, but that's something you have to decide."

Murphy nodded. "Were you trying to scare me into doing what's right by talking about all that heaven stuff?"

Alan smiled. "No. It's just that you never know when you're going to die. Death is an invisible pattern. You have to make things right while you're still here. Don't worry, Murphy—if you die, I'll be there for you. I got your back."

Murphy laughed heartily. "I know you do, Sarge. You always do. And I appreciate it."

Dispatch came over the radio and called, "Three-twenty-one."

Murphy grasped his walkie-talkie and replied, "Go ahead."

"Three-twenty-one, we had a motorist advise that they'd observed the gate to the street maintenance division had blown open. Can you run by and re-secure it?"

Murphy replied, "Ten-four, City, I'll be en route." He shook his head. "Second time this week. I'll see you back at the station."

CHAPTER FORTY-FOUR

"Success is not measured by what we have,
or who we know, or even by how we live our lives,
but rather, by where we spend eternity."

—Rev. Robert N. Thompson's last words to his daughter, Kathe

RICH MAVERY SAT NEAR A LARGE stack of tires propped up against a chain-link fence. Only twenty-four hours ago he had been released from prison on three armed robbery charges. As he slid his finger over the deep scar that started on his forehead and ran over his eyelid down to his chin, he reminded himself that he was not going back to jail, no matter what he had to do. He knew that he needed money and fast, or he would have people after him. His plan was to make his way down to the Southside Liquor store, where he knew there would only be one employee working and about $300–$500 in cash for the taking. The only hang-up was that he had no gun. Luckily, the cell phone he had stolen earlier today was still working when he called the police department to report the unsecured gate.

He sat and waited, clenching the tire iron he'd found on the ground near the stack of tires. Trying not to move, he watched as headlights illuminated the driveway approaching the gate. He heard a car door close and saw a uniformed figure coming his way. The cop walked up to the gate, which was swinging freely, and began to examine the damaged lock. Rich moved as quickly as he could behind the cop and swung the tire iron down on his head with a heavy grunt. As he raised it above his head to strike a second blow, he heard three loud pops and felt a burning sensation in his chest. As the warm, salty taste of blood filled his mouth, he found it difficult to breathe. His knees buckled.

Alan holstered his gun and ran up to where Murphy lay on the ground. Murphy looked over at the body of his attacker and noticed the three holes in his chest where Alan had shot him.

"Thanks, Sarge, that was a close one. I appreciate it."

"Yeah, don't mention it. Here, take my hand."

He pulled Murphy to his feet and asked, "Did you happen to speak to Janine or Alice?"

"Actually, I called Alice on the way over here and told her we were through, and how I felt guilty about the whole thing. She said that she was feeling the same way and understood. I called Janine just as I pulled up here and told her that we had to talk when I got home. I'll take your advice and come clean. I know it won't be easy, but I'll try to work through it. We'll see how it goes."

Murphy began to walk back to his car, but Alan called, "Hey, Jeff."

Murphy stopped and turned around. "Yeah?"

"You're going the wrong way," said Alan with a solemn look on his face. "Follow me."

Murphy seemed confused, but he followed Alan back up to the back door of the street department. Alan opened the door and stepped into the dark hallway with Murphy, who nearly jumped out of his skin when he saw the man Alan had just shot sitting up against the wall. Alan bent down close to Rich Mavery's worn face and whispered, "I'd take you into the realm of the light as a prisoner, but you haven't fallen in battle yet. But soon…we'll meet soon."

Rich Mavery stared back at him with cold, black, soulless eyes and said nothing.

Alan stood up and said to Murphy, "Pay no attention to him. He's waiting for someone else. We need to go this way."

As Alan turned the corner, Murphy felt a stab of clarity. Realizing what had happened, he said, "Janine—I never got to tell her. I need you to tell her—"

Alan interrupted him. "I'll tell her that you loved her very much and that, although you weren't perfect, you wanted to do right by her in every way you could. The door you see ahead of you is where you need to go. Farewell, Murphy."

The door stood before him, and Murphy walked forward into the brightness illuminated there. At the last moment he paused in the doorway and turned.

"Good-bye, Alan," he said. "We'll meet again soon."

"Not too soon," Alan said with a smile, his face lit by the light from beyond.

ACKNOWLEDGMENTS

W E OWE A SPECIAL DEBT OF GRATITUDE TO all of those people who made this endeavor possible, especially Tom and Betty Hill whose encouragement and direction kept driving us forward and changed our lives forever. To Roberta Van Haag who helped with our initial edits. To our mentor and literary agent and friend, Linda Langton, who truly brought our writing to a new level and instilled confidence to continue onward.

We would also like to express a very special thanks to Dennis Cummins for his honesty, candor, and advice. Terri and Mickey Olsen were two friends who continued to cheer us on through the long journey as they continually offered their encouragement. And a special thanks to Sue Rector who was one of our initial readers that offered so many kind words and praises that sparked us to push this project into what it has become.

A special thanks to our good friend Jim Modglin for his dedication and creativity in creating our book trailer.

A sincere thanks to Dr. Steve Parkin for his encouragement and support.

We would like to recognize all of the amazing people at HCI Books who believed in us and helped us through the publishing process. What an outstanding organization.

Most of all we need to mention two very special people who kept us going throughout this adventure—our wives, Nicole DiGiuseppi and Patty Force, who supported us through all of the ups and downs of creation, editing, and completion of *The Light Bringer*—Thank you for putting up with us!

Lastly, to all of the other people who read the drafts at different stages and gave us the needed compliments, criticisms, and endorsements that enabled us to mold the story that we now have.

From us to all of you—Thank you, God bless, and stay safe.

Chris and Mike

In great moments of despair,
there comes great clarity.

About Chris DiGiuseppi

C HRIS DIGIUSEPPI has more than nineteen years in Law Enforcement at various levels, including Assistant Chief of Police. He is a graduate of the FBI National Academy and Northwestern University School of Police Staff Command. Visit the author at www.thelight bringerbook.com.

About Mike Force

M IKE FORCE has spent more than thirty years in Law Enforcement, the last nineteen as a Police Chief. Mike has numerous certifications in various areas of law, forensics, investigations, and criminology. He is a graduate of the FBI National Academy and served twenty-two years in the U.S. Marines, where he retired as a Captain. He oversaw operations for twenty-seven military installations worldwide. Visit the author at www.thelightbringerbook.com.

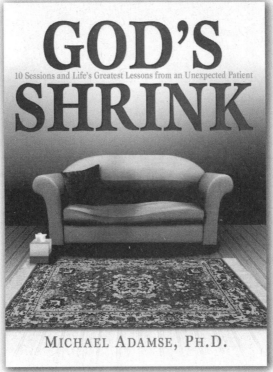

A Journey of Discovery and a Return to the Deepest Truth

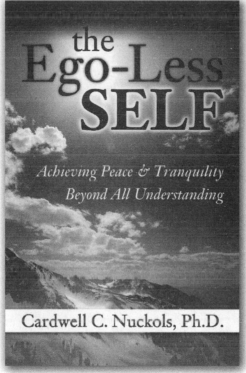

the Ego-Less SELF

Achieving Peace & Tranquility Beyond All Understanding

Cardwell C. Nuckols, Ph.D.

Code #5410 • Paperback • $14.95

With a broad range of spiritual influences from the Bible to Zen Buddhism, *The Ego-Less SELF* sets out to deflate the ego to let the true self shine through.

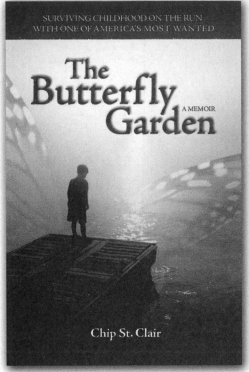